Olivia is a former software engineer who writes contemporary romance. She lives in Atlanta with her husband, two kids, and two naughty cats (Hairy Houdini and Bess). Besides writing, she enjoys traveling and experimenting with cooking, and most of the time, she ends up eating the new meals herself because her family has a limit on how much they love her.

She is a member and volunteer at the Atlanta Writers Club. Olivia is represented by the lovely Helen Lane.

www.oliviajacksonbooks.com

instagram.com/oliviajacksonbooks

Also by Olivia Jackson

Digging Dr Jones

HUNTER'S TREASURE

OLIVIA JACKSON

One More Chapter
a HarperCollins*Publishers* Ltd
1 London Bridge Street
London SE1 9GF
www.harpercollins.co.uk
HarperCollins*Publishers*
Macken House, 39/40 Mayor Street Upper,
Dublin 1, D01 C9W8, Ireland

This paperback edition 2026
25 26 27 28 29 LBC 6 5 4 3 2
First published in Great Britain in ebook format
by HarperCollins*Publishers* 2026
Copyright © Olivia Jackson 2026
Olivia Jackson asserts the moral right to be identified
as the author of this work

A catalogue record of this book is available from the British Library

ISBN: 978-0-00-872967-7

This novel is entirely a work of fiction. The names, characters and incidents portrayed in it are the work of the author's imagination. Any resemblance to actual persons, living or dead, events or localities is entirely coincidental.

Printed and bound in the United States

All rights reserved. No part of this publication may be reproduced, stored in a retrieval system, or transmitted, in any form or by any means, electronic, mechanical, photocopying, recording or otherwise, without the prior permission of the publishers.
Without limiting the exclusive rights of any author, contributor or the publisher of this publication, any unauthorised use of this publication to train generative artificial intelligence (AI) technologies is expressly prohibited. HarperCollins also exercise their rights under Article 4(3) of the Digital Single Market Directive 2019/790 and expressly reserve this publication from the text and data mining exception.

For my children, Alexander and Catherine. You are my most precious treasure. Please never stop believing that you can make your dreams come true, as self-doubt is the greatest obstacle to success.

I love you always.

Playlist

Golden - Harry Styles ♥
Rein Me In - Sam Fender ♥
Mess It Up - Gracie Abrams ♥
Pure Shores - All Saints ♥
supernatural - Ariana Grande ♥
Jump - Madonna ♥
Wood - Taylor Swift ♥
Rush Rush - Paula Abdul ♥
Read your Mind - Sabrina Carpenter ♥
National Anthem - Lana Del Rey ♥
Nobody Knows - Shawn Mendes ♥
I know it won't work - Gracie Abrams ♥
Unwritten - Natasha Bedingfield ♥
I Know Places - Taylor Swift ♥
Everywhere, Everything - Noah Kahan ♥
Light On - Maggie Rogers ♥
Landslide - Haley Klinkhammer ♥
Sally - ROLE MODEL ♥
Out Of The Woods - Taylor Swift ♥
Stargazing - Myles Smith ♥
Want You Back - HAIM ♥
Miracles Happen - Myra ♥
Opalite - Taylor Swift ♥

Chapter One

Being lost on a sailboat in the middle of the ocean seemed romantic in the movies, but in all those movies the captains were handsome, capable men, not the drunkard woman I hired. I should have known better than to venture into the South Pacific on a whim and while this wasn't my dream, it had become my nightmare. Trying to focus, I reminded myself that every challenge could be turned into a learning opportunity, but it didn't work. The only wisdom I could extract from this particular situation was not to trust strangers, and not to be so cheap the next time I chartered a boat. If there was a next time.

Below deck, I slammed a drawer shut and glared at the mess of clothes, charging cables, books, kitchen tools, towels, broken Christmas lights, and other whatchamacallits now on the floor. I'd turned this piece-of-shit boat upside down twice and still nothing. Leaving the galley in chaos, I marched up to the lounge and found Bambi—the halfwit captain I'd hired a month and a half ago—on a chair near the helm. The small-framed woman with leathery, sun-darkened skin had fallen asleep in the sun. Eyes closed, her head bobbed from side to side, lolling with the boat's movement. Her right arm hung down with the other curled inside her light windbreaker.

"Wake up!" I yelled. She didn't flinch. "Where's the GPS? And the satellite phone?"

Bambi mumbled something incoherent.

At the last marina, I caught her trading my solar charger for a small bottle of liquor. I leaned in closer to hear better. "Did you sell them?"

She opened her eyes and squinted at me. "Hi, Sydney," she said with a crooked smile. Her breath reeked of alcohol. "Whatcha want, babe?" she garbled, sounding exactly like the radio on the boat, and took out a nearly empty bottle from under her shirt.

I grabbed it from her hand, almost pulling Bambi out of her seat along with it.

"What is this?" I made a big show of checking the label on the bottle as if I didn't already know what it was. "Where'd you get it?"

Soon after we'd sailed from Australia, I'd learned Bambi was a not-so-recovering alcoholic. She had conveniently forgotten to mention this detail during our interview regarding captaining a sailboat for a three-month journey. Her face was kind, but battered by weather and sun. She spoke knowledgeably about the areas where I intended to scatter my father's ashes on the tropical islands. Her résumé listed as many years of experience as any other captain I'd met. But I was a thirty-year-old software engineer, with no self-defense training. If a man were to attack me on a boat in the middle of nowhere, all I could throw at him would be complicated algorithms and lines of code. Bambi seemed a safer bet.

Turned out, I was wrong. Shocker.

Bambi's head sagged, and her body started to slide off the chair. I caught her just in time and propped her up, steadying her against the back of her seat. "We agreed you wouldn't buy any more booze." I fought to keep my voice even.

After her last bender, Bambi had surrendered her cash willingly and showed me where she had stashed bottles, which I poured out. At each island, we shopped together for provisions, then a taxi would take us to a peaceful cove. Bambi would stay in the car with our hired driver while I said goodbye to my father one more time. Not much booze-buying to be done there. The only other times we'd been separated on the trip were when she had to do whatever captains did to take care of their boats—maintenance or whatever. I'd used that time to find a place with decent Wi-Fi and reconnect to the life I'd left behind. It wasn't that much of a life, really. Still, I needed to check my email and send my friend Tina an "I'm okay" note at every stop or she'd worry.

"Open your eyes, Bambi." My hands started to shake from anger or nerves (or both) and I inhaled the salt air and slowly let it out. "Tell me the truth. Did you sell my GPS and the phone to get this brandy?"

"It isn't brandy. It's rum," Bambi slurred.

I gritted my teeth. "Answer the question."

"Maybe?"

"Maybe?" My eyes went so big they hurt. "What the hell? How are we supposed to know where we are or where we're going? The navigation on this stupid tin can of a boat has failed, and you sold our only backup. We have no way to call for help."

"We'll be okay. The stars will guide us." Bambi threw her arm out toward the sky, nearly falling out of her chair again.

"Damn it!" I hurled the glass bottle into the ocean.

A brief wave of regret coursed through me—should I have placed a message inside? A harsh chuckle escaped me. We were probably goners. In all my meticulous research I knew that in *normal* circumstances, a sailboat would have at least one backup GPS device, if not several. But *Bloody Mary* was clearly anything but normal. In retrospect, the boat name should've been my first red flag.

I walked as far as I could from the drunken fool, making it to the foredeck. A full forty feet away. Not far enough.

"Well done, Dad," I muttered staring into the vast expanse of nothing but blue water and sky. "Well. Done."

Okay, so it wasn't technically my father's fault I was in this predicament. He wasn't to blame for my rock bottom after mom died and he got sick, and it certainly wasn't his fault that my husband had filed for divorce.

It took two years of suffering before I decided to change my life. At first, the thought of me chartering a boat for three months was absurd. But the more Tina pressured me into it, the more the idea grew on me. Until in the end it seemed to be cathartic, necessary even, and with each passing minute, the idea of *not* sailing worsened.

Until now.

Standing at the bow's edge, holding onto the lines, I let the cool mist from the waves bring back some semblance of normality.

Returning below deck, ignoring a moaning Bambi, I tidied my stateroom and the galley, both in shambles after my frantic search. I ran my finger over the engraving on the urn, allowing myself a smile, "Follow me at your own risk." My father had always been a wisecracker. He'd written those words into his will, but I bet he hadn't thought it would be used before he turned sixty. Or that I'd follow his mapped-out sailing pipedream. I carefully placed my father's ceramic urn back into its bright green flotation bag, having pulled it out earlier in my frenzy—even though there'd been no reason the GPS or phone would've been inside it.

Damn it, Bambi. The reason I'd bought a portable GPS at our second stop a month earlier was because she didn't have navigation aboard the *Bloody Mary*—correction: the navigation was spotty. Up until tonight, secured with a functional GPS (or I foolishly thought we had them), things had been going well. Bambi taught me to catch and fillet fish, some boating etiquette, and how to tie different knots. I got used to short showers and sleeping without air-conditioning, and I enjoyed sunny days filled with trouble-free tasks.

Except nothing Bambi had shared about sailing was valuable right now.

For the next two hours, with my head clutched between my hands, I studied the nautical charts strewn across the desk, trying to guess where we were. I had no clue, but we for sure had arrived at Destination Fucked. Our last stop had been Talava Arches, Niue, and we were supposed to be on our way to the Cook Islands. With no major issues, it would've been a six to seven-day trip. Today was day nine, and the weather conditions had been mostly perfect.

"Shit." A frustrated groan left my mouth, and I shoved the maps off the table, as I spotted that the cooktop—on a gimbal to keep it level—swayed more than usual. Double shit. I'd been so consumed with figuring out our location, I hadn't noticed the increasing rocking of the boat. Thunder rolled not far away. Peering through the narrow window, I realized the line where the ocean met the sky had disappeared, both blending into blackness. On the horizon lightning flashed every few seconds, piercing the dark.

Abandoning the maps, I hurried into my berth and yanked my lifejacket from its spot. Just in case we'd have to desert the sailboat, I stuffed the plastic baggie with my passport and wallet between my chest and the vest. With alarm settling deep inside my bones, I climbed to the main deck to check on Bambi.

The wind was no longer a friendly breeze but a full-on gale. Lightning lit up the unsettling skies, and a chill of panic pelted me along with the cold rain. In the distance, two monstrous waterspouts scudded across the ocean. They were miles away, but *Bloody Mary* was in their path. This was the moment when I needed a stronger word than "fuck."

Loose strands of hair lashed my face. I tried to smooth them away, but it was pointless. Bambi was lowering the mainsail. Bracing against the wall for balance and gripping the lines, I staggered to help her.

"Sydney, tighten the—"

The wind in my ears blocked most of her instruction, but I scrambled to snatch the line she threw at me, my fingers missing it by inches. Bambi rushed closer, grabbed the rope, and began to secure it. She finally looked like a captain, her face sober with fear.

"Where's your lifejacket?" I shouted.

"You'll go overboard. Get back inside."

Bambi was a captain, but I wasn't about to take her orders and let her risk her life. "I'll get it for you."

Waves buffeted the boat as I struggled to make my way to the galley. The cabinet doors flapped open, their contents rolling around on the floor. Every single thing had fallen out: books, papers, cans, water bottles. I'd envisioned this situation countless times—what I'd do if we were caught in a bad squall—but right now, my thoughts were scattered in different directions. Standing near the door to Bambi's cabin, I pressed my hands hard against the walls on either side as another big wave hit, and the books, secured by a wire, broke free and showered down on me. My hands flew to my head. The next wave jolted the boat and drove me headfirst into the table.

Ignoring the sting of pain in my forehead, I braced myself on hands and knees and moved through the mess to where Bambi's lifejacket hung on a hook. I snatched it, then crawled as fast as I could to the steps leading up to the deck. My pulse hammered beneath my skin, and beads of cold sweat covered my face as I forced the hatch open and fought my way outside. The sky looked awash with fireworks of electrical discharge stealing my breath for a moment, long enough that I only caught the boom that swung with force to my left out of the corner of my eye, sending my heart to my throat. I ducked, avoiding a direct blow to my head.

The wind screamed like a band of coyotes, rain battered my face, and waves crashed against the boat with terrifying power. Holding the helm, Bambi battled the rogue waters.

"Put this on!" I thrust the lifejacket at her and grabbed the handles as if I knew what to do.

Struggling with her balance, Bambi threw the lifejacket over her shoulders and threaded her arms through the openings. A sudden gust heeled *Bloody Mary* low, knocking Bambi and me off our feet. My left hand lost its grip on the helm, and my body jolted with a sickening twist. The lightning struck, and my gaze locked with Bambi, her eyes wild with fear and—

She hurtled overboard.

My God!

I swallowed a surge of nausea, both from panic and the endless tossing. The boat pitched, and I stumbled to the rail where the life ring hung. I released the red lifesaver from its cradle and readied to toss it, but I wasn't sure where to throw it.

"Bambi!" My eyes frantically scoured the waters, searching for my captain. Hoping the life ring would find her, I tossed it over and grabbed the helm. With all the energy left in me, I pointed the stern into the waves. Wasn't that what she once said to do?

As the sea violently thrashed *Bloody Mary*, sobbing and praying for Bambi's and my survival, I rode out the storm for what felt like long, terrifying hours. I should have listened to my first gut feeling weeks ago that pursuing someone else's dream unprepared was foolish and definitely not honorable. My drenched body trembled, and my fingers lost any feeling in them as I gripped the helm tight. There was no end to the unutterable abyss … until a bolt of lightning split the darkness, outlining an island on the horizon. I blinked then turned the wheel, desperate for land, safety, survival. A sudden screeching sound came from deep within the boat, and I was propelled forward, hitting the steering wheel. Another jerk pushed me back, then tossed me sideways. My fingers slipped from their grasp, my hands clutching thin air, searching for a hold on anything and finding nothing. The next moment, I was thrown into the raging murkiness of the water.

Chapter Two

I opened my eyes, disorientated, my skin damp with sweat or ocean water. A moan escaped my lips as I tried to move. My mouth was dry. When I swallowed, what little saliva there was scraped my throat. I pushed myself upright, and my sore muscles screamed as my mind struggled to make sense of where I was. The room spun out of control. Shutting my eyes, I fell back and waited for the queasiness to pass.

I repeated the breathing technique the nurse who visited my dad taught me: breathe in through your nose for four seconds, hold breath for seven, and then exhale through your mouth for eight, repeat three more times. After several repetitions, when the dizziness and nausea subsided, I stared up at a wood ceiling with blue flaking paint. Probably lead-based since it appeared to be old. Focusing on something, even something small, like chipped paint, would calm me, so I gave it full rein. My dad had watched *This Old House* religiously. Even after his condition had worsened and he hadn't been paying attention to the television anymore, I'd kept his favorite DIY show playing in the background.

Turning my head to the right I spotted an old bookcase against the wall. Books of different heights and thicknesses were crammed in every available space. Romances and beach reads neighbored classics and non-fiction. A small brown lizard rushed across the shelf, its long tail dragging behind, before it quickly disappeared around a large conch shell.

Sitting on top of the bookcase was a stack of identical metal boxes, one of which had a small lock. What was so important about that particular box? Money, perhaps, or important papers and documents were secured inside. Passport. My hands flew to my chest. The lifejacket I'd worn was gone, along with the baggie that held my papers. My jean shorts and shirt were gone too, and I wore an unfamiliar, wrinkled linen shirt instead. Too large. I peeked underneath and breathed a sigh of relief—my green bikini was still on.

A sharp pain of memory sliced through me. Bambi's eyes before a wave swept her away. My breath caught in my chest as if my lungs had collapsed under the weight. She was dead, had to be. She was a drunken fool and a thief, but still, I'd liked Bambi and her very likely made-up adventure stories. She would start with, "This was interesting…" and then continue telling me something that wasn't interesting for the first ten minutes. At first they annoyed me but now I would give anything to hear them again.

My heart throbbed in agony, and a raw sob ripped out of me. I should have gone after her right away. I'd had my lifejacket fully secured on me. I might have saved us both. And then the swoop of old sorrow seized my breathing, the weight of another realization so heavy I physically couldn't bring myself to take the next breath.

"Oh God," I gasped as if I had come from under the water. My father's ashes. They were on the boat. Because of my ignorance, I wouldn't be able to finish honoring his dream. If only I could go back in time and talk myself out of going sailing.

Closing my eyes, I laid my head back on the pillow and cried until I was empty of tears and my throat burned.

After a while, when my breathing normalized, and I convinced myself that crying bore no results, I faced left. An oil lantern and a tired aluminum mug holding a cluster of bright pink and purple tropical flowers sat on a nightstand beside the bed. I reached out and touched the petals, my hand a visual medley of the pain as I noted bruises and dry scratches that hadn't been there before. I had no recollection of what had happened after my fall overboard. This place didn't look like a hospital. Leaning on my elbows, I raised myself to survey the rest of the area.

Along with the queen size bed I was in, the room housed a sofa with sagging cushions that had seen better days, and several other mismatched bookcases. Next to the couch was a tall cabinet packed with cans and dry food bags. A table with two chairs divided the space. The room had three glassless but screened windows and a wide-open door.

Pulling myself up, a dull pain pinged in my right thigh. I tugged aside the flat sheet that covered my lower body. Good news: both of my legs were attached. Bad news: my right thigh was bandaged. Just like my arms, large bruises and scrapes coated my legs as if a bobcat had used me as a scratching post.

I scooted to the edge of the bed and slowly swung my legs

off. One leg then the other. Through the window lay a tropical jungle. A beautiful vista if I were on vacation—an intimidating and frightening sight now that I wasn't sure where I was. Under the window stood an antique bureau with a large oil lamp and an open journal atop its unlocked flap. A green gecko, sunbathing to the left of it, stared at me, its eyes turning in a funny way.

Heavy footfalls outside alarmed me, and I froze. A broad-shouldered, bearded man entered, ducking his head through the doorframe. The wood floor creaked in protest under his weight. He stopped when his large blue eyes locked with mine. He had on knee-length beige shorts and wore a shirt similar to mine, sleeves rolled up to his elbows. This must be his place. Did he rescue me?

He studied me for a moment, his long fingers clenched around the cup in his hand, then gave me a friendly smile. "How are you feeling?"

In pain, shitty, and confused. I'd gone sailing for a new beginning, and ... Bambi. My heart was back in my throat. Prickly tears filled my eyes, and I wrinkled my nose.

"Don't be scared," the man said in a soft tone, his smile fading. "I won't hurt you. Do you speak English?" He raised an eyebrow. "Est-ce que vous parlez français?"

"What?" I croaked. "Yes, I speak English. Where am I?" I pressed my hand to my head. "I'm sorry ... I'm a bit confused."

"That's okay. My name is Hunter Holden."

"Where is my captain, Bambi?"

"I'm sorry." His brow creased in sympathy. "You're the only one I found yesterday morning."

The thought of her drowning squeezed my soul, and tears pooled. I wiped my eyes with the heels of my hands.

"Do you remember your name?" Hunter had a calm and welcoming aura about him, and the earlier tension in my muscles abated and I relaxed in his presence. His sun-bleached hair with slight curls hung over smoldering eyes. He was probably in his thirties, the scruffy beard smoothed what I imagined was a sharp jawline.

I nodded. "Sydney York."

Hunter went to the hutch, opened a cabinet and retrieved an olive-colored medical box. "I need to look at your leg. You had a cut when you washed up on shore. It wasn't deep but it did require stitches. So far, it's healed well. I'll clean it again, and we'll leave it open until this evening to breathe."

He walked closer and offered the mug he still held in his other hand. "Drink some water."

His left inner forearm had a tattoo in black ink, and the details were stunning. A sea chart with schooner, an old-fashioned compass in the center, and compass rose below. It shouted *wanderluster searching for the beginning of a happier life.*

Hunter cleared his throat and shook the cup to bring my attention to it.

I hesitated. Accepting a drink from a strange man was a bad idea, but if he wanted to do something sinful to me, he would've already done it. Thanking him, I drained it, my thirst only getting worse.

At the table, Hunter poured water from a kettle I hadn't noticed before into a bowl, then emptied a packet of dry powder into it. After stirring, he approached the bed, holding a small glass bottle filled with liquid, clean gauze, and the bowl.

"Lie down," he instructed. "I'll unwrap the bandages and clean your cut. It shouldn't hurt much."

I didn't see any harm in complying.

"Hold these, please." Hunter handed me the medication. "You can be my helper today." He smiled, and I returned it automatically, but my body stiffened as soon as his fingers brushed my leg. "Does it hurt?" He met my eyes, concern there.

It wasn't pain that had caused me to tense. The last time a man touched my leg was a long time ago. Well, technically, three years, two months, and a few weeks, but who was counting? The little magic Phill and I had to begin with had ceased after my mother died. I'd spent so much time at my father's house, we'd rarely seen each other, and when we had been together, something had changed.

"No," I admitted.

Hunter began to unwind the gauze. He slowed down when he got to the last layer of the bandage. It was coated with brownish-yellow stains, and Hunter cautiously unpeeled it. The skin near the opening was tender and red, while the rest of my thigh was one large bluish-purple bruise. The wound was at most two inches long, patches of dry blood blotted here and there. With my limited medical expertise (none), it appeared promising-ish.

"Doesn't look bad at all. No trace of infection," Hunter said, as if reading my thoughts. "The swelling is down. That's a good sign. In a few days, you can run a marathon."

"I don't do sports," I said, watching his gentle strokes, as he cleaned the wound and patted the cut dry, not causing too much pain. Then, Hunter took the bottle and applied some liquid on a clean cloth.

"This is a salt mixture to accelerate healing," he said and then chuckled. "Talk about adding *insalt* to injury." His kind gaze met mine before he dabbed the cut. "This may sting a bit."

By that, he must have meant it would hurt like hell. I flinched, sucking my breath through my clenched teeth.

To keep it together, I focused on Hunter's forearm flexing as he tended to the wound. Many scars, each the size of a grain of rice were scattered across his tanned arm. The time on his solar Casio watch displayed seventeen thirty-five. The only person I knew who used military time was my neighbor, a retired Navy surgeon.

"Where did you learn to take care of cuts?"

"I've had some basic medical training in the last couple of years. During fishing trips, people slip and fall, get minor injuries, and sometimes deep cuts. What happened to you?" Hunter retrieved the bottle from my hand, collected the soiled bandage, and returned to the table.

"I was on a sailboat with Bambi. She's my captain. Well, was..." I drew in a ragged breath. "The storm was so bad I think it broke our sail in two. She went overboard first, and sometime later, I fell too. The last thing I remember is being dragged underwater, and then pain."

"It was one of the worst storms I've seen." Hunter slid the medical case onto a shelf and closed the cabinet. "I'm sorry to hear about your friend. Let's hope she survived and was rescued."

I nodded, but dreadful doubt seized my heart. Bambi hadn't fully put on her life jacket. Tears blurred my vision, and I rubbed my eyes on my forearm. I had to report her missing and maybe, just maybe, the recuse team could find her. "Do you have a phone I could use?"

"I'm sorry, but I don't."

"Do you mind taking me into town? I'm sure I can find a bar or a hotel with one."

Hunter remained still, his back against the cabinet. He looked past me at the open window, then to me. I had a sinking feeling that I was about to be disappointed by a man once again.

"There's no town," he said, a pained expression on his face, his eyebrows furrowing in the center. "I'm the only one who lives on the island."

And there it was.

I sat up. "Do you mean you live here all by yourself?"

"Correct."

I smiled to hide my growing alarm. I'd gone out of my way not to be alone with a man during my sailing trip, just to end up with one after all. Deep breaths. It was just for a short time. For a few hours tops. "Could you please ferry me to the next island with a town?"

"I can't."

"Why not?"

"Because…" Uncertainty flickered across Hunter's face, but he quickly erased it. "I don't have a boat anymore." He inhaled gradually and exhaled just as slowly, his face calm but serious. "The storm damaged it."

My heart sank. "And you don't have another one?"

"I do but regrettably it's at Avarua."

Perfect. Rarotonga was the largest of the Cook Islands, and Avarua was the city where Bambi and I had been heading. "Can you take me there?"

His forehead wrinkled, and he mouthed *wow*. "You must have hit your head hard," he muttered, pushing off the cabinet. "I don't have a boat."

Without meeting my eyes, Hunter walked over to the table and pick up the used bandages and wound them into a loose ball. His calmness, which I found comforting before, now pissed me off. Of course, maybe he wasn't worried about the fact that we were boatless because he had already called for help. I shouldn't just assume he wasn't prepared, like Bambi. Or me.

"Do you have a satellite phone?"

He scrubbed his cheek like his beard bothered him. "The phone is somewhere in the bay."

My mind exploded with panic. "What about VHF radio? A walkie-talkie? Something to reach other people."

"A walkie-talkie?" he said, as in *are-you-serious?* "How about we tie two paper cups with a string and try to reach other people that way."

Har-har, Hunter was a comedian too.

"So, we're stuck on this damn island?" I asked with an accusatory tone, as if it was his fault he didn't have an extra vessel, or that I ended up in his bed, or that he made me go on my trip.

"No," Hunter said, his voice low. "*You* are stuck here. *I* live here."

A hoot escaped me. This situation was more than I bargained for. I'd been so unqualified for this sailing trip, and much less so for surviving in a jungle. God, I'd been stupid.

"Well, fuck," I said and slapped my hand over my mouth. "Apologies ... except what the actual fuck?" I wanted to laugh and sob at the same time. "Of all the stupidest, idiotic, ridiculous—"

"I hate to interrupt this display of your vocabulary glory, but I must wash and sterilize these." With a tight smile, Hunter crumpled the dirty dressing in his hands. "You should rest. I'll check on you when you've run out of fucks and adjectives." And he walked out.

Chapter Three

I sank onto the bed and lay there dumbfounded. "I'm stuck here," I mumbled.

For how long? Certainly, we couldn't be that far from other islands for someone not to come by (I ignored the fact that Bambi and I had sailed for days without seeing an inch of dry land or any other boats). We would be okay as long as we had enough supplies to last until rescue came. Hunter lived here, he must have what we needed to survive. Surely anybody who lived on a remote island had the tools and the know-how to fix a boat. Only an idiot came to live on an island unprepared. Of course, some idiots sailed with a drunk captain, not knowing a damn thing about navigation or boats…

Perhaps Hunter and I could build a raft! I smacked my head and then wished I hadn't, I must have another bruise. All the HGTV shows I'd watched with my dad were no help; all they talked about was how to flip and not flop with a fixer-upper, how to change a faucet, and other crap that was useless in my situation. My head pounded.

Fucking fuck.

Well, it could have been worse. I could have washed up on a deserted island, died a slow, painful death from an infection, or been eaten by a wild pack of squirrels. That said, lucky me, at least Hunter was here. He knew how to handle life on Gilligan's Island, right?

He'd said this was his home, which seemed odd for a man in his mid-thirties to live alone in the middle of nowhere. Maybe Hunter was on the run, and this was his hiding place! He could be dangerous or mad or—

If I didn't stop this train of thought, I'd give myself a heart attack. My mom warned me to stay away from men with large tattoos, and she also said I could learn a lot about a person by what was in their house.

Sitting up, I scrutinized the hut. It wasn't a luxurious bungalow, but the area was clean with a rustic, tropical-hut look. No heads in jars. No weapons on the walls. No obvious red flags. Yet. If I wanted to find out what kind of man Hunter really was, I'd start with the journal. Just three feet away. Yes, I knew it was wrong to read someone else's diary but in the current situation this was necessary. I wouldn't read much. Just enough to understand if he had lotion in a basket.

Listening for footsteps to ensure Hunter wasn't coming back, I planted my feet on the floor and stood. Too quickly. A lightheadedness fogged my mind and my head swam. I grabbed the back of the chair to stabilize myself, and hey, my jeans shorts lay on the cushion, dry and folded. Breathing through my nose I counted to ten and then with slow movements, I carefully put them on.

A green lizard skedaddled across the table and over the journal. Reaching out, I flipped a few pages. The sheets included dates, weather descriptions, tide times, and tidal ranges written in neat, boxy penmanship. The last recorded date was May twenty-first, the day I discovered Bambi had nicked my GPS and satellite phone. My earlier anger yielded to sorrow. She paid for her mistake with her life.

The humid breeze carried the sound of waves and a rattle of pots. I looked out the window at a porch with a drooping hammock. Rows of swaying palm trees, low ferns, and magenta-red blooming bushes separated the hut from the beach. The soft undulation of the ocean and views of emerald water filtered through the palm grove.

The journal told me nothing about who this man was or why he lived here. There must be something to it, or he was simply a recluse. Of course, I'd seen YouTube videos of people in their late twenties selling their homes, quitting their jobs, and going on sailing trips for years. There was not much difference between living alone on a boat or on a remote island. I shouldn't be too quick to judge Hunter, but that didn't stop me from poking around more.

Moving at a tortoise's pace, I staggered to the closest four-shelf bookcase. A topographic map, presumably of this island, hung on the wall above it. At the torn bottom right corner, the map had a stamp, "Teaku." The name didn't ring a bell. The scale was missing, so it was hard to say how big the C-shaped island was, but I'd seen enough maps to know this one was close to five or so square miles. Green dominated most of it (jungle), some light brown with steep terrain to the west and north (hills), two blue spots (small lakes), and a flat line on the south side (beach). Tiny holes dotted the map as if someone had previously stuck pins there, or it was used for mini-dart practice, like Tina and I used Phill's photos.

Unsatisfied with my location assessment, I lowered myself to the floor and examined the bookshelves packed with paperbacks with diverse titles like *Fiji Week-by-Week Gardener's Handbook, The Selected Poetry of Lord Byron,* and D'Aulaires' *Book of Greek Myths*.

The next row that caught my eye was a series of Julia Quinn novels. I huffed in surprised. Hunter was a romantic. Could a romantic also be a serial killer? Perhaps a woman lived here too. But the room was bare of photos or feminine, homey touches besides the fresh flowers by the bed.

From there my gaze dropped to the lowest shelf holding a stack of *Spies and Science* magazines. I picked up the top copy with a sun-bleached cover and flipped through it. It was a British publication with articles like "WWII Spies," "Shaken, Not Stirred," "Holmes New Discoveries." Security systems and spy gear advertisements were plastered over nearly every page and looked comical in our modern day of technology. Toward the back the magazine had crosswords, puzzles, and encrypted messages. Judging by the penciled-in scribbles, someone had tried unsuccessfully to solve them. I smiled to myself. My father would've loved something like this. He'd been a diehard superheroes and spies fan.

With my energy level depleted, I returned the magazine to the stack and sprawled out on the floor, staring at the map on the wall. A few days ago, I'd been on my voyage, following my father's mapped-out islands, spreading his ashes. Now, I was lost on a remote island with a stranger. Admittedly a good looking one (minus the beard). But a beautiful man could still be dangerous. In more ways than one. When Bambi had steered us off course was anyone's guess. It could have been the first day we left the last stop, or it could have been just a day before our arrival to the Cook Islands.

The porch's wooden planks squeaked, and a split second later, Hunter walked into the room. From my current point of view, he seemed even taller and broader.

"Are you okay?" He knelt near me, his eyes wide. *And wow.* What incredible eyes he had. The color of a crystal-clear mountain lake, ringed by long dark lashes. "What happened?"

I couldn't exactly tell him I'd been snooping around his room and got tired. Instead, I said, "I need to use the bathroom. I got out of bed but didn't make it." He creased his brows, and his gaze darted to my jean shorts, then back to my face.

For real?

"I didn't pee myself." I rolled my eyes. "I just didn't make it to the door." Come to think of it, I wouldn't mind finding a bathroom. "Is there a toilet nearby?"

"It's not far, but given your condition, it may feel like it is."

My desperation to get outdoors outweighed my weakness, so I sat up on my elbows, and reached out with my right hand. Ignoring it, Hunter bent forward and wrapped his arm around my torso. His face was inches from mine, and I didn't dare blink. No doubt I had a deer-in-the-headlights look because what the hell was he doing?

Perhaps sensing my uncertainty, Hunter paused. "I don't think you have any internal injuries, but it's safer to help the injured get up this way. I don't want to pull you by your arms. It might cause you more pain." His breath brushed softly against the side of my face. "Lean on me as much as you need but look forward. We're going to stand up now. Ready?"

Something about the way he explained his actions—though

he could have first clarified his intentions—calmed me, and I moved my arm over his shoulder.

"Okay, I'm ready," I said, my focus aimed on the blue water ahead.

Once he had me standing, he didn't let go. My head spun for a moment, my fingers clasping tight around his forearm, and I shut my eyes. When Hunter's arm tightened around me, bringing me back against him, I relaxed into the comfort of leaning against his warm muscular frame. For a jungle man, he smelled rather pleasing—like the ocean and the sun, with a hint of citrus.

"Do you want to sit down?"

"No," I breathed out.

He allowed me time to gather myself. "You need to eat."

And I needed something to drink. Preferably hard liquor.

My dizziness had passed, and I opened my eyes. "I'm good now. We can go."

With my arm around his, we shuffled onto the porch.

"We'll rest when you get tired." He stopped at the top of a four-step staircase. "Can you make it down? If not, I'll carry you."

I whipped my head around so fast to look at him, it took a second for the rest of the world to catch up with my vision. I was weak but I wasn't totally helpless. "No, thank you, I'll be okay."

We gingerly descended, one plank at a time, until we reached a dirt footpath. Hunter pointed to the left and we trudged around the hut, small rocks and wood chips poking at my bare feet, then shuffled past an outdoor kitchen sheltered by a large tarp. The setup was basic: a wooden picnic table, some shelving attached to trees, and a stone fireplace.

I couldn't make out any other details as we stepped deeper into the overgrown jungle.

I was hyperaware of each point where our bodies touched. It wasn't a zap of electricity that shot down my spine at how Hunter's fingers pressed into the skin near my waist or how his gaze was so intent, but a warmth originated in my chest.

It had to be heartburn.

As we slogged down the path, he moved low-hanging tree branches out of the way.

"So," I said, disregarding the growing pain in my feet, "how long have you been here?"

"I moved to the South Pacific from Atlanta about six years ago. Lived most of the time in Avarua and now here."

Over one hundred islands and atolls—most of which remained uninhabited—were sprinkled throughout Polynesia, so perhaps this one was close to my original destination.

"Is Rarotonga far from here?"

"About four to five hours depending on weather conditions and the boat."

For the first time today, joy sprouted inside of me. Bambi hadn't chartered us on the wrong course after we left Niue. Maybe she had been honest about reading the night skies. Or we just got lucky. Well, not really…

A pointy stone stabbed my foot, and I winced. "Shoot." I paused and scraped my foot against the dirt until the pebble shook free. "Were my passport and credit cards still inside my lifejacket when you found me?"

"No," Hunter said.

Well, shit. Getting home would be a double headache.

Hunter stared forward, his brows together as if in deep concentration. The forest thick with tropical trees, various shrubs, and tangled vines resembled a living and breathing creature. My stomach muscles tensed with worry that some danger lurked in the jungle.

"What are you looking at?" I peered up at him and searched for traces of fear or concern on his face. "Is there a tiger or a dinosaur?"

He looked at me, a humorous glint in his eyes. "No dinosaurs."

"A tiger then?"

"No." His cheeks creased into a smile. "I was cataloging what materials I have here to pull my boat out of the water."

Good, at least he had a plan to get a boat. I was one step closer to getting the hell out of here. "And do you?"

"I think so. I'll check the workshop." The hut, the kitchen area, and now the workshop. He indeed resided here.

"Why do you live here?" Alone.

"Not long ago, I worked with my uncle. This was his place, and I lived on a boat." We started to walk again. "He died a year ago, and left this place to me."

"I'm sorry."

"Me too." He cleared his throat. "So why were you sailing in the South Pacific?"

"I was living my dad's dream. He had a lot of sailing routes mapped out, and we picked this one because of my name."

Hunter gave me a sideways glance. "Was he with you on the boat?"

"He passed away a few years ago."

"I'm sorry to hear that, Sydney."

The ache of losing both of my parents in a matter of two years pinched my heart. Time softened the unceasing pain that at first felt like a sharp stab, but it was never gone. My throat closed, and my face prickled. The earlier lightheadedness returned, and I didn't want to lean on Hunter more than I already did. "Can we take a break?"

Hunter navigated us to a large rock where he helped me sit.

"I must be tired." Pressure formed behind my eyes, and I sniffled. "I usually don't cry"—*well, not anymore*—"but right now, for some reason, my emotions are getting the better of me."

"Grief is complicated. After you think you've got hold of it, it returns when you least expect it. And being stranded on a deserted island doesn't help." He sat on the ground, hauled his knees up, and rested his back against a tree. His tanned ankles and calves had several small, white scars in pairs. I would ask why he had them but then I didn't want to appear too prying. Hunter plucked a twig off his shirt. "What made you want to live your father's dream?"

I shrugged, letting fat tears run down my face. "Stupidity."

And Tina… Tina, who had stayed by my side through all these years while everyone else had slowly drifted from my life, was the closest I had to a family. Soon she would probably be worried sick over why I hadn't sent her another note.

"I thought it would be a nice gesture to honor him." I tilted my head skyward. "I came across Dad's detailed sailing notes and played with the idea of whether I could do it for him and me. I had several months free before starting a new job, so I decided to charter a boat in Australia, and thought I'd figure the messy stuff out later. And look at me now. In a jungle with no sailboat and no ashes."

Phill was right: I wasn't good at anything but being book-smart. I couldn't prepare a meal, wasn't crafty, and definitely couldn't plan and execute a successful trip. I wasn't built for an adventure.

I let out an exaggerated groan. "I'm so stupid chartering a boat without knowing anything about sailing."

"Do you know how to fly a commercial airliner?" Hunter asked.

I looked at him sideways. "No."

"But you bought a ticket and got on the plane to fly from the States to Australia. You are not stupid. You counted on your captain to do their job just like you trusted the pilot."

He had a valid point. I sighed. "I need to get back home."

"I'll drag my boat out of the water and see if it's fixable. But if I can't fix it"—Hunter rose to his feet and brushed the dirt off his shorts—"we'll find a way to get the attention of a boat passing by and catch a ride with them to Rarotonga."

"That's good." I smiled, relieved that Hunter already had an extra plan to get us out of here. "How often do people sail by?"

Hunter hesitated for a moment, ran his hand through his hair. "Maybe a few times a year."

There were just not enough middle fingers to make it through this day. I snorted, and a snot bubble popped out of my nose. *That's embarrassing.* I wiped it with the back of my hand. "You mean I'm stuck here with you for months?"

"Trust me"—his forehead wrinkled in the expression *I know, that sucks*—"I'm not thrilled about it either."

My chest tightened, and my stomach cramped. I felt truly nervous. No—scratch that—I had a full-blown panic. What in the hell would I do for that long on a deserted island? Not to mention my job as a senior cybersecurity architect at Global Aegis waited for me. They had the highest-paid jobs in the

States, and the most exciting projects. And I got in. I was born to design networks, write algorithms, and get lost in a constant battle of identifying security gaps. This was my job, the one I'd fought for, it was the bright spark in the crap sandwich of my life so far. It was the fresh start I needed.

I screwed up. Big time.

"It's just ridiculous." I laughed, this time covering my face to avoid another snot mortification. "I had a good plan to get my life back on track. But *this*"—I waved my hands around—"wasn't part of it."

"Don't get worked up just yet. Let me first figure out the situation with my boat. Maybe it is not as bad as I think."

I wanted to slam my fist into something, but all around me were hard surfaces: trees, rocks, and Hunter. A fly landed on my left thigh, and I smacked it—totally missing the bug but leaving a hot sting on my skin. I glanced at Hunter. His eyes had an intense focus. I was so far out of my environment it was comical, in his domain. What if he was a recluse who hated damsels in distress? The less I appeared to be a problem, the better the chances he wouldn't mind sharing this wretched jungle.

I straightened my back. "I've had enough rest. Are we near the bathroom?"

"You can almost see it." Hunter reached his arms out to help me off the stone.

"It's okay," I said, ignoring his offered hand and stood (slowly) up. "I feel much stronger," I lied.

The walk from the hut to the rickety shack in front of us wasn't far, but because of my condition, it took a good five minutes, including time for me to rest.

"Oh, crap," I grousede.

"Literally."

The use of a porta-john, no matter how fancy, was one of my biggest nightmares. Yet, I stood before a small wooden box with a half-moon carved into a door and a plank above it with the word "outhouse" burned into the wood as if someone would confuse it with a day spa. The hope was that Hunter wasn't a teenager who would think it was hilarious to block the door.

"Are there any snakes inside?"

"No. They don't like the smell." He snorted, rubbing the nape of his neck.

"I think I can take it from here." I made a step closer and reached for the handle.

"I'll wait for you."

Not in a million years. I didn't want him to stand here and listen.

"Um, do you think you could go back to your camp? I'll call you when I'm out. Or I'll find my way back."

"Are you sure?"

"Yes." I opened the door. Its hinges squeaked and the stink was enough to turn my stomach. I understood the snakes' decision.

"You might want this." Hunter took a two-foot stick next to the door and handed it to me.

"What for?" I was puzzled by his suggestion but took it anyway.

"Hit the seat a few times. Spiders like to hide under there."

Oh, for fuck's sake. I'd only been on the island for a day and I already hated it.

Scrunching up my face, I tapped the wooden ring with the stick twice and sure enough, four giant brown spiders ran out and disappeared through a crack in the wall. *This is the tenth circle of hell.* I peeked my head inside: cobwebs decorated each corner, a buzzing sound of flies, and one valuable item absent. I turned to Hunter.

"There's no toilet paper."

"Oh, yes. Sorry." He reached out to a tree, tore off two big leaves, and handed them over. "Here you go."

Oh. My. God.

I stared at Hunter. "You must be kidding."

Hunter shrugged and turned on his heels. "You'll get used to it," he called over his shoulder as he disappeared into the jungle.

Uh, fuck.

Chapter Four

Basically, I had been thrown into the bizarre show *Hungry and Naked*. Or maybe it was called *Lost and Naked*. Whatever the heck it was called, it had a troublesome combination of two words. I flung the door open and limped out of the hot box as quickly as possible, waiting to inhale until I was clear of the area.

I drew in moist air and evaluated my situation. If Hunter was right and a boat wouldn't pass by for months, I had to share a hut with a man I'd met only hours ago, stuck in a jungle without contact with the outside world, with a literal shithole as my toilet. All while praying for a passing boat to notice us.

Sweat ran down my face, down my neck, and between my breasts. I peeled the shirt away from my chest and puffed it a few times, creating a little breeze. Lowering myself to the ground, I leaned against a tall tree. I had to return to camp, but my body didn't respond to my brain's command.

My eyes grew heavy. Maybe sailing and the island were all

a dream. Maybe I could open my eyes, and I'd be back in time when my parents were alive—definitely before I married Phill —and I was in my happy bubble. I would urge my mother to go to the doctors and get an MRI—perhaps saving her life and Dad's. Bambi would still be alive because I wouldn't have gone on this sailing trip.

A rustle in the bushes jerked me out of my drowse and sent my heart racing.

My eyes locked on the low fan-leaved bushes a few feet away. The noise stopped. I had no idea if this island had dangerous animals. If a predator was out there, was it watching me, getting ready to pounce on and devour me? I should have asked Hunter to wait. My condition wouldn't allow me to outrun whatever was hiding. Barely breathing and not daring to blink, I listened.

Another sudden rustle plunged me into a frantic panic, and then a black-feathered chicken strolled out from under the bush, its feathers ruffled up as if it had taken a dirt bath. It pecked at something on the ground and continued on its merry way as if I weren't even there.

"Stupid chicken." I closed my eyes again.

If there were threatening animals around, Hunter would've warned me. He'd pulled me out of the water after all. Or had he said I'd washed up on the beach? In any case, he hadn't let me die and had taken care of me.

"Hey." A voice spoke as if in a dream. "Sydney, wake up." The touch on my arm felt more real than any dream could fabricate. I opened my eyes to Hunter crouched next to me. His hand slid under my knees and around my back.

"I'll take you back to bed." He swung me into his arms.

Oh, good. *So much for being less of a pain in his ass.* I mocked every movie and romance novel when a handsome stranger carried a passed-out woman, and there I was, living the cliché. My arms looped around Hunter's neck, and I rested my head on his shoulder, the touch of his old shirt soft against my skin.

"Ohhhh, *Naked and Afraid*," I mumbled.

Hunter paused his walk. "What?"

"Just thinking out loud," I said, inhaling the ghost of citrus on his clothes. "You smell like oranges," I murmured. "Is that your detergent?"

"No." He chuckled.

At his hut, Hunter carefully set me down on his bed and pressed his hand to my forehead. "You need to eat. I'll be right back."

A few minutes later, he returned with a tin plate and a Mason jar filled with a yellow liquid. He set it all next to the journal on the desk and took a seat on the chair.

I sat against the headboard and Hunter helped to adjust the pillow higher behind my back for more comfort. "A common drink on this island—fresh orange juice." He passed me the jar. That explained his citrusy smell.

I drained the entire cup, instantly craving more of its sweet taste. "That was so good."

"I wouldn't offer anything bad to a guest at my house."

I arched an eyebrow. "You gave me a leaf to wipe with."

"The best tree I could offer." The corners of his mouth inched up and his eyes crackled with humor. "I do have toilet paper. I'll replace the empty roll today. But we have to agree that since we are here for an unknown amount of time, toilet paper is only for more serious business." The tips of his ears turned a shade of red. "Is that okay?"

Even in my current unwell state, next to this man, my grin

annoyingly refused to be contained, and I responded with a broad smile of my own. "I understand."

"Good." Hunter broke our eye contact and reached for the plate. "Ready to try the finest food in the South Pacific?"

Aside from my parents, nobody had ever taken care of me. Certainly not my ex-husband. Hell would freeze over before he would cook me food when I was sick. Once, when I caught the flu and could barely get out of bed, I'd had to drive myself to a doctor because Phill didn't want to be in the same car with me, even though we'd shared a bed the night before. Yet here was a good-looking man—even with a rowdy beard—a total stranger who saved my life and didn't mind taking care of me. My lips urged to smile.

"What? Why are you staring at me like that?" he asked, amusement in his expression.

"No reason." My cheeks grew hot. I hadn't realized I was gaping at him.

"Hungry?"

"You could offer me roasted squirrel, and I would eat it," I joked, accepting the plate, but prayed it wasn't a fuzzy-tailed animal. The plate held a fish fillet, a small boiled potato and avocado, with a side of cut-up mango.

"There are no squirrels on this island," he said. "Mostly lizards, iguanas, snakes, cats, and lots of birds, including chickens."

A brown gecko climbed up the screen on the window above the desk. "You have a lot of lizards inside the house."

"Don't hurt them. They eat bugs and mosquitos."

"I'm not scared of lizards, but in the woods, one of your chickens scared the bejesus out of me."

"Yes, they are terrifying creatures." Hunter widened his

eyes in mocking shock. He seemed to be in a top-notch mood for someone stuck on the island for the unforeseeable future with a complete stranger in need of medical attention.

I lowered my eyebrows in alarm. "Do you have enough supplies for us not to go hungry?"

"We won't starve," he said with calm confidence, his gaze flickering at the cabinet on the other side of the room. "There is plenty of food in the ocean. If we stay healthy, we should be all right."

Gratitude swelled inside my chest as I watched him appraise the shelf of dry and canned food, then his kind eyes cut to me and he smiled.

"Thank you for saving my life," I said, my throat thick with emotions.

"I didn't save your life. You were on the shore when I found you. Alive."

"You took care of my injury, and now this." I motioned to the food.

"Any decent human would have done the same." His gaze cast down to his hands, linked together on his lap. *And here I was, hoping you were indecent,* I wanted to joke. My ears burned with embarrassment. I glanced at Hunter to make sure I didn't say it out loud. He was looking down.

Before I could say something unwise, I took my first bite of the fish. A wave of unfamiliar spices mixed with a sweet, flaky fish flavor exploded in my mouth, sending my taste buds into ecstasy. A moan escaped my lips. "This is good." I stuffed in another bite—a bigger one this time.

"Was your father a sailor?"

"No," I said, between chews. "I discovered his journals from his college years, with mapped-out routes he wanted to sail after graduation. There were article cutouts from National Geographic and other magazines about a teenager, Robin Lee Graham, who set sail around the world at the age of sixteen. I guess my father wanted to do something similar."

"I have heard about that guy."

I speared a piece of potato with the fork. "His journey was terrifying. He starved, battled storms, and even encountered pirates." Selfishly, I was glad that my father had met my mom, fallen in love, and given up on his dream because there might not have been me if he had copied Robin. He could have died. My eyes welled up at the thought that he *was* dead and never got to explore the world the way he wanted. I had to focus more on Hunter and not let another wave of sadness take me under. "If you don't mind me asking, what exactly do you do here?"

The smile on Hunter's face wavered, and something in his expression changed, but he recovered quickly. Stretching his long legs and leisurely linking them at his ankles, he crossed his arms and studied me. "I run a deep-sea fishing rental that used to belong to my uncle."

"And what did you do before you came here?"

I sounded like a police interrogator. It was a good thing we weren't on a date, but as long as Hunter gave me answers, I would continue asking questions. In my defense, the need to piece together as much information as I could about him to understand if I was in peril outweighed politeness and etiquette.

"I was a driver for a drug lord," he said, looking me straight in the eye.

My hand with the fork paused midair, and I stared back at him. He couldn't be serious. Or perhaps he'd told the exact truth, but it was so far-fetched that he was sure I wouldn't believe it. I blinked, not sure what to think now, and then I snorted. "Yeah, right. Nobody openly admits to a stranger that they are a criminal."

A smile seemed to teeter on the edge of his lip. "What about you? What did you do before you went sailing?"

"I'm a software engineer. For the last two years, I was a freelance developer for several companies based out of Europe."

He cocked his eyebrow. "That's interesting. Why did you stop working for them?"

I stuffed the last piece of mango in my mouth and placed the fork on the empty plate.

"Short story: AI." In truth, I was too tired and didn't feel like sharing the saddest moments of my life.

A black cat sashayed into the room through the open door. It looked like it was on a mission, its tail up and its yellow eyes fixed on us. The cat disappeared before the bed and then jumped up on my feet. Nonchalantly, it sauntered over to me, paying no attention to my empty plate, rubbing its head against my resting arm.

"Hi there." I ran my hand over its short fur. "What's your name?"

"This is Tuesday. I have two cats."

A snort escaped me. "I'm not sure if the name is creative or ridiculous."

Hunter's full lips curved into a smile, deepening the wrinkles around his eyes. I'd always been a sucker for big, blue eyes. And right now, Hunter's ocean eyes—with long, dark eyelashes—regarded me with a steady, assessing gaze.

I forced my attention on the cat. My fingers kept scratching

Tuesday's neck, behind its ears, sending the cat close to the gate of nirvana. It dropped on its side, purring. "Where did you get him?"

"I was in town, loading goods I'd purchased, and a black cat jumped into my boat. He sat in my seat and stared at me. I didn't need a cat, so I set him on the dock and left the harbor. The next time I returned, the same damn cat was in my sailboat when I came back. It wouldn't leave. So, I brought him here. It was on a Tuesday."

"Where did the second one come from?"

"Same place. Only that time, Monday followed me back from the bar to my boat. I couldn't say no. I thought maybe he was a friend of Tuesday. It was on Monday." Hunter took the plate off my lap. "How are you feeling now?"

"Better." The sensation of weakness wasn't as noticeable as before. A little food made me feel like a human again, but it didn't fully recharge my batteries.

"Good." Hunter rose, collecting the dirty mug off the nightstand. "I'll come by later to check on you."

"Hunter," I said, tucking the strand of hair behind my ear. "Where are you going to sleep tonight?"

He paused at the door. "In the hammock on the porch."

Guilt that I had taken over his bed ground its teeth at my consciousness. "Tomorrow, you can sleep here, and I'm out there." I tipped my head toward the window, my eyes landing on the worn-out sofa that looked even less comfortable than the hammock. "Or maybe I can take the couch?"

A relaxed smile crossed Hunter's face and shook his head. "That's all right. If I stay inside, it leaves you no privacy. I'm perfectly fine outside."

Thank goodness. There was no way I could shut my eyes in the open jungle.

"Try to get some rest," he said before exiting.

Tuesday jumped off the bed and darted through the door after Hunter.

I nestled in the bed, cradling my hands on my chest, and stared at those same paint flakes on the ceiling. This situation —alone on a tropical island with a (so far kind) man—was so surreal. If Tina knew, she would jump up and down, clapping her hands, saying this was the first chapter of my new beginning.

I just hoped that it wasn't a thriller.

Chapter Five

Darkness lingered outside when I opened my eyes. The steady flame of the kerosene lantern on the nightstand gave off enough light to illuminate the desk. Turning the light's knob to its highest setting, I rose off the bed. My head wasn't dizzy, and my energy level seemed to have returned to normal. Sticky sweat covered my skin, and my scalp itched. I'd give anything for a long, hot shower. A bird crooned, and waves calmly lullabied the island and beckoned me to the beach to wash off my filth.

With the lantern in one hand, I walked to the open front door. The encroaching jungle had a mysterious absence of movement with an ocean soundtrack.

A furry body shot between my legs, sending my heart to my throat. I yelped, jumping to the side, as a cat dashed down the stairs and vanished into the inky shadows.

"Stupid ass," I mumbled, peeking around the door to see whether I woke up Hunter.

The full moon's silver light outlined Hunter's tall frame in the ragged hammock, his arms crossed on his chest and his face turned to the forest. A tremor passed over his shoulders, and his hands jerked while his eyebrows pinched together. He shifted his head to the opposite side, the suspended bed swaying ever so slightly. It didn't look very comfortable to sleep like that and for not the first time I was grateful for his kindness and generosity in allowing me to occupy his bed.

I took a step. A wood plank creaked, and an animal—probably the same cat—yowled somewhere in the woods, making my pulse thunder in my ears. I could wait for the morning. Scratching my head, I retreated into the hut and lay back in bed. After several minutes of staring into nothingness, trying to go back to sleep was out of the question.

Placing the lantern in the center of the table, I looked around the dimmed room. I could snoop, but with Hunter sleeping just outside the door, I was doomed to be caught red-handed and that would be embarrassing. My eyes scanned over the bookshelf, stopping at the spy magazines.

Every Sunday morning, for as long as I could remember, my father worked on magazines, crosswords and logic puzzles with a cup of coffee. His love for logic problems and anagrams had developed as a child when my grandfather had subscribed him to Scientific American. Until age ten, I had often sat on my father's lap and pretended to work on them with him. When I turned a teenager, he dragged an extra armchair for me into his office, and we worked across from each other at his desk: he on a magazine, me on my Sudoku book.

My father's ghost settled beside me, readying to look inside the magazines. My throat burned as the old ache flared. I urged it back into my chest, but it brawled its way out, and I choked on a sob. Pressing my face into my hands, I took slow, controlled breaths through pursed lips, willing myself to calm down.

"It's just fatigue and exhaustion," I whispered and rubbed my nose on my shoulder.

Snatching a magazine from the top and getting a pencil off the journal, I took a seat at the table. I flipped it to the page with a puzzle of squares and incomplete triangles, some with and some without dots. The hint under the message suggested using a pigpen cipher from the previous issue. I turned the page. Among ads for spy and deductive classes, I found a cryptographic puzzle with a hint of "movie quote." Since it was a spy magazine, perhaps it was from a James Bond movie. A martini. Shaken, not stirred. The phrase didn't match the encoded pattern. I bit the end of the pencil, then pulled it out of my mouth. Yuck. Someone else had already chewed on it.

Back in college, one of my computer science professors spent a great deal of time on cryptography instead of teaching Java language to the class, which was annoying because it was a complete waste of students' money. He taught us that to solve a cipher was a matter of looking for high-frequency letters and making educated guesses—like anything else in life. I smiled as I wrote my first probable variation in the space next to the puzzle. The money spent on that class was finally about to pay off.

Soon, the lantern flame sputtered, and my scribbled ideas left no room on the page. I needed paper to organize my decoding chaos in an orderly fashion. I tore a few pages from Hunter's journal—I'd ask for forgiveness tomorrow—and started a complex chart of letter combinations.

Sometime later, the sound of Hunter rattling pots in the kitchen reached my ears. I sat up straight, a magazine page peeling off my face, leaving a wet spot of drool on my cheek. Rubbing my eyes, I glanced around the room, my mind in a haze. Empty of oil, the lantern's flame had died, and bright light seeped through the cracks of the shutters. Wiping the drool off my chin, I went outside.

Hunter had pinned a torn notebook sheet on the porch post near the steps. In pencil, inside a cartoonish-shaped speech bubble with a tail pointing down, was a handwritten note.

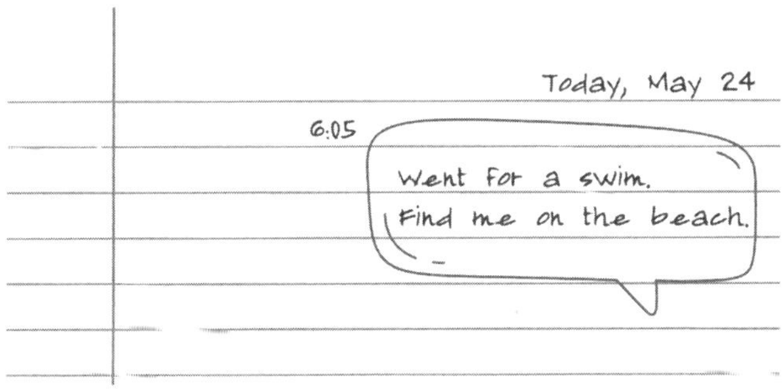

I snatched the paper off and carried it with me.

Hunter stood next to a stone stove that resembled something I'd seen during tours of historic buildings in Savannah, GA. One side had an open area for roasting, and the other had a firebox with a door and a flat cooktop. He moved a skillet aside, picked up a well-used saucepan, and poured brown liquid into two tin cups. Fire pit smoke mingled with the warm tropical air, but I also recognized the distinct aroma of—

"Coffee?" I stopped at the wooden picnic table under the kitchen tent and inhaled deeper.

"Morning." He glanced at me. "I fixed the bean grinder. It's not Starbucks, but it isn't terrible."

My fingers clutched the page I found on the porch, my lips curling up. "Is this a text message?"

"Yes." Hunter rubbed his brow, appearing a bit shy. "I left it in case you woke up before I returned and couldn't find me. I didn't want you to get scared. I drew a speech bubble around it to make it fun." He ran his palm over the beard stubble. And I wondered—for not more than a microsecond—if it would feel soft under the tips of my fingers. *His*. Not mine. I meant to think *his*. Hunter sheepishly smiled and said, "I know, it looks stupid."

I'd known this man only a matter of hours, but after a much-needed sleep, my gut feeling was that it was a good thing I'd stuck with him. Hunter knew how to fix things, had a sense of humor, and maintained a positive mood in this shitty situation. If I were here with Phill, he would have no doubt sulked for days, blaming me for the sailing trip's misfortune, for hiring the insufficient captain (as if he would've done a better job choosing one), and most likely, somehow, the dreadful storm would have been my fault too.

"It's a cute idea. I like it." I smiled, then ran my fingers through my greasy, tangled hair. If I waited any longer to take a proper shower, a family of lice could soon become my pets. Just the thought of the wingless parasite worsened the prickling of my skin.

He offered me the mug. "I might have some sugar. Would you like some?"

"Yes, please."

Hunter disappeared into the hut and soon returned. He retrieved a teaspoon from an aluminum jar on the shelf and presented me with an Organic Brown Coconut sugar paper bag.

I wrinkled my nose. "Coconut flavor is my least favorite."

"Take it or leave it, Wonder Woman." He left everything on the table and moved around me.

Wonder Woman? My mouth twitched at its corners. Phill always called me a Silly Ducky, which he usually followed up with, "You're book smart, but you aren't clever." I hated when he said that to me. Where did that nickname come from? And a better question was, why had I allowed him to use it? Hunter's nickname for me was much better. I wished I were Wonder Woman. I could have saved Bambi.

"Why did you call me that?" I asked, trying to hide my reaction that I liked it.

"Because I *wonder* where you came from." He turned away but not before I caught a kind smile on his face that gave away that it wasn't the only reason. Many people have commented over the years that I resemble Gal Gadot. I felt an unexpected curiosity about whether he found her attractive.

I added some sugar to my coffee and then took a sip. It was flavorful—a bit weak—but had no trace of coconut grossness. All things considered, it was superb.

Hunter placed plates with scrambled eggs and cut-up mangoes on each side of the table and gestured for me to take a seat. "How is your leg?"

"It hurts if I press on it, but overall, I feel great."

After long minutes of us eating in silence, stealing curious glances at each other, he asked, "You made a hell of a mess on the table back there." He peered at me over his mug, then nodded at the hut. "What were you doing?"

"Decoding messages in the magazines. I'm not sure how long I was up. I fell asleep while working on a phrase from a movie from 1995."

"What movie?"

"It doesn't say."

"What words do you have so far?"

If he wasn't interested, he wouldn't be asking. Or maybe he was just trying to be polite. Either way, this was an excellent opportunity for us to bond, get to know each other, and make this castaway situation less tormenting.

Stuffing the last bit of food into my mouth, I held up an index finger and went inside to grab my notes. On my return, I pushed aside my empty plate and spread the sheets on the table, pointed at the magazine page, and then at the paper with my scribbles. "I think these are correct: 'a box of chocolates', 'you', 'you're', but the rest of the words I partially guessed."

Hunter picked up the sheet and twisted his lips to one side, reading my chicken scratch. My handwriting was never beautiful, especially when I rushed or was tired.

"My momma always said life is like a box of chocolates. You never know what you're going to get." He handed me my notes back. "*Forrest Gump*."

I couldn't believe I didn't think of it. My eyes matched his words to the scripted ones. The length of each word equaled the number of letters in each scripted word. "You're right." I beamed. "You were quick to break this code."

"I just guessed the movie." Hunter flipped through the rest of the pages with my decoded puzzles, taking in every note and chart. His eyebrows went up and his eyes flicked to me, questioning. "What was your job again?"

"A software engineer. You know, a geeky girl who hides behind lines of code while wearing sweatpants covered with old mustard stains and munching on Twizzlers." My fingers stiffened as I said those words out loud. I wasn't always that girl. I used to wear stylish power suits and leather pumps, had a corner office overlooking Biscayne Bay, and was the lead developer, driving my career forward ever since college graduation before everything shattered.

"Did they teach you how to decipher messages at school?" he said, sounding genuinely curious. It was just a couple of puzzles. Not that big of a deal.

The black cat rubbed against my leg, and I reached out to scratch his head. "I think writing code is like working with a jigsaw puzzle. Long before my fingers touch a keyboard, I must imagine the big picture. I work with the data I have and spend time carefully looking at each small or big part of the project, figuring out how they all fit together."

"Interesting." Hunter picked up the magazine, bringing my attention to his tattoo. Yesterday, I wasn't in a state to notice all the details. Most people had tattoos to tell a story of their experience or struggle or to honor someone. Of course, some (Tina) get a poo emoji tattoo on their left buttock during spring break in Panama Beach. Hunter didn't strike me as someone who would get a tattoo because his favorite phrase was "little shit." There was a story to his tattoo. And my guess was it was a tragic one.

"May I see your tattoo?" I asked quietly. He hesitated, but then stretched his arm out. I took in the fine details of a three-masted ship sailing across the nautical map with multiple islands. Near his wrist was an ornate wind rose, and above it, closer to the inner part of his arm, was a beautiful compass with roman numerals, one to twelve, on the outer bezel, and degrees 0 to 360 in regular numbers edged into the inner rim. Four fine arrows shot down along the longitude lines.

"It's remarkable." I looked up at Hunter and smiled. "Were you in the Navy?"

Hunter's gaze rested on me, and his eyes had a gentleness that hadn't been there before, but then he blinked, and it was gone. "No, I wasn't. I just love the look of the three-masted barque. For the rest of it the tattoo artist used her imagination."

I tore my eyes off Hunter's face and traced the digits above the longest arrow as if my hand had a mind of its own, finding an excuse to make contact with him. "What are these numbers?"

"Just numbers." Hunter flexed his forearm, making his muscles dance, then broke away from my touch, got up and collected our plates and his cup. I got a feeling he knew the meaning behind the numbers but didn't want to talk about it. That was fine, I could let it go.

"When I return home," I said, "I should get the shape of this island, or its coordinates tattooed as a reminder of my mistake." I gave a short, nervous laugh.

Hunter furrowed his eyebrows and opened his mouth as if to say something but then closed it and walked away to where water ran out of a barrel. On his way, he grabbed the pan off the stove and placed it all into a makeshift sink made from a small, galvanized tub. He probably didn't want a stranger to have his home location on their ass.

"I'm joking." If I had to pick one as a reminder, it would be the *Bloody Mary*.

Tuesday sat down near the tub, his tail wrapping around his butt, and then, instead of lapping up water that ran out and down to a stream, he tapped it with his paw and licked drops off his pads. Then he repeated the motion again and again.

"That's an odd way to drink." I gestured with my cup at the cat.

"Tuesday is an oddball. He likes most fruits and enjoys swimming in the ocean."

"Really?"

"When the waves are calm, of course. It started as him trying to catch fish and then, I guess he liked playing in the water."

My eyes flickered to the note he wrote to me. "Is he accompanying you in the morning for your swims?"

Hunter shook his head, smiling.

My scalp prickled again, and I scratched it. A bamboo halved pipe that ran to the barrel connected to a bigger channel that disappeared into the vegetation. Hunter had running water and didn't appear as filthy as I was. "Is there a place I can take a bath? I feel like I'm starting to stink."

He wrinkled his nose. "I didn't want to say anything." Then he smiled. "Just kidding. There is a waterfall."

"You have some soap?"

"I have more than that. Come on. I'll show you where everything is."

"How about you get stuff while I run to the bathroom?" I pointed over my shoulder.

"Need help finding it?"

"I think I can manage."

A few minutes later, we regrouped in the kitchen again. Hunter handed me a towel with a toothbrush, a tube of cinnamon-flavored toothpaste *(gross)*, a pure coconut oil bar of soap *(the worst kind of scent)*, and *(just kill me now)* coconut shampoo. Oh, for crying out loud. Was there anything here not made from this awful turd-colored fruit?

"These are yours. I suggest using it sparingly." He added a folded light blue T-shirt and brown cargo shorts, pulled a piece of twine from his pocket, and placed it onto the pile in my arms. "For you to tie up the shorts."

A smile pulled my lips at his thoughtfulness. "I'm not sure if blue is my color, but it will do."

The corners of his eyes crinkled, and he motioned to the left. "It's this way."

With my toiletries and towel in hand, I followed him, mentally mapping out the island, orienting what was where. We went in the opposite direction from the outhouse, passing a small open area with clothes hanging on a line stretched between trees, and two small birds balanced on the wire. I recognized my white T-shirt with *"Mind The Gap"* that Tina bought me several years ago from London.

The path meandered through a tangle of tree ferns, flowering bushes, palms, and hardwoods with twisting brown roots. The bamboo piping system carrying water ran above our heads, propped up by timber, or fed through tree branches. Hunter walked at a slow pace with his back ramrod straight, from time to time moving large leaves out of our way and holding them until I passed. About three hundred feet from the hut, the walkway opened at the mountain's base.

My bare foot stepped on a rock, and I yelped.

Hunter paused, turning to check on me. "You okay?"

I hopped on one foot, brushing off a pebble. "Yes."

"I totally forgot," Hunter said. "I found shoes for you."

"My shoes?"

"No. My uncle collected everything that turned up on the beach. I do the same. I have piles of washed-up junk, including an assortment of different shoes. Last night, I picked some out for you. Not a pair but they are similar in size and style."

A teeny-tiny bit of gratitude for marine pollution passed in my mind. I was not proud of that. I lived my entire life in Miami, and even though I wasn't the most eco-friendly person, I participated in organized beach clean-ups. Every time I went to the beach, I brought a garbage bag to collect whatever I found. And now I was grateful for trash. *Yep, definitely going to hell.*

We maneuvered through a break in a stone barrier overgrown by vines (I kept my eyes on the ground to dodge another mean stab), and came out to a waterfall framed by lush plants, plunging into a crystal-clear pool so loud it drowned out the murmuring ocean. Brightly colored flowers of different shapes and sizes were embroidered into the greenery. We stood in complete and total splendor.

"It's so beautiful here," I said, taking an awed breath.

"The world's best shower comes with only one temperature setting." Hunter planted his hands on his hips and rocked back on his heels. "But you'll get used to it."

I looked up at him. "I'm not sure I'll ever get used to the Neanderthal lifestyle."

"Cavemen didn't have coffee and eggs for breakfast."

"You sure look like a caveman with all that." I motioned at his face.

Hunter rubbed his cheek. "You don't like my beard?"

"It's great if you want to join ZZ Top. You'd fit right in."

"I think you secretly like it."

"I assure you, I don't," I said, trying to sound stern, but my stupid mouth betrayed me and pulled up at its corners.

A teasing glimmer played in his eyes. I should have rolled mine back at him, but looking away from his blue gaze was impossible. The scruffy look wasn't my favorite, even if Tina proclaimed that beards were hot, and that it added a certain tickle when—well, never mind where the man's face was.

Hunter pointed to the right of the waterfall. "There's a nice flat rock where you can set your stuff, and there is a smooth entrance into the lake next to it. I'll meet you by the house."

Once he was gone, I dropped everything on the rock and removed my shorts first and the shirt but kept my bikini on.

I dipped my toe into the water, and goosebumps stippled the skin up my leg. As I went knee-deep into the lake, painful prickles spread all over me—another rude awakening. If Hunter's boat was unfixable, this was my bath for the next few weeks in the best-case scenario.

My hands worked hard and fast, scrubbing my body with soap and stripping days of grime, sweat, and ocean salt. I squeezed a hefty amount of shampoo into my palms and massaged it into my hair, trying not to gag at the coconut scent but enjoying the feel of my nails digging into my scalp. And then I had to do something I *really* didn't want to do. Holding my breath, I hurried farther in until the water was chest-high and submerged myself. A few seconds of brutality. There was no other way to describe it.

By the time I squeezed the last drop out of my thick hair, my teeth chattered, and my skin had a bluish tint. I was a five-foot-five-inch popsicle. Drying off, I changed into the clean clothes and collected my belongings. I paused with the shampoo in my hand. I usually washed my hair every other day, and this bottle wouldn't last me long. The amount I used a few minutes ago was a colossal waste. I should be more mindful since we didn't have a store to run out to to get more. At least I didn't need to worry about tampons. I lifted my face skyward, sending small thanks to my OB-GYN for talking me into getting an IUD.

On the way back, I threw the wet towel and bikini over the wire. In the kitchen, a calico cat—must be Monday—rested on a bench and licked his outstretched leg. He gave me the once-over, one ear turned to the side, and resumed his bathing.

Hunter stood before a small mirror attached to a tree near running water. Foam covered half his face as he carefully ran a straight razor against his skin. He cocked his head to the side to shave his strong neck. I remained motionless, watching him as if he were an exotic animal, my eyes wandering the broad planes of his back. A wave of heat swept through me. To me, broad shoulders and a strong back were like cleavage to a man. I could stare at it until someone told me I was rude.

Hunter wiped his face with a wet towel and turned to me. My focus was everywhere at once. And, well, shoot.

His jawline was sharp, and his attractive mouth had soft-looking, reddish-pink, inviting lips. He was so damn striking I wanted to high-five his mom.

"Why are you looking at me like that?" Hunter traced his hand on his face. "Do I still have some foam?"

"Because..."

His tan body with just the right amount of hair running from his chest down to his navel trumped my words. My gaze roamed over a vast expanse of torso and muscular shoulders, then down his defined abs. Unashamed, I allowed my eyes to follow his happy trail down before it was no longer visible.

Tina was thousands of miles away from me, but I could hear her making a drooling noise and felt her elbow jab into my ribs as if she were standing next to me right now.

"You don't have a shirt on," I said, a little breathless.

He glanced down at his body. "Good observation."

Swallowing, I blinked and finally snapped out of my awe haze. I forcefully dragged my eyes away from his body. My hand went to my head to smooth my wet hair. I looked like crap, especially wearing way-too-big-for-me clothes. I wished I had some lip gloss and mascara. Tina may have been wrong about a lot of things: signing us up for the Cockology conference (it was *not* about cocktails—I had to bleach my eyes after), a surprise sleepover at an ophidiarium (her attempt to break my fear of snakes), the Fish Fling (it hurts when a fish hits you in the face). But her suggestion to do the full-body laser treatment was coming in handy.

Hunter swiped his T-shirt off the branch and pulled it on, the lean muscle of his stomach tensing with the movement. "Is this better?" He smiled, and dimples appeared on his cheeks. Dimples? He had freaking dimples. Everything inside me fluttered as if I were back in ninth grade, with acne-pocked skin and teeth caged in braces, and a popular kid asked me to dance.

I smoothed my hair back again, then gestured to my clothes. "I look terrible in these."

"You look beautiful."

He was trying to be polite and lift my spirits, but my insides turned to mush anyway. For a split second, I wished we could have met in the Speakeasy bar near my house, and I wore something sexier, and smelled better, too.

Off the ground, Hunter picked up two different running

shoes and a pair of mismatched flip-flops and placed them by my bare feet. "I hope they'll fit."

One purple Nike shoe, one green and yellow sneaker, a left flip-flop with a single green jewel, and a right one with a golden Tory Burch buckle.

"I always wanted to try this brand." I wiggled my toes into the flip-flops. "Thanks. They fit." I moved my wet hair off my shoulders, wishing I had something to tie it up. It was early in the morning, and the air was already so humid and hot. Or maybe it was Hunter.

Hunter's hand slipped into his side pocket and pulled out two hair ties. "They wash up too sometimes."

"You're the best." I twisted a bun on my head and stretched the hair tie over it. The band broke, flying in some unknown direction. "Oops." I tried the next one, and it held together.

Since I was in an *up shit creek without a paddle* situation, the *if you can't beat them, join them* approach was the best one for now.

"What else do you have on this island?"

Hunter shrugged. "A lot of really neat spots and a bunch of useless junk."

"I wouldn't mind checking it all out."

Hunter tipped his head for me to follow him to the beach. "You might never want to leave once you explore."

I scrunched up my face to hide yet another smile (today, they were very persistent). "I doubt that very much, but let's see if you can prove me wrong."

Chapter Six

"The beach is a little dirty since the storm," Hunter explained when we walked out of the shade of the last palm. "I haven't cleaned it yet, but you can see why I don't mind calling it home."

"Oh wow," I murmured.

Even with lumps of washed-up seaweed, plastic human trash, and driftwood peppered across the white sand, it was out-of-this-world beautiful. The crystal-clear blue water and palm-fringed coast was nothing like I had seen before. It was like what you would see an influencer post with the hashtags #tropicalparadise #nofilter. Unreal beauty, unbelievable tranquility, and unarguably not my home.

My eyes scanned for the bright green bag with my father's urn, hoping it was among the washed-up litter. It wasn't.

I took off my *fancy* flip-flops and moseyed ankle-deep into the water. Turning my attention to the rocky borders, I asked, "Do you think the *Bloody Mary* crashed on those rocks?"

"If it had, more debris would have washed up. I think your sailboat sank a few miles away from here."

My heart broke for the millionth time at the thought of Bambi being lost somewhere out there. Maybe she caught the life ring or something else from the *Bloody Mary,* and as Hunter had said, a passing boat had picked her up and brought her to safety. Holding on to this hope, I willed myself not to cry. I had to focus on the present moment, on something that was in my control: get acquainted with my island mate and then help him to fix the boat and get the hell out of here.

I walked back to where Hunter sat on the sand next to my shoes, arms resting on his bent knees, and found a spot near him.

"Tell me more about yourself," I said. "You said your uncle lived here before. Why?"

He plucked a seashell out of the sand, brought his arm around, and sent the shell flying into the water.

"I moved from Atlanta here to work with Edward. I was in between jobs. His business was booming, and he needed help. We worked half a year during the busy season, and the other half we just enjoyed a slow life in paradise. Sleep, fish, snorkel, take it easy. We worked together for five years until he passed away. Now I run a deep-sea fishing business." He winced, squinting at the dock where his boat's white side barely peaked above the surface. "Well, as you can see, my business is closed for the unforeseeable future."

A breeze blew the loose strands of my hair, gently brushing my face. I inhaled the salty air, concentrating on the sound of small waves that refused to stop kissing the shoreline and chewed my bottom lip, taking in Hunter's features. Perhaps he had a totally different personality from me. Something or someone rubbed him wrong in his past, and he was so fed up with people that he would rather play *Cast Away* for six months. I could see myself leading a slower-paced life on a tropical island like St. John. I'd have a simple job, like running a trinket shop in a touristy area. I couldn't imagine living in total isolation with no connection to other people. Of course, I spent close to two years barely leaving my house. But I had work Zoom meetings, and Tina visited me at least once a week, and that should count as staying in touch with the world.

"Sounds nice, but doesn't it get boring?" I asked. "What about modern comforts? Internet? Electricity?"

Hunter rubbed his freshly shaven chin. Light freckles speckled his cheekbones and all the way past the crinkles by his eyes. "I'm getting there. I already ordered solar panels. It will be a nice place once I fix it up." He looked over his shoulder at the hut tucked in the woods. "Keep in mind that this wasn't my home until recently. I lived on the *Nauti Guy*, where I had all the modern comforts a guy needs."

"A naughty guy?" I arched an eyebrow. "Sounds like a brothel."

He chuckled, rolling dry seaweed in his palms. "Nauti like nautical. Edward came up with the name."

"Edward sounds like a fun man to hang out with."

"He was," Hunter said, with a ghost of a smile. "There isn't a day I don't miss him."

"I know the feeling."

I missed my parents every day too. Burying myself under a lot of work was the easiest escape for me. It didn't help I also lived in their house. More often than not, when I thought grief and I, at last, had called a truce, a simple item like my mother's favorite margarita pitcher I came across while rummaging around for a Tupperware would send me into the dismal vacuum. And it had felt like I wouldn't ever find my way back. One of the agreements I made with Tina was that while I sailed, she would pack everything up, move it to storage, and then put the house on the market. If I truly wanted a new beginning for myself, I had to let go of everything that was old me.

I pulled my knees closer and rested my cheek on them, my face to Hunter. "What did you do before you moved here?"

"I was an on-call doc for a mobster," he said, with a twinkle in his eyes.

I shook my head, suppressing a smile. "No, you weren't. You said you were a drug driver."

"That was my job, too." Hunter laughed, the sound rich and free, and my heart fluttered again. "Before I was laid off, I worked in finance."

I shifted my legs in the white sand and formed a mound with my feet. "Sorry about that."

"That's all right. I didn't enjoy my job and I'm in the better place now. Anyway, you see those rocks." Hunter pointed at the sizable stones in the water about three hundred feet away from the beach. "Most of them have poisonous sea urchins. Four out of five people die from their toxins."

Jesus, I could have died during the storm if a wave slammed me into one of those. I shuddered at that thought. "Do these urchins wash up on the beach?"

"I've never seen them anywhere but on those rocks."

At least now I could go in the water. Knee-high.

"Is there anything else poisonous here?"

He gestured toward the right side of the bay, where a set of dark rocks lurked. "There are snakes. I call them Medusa snakes because they turn you into stone."

A prickle crept up my spine, one vertebra at a time. I stared at Hunter with my eyes wider than a pufferfish. "What, and I can't stress this enough, the fuck?"

"Their venom temporary paralyzes you. The bite won't kill you, but it's hard to swim when you're paralyzed."

"They're water snakes?"

"Sort of. They live on rocks near the water. Over there. It's the only place I've seen them. They don't swim in the ocean or really go on sand. Until we figure out my boat situation, don't go there. But if we're stuck here for a month or longer, you need to build an immunity to their venom, and the only way to do that is to let them bite you." He brought his arms up so I could see them. "You see these little scars on my forearms and my ankles? The snakes have bitten me a dozen times, and now it just hurts a bit. Like a bee sting."

I scuffed. "A bee doesn't leave a scar. How about I'll stay away from that area."

"It can save your life."

"How and why?"

His eyes swiped over my face. "Let's say something happens to me and I die—"

"Let's hope not."

"But if something goes wrong and I'm not around when a snake bites you while you are in the water, you will drown."

First an outhouse, then a freezing lake instead of a shower, and now killer sea urchins, and fucking snakes. Out of all living creatures, snakes—and Phill—were my least favorite. Soon, there wouldn't be enough fingers to count reasons to despise this island. My eyes scanned the beach, my mind searched for a better subject, but it kept tripping over the snakes. What a stupid idea—getting bitten on purpose. I really hoped that the boat under the water in the bay was fixable, and I wouldn't be here for long.

We sat in silence for countless heartbeats, my face warmed by the morning sun. I finally came up with a question. "Do you have a family in Atlanta?"

"I never knew my father." Hunter stared ahead into the ocean. "My mother joined a hippie cult and left me when I was nine."

"That sucks." I frowned. "Who did you live with?"

"Edward and Annie."

"I thought your uncle lived here?"

"Once I left for college, Annie divorced Edward, and he moved out here." Hunter looked at me. "What about you? Any friends back in Miami?"

"I have a few friends. Well, acquaintances," I said. My heart lurched, and I added, "Tina is my only real friend. She's a large part of the reason I'm in this mess."

Tina was a hand that reached down and pulled me back up—a little forcefully, perhaps, but she didn't know any other way. One morning, she barged into my house and literally tackled me to the floor and pulled my sweats off. I thought she'd gone mad. Tina proclaimed she wasn't leaving until I agreed to change my life. She wanted her friend back, and I'd turned into some rat that just sat in the house and only went out to get the mail once a week. I wasn't even going grocery shopping anymore. Thanks to DoorDash and Instacart, everything was delivered to me. Dammit to hell, those convenient services.

We fell silent again, watching the sapphire water for a few

minutes. Hunter glanced at me from time to time but said nothing. Then, at last, he rose to his feet. "Come on, Wonder Woman, I'll show you my junk."

I blinked a few times, suppressing a laugh. "Don't you think we should have at least one proper date and maybe kiss first?"

He opened his mouth and then closed it. A flush rose on his face and he laughed and goddamnit that pulled on the strings of my soul.

"You know what I meant—the washed-up trash," he clarified, offering me both hands.

"Let's take a look at your *junk* then." I released a short, laughing breath and pressed my small palms into his large ones, my skin warmed at our contact. "It better be impressive."

He smiled wide, his cheeks showcasing dimples. "I've never had any complaints."

Chapter Seven

A spotted brown bird with a rust-colored tail hurried ahead of us, occasionally picking in the sand, as we strolled for a few minutes along the beach until we reached the dock. At its end, the white side of the boat peeked from under the water, calm waves stroking it.

"How are you going to get it out?" I asked as we turned into the jungle, where the thick vegetation provided an instant cooling shade.

"How *am I*? I think you mean we. You and I are partners, Wonder Woman," Hunter said, moving his finger between us.

"If I'm Wonder Woman, does it make you *my* Steve Trevor?"

My dad was the geekiest Marvelite in the university and, hence, one of the most beloved professors on campus. He'd chat with students for hours about comics and went with them to comic cons a few times. So naturally, I was more into Marvel superheroes than any boy in my middle and high school. While all the girls plastered their bedrooms with boybands and

Twilight posters, my walls were covered with Captain America and Thor (for obvious reasons).

Hunter's lips pulled into a cheeky smile. "I'm impressed."

I rolled my eyes. "Of course I know who her partner is." *And lover.*

At that point, our eyes met and Hunter's impish look, with a slightly lifted eyebrow, told me he had the same thought: those two had sex. Probably a very superhero-kind-of-great sex. And, for an unexplained reason, Hunter thinking the same thing shot sparks up my veins.

He averted his eyes before I did, "*We* will build a block and tackle, and then drag it onto the beach."

Under a stretched tarp was a working bench with scattered tools and parts of the boat motor, closed canisters beneath it, wooden crates, heavy-duty plastic bins, ropes, and other stuff next to it that I couldn't name. It reminded me of a ramshackle auto repair shop where I used to take my car when I was in high school. The place and its owner gave off a total serial killer vibe. Only the old man knew how to fix anything and didn't charge much.

Hunter tapped his knuckles on the stacked wood beams near a pile of pulleys and cables. "We need more wood, but I have enough ropes and pulleys to drag the *Reely Nauti* to the beach. Then—"

I snorted. "Another naughty?"

"Edward named all his boats Nauti something." He scratched his forehead, looking around the space. "Once we take it out of the water, we'll build a hoist. And if we are lucky, once we lift the boat and the damage isn't bad, I can patch it well enough to get us to the Rarotonga."

"I know nothing about fixing boats, but I'm a quick learner.

I can help you with whatever you need," I said, picking up a hammer and inspecting it as if it were an alien object. A large green gecko darted between cans of polyester resin, jolting my heart, and I dropped the tool.

Hunter and I continued meandering, occasionally pausing as we caught sight of various lizards or birds. The paths and trails weaved through the island like a spider web. He told me more about Edward's business. During the off-season, his uncle used to reside on the island, but throughout the busy fishing season, he lived in a rented studio in Avarua.

We periodically strolled side by side, sometimes with Hunter leading, before we arrived at a wooden structure covered in green vines and buzzing bugs. Human-made (helpful-during-a-crisis) garbage surrounded the ramshackle shed, piled in groups, from shoes and plastic bottles to large synthetic buckets and barrels. Two chickens pecked at the ground near the fishing buoys. Hunter suggested I look inside the shed later because it might have some valuable things Edward's girlfriends had left. Edward had many ladies, from bartenders to surgical doctors, who never lasted more than a few months. For a brief moment, I wondered if Hunter also discarded lovers like shrimp shells. But then, what did I care?

We reached a garden, surrounded by wattle fencing, overgrown with various plants and invading weeds. My mother had loved her garden. Taking care of plants was her idea of relaxation after long hours at work. If she had seen this mayhem she would have cried out in horror. Using my limited gardening knowledge, I tried to figure out which plant was what on the brief tour. Tomatoes? Peppers? It was hard to say.

From there we went to the kitchen where Hunter added the egg we found in the grass to a basket and removed a bowl and a knife from the shelf near the firepit. He dropped an ear of corn, avocado, and mango on the table before me, his forearm brushing my shoulder. Like a dragonfly landing on a lake, our briefest touch set off soft ripples over my skin.

"Can you make a chunky salsa?" he asked, hesitantly.

"Sure."

While my mother possessed remarkable culinary skills, my attempts at cooking served as prime examples of what not to do. I was good at enjoying the delicious plat du jour and helping to clean the kitchen afterward, but salsa was easy enough even for me not to mess up.

"While you're making this, I'll catch a fish." He reached behind a shelf and pulled out something resembling a diminutive version of Triton's three-pronged spear.

"You're fishing with that? Isn't it hard to do?"

Hunter checked the sharp tips with his finger. "Not anymore."

I smiled, realizing how much Hunter's name suited him. Picturing a shirtless Hunter standing waist-deep in the water, one hand above his head, brandishing his weapon, fearlessly watching his prey, and then confidently spearing fish for us to eat was enough to make me blush. This was something I had to see for myself.

"Can I go with you?"

Hunter shook his head. "The easiest place to catch fish is at the small lagoon, but to get there you have to pass by the black rocks with snakes."

Never mind.

"Have fun fishing." I picked up the avocado.

As minutes passed by my stiff fingers clutched the fork as I mixed the raw ingredients in the bowl, and my heart raced as I grasped the seriousness of my current dilemma. If something happened to Hunter, I would be doomed. Firstly, I didn't know how to fix a boat let alone operate it. There would be no fish for me because of the stupid snakes. My eyes cut to the firepit —I had no idea how to make fire. I didn't even know how to kill a chicken—if I could catch it first. I had no survival skills.

"Don't mash the avocado so hard or you'll make guacamole."

I looked up, surprised by the force of how happy I was to hear his voice. His shirt was dry, only the hems of his shorts were wet, and a large fish was speared atop of the sharp blades. His return unmoored me from my defeatist thoughts for a second, but then they were back. My pulse drummed, and I cautioned myself not to overreact, but *really* how could he be so calm?

"I have to get out of here," I blurted out, not hiding my panic. "We need to fix the boat."

Hunter's easy smile waning. "I know. One step at a time. Let's have lunch, and then we work on our plan."

Hunter pulled the fish off the metal tips and deposited it on a flat stone just outside the tent. He collected a folded plastic tarp with a thin fillet knife off the shelf. I might need to learn how to catch fish with a spear, but one helpful skill Bambi taught me was how to fillet fish. I rose off the bench and extended my hand. "I can gut and clean the fish."

"Do you know how to do it? Because if—"

"I had a month and a half of practice on the sailboat," I said (a bit too harshly), taking the knife from his hand. "I'm not totally useless."

Hunter tilted his head, his eyes softened. "I didn't say you are useless. If you want to learn how to fish, I'll teach you. We don't have to go to the lagoon," he said, his tone earnest. "Everything I know at some point I had to learn first."

Something shifted inside me, and I had to look away, my cheeks burning from guilt. Maybe I shouldn't assume all men were like Phill, who constantly shamed me about my inability to be useful around the house. The ironic thing was that Phill wasn't a handyman. He enjoyed pointing out what I didn't know and gloated over my failed attempts at minor repairs and renovations, but I'd never seen him do anything either.

"I appreciate that," I said, staring at the running water, unable to meet Hunter's gaze. "Sorry. My ex-husband berated me … often, and sometimes, I can get defensive when people assume I can't do things, when I know how to do them."

"That's all right." Hunter shrugged. "You take care of that while I work on stoking the fire."

After I gutted and cleaned the fish, I passed it to Hunter. He sprinkled some spices, wrapped it in leaves, and laid the fillet on a wired basket. I discarded fish guts into the flames and washed the knife and tarp.

Hunter moved with ease in this primitive kitchen, reminding me of my father in our house when he was helping my mother during the holidays. He tried to take a scientific approach to cooking, and Mom teased him that there was no science in the kitchen, just magic and a harmony of flavors and aromas. They never danced while they cooked like happy couples in the movies, but Mom and Dad did exchange plenty of butt squeezes and neck kisses. My heart ached under the weight of pain and longing. For what they had. For them.

"You okay?" Hunter asked, drying his hands on the dish towel.

"I was just thinking about my parents. I miss them so much."

I missed our puzzle Sundays, our summer outdoor movie nights. I missed phone calls with my mom on my way home from work while stuck in traffic. We talked about mostly the same things (my work projects, her cooking or garden, their neighbors' car parked again too close to my parents' mailbox). A lump grew in my throat. I longed for her to tell me the same darn story just one more time.

"What happened to them?" Hunter asked in a low voice.

"My mother had an aneurysm. At the funeral, when they lowered her casket, my father jumped into the hole after her. He cried and begged them to bury him with her… It was awful to see him like that." My lips trembled, and hot tears landed on my lap like fat thunderstorm raindrops. "He fell into a depression. I didn't grasp how bad he felt at first. I thought he would recover with time, but it only got worse. We tried different treatments and therapies, but nothing helped. His body was present, but his soul had died with my mom." The familiar pain ached in the pit of my stomach.

Hunter sat beside me. "That's a special kind of love."

Despite all the issues I saw in Phill, I'd desperately wanted to recreate with him what my parents had—deep love for each other. But it took two for a marriage to succeed. In my case, it was only me trying, while Phill each year created more reasons for me to give up.

I nodded without looking at Hunter and attempted to control my next wave of emotions. I inhaled deeply and let out a shaky breath. "Then one night, my dad went to sleep and never woke up."

There were times when I felt that the entire world was

against me, when nothing seemed to work, when it felt like everything that could go wrong had. My mother died, my father got sick, I had to let go of an excellent job to take care of him. And then Phill divorced me. There were innumerable nights when I cried myself to sleep, wishing I could wake up as a different person, in a different life, and that yesterday was just a nightmare.

"Sorry." I wiped my eyes and managed a bleak smile. "Most days, I'm not an emotional basket case." I was sure I looked atrocious, with red-rimmed eyes and a puffy nose. "I must be really, *really* tired."

"You're fine," Hunter whispered. "When Edward died, I cried too. A lot."

"What happened?"

"Cancer." Hunter turned his attention to the smoking fire. "I had some time to prepare myself, but it wasn't easy when it finally killed him."

I took his hand in mine and squeezed it lightly. "Tell me more about him."

Hunter glanced at our joined hands. I had probably overstepped so I released it and moved mine onto my lap.

"Edward and Annie fostered me and raised me as their own. They were kind people. They took good care of me." Hunter's lips curled up at corners. "The three of us traveled to various parts of the world every holiday and school break. We went on several long sailing trips in the Caribbean and the East Indies."

"That's amazing. My mom was terrified of flying. Her only flight was from Montenegro to the States when her parents migrated. She was six, and it wasn't a smooth flight. We only took road trips around the states. She and Dad have been to all the states except Hawaii."

Well, shoot. I dropped my head, shaking it in disbelief. How dumb of me. Hawaii would have been a much better place to spread my dad's ashes than a sailing trip.

"Even Alaska?"

I pulled on the loose thread on the hem of my shorts. "Yep. It was the longest trip of their lives, but they made it."

"Did you grow up in Florida?"

"Born in Miami, went to school in Miami, worked and lived in Miami. What was your favorite part of your childhood, apart from traveling?" The need for him to continue to talk and share about his past grew as my interest in him was piqued. It also helped me feel safer and more at home.

"Edward often left maps and coded notes for me around the house. He left them for Annie, too—on her birthday or their anniversary. He'd write her a poem, and she'd have to guess where he was taking her. It could be a fancy restaurant or a lavish trip."

"Were you any good at these games?"

A huge smile adorned Hunter's face, and my heart stuttered. It was impossible not to notice how handsome he was without the beard, and I had to drop my gaze to my hands as if my broken fingernails were captivating.

"On my fourteenth birthday, Edward hid my present and gave me a page with a text that made no sense. It took me a week to get all the clues to crack his puzzling message. I suppose I'm not good at it."

"What did you have to do?"

"I don't remember all the details now, but he had a built-in bookcase in his home office. Behind it was a broom-sized hidden closet. I knew about it, but didn't know how to unlock the secret door. Edward decided I was old enough to be trusted with the safe combination, except I had to figure it out on my own. One shelf had weight-sensitive spots. I had to place books in a certain order and shift an antique brass horse and other knick-knacks around until they were all in their correct places simultaneously."

"That's neat. I hope it wasn't a puppy in a box." I smiled, thinking how much fun it would be to treasure hunt as a child.

The calico cat leaped onto the table. Hunter gently picked up Monday and scratched its neck, turning the purring button on.

"They're not allowed on the table." He set the cat on the ground. "But after all this time, they still break the rules."

"So, what was at the end of Hunter's treasure hunt? What was the birthday gift?"

"A Nintendo."

"I loved video games. I bet you were stoked."

"I was," he said, turning the fish over on the grill. "Unfortunately, the same day, Annie grounded me for lying about reading for an hour, so I couldn't play it the rest of the month."

I couldn't think of any time my parents grounded me. But I was an annoyingly good kid and rule follower. "Wow, that's a bit extreme."

Hunter shook his head with a *you have no idea* expression, his eyebrows rising and eyes going big. "Annie loved two things: rewatching old movies and reading. And she took both activities very seriously."

We continued to exchange stories, and bursts of laughter charged our lunch as we shared more about our upbringings between mouthfuls. So far, if I had yet to find any red flags about Hunter, I wouldn't be able to. Of course, Phill was also perfect until one day he wasn't.

When we cleaned the dirty dishes, Hunter broke down the strategy of dragging the *Reely Nauti* out of the water and hoisting it. He sketched the pulley system we were going to build and explained the physics behind it. His drawing resembled a stick figure house hit by a Category Five hurricane; nonetheless, I understood his master plan. He warned it wouldn't be easy but had great hopes that he had enough material to fix the boat—depending on the damage.

Hunter was an animated talker. He used his hands a lot, and his face used millions of different expressions, his smile always reaching his eyes, making them somehow even brighter. His enthusiasm gave me enormous hope that soon I'd return home to hot running water, a pool without snakes in it and a bedroom all my own. The logistics of getting to an embassy and sorting out my passport and money to buy a ticket to Miami could wait until my feet hit Avarua's ground.

Today, May 25

~~Dear Diary~~

Just kidding

5:35

Couldn't sleep.
Went for a swim
H.

I don't have a watch, but the sun is about three fingers high off the horizon

Where are you?

show off

Chapter Eight

In the kitchen, I brushed my teeth as Monday begged for attention, rubbing his body against my legs. This morning he acted needy, jumping on the bed when I was asleep, following me to the outhouse, and trying to open the door while I was inside. Maybe he was just happy to see me.

Yesterday, Hunter spent all day deconstructing part of the dock, while I dragged the salvaged timber into the shade to remove nails, then tried to straighten them so that today we could start building a pulley system. I looked at my bruised left thumb, which the hammer had whacked instead of the nail. Three times. By the end of the evening, Hunter and I were so tired we barely talked during our dinner of fresh fruit and grilled oysters.

Monday leapt up on the bench and bawled a meow, and my stomach growled in response. There was no need to wait on Hunter to make breakfast, and I shouldn't always depend on him. If he got sick or injured, we would have to rely on me. I was capable of doing it myself. All I needed was fire. Last night Hunter showed me where the logs were, and I knew where the lighter was.

"Let's go get some firewood." I motioned to the cat, not that he would understand, but he jumped off the bench and ran after me.

Just outside the kitchen, the path curved deeper into a jungle. The chirping insects serenaded us, and Monday led the way as if he knew where we were going. Humming the Destiny's Child song "Survivor" I pushed straight ahead, moving big green leaves out of my way. After a minute, striding through the shadowy thicket, I came upon an open space with logs neatly stacked inside a woodshed. An ax rested on top of it.

I picked a log and laid it in the crook of my arm. My hand went to get the second one, then a clinging sound, metal on a rock, resonated, and then it turned into a clank. I cocked my head to the side, concentrating. There it was again.

Dropping the wood, I walked around the woodpile and stepped again into the jungle gloom. I moved slowly, listening for the clanging noise. Ahead of me, leaves ruffled, and twigs broke. I kept moving. My right foot sunk into something soft, and I lurched back, muffling a yelp, my flip-flop swallowed by a new heap of recently turned-over dirt.

My chest tightened, fear stirring within me. I brushed my hair off my face. A five-foot-long and two-foot-wide lumpy dirt pile could have been many ordinary things like a new garden or a place to bury garbage … or it could be … a fresh grave.

"Shit," I muttered.

My heart rate escalated, and each breath turned into a knife-stabbing pain. My brain struggled to come up with a reasonable explanation other than this raw pile of dirt was a fucking grave. There was another mound, a yard or two away, about the same size, with flowerless plants claiming back the soft layer of black earth.

The sound of a shovel hitting the ground snapped me back to attention. I pulled my flip-flop out of the wet mud and slid it back onto my foot.

Swallowing my fear, I edged around the berm and trudged onward.

Pushing another giant banana leaf out of my way, I halted mid-step. Hunter was knee-deep in the ground. He struck the ground with a shovel and heaved the dirt to one side. Filth and sweat covered his shirt and arms. A few freshly dug-out rocks sat near the dirt mound. Panic ricocheted through me, and hairs rippled down my backbone.

The flat blade hit something hard, and I flinched. Hunter struck the earth again and then pushed down on the handle. The metal screeched against the hard stone. Dropping the shovel, he bent and pulled out a large stone. *Quietly retreat and go back to the hut.*

At my feet, Monday bellowed, announcing our presence. *Fuckin' A.* Hunter swiveled with the rock in his hands, and froze when his eyes met mine.

My mind jammed with horror. My muscles tensed to the point of agony. The over-the-top images flashed through my mind—Hunter was Patrick Bateman in disguise. He had enough sex appeal, charm, and charisma to make himself irresistible to others. I hated myself for ignoring that Hunter *was* a stranger and sleeping like a dead man. Oh God. Dead man. The first pile was for his uncle, or Edward's mysterious girlfriends, whose things were in the shed. Or maybe it was someone else entirely. Fuck. He was going to murder me, and nobody would ever find me. I should have searched his place better for clues that he was a murderer.

I spun around and darted back between the greenery to the hut.

"Sydney!" Hunter yelled. "Wait!"

My feet carried me through the woods, branches striking my face and shoulders as my heartbeat banged like gunfire.

Breaking out of the jungle, I picked up the pace and ran toward the woodpile. I skidded to grab the ax, but my flip-flops slid on wet grass, and I crashed hard on my right side, my elbow driving hard into the dirt. Pain shot up to my shoulder.

"Stop!" Hunter's voice boomed from somewhere right behind me.

"Shit." I scrambled to my knees just as Hunter pushed his way out of the line of trees. Forget the ax. I bolted off the ground and dashed into a massive wall of greenery, hoping to reach the kitchen soon, reach the hut, reach safety … but was I safe there?

Hunter caught up to me. His hand went to my wrist, but I ducked and pivoted to the left.

"Stop running!" he shouted when we were under the kitchen tent.

I beelined for the shelf with the utensils jar and reached for the biggest knife. My fingers gripped the handle, and I yanked the blade out, tipping over the jar. Forks and spoons spilled all over the ground. I kept moving until the picnic table stood between Hunter and me.

"Stay away." My hand stretched out with a knife at him, my pulse beating unpleasantly hard. There was no way I could out power the large man before me, but it didn't mean I would go down without a fight.

He stilled and lifted his palms. "It's not what you think it is," he panted, his chest heaving.

"I saw the other grave. I stepped on it." My right thigh throbbed with hot pain. I wanted to make sure it wasn't bleeding, but my eyes didn't dare shift away from Hunter. "Are you going to kill me next?"

"No!" Hunter bent and pressed his hands onto his knees, trying to catch his breath. "Shit, you run fast."

I was the least athletic person on the planet and ran at the speed of a manatee (barely passed high school PE), but I also never had to escape a killer before. I wiped my face with the back of my free hand. "Why are you digging graves?"

"Those are not graves." He shook his head. "You can put your knife away. I have no intention of killing you or anyone else. If I wanted to hurt you, I would have already."

He had a good point there. I lowered my arm a degree—offering a detente.

"Okay." I swallowed, shifting on my feet. "Care to explain what the hell you were doing?"

Scrunching his face, he said, "I'm searching for something."

"What do you mean *something*? Did you just wake up one morning and decide to dig for things?" My palm patted the cut on my thigh. It was wet. I brought my fingers up for a quick glance. Just mud. No blood.

He looked skyward for a count of three, then said, "I'm searching for treasure."

Was he making this shit up? Just like how he joked about working for the mob. *This* couldn't be true.

A nervous laugh escaped me. "Treasure?"

Hunter hung his head in defeat. "Edward and I searched for it for years. Last night, I thought of a new place. I hoped I'd be done before you woke up."

It took all my power to suppress a laugh at how unhinged and delusional this all sounded. He sounded. Frankly, it wasn't a lousy pretext. I probably would've said the same thing. Most treasure-hunting stories were set in remote tropical locations, and we were on an island in the middle of nowhere. But let's be serious. This was just too far-fetched.

I straightened, pushing my shoulders back. "I'm sorry, but this sounds like bullshit."

"You asked what these numbers are." He pointed at his forearm with the tattoo. "These are the coordinates. At least, we think they are."

If I wasn't scared to lose eye contact with Hunter, I would have rolled my eyes so far, I would have needed a surgeon to put them back in place.

"Let me tell you how I see this. You lied about what you and Edward were doing here. You lied about the numbers on your arm. So you probably lied about running a deep-sea fishing rental too." Hunter opened his mouth to say something, but I shushed him. "You've lived here for five years —if *that's* true—and you haven't found anything? You're either terribly bad at searching or your story is BS."

"I did not lie about Edward's business. The *Nauti Guy* is docked at the pier. At least I hope it's still there in one piece. I moved here six years ago to help Edward. He lived here and also rented a place on Avarua. I lived on a boat. Edward passed away, and I'm changing this place to be mine." He closed his eyes, rubbing the back of his neck. "I didn't tell you about the numbers or about the treasure because you are a stranger to me just as much as I am a stranger to you. And yes, six months out of the year, we were out in the water searching for the lost Treasure of Lima."

Silence stretched between us as my mind processed this information. Either it was true, or Hunter had an insanely overactive imagination. I once worked with a software developer who came to work each day sporting a Spock costume, believing our office was a spaceship and that he was writing code to fight aliens. He was a brilliant and friendly guy, but seeing his cubicle turn into a mission control out of *Star Trek* and him calling me Admiral York (Kirk–York, you get it?) was a teensy weensy strange.

My coworker had a fantasy-prone personality, but he was harmless. Perhaps Hunter had the same disorder. Or maybe he had been shipwrecked here so long (who knew how long his boat was in the water), and living alone on the island was messing with his head. Hunter might have needed a hospital bed instead of a hammock.

Taking a deep breath to bring back oxygen into my lungs and gathering myself, I put on a sympathetic but stern expression. At least, I hoped that was how it looked. "Hunter, I want to believe you, but—"

"I'll prove it. Wait here." Hunter marched in the beach's direction, and once he reached the sand, he pivoted left and continued down the shoreline, soon disappearing out of view.

My week just escalated from crap to apeshit.

Chapter Nine

My immediate urge was to follow Hunter and not let him out of sight, but I stayed behind. If Hunter had wanted to hurt me, he would have done so already. Easily. With his six-something-inch muscled frame to my everything-opposite-of-that body I stood no chance. Even when I held a knife. I *usually* had a good instinct about people (except Phill, but life with him taught me lots about narcissists). Meeting Hunter for the first time didn't alarm me. It was quite the opposite—it gave me a sense of security. I had to trust the first feeling that Hunter was a good man.

The lost treasure twist was, I must admit, a bit … dodgy? Iffy? Cuckoo?

All of the above?

I busied myself by cutting mangos and squeezing juice from the oranges we'd collected last night. I wasn't hungry, but my body craved a little pick-me-up sugar, and if the day ahead of me still held a chance of combat, I might as well make sure my bloodstream had some fuel to burn.

By the time Hunter returned, carrying a light brown mailing tube and several journals in his hands, I had made two full glasses. We settled at the picnic table with two diaries, a rolled-up map, nautical charts covered in a grid of crossed-out or shaded-in squares, and pencil scribbles in two different handwritings—Hunter's neat, boxy writing with perfect and equally spaced letters, and the other, sloppy and similar to mine, must have been Edward's. The journals had newspaper cutouts, some dating back to the 1950s, multiple printouts, and photocopies of book articles about the Treasure of Lima.

The remarkable *National Treasure* meets *Indiana Jones* movie props presentation in front of me eased the prickling sensation at the back of my neck. Pushing skepticism aside, I willed myself to believe that Hunter was honest with me about his reasons for being (and digging) on this island. Whether or not the treasure was real was another matter.

"In 1820, Peru started a war against the Spanish Empire colonizing the Americas. The Spanish Viceroy decided to remove all their treasures, so they commissioned British Captain William Thompson and his vessel *Mary Dear* to take them to Mexico for safekeeping. Unfortunately, Captain Thompson was more greedy than honorable, so he and his men killed all the Spanish soldiers and priests on board. Historians believe they arrived at Cocos Island on the coast of Costa Rica and buried the bounty there." Hunter eyed me over the brim of his mug. "Later, a Spanish warship captured them, but Thompson and his first mate escaped, and were never recaptured."

"I hate to break it to you, but this is the wrong island," I said. At least I knew that much. "We are nowhere near Costa Rica." The knife now rested at my thigh on the bench.

My curiosity had shoved my fear aside, but not to the point where I was convinced this wasn't some elaborate cover-up story designed by someone who failed high school geography.

Hunter put down his mug and grinned. "Everyone thinks it is on Cocos Island. Hundreds of explorers have tried to locate the Treasure of Lima over the decades, but all have failed, because Captain William Thompson never went there. He sailed to Australia, and on the way, he hid all the treasure somewhere around these islands." Hunter circled the area between French Polynesia and the Cook Islands on a map with his finger. "Legend has it they sank it somewhere with the idea to come back later and retrieve it. In 1955, during his vacation, my grandfather caught a two-hundred-pound blue marlin. Inside the fish, he discovered not one but two gold doubloons."

I bit into a slice of mango. I could humor him in return for a good story. "Really? Spanish gold coins?"

Pulling a journal out from under a map, he opened to a page with taped yellowish newspaper cutouts, then flipped a few pages more, before stopping on a pencil sketch of the coin. "Like this."

Pressing my elbow on the table, I leaned sideways to take a look, my shoulder brushing Hunter's arm. Somehow, in the last few minutes, we'd moved closer.

"And where are they now?"

Hunter's face dimmed. "Edward gambled them away."

"So you have no proof it's true?"

"I don't need the proof. I know it's true." His voice was gruff and hard in a way I hadn't heard yet.

I shrugged. "Okay. What happened next?"

"Grandpa got invested in research. A few years later, he

purchased this island as his base and began to explore these waters. He lost his family and eventually his sanity because of the Treasure of Lima. Everyone in my family thinks Grandpa brought down some kind of Holden curse upon us when he found these coins."

I was a firm believer that there were no jinxes or curses, just consequences of our actions and human error. But I was curious to know Hunter's thoughts. I raised an eyebrow. "A curse?"

"There are no curses." Hunter waved his hand in dismissal and flipped a page in the journal. "As a kid, I always thought his stories were just crazy tales an old man told me when we visited him, but now, I believe him. Edward and I found ship parts that dated back to the mid-1800s about half a mile from here and then…" He held my gaze. "Don't be alarmed."

I wouldn't say I liked the sound of that, but I desperately wanted to know what he would say next because a tiny part of me was intrigued now.

"Edward found a skeleton holding a brass compass with numbers etched into its base." He turned to the page with a detailed sketch of a compass like the one on Hunter's forearm. "It was missing its lid and gnomon but that's not important."

"What is a gnomon?"

"It's a piece that you'd use on a sundial to cast a shadow to tell the time. In this case, it would be a triangular one that you'd put over the glass connecting its points from here to here." Hunter pointed to the drawing, placing the pencil tip to a dot above north, and then to a dot in the center of the glass.

Wait a minute.

"Did you say a skeleton?"

"Yes."

"You have a dead body on this island? And you're just now telling me about it?"

Hunter outstretched his arms. "How would it sound if I told you there is a skeleton in the jungle?"

"I don't know." Chills ran down my spine. I would've died if I found it on the way to the bathroom or something. "How about why didn't you tell the truth from the day we met?"

"Because I didn't know who you were."

I dropped my chin and pinned him with a look from under the brows. "And what makes you trust me now?"

He mimicked my stare. "I have no choice now, do I?"

Touché.

I wouldn't have spilled the beans about the treasure the first day to an outsider, especially one who so conveniently washed up on his island.

"Is there someone else who is looking for it?"

Hunter's gaze dropped to the notebook, and he ran a finger along the edge of the pages. "Many are looking for this treasure."

"But you said everyone thinks Captain Cook hid it on Coconut Island."

"It's Cocos Island. And Captain William Thompson, not Cook." Hunter let out a resigned sigh. "You are not taking me seriously."

"I am." I cupped the back of my neck, my fingers kneading a tensed muscle.

Everything Hunter said about his grandfather and Edward no doubt was true. Even Captain Thompson's story could be true. I never was interested in sunken treasures, but I had lived my entire life in Miami and heard a lot of stories about a friend of a friend who found silver or gold coins, bejeweled daggers, or ship's bronze bells while snorkeling or scuba diving in the Bahamas or even around the Florida coast. So it was all possible. I just didn't expect to end up in the company of the treasure hunter in the middle of a hunt.

"Can I see this compass?" I asked. Hunter flattened his lips into a tight grimace. "Ah, Edward gambled that away, too?"

"Yes."

"Well, that sucks." I pulled the page with numbers closer.

7863221 1698 2232626311 1526231019 1698 18191518 2327231819

2126 2613674175 1814641755 9131617 212661 1617172
1417181417 1117 5171723

1021181 72118 21618141 152106 25210 227 1811326186
141621222525186 191471425 19251410

194110 211117 223251 1611 223251 195164 26123164 211117
23141 510 1641 1453416 12823251

"This is exactly how they were written?" I glanced at Hunter. "It looks like a message, not coordinates."

"Yes. Edward was sure they were cryptic nautical coordinates. But the more time I spent on this island alone, the more I thought, why would you hide something in the water when there are many islands between the two continents? And why not this place? Why leave a trap if you have nothing to hide? I stopped searching in the ocean and explored here. I've measured, sorted, jumbled, added, and subtracted numbers in every possible way and marked it on this map."

"Why are two, three, six, and nine standing out more than the other digits?"

"I wish I knew."

I studied Hunter's handwritten notes, sketched maps, and his mathematical calculations. "You have been doing this for a year?"

"I don't work on it every day. During the tourist season, I stay in Rarotonga and barely spend time here, just enough to check on the cats and chickens. I work on it nonstop in the off-season. When I grow frustrated with constant defeat, I stop. Then, when I have a new idea, I work on it, but then it leads nowhere, and I lose interest, again."

Hunter picked up another journal and turned it toward me, showing a page with an itemized list. "This is presumably what we are looking for."

I arched my eyebrow at him. "We are?" I must have misheard him.

"Don't you want to help me?"

I shot him an incredulous look, but my eyes kept darting back to the numbers again. Did I want to help him? I was curious about it (a bit) but I didn't know the first thing about treasure hunting—just what I'd seen in movies or read in adventure books when I was a child. I was good at puzzles, and I loved math. I looked at the numbers again, willing a pattern to emerge. My mind was far from John Nash's, but I couldn't help but recognize that this all sounded like fun. Plus I was stuck here with nothing better to do; it could be a good distraction from the painful thoughts about Bambi, my parents and my failed trip. I could help Hunter figure out the meaning behind the digits—if there was one—while we were fixing the darn boat.

I could hear Tina in my head, cheering me on, saying this was a unique, exciting, and *spellbinding* adventure on a tropical island with a good-looking man. For the first time, I was glad she wasn't on this trip with me, as she probably would have tried to sabotage our chances to repair the boat and return home. And I needed to get back. My new beginning I'd been working on, that exciting new life awaited me in bustling Miami, complete with a hot shower, an air-conditioned house, and a well-paid dream job.

"Fine," I said, motioning to the maps. "I'll try to help you figure out these numbers, but we're also working on getting your boat out of the water and fixing it. Once we return to Rarotonga, you're on your own. I'll be rooting for you from the sidelines and hoping one day to see you on the news announcing the discovery of the great lost treasure." I placed my hand on my chest. "And rest assured your secret is safe with me."

Hunter's face saddened for a split second, but he quickly masked it with a brilliant smile. "Maybe this can change your mind." He tapped his knuckles on the sheet. "Read this."

The record listed multiple chests containing gold cloth with canopies, monstrances, chalices all coated with gemstones, a gold relic with topaz, carnelians, emeralds, rubies, diamonds, thousands of gold doubloons, silver, Spanish swords, daggers, crowns of Mexican Gold, thousands of cut and uncut stones, and twenty-two candelabra in gold and silver. The list went on for two pages, but the last item made me gasp.

"A 780 pound, seven-foot solid gold statue of the Virgin Mary with Baby Jesus, rolled on her gold chasuble adorned with 1,684 jewels including four-inch emeralds, six-inch topazes, and seven crosses made of diamonds. Holy shit." I gawked at Hunter. "What is this treasure worth?"

"Over two hundred million dollars," he said, finishing his juice. "Of course, when we find it, we wouldn't be able to keep it, but should get at least ten percent as the finder's fee. Edward had a list of firms to contact."

I liked how he said 'when' and not 'if'. His determination was admirable and maybe alarming. Was he willing to sacrifice his life like his uncle and grandpa over what could be just a rumor, some big historical joke? I unrolled the map again and reviewed the penciled-in lines crisscrossing the canvas. Hunter pressed his elbows on the table, bumping my shoulder with his, and held the end of the map.

After a minute, he got up and said, "Come inside and look at the map there."

Taking the knife (just in case) with me, I abandoned the table and followed him to the hut, where Hunter walked to the low bookshelf and, with a pencil, he pointed at the pricks on the map near the foot of the mountain, not far from the waterfall. "This is where I'd placed pins to mark where I had thought the hidden treasure could be, but I removed them when I found you."

"Why?"

"To eliminate additional questions."

"And you think a bunch of holes in the map didn't raise any?"

He wrinkled his nose in an adorable way. "I hoped you wouldn't notice them."

"I saw them the first day." I returned my focus to the map and studied the elevation contour lines showing the height and shape of the island's surface. Did a similar topographic map exist in the early 1800s? The creation of a coordinate system dated back to Eratosthenes, so the cryptic message on the compass could be a combination of elevations with latitude and longitude. "Want to put the pins back and tell me how you came up with these locations?"

"Want to put down your weapon?" He gave me a sideways glance. "You make me a little nervous."

I snorted. "A five-foot-five woman makes a six-foot-something large man nervous?"

"I saw you running today. Who knows what else you're good at. You might be a Mr. Miyagi in disguise."

That made me laugh, and my tense muscles relaxed. I stepped back and lowered the knife onto the nightstand.

Hunter placed multi-colored pins back in position, we backed away and studied the map again as he gave me a short reason why he thought each place had treasure, and then he said, "Why don't we walk?"

This was going to be a lot of walking, but if I was going to help him figure out where the treasure was, it was best to familiarize myself with the island. Only where to start first? Teaku wasn't exactly a small patch of land.

"Okay."

"Do you want to see the skeleton?"

Not really. "Why the hell not?" I shrugged as if checking out skeletons was something I regularly did. I've seen a mummy at the Lightner Museum in St. Augustine, so what if there wasn't a two-inch glass case this time?

Chapter Ten

Ten yards before the break in the stone barrier that led to the lake—aka the cold-ass nature shower—we took a right turn and walked deeper into the jungle. No more than a hundred feet from there, we stopped at a gap about eight-by-eight feet in the ground.

"This is John." Hunter squatted at the hole's edge, resting his arms on his knees.

"You gave him a name?"

I dropped to all fours and peered over to look inside. At the bottom, roughly twenty feet down, rested a grayish skeleton dressed in torn brown pants, a dirt-covered what-once-was-white shirt, a belt with a buckle, a sword, and a leather tricorn at its feet. The skull was turned skywards, its hollow eyes staring at me. Instead of raising horrified emotions, pity enveloped me. He looked sad and disappointed, like someone whose last thought was, *What the fuck was I thinking coming here?*

"Edward and I didn't want to say 'a dead guy' or 'a

skeleton' when we discussed him in public places. So Edward named him after William Thompson's friend, John Keating. Before Captain William Thompson died, he left the treasure's location and instructions with Keating. And since we found him here with the compass, Edward thought it was John."

"Are you sure this wasn't a Halloween party gone wrong? He looks like Captain Sparrow."

Hunter chuckled. "I'm pretty sure he is John Keating."

"This is your rope?" I pointed at the cable, tightened to a healthy tree and tossed into the hole, its end reaching the bottom.

"Yes. I left it there on the off-chance I accidentally fell into this trap."

"Why do you think it was a trap?" I stood up and rubbed my palms on my jean shorts. "What if he was digging the treasure up? What if he dug it all out and then accidentally fell into it and broke his neck? And what if he didn't dig deep enough and was sitting on it?" Good grief, the questions piled up in my head quicker than sand in an hourglass.

"He didn't have a shovel, and at the base, there were stakes. I removed them all just in case, with the exception of the one in his back. I didn't want to disturb the fellow much."

"Do you think there are more traps?"

"I crisscrossed this place a million times and haven't found another"—he gave me a warning look—"yet."

Hunter rose and motioned for me to follow him around the hole. "I numbered each landmark that would have been here two hundred years ago and used the numbers to measure in feet. I marked the waterfall landmark number one."

I scrunched up my face. "Why did you decide the waterfall was number one?"

"Because John was here. I rotated landmarks. First, I tried the waterfall, then the cave."

"The cave?"

"Yes, I'll show it to you soon."

From there, we went to the beach, where, not far from the black rocks at the edge of the woods, Hunter pointed out remains from the old sunken vessel he and Edward discovered in the ocean half a mile from the island and dragged onto the beach.

"Edward believed it's the barkentine John and his men sailed on to here," Hunter said. As he and I got closer, medium-sized crabs raced sideways to the water while smaller ones dashed into the nooks and crannies of the debris.

"I don't know what barkentine means."

"It's a smaller three-mast ship with only the foremast square-rigged, whereas a full-rigged ship is square-rigged on all three masts."

"Ah." I smiled, shaking my head. "Yeah. I still don't understand, but it doesn't matter. I'm trying to understand the story. So they came to this island, then John got killed, and then their ship sank somewhere nearby. Or did it sink first, and he was the only survivor and somehow made it to this location, just to fall into a trap?"

Hunter scratched the back of his neck. "We don't know. It might be someone else's boat. I haven't found any markings on the pieces."

"Assuming it was John's, wouldn't he need a bigger ship to take all the treasure back?" I asked as we meandered our way into the jungle and strolled north.

"What we found is just a small part of it. From what we can tell it was a large vessel that could fit all that treasure."

My head spun slightly from all the ship types and too much uncertainty. In reality, the only boat we had to worry about was the *Reely Nauti,* but Hunter seemed to want my help to figure out the location of this loot, so we needed to focus more on what he knew and not what he didn't know about old scraps of wood on the beach.

"Go back to how you searched the island," I said.

"With each starting mark," Hunter explained, holding a large branch out of my way and letting me pass, "I first walked seventy-eight north, then turned right and walked sixty-three, then turned left and moved two hundred and twenty-one, then—"

"Do you know the numbers by heart?" I glanced at the digits above the arrows on his tattoo.

"I do." He frowned. "I can recite it backwards too."

Shaking my head, I walked on. "And when you found nothing, you started all over, but with a different turn order. Instead of going right, you went left, and so on?" Hunter gave me a pitiful glance. "Ouch." I cringed at the idea of how many possible patterns there were. "In one of your journals, you have a complicated table with digits that went on for days. Was it the list of combinations you completed?"

"Yep."

I came to a stop. If I had my laptop, I could easily code a simple program that could spit out results within seconds, but doing it by hand … my brain hurt just thinking about it, and my feet ached at the miles it would take too. "And you have walked them all?"

"I'm not even sure if I finished writing all the combinations. I did it for some time, then gave up. Once in a while, I'd pick up where I left off."

We returned to the kitchen for a quick bite of boiled eggs and avocado. While we ate, Hunter described more of his grandfather's fruitless treasure quests. After a short break we ventured further into the jungle, where lush greenery blocked out the sun, crafting cooler air around me, as our path ascended. We were at the foot of the hill with the highest peaks when the sound of rushing water mixed with my heavy breathing. Hunter showed me a carving on a bare wall, which he discovered soon after Edward's passing. It was a pirate ship drawing that could have been left by John Keating or Captain William Thompson. The mark theoretically matched the one found on Cocos Island, per a Wikipedia printout he had in his journal.

"It must mean this area is important." I ran my fingers over the grooves engraved into the stone. It was mind-blowing that two hundred years ago someone stood where my feet were and etched this image with their dagger. Maybe it was the pirate's way to say, "I was here."

"In a second you can decide for yourself," Hunter said and slid between two stones blanketed with soft green moss. I followed him around the bend and found myself in a place that looked like it had been ripped out of a storybook.

Enclosed by a mountain, a cascading low waterfall flowed through a tremendous arched opening, spilling into a small pond. A hundred feet above us, tropical flora surrounded the aperture to the blue sky. Past the arched gate, a giant, gnarled tree grew in the center, its snake-like roots twisted and spread out, reaching into the water. The tree's meaty branches grew outward toward the sky, creating a vast canopy that cast us into a shadow, where some of its thinner branches dripped down, brushing the ground.

"This is amazing," I breathed, gazing at the green Gulliver.

"It is something, isn't it?" Hunter walked past me. "There is nothing like this anywhere else on this island."

"How big is it?"

"At least six feet in diameter."

I made a low whistle. "It's the perfect place for it. There's enough daylight and water, and the tree has protection from strong winds. It must be so old. I bet it was already here when what's-his-name's skeleton wandered around searching for treasure."

"Probably."

Hunter first climbed the slippery rocks up the stream, then held out his hand to help me. Pushing hanging vines out of our way, we curved around the trunk, my fingers brushing reverently along the mammoth's bark. On this side of the tree the space darkened, as if rain clouds had gathered above, but when I craned my neck to look up, the sky was still blue. Before us, a ravine ripped the mountain apart, and to our left, the wall held two large circular cavities, ten or so feet high, with a dark aperture at the bottom.

"If I were a pirate, this would be where I'd hide my stuff. It's far from the shore and not easy to reach through the jungle," I said, standing in the middle of the spacious, ghoulish area.

Hunter walked past the murky entrance, and I followed him but stopped by the cave.

"Did you check inside?"

He nodded. "Yes. It's empty."

I stepped one foot deep and sang, in my very best Adele voice, "Hellooooo..."

My word echoed into the cave's depths, and an odd noise

drifted back, accompanied by a squealing sound. My eyes fixed on the darkness, my body tense. A bat swooped past my head, followed by another grazing my hair, and suddenly dozens of black flying creatures rushed out.

"Shit!" I shrieked and flapped my arms in the air, hitting some of them by accident. Gross.

Hunter grabbed my forearm, and we ducked to the opposite side. We were jammed into a small corner, crouching, Hunter's broad frame folded over me, shielding me from the outside elements, his chest to my back, his arms around my shoulders.

"You said it was empty," I hissed.

"I meant there is no booty," he said, his hot breath on my neck.

Talking about *booty*. Mine was firmly pressed into Hunter's manhood terrain. And now I was hyperaware of Hunter's breathing, his face in my hair—I hoped it smelled borderline clean. My temperature rose a few degrees, and I shivered.

"Are you scared?" Hunter whispered, tightening his strong arms around me.

"No, but I'll have nightmares now about them eating me alive," I said in a low voice as if we were playing hide and seek with the flying creatures.

"I don't think bats can eat you." His voice caressed my ear, and I shivered again.

The squeaking noise died out, but we stayed sandwiched, neither of us moving. As much as I hated to admit it, I enjoyed Hunter's closeness. Something about him using his body to protect me felt gratifying.

"I think they're gone." Hunter released his embrace and leaned away, robbing me of his heat. "It's safe to continue."

He backed away and carefully directed me from under a low-hanging boulder I hadn't noticed earlier.

"Where did they go?" I asked, whipping my head to the left, to the right, then up.

"Not sure. Maybe back into the cave."

"If we find out that the treasure is in there"—I pointed at the dark entrance—"you're going inside alone."

"Sure, but I promise you, there is nothing inside."

We shuffled past the eerie cavern and walked between two giant rock walls, with dense vegetation masking the sky, vines, and tree roots hanging above us. At times, the path would open wide enough that we could stand side by side, and then it would narrow again. Small broken rocks and a few lonely green ferns carpeted the trail. The way before us weaved this way and that, there was a constant breeze moving against me and the deeper we went, the louder the crash of waves became. After the last turn, the passage grew wider, and nature's window opened before us with a view of the endless sky and sea.

Not daring to get any closer, I stopped a yard away from the edge of a cliff and dropped to the ground, stretching my legs. After so much walking in flip-flops, my feet couldn't carry me anymore. Hunter crept forward until the toes of his shoes hovered near the rim. The strong wind smoothed his T-shirt around his body, the hem flapping like an unfurled sail.

My heart was in my throat at how close Hunter stood to the edge. "Aren't you afraid to fall over?"

"Nah. Never been scared of heights," he replied casually, looking over. His forearm muscles flexed and strained as his right hand gripped the rock wall, fingers digging into the creaks. "But if it makes you feel better, I can step away."

He stepped back and moved to sit next to me, leaning back on the heels of his palms and crossing his long legs at the ankle. A sudden gust pummeled us, awakening goosebumps over my skin. I restrained myself from shifting closer to Hunter and stealing some of his warmth.

We fell into companionable silence, staring out at the unmeasured horizon fading up into the red-hued sky. Waves rose gracefully, whitecaps forming atop their peaks, arching their backs and curling under with deliberate practice. They appeared merciful and calm from a distance, but I'd learned firsthand how cruel and unforgiving they could be. I wondered if the *Bloody Mary* had trapped my father's urn forever on the ocean floor or if it had escaped and he was now freely traveling in continuous undercurrents, finally exploring the world as he had always wanted.

"Tomorrow would be a nice day to sail," Hunter said.

I could hear Bambi's raspy voice saying the same thing to me: "Babe, tomorrow the wind and the waves will be on our side." I hated when she used that nickname for me, but what I wouldn't give to hear her say that again. My chest hurt at that, and then anger rose in me at her stupidity for not wearing the lifejacket from the start, for my stupidity of not noticing it was below the deck when I went out the first time, for not getting it sooner. She could have been here with me and Hunter, shooting the breeze. My mouth twitched. She would've loved to hunt treasure.

I wondered if my father would have also enjoyed the treasure hunt. I could without doubt picture him becoming friends with Edward over their passion for puzzles. But he always advised against gambling. Was treasure hunting considered gambling? Risk vs worth of pursuing. It came with thrill, hope, disappointment, and wasted time and resources. But then again, pursuing any dream, whether getting an oddball (but cool) college degree like puppet arts or turfgrass science, could be a gamble. Opening a business or choosing a life partner was a huge wager; one could lose so, *so* much. Look no further than my mangled heart and impaired bank account.

Soft sunlight bounced off the walls and gave Hunter's skin a healthy glow and a hint of gold to his windswept dirty-blond hair. He had an irresponsibly handsome profile with a straight nose, a razor-cut jaw, and a gorgeous mouth. The idea of adventure somehow made me see him in a different light. Of course, I had noticed all his heartthrob features before, but for some reason, right now, everything came in with ultra-sharp focus, making my cheeks burn.

"Do you have someone waiting for you back at Avarua?" Of course, if he had a special person, he would have mentioned it the first day we met, that soon someone would come to rescue us.

He side-glanced at me. "Like a girlfriend?"

"Or boyfriend or partner, or whatever. I won't judge."

"No girlfriend."

I wondered what Hunter's reason was to be a bachelor. Maybe he was busy with his job (was treasure hunting a job?), or maybe he was a player (no, he wasn't cocky enough to be one), or maybe he was recently single (then I certainly wanted to know why). But to be nosy was rude, and really, I didn't care. We didn't need to become BFFs, we needed to get through fixing the boat while decrypting a pirate's old message. So, with startling regret, I steered us in a different direction.

"Have you considered maybe selling this island?"

"Even if I wanted to, and believe me I thought about it, I can't. The original purchase contract has a clause that the island has to stay in our family for at least a century before we can sell it."

"Oh." I smoothed strands of hair out of my face as I retied the bun on my head. "What will you do with the money if you find the loot?" Asking hypothetical questions about possible wealth was okay. It was similar to how each time Tina bought a Powerball ticket, we daydreamed about how she would spend the jackpot if she won. Most of her ideas changed, but two always stayed the same: build a house with a Sephora replica as her makeup room and have a million-dollar charity dinner date with Glen Powell for her, and Henry Cavill for me (she was, after all, a good friend).

Hunter's chest expanded with a deep breath, and something in his face shifted. "I'd pay off my debt."

"What kind of debt?" *Okay. I know.* It was rude of me to ask but it just slipped out. The debt that Phill dragged me into was such a shock to my system that if I even considered dipping my toes into the dating pool again, I would want to do a full credit history check before accepting a date invitation. Not that Hunter and I would date. Or be interested in dating… I really shouldn't have asked it. So, I quickly added, "Like student loans?"

Student loans were okay to talk about. Almost everyone had them, and it was *sort of* a proper loan to have, right? I should have kept my mouth shut.

"Yeah." He slightly nodded as if in a daze, his eyes focused on the horizon. I had a feeling there was something more. Maybe he had defaulted on his credit cards and wasn't comfortable discussing it. I opened my mouth to apologize for prying into his finances, but then his expression reanimated into a smile. "Then I want to open a low-key resort on this island. Nothing big. Maybe four or five bungalows over the water, a small restaurant, and plenty of fun water and land activities."

"What about your deep-sea fishing business? You don't like it?"

"It's okay and can make good money, but it's not something I want to do for the rest of my life. I always wanted to be in the hospitality industry. I could run deep-sea fishing as part of the water sports package."

"If you want to stay closer to the water and sand, there are plenty of nice resorts in Florida," I suggested, unsure why I had to throw in my home state. I wasn't inviting him or anything like that.

Hunter regarded me for several beats with a ghost of a smile on his lips, but then he looked away. "I don't want to go back to the States. Until I moved to the Cook Islands, I didn't realize how not myself I was back there. The demands of modern culture were too much. My life was hectic. I was rushing to keep up with my friends, coworkers, heck, my next-door neighbor. I felt I was running a never-ending race. But here, my life slowed, and with it, my mind too. I feel so much better now. I'm not saying that the way the majority of people live back home is the wrong way to live; it's perfect for most people, but it just wasn't for me."

I was that person. From a young age, the tempo of my life was go, go, go. I was busy with school, multiple clubs, then college, and later, a demanding job. I wasn't even sure if I liked a fast-paced, frenzied life or not, because it was the only way I knew how to live. Then the only way I knew how to deal with my grief was to throw myself back into challenging work. I might have turned into a pseudo-recluse like Tina liked to call me (I preferred the term *homebody*) but it helped. At least I thought it did; my mind was too preoccupied to notice my heart was broken.

"And maybe one day," Hunter continued, "I'll change my mind and go back, but right now I don't see it happening. This part of the world is my home now." An unexplained fracture formed somewhere deep in my heart.

"But running even a modest resort could still be a lot of work. The headache of dealing with the government and unappreciative customers," I said. "Are you not afraid it will make your life hectic once again?"

He hummed, pulling his lips to the side. "Possibly. Difficult customers don't bother me. I have dealt with those types of people many times on fishing trips." He smiled. "What about you? What will you do with your share?"

"What is my share?" I mimicked his pose and leaned back on my palms, flat on the ground, my thumb barely touching his. The most minor point of contact, yet so much heat streamed through it.

Hunter looked at our hands then at me. "Half, obviously."

I never thought of having so much money. I was comfortable with what I made at my job (of course, because of AI, I might soon be unemployed), and it never crossed my mind to stop working until perhaps my late fifties (if I invested well), but I was sure I could get used to the idea of even earlier retirement. What would I do with myself? I could sail the world for a few years in honor of my father, visit places he'd mentioned in his diaries, and perhaps understand why he had wanted to do it. I could donate some money to the animal shelter a few blocks from my house, and volunteer there several days a week. Or maybe I should donate right away and then go traveling. Something to think about later.

"You'd give up that much?" I said, my eyes never leaving his. "But I just got here. You have been doing this for much longer."

It was his turn to tilt his head. "Trust me, I'm still at square one."

"No, you're on square two because you narrowed your search to this island."

"I *think* it's here," he said, arching an eyebrow. "I could be wrong. I've been mistaken about many locations before."

My gut feeling was this time Hunter was right. The island had a skeleton with a compass containing a cryptic message and a pirate's ship carved on the side of a mountain. There was obviously something special about this place.

"You're saying if we find the treasure by the time you fix your boat, I can keep half of the finder's fee?" I asked, and he nodded. A flare of eagerness fizzed through my veins. I had several days to a few weeks to find a two-hundred-year-old lottery ticket. Challenge accepted. I stuck my hand out. "Deal."

Hunter's large, callused hand enveloped mine, his warmth seeping into my skin. "Deal."

Today, May 26
7:12
I don't know the time
Hunter, wth is that?
A pic of a squashed bug?
17:05
I texted you my breakfast. It was an attempt at food porn.
You have many talents, but drawing isn't one of them
sad emoji
17:23
Since you just wrote that, it's 17:23
I figured that
Today, May 27
6:35
At the workshop

Chapter Eleven

Dressed in my bikini and jean shorts, I followed a thumping noise to the beach, where I found Hunter erecting a part of the block and tackle system. Yesterday, as we gathered all the lines Hunter had and selected the healthiest and strongest-looking trees, he explained the simple engineering behind the pulley and lifting design we were building today. The easiest part was assembling this system and the structure where the *Reely Nauti* would be lifted or something like that. But the challenging part was reeling the sunken boat out of the ocean—a many-thousand-pound beast, full of water, resting on its side on the seabed. Several days max.

A few hens pecked the ground, a group of young chickens following them. Tuesday sunbathed on driftwood on the beach, and Monday hid in low bushes, his tri-colored face not blending well with green. I kept in the shade and watched Hunter work as if I'd never seen a man before. Hunter's shirt hung on the corner of the workbench as he stood tall with both hands holding up a large joist, trying to connect it to a structure with pulleys and cables attached and threaded between other timbers.

As he lifted it, sweat ran down his muscled back and disappeared in the waist of the shorts which hung low on his hips. His broad shoulders and clean-cut muscles were those of a man who didn't spend hours in the gym huffing in front of a mirror but earned through hard labor. This wasn't the first time I'd seen him without a shirt on, but right now, scorching heat spread in my chest and reached deep down into my core.

Before I forgot how to breathe (and that we should be a team), I asked, "Need my help?"

Hunter peered over his shoulder at me. "Please."

Joining him, I flattened my palms next to his on the beam.

"Hold it in place." Hunter wiped his damp forehead with his forearm and stepped back to grab a hammer. "Watch your fingers." He came up behind me, so close the heat of his body gave me a long-forgotten lustful thrill of being so close to a hot (figuratively and literally) man. He hammered nails into the wood's top corners. Then we shifted to work on the lower corner, my shoulder brushed his side. Or did he brush against me?

"You slept late," he commented.

"You should have woken me up. And thanks for the breakfast." And fresh flowers in a jar next to the bowl of scrambled eggs and cut-up fruit salad. "What time is it?"

He glanced at his watch. "Almost eleven."

Hunter hitched his right shoulder and rubbed the side of his face, then returned to aligning the two boards above our heads.

"You need a clock in the hut or the kitchen," I said.

"I'll make you a sundial," he grunted, through squeezed tight teeth, concentrating on the board that wouldn't go in its place.

Tilting slightly toward him, I took a deep breath. He smelled ... well ... sweaty. What else did I expect? And Heavens to Betsy I loved this smell. What was wrong with me? I needed a distraction. Quickly. Anything.

"Do you want to get acquainted more? Or talk about anything?" I said louder than intended.

"I'm right here. You don't have to yell," he said around a nail between his teeth. His answer wasn't a splash of cold water, but it calmed my inner crazy. "I'm not sure I want to talk right now."

I focused on the small grains in the wood. "We don't have to talk. We can play This or That."

"*That* involves talking," Hunter grumbled as he tried to pull a broken nail out of the wood that didn't go in quite right.

"I know, but we could learn more about each other since we are roomies for the next few days or weeks." I couldn't resist and glanced at the dance of Hunter's muscles as he moved.

Pinching the crooked nail, he pressed it against the beam and slightly tapped it to straighten it. The nail didn't cooperate. Hunter took a deep breath and tossed it into a bucket. "Fine. I'll go first."

"But we should set rules."

"Rules?" Hunter gave a huffy laugh and started to hammer the nail, shaking his head at whatever thought he was thinking.

"You can ask five questions, and then it's my turn."

"Any other rules?"

"Answer quickly with what comes first to mind. And nothing too personal."

"I thought the point of this game was to learn more about each other," he said, his voice tinged with irritation. Hunter dropped the hammer, grabbed his shirt off a post, and wiped his face with it.

"Yes, but you can't ask me, say, if I'd prefer a strawberry or a banana-flavored condom." I needed to smack myself for saying that.

Hunter's movement paused, and then he chuckled. "I know for sure it won't be coconut flavor." He cleared his throat. "Okay. No condom questions." He did a quick sweep around the beach with his eyes. "Watermelon … or vanilla-flavored…" His gaze turned to mine. My temperature skyrocketed, and I tilted my head in a warning. His mouth turned into a cocky grin. "Chapstick."

"Vanilla."

"Fiction or nonfiction?"

"Fiction."

"City or countryside?"

"City."

"Rain or snow?"

"Sun."

"That wasn't part of the question," Hunter said.

"I know, but I didn't like either option."

"The last question is…" He drummed his fingers on the wooden beam we worked on. "Over or under?"

My skin lit on fire again. "Hunter!"

"What?"

"We agreed. No personal questions."

He did a double look at me with surprise. "Was that too personal?"

"Of course it was. Asking me if I enjoy having sex on top or not is way too personal."

He stared at me. I stared back at him. He threw his head and laughed. "That's not what I meant."

I was confused now. "Then what did you mean?"

"Toilet paper: over or under?"

I banged my forehead on the tree trunk and my shoulders shook with laughter. "I'm such an idiot."

"Not an idiot. But we know where your mind goes."

"It doesn't go there," I lied. In Hunter's get-your-panties-wet presence, it was hard not to fantasize about dicktopia. Especially after three years of not shagging. Sex with Phill was like having wham-bam-thank-you-ma'am with a male blowup doll: clinical, quick, and slightly deflated in crucial places.

"Your turn to quiz me." Hunter placed a nail on the wood and slammed the hammer on it. To look away from his washboard abs as he worked would've been a sin. Was it a good idea for us to continue this game? I was doomed to ask a question I'd regret for the rest of the day, or worse, until we could get off this island.

"Perhaps we should just focus on the boat rescue," I said.

"Wonder Woman, are you afraid you'll ask a dirty question?" His teeth grazed his full bottom lip.

"No. I lost interest in the game."

"Sure you did."

Hunter linked his arms behind his head and bent his torso, first to the right, then to the left. As he stretched, his body got leaner, and his shorts dropped even lower on his hips, exposing a little more of where the happy trail led. Was he doing it on purpose? Was he showing off his well-cut body in front of me?

What a bastard.

I swallowed with difficulty. "Your shorts are missing a button. And you should put your shirt on. Protecting your skin from direct sunlight keeps the body temperature lower."

Hunter stopped his peacock act, gave me a playful *whatever* look, and then picked up a pulley with a bundle of thick cable. "Can I ask you why you dislike coconut flavor so much?"

I groaned. "You will think it's stupid."

"Try me."

"Phill, my ex, loved coconut mojitos. After he stripped me of half of my money during our divorce, I woke up the following day just absolutely hating the taste. At first, it was so bad I would gag if I came close to it." I chanced a glance at Hunter. His face held no trace of judgment, but his eyebrows were drawn together like something bothered him.

"From now on, I'll avoid cooking with coconut. I wish I could offer you a different shampoo, but that's all Edward stocked up with on the island."

"Don't worry." I planted my hands on my hips. "Okay, what's next?"

"Grab the blue ropes and follow me."

Once we had a sturdy system, Hunter swam to the *Reely Nauti* and dived to hook it up to the rope (thank goodness we had enough of it to reach). Then he linked ten lifejackets and six old fishing buoys together and attached them to the boat in the hope that it would give some buoyancy and help to fight against the laws of pushing force and friction.

Well, it didn't. No matter how many times we tried to pull on the cable.

After several attempts, my hands and arms were tired, and I sweated more than I had ever done in my life. Hunter also grew frustrated. His answers became short grunts, and the groove between his eyebrows grew deeper than the Mariana Trench. Finally, I had to call it a day and suggest using the rest of our energy on cryptic numeric messages.

Hunter and I took turns in the ice lake, and regrouped in the hut to work on the numbers. We agreed that if the digits were indeed an enciphered message or instructions, they would surely (hopefully) be written in English. Even more hopefully, the words would be close enough to modern language that we could understand their meaning. Without the internet and limited knowledge about the cryptography used in the 1800s, our next best bet was to use mathematical concepts and principles. The obvious thing was that numbers two, three, six, and nine held the key or keys to solving the puzzle or puzzles.

"Okay. One of the problem-solving principles my father liked to follow was Occam's Razor. The law of parsimony. The simplest explanation is usually the correct one," I began. "We'll start with replacing each occurrence of a number with the designated letter."

Hunter wrinkled his forehead. "There are thousands of possibilities."

"And that's half of the fun." I wiggled my eyebrows.

"That doesn't sound fun at all."

"Oh, come on." I reached over the table for paper and a pencil, my arm brushing against his.

Using a trial-and-error approach, I drew a complex network with vertices and degrees, rotating numbers and moving them from place to place. Then we scribbled arrays with numerals, and shifted them by a certain quantity, assigned letters from the alphabet, and copied the results into a grid. This would have gone much smoother if my fingers could access my computer.

We counted how many times each digit appeared. On a separate page, we created charts containing the most common vowels and high-frequency consonants and paired them with some numeral combinations.

Hours later, the flame of the second lantern danced and guttered as we continued to decode, but despite making countless letter pairings, nothing reasonable came to our minds. An idea of a Braille code surfaced in our debate, but without Google, it was useless. We didn't know the amount and position of the dots, and we weren't sure if Braille had even been invented by the early 1800s.

The following morning, we were able to drag the *Reely Nauti* about twenty feet closer to dry land. When the sun reached the point of turning us into ants under a magnifying glass, Hunter and I returned to interpret the meaning behind the numbers. So many numbers.

The thick, hot air took up too much space in the room, and a drip of sweat ran down between my breasts. Judging by the numbness of my butt and where the sunlight bleached the tattered sofa's armrest, we'd worked for long hours.

"What's this?" Hunter tugged on a piece of paper with an outdoor shower I had sketched last night after we said goodnight. I tried to smash my hand on it to stop him from pulling it out from under the journal, but he was too quick and yanked it out. Abandoning my chair (and lucid thoughts), I launched for it, but Hunter raised it above his head, then behind it, then out to his right, not letting me catch it.

"Goodness." He laughed. "What is it?"

I climbed onto Hunter's lap, reaching for it, my boobs smashing Hunter in the face, his exhaled "oof" skimming my skin. The move brought our bodies flush together. The chair tilted back too far and gave a warning wobble. I squealed, my thighs squeezing his waist, readying for impact with the floor.

"Whoa!" Hunter's arms went under my butt, and he jerked forward, standing up and saving us from falling backward. The chair tumbled with a loud thud.

Hunter's body was a hard wall of muscle. Of course, I knew that from observing him for hours, but I'd never imagined how it would feel when one hung on to it like a buoy in the middle of the ocean. The heat radiating from him was enough to burn down this hut, especially where his forearm propped me up under my ass. His gaze was no longer playful, but scorching, yearning. My breaths resembled those of a triathlon winner, and my eyes were trained on his. And his were … on my mouth. From my very center, something spread like warm, soft honey in every direction of my body; the feeling amplified as it reached certain parts of me and turned into throbbing.

Another beat passed before Hunter cleared his throat, and his arms relaxed, releasing me. I didn't want to let go of him. I wanted him to touch me more. My legs trembled, but I managed to stand without falling. Hunter bent and reached for the chair, and I used that moment to yank the page out of his hand and flip it face down on the table.

"Wonder Woman, why are you so protective of that?" Hunter chuckled, setting the chair upright. "What is that? Did you figure out the message?"

"It's nothing." I smoothed my frizzy hair and sat down, my heart racing at the speed of light. "Just a stupid idea."

How Edward had lived on the island without proper plumbing forever would remain a mystery, but I imagined what I would have done if this was my place. My dad built a rain barrel watering system for my mother's garden. During hot days, we used to joke that the sun had heated the water to the point it could be used for showering instead of watering the plants. And that made me think about designing an outdoor shower. On the island, there were plastic bins and an endless supply of fresh water and sunlight. Everything we could need.

"You don't have to tell me if you don't want to," Hunter said, swiping one of the bigger journals off the table and placing it on his lap as he sat down. His blue eyes stood out more against the red hues spreading across his cheeks.

"Fine." I blew my fallen hair off my face and turned the sheet over. "I just thought that you have enough junk here that we could build this."

Hunter leaned in, pulling the page closer, and studied it. I used the pencil to point at the top of my sketch to eliminate accidental or non-accidental body touching. We'd had enough of that for today.

"That's the large blue plastic drum you have by the shed," I said. Hopefully, it wasn't used for toxic waste and had no holes. I move the pencil's tip to the bottom of the barrel. "And this is an awful illustration of the watering can toy we could use as a showerhead. We could build it in the open area with a damaged tree halfway between the hut and the waterfall. These are plumbing pipes overhead."

The "hmmm" Hunter made didn't sound as if he was all that convinced. But I went on since he asked, and I had nothing else to lose. "We'll secure this drum on this trunk, stick the hose inside, add the watering can on its end and divert water into it from this pipe." I circled the bamboo tube. "During the day, the sun will heat the barrel, and voilà, in the evening, we'll have a warm shower." Just thinking about it made me ecstatic. I flashed a triumphant smile.

He hummed. "It's a fine idea, but it won't work."

My smile dropped. "Why not?" That came out whiny with a touch of defensiveness.

Hunter was about to lecture me, just like Phill often did, about my inability to assemble even a simple IKEA bookshelf without connecting it to my laptop. And yes, I was sure I'd have figured out how to make an even better outdoor shower if I had internet. There were enough YouTube tutorials available that anyone could build a space rocket in their backyard if they wanted to. In our situation, I would have looked up how to construct a motored raft.

"It'll leak all day long."

"I thought about that, too. We'll use that sticky goo you use on the boat to fix any leaks."

"Okay." He tugged on his bottom lip with his teeth as he eyed me. "What about the faucet? You could bend and pinch the hose a few times, but eventually, it will break."

"Didn't you study physics in high school?" I teased him with the exact phrase my dad had used on me. "I don't know the specific law, but it has something to do with the water level always being at the same elevation. With a rope, we'll lift a hose above the water level in the barrel, and it shouldn't leak.

When we're ready to shower, we lower it down." I beamed proudly and wished my father could see me now. At last, I was doing something besides sticking my nose into a computer screen or book. He would be so pleased with my inventiveness. I also pondered, not for the first time, if he would be pleased with me for trying to fulfill his sailing dream, or if he would tell me it was solely meant for him?

Hunter hummed again, nodding. "Okay," he said, straightening in his seat.

That was all? He did not find it impressive. I knew it was a stupid idea. I wanted to ask (shout), "What do you mean, okay and hmm?" but I was afraid he would turn into Phill and belittle me with cheap and baseless facts, twisting them in such a way that it would crush my self-confidence. I didn't want that.

Plastering a fake smile, I removed my sketch from his view and added it to the pile of papers with our dismissed ideas about the puzzling message. "Let's get back to working on these numbers."

"I don't think I can take this anymore," Hunter said about an hour later, leaning back on the chair and linking his long fingers behind his head. His plain, light green T-shirt stretched across his broad chest and clung around his biceps. "Do you want to go for a swim with me, and then I'll start on our dinner?"

"I came from a family of robotics engineers and financial modelers. Math is my second nature. Algorithms were my second language. I can't give up just yet," I said. "I need to beat this."

In truth, it wasn't a genuine excuse for me not going.

Working so close together we frequently touched and leaned on each other more often when it could have been easily avoided, his knee pressing to mine, or my hand resting on his forearm. And I think it was all my doing.

"I'm not in a swimming mood." I nudged his foot slightly with mine—see, I could have avoided that—while my gaze pointlessly zigzagged across the five diagrams we had created. "If I get tired of this, I might read a gardening book. You have fun." I saluted him and flipped to a new page.

Pressing the pencil tip on the sheet, I closed my eyes and tried to envision the numbers for a minute, but all I could see was water, Hunter, and me next to him. *Oh, why not*. I dropped the pencil on the paper and stripped to my bikini.

On the porch, I glanced up just in time to see Hunter stopped short before the water. The sun was already down but there was enough light for me to see him fidgeting with his shorts, and then taking them off. Oh. My. God. I should have felt some embarrassment, but I didn't. And that mortified me. I stumbled backward into the house and knelt before the bookshelf, the vivid image of Hunter's naked ass imprinted in my vision. Naked everything. Well, not everything. He didn't turn around. Shame.

There was no way I could go for a swim now. *Or maybe I should.* Nope. I wasn't that brave.

I yanked a T-shirt and shorts back on and sunk onto the couch with the *Coastal Gardening* book, the metal springs inside the worn-out cushions jabbing at my butt. I turned to the

"Crops" chapter. Educating myself with something new should have taken my mind off Hunter's nakedness. Hunter wore nothing under those shorts. Was it every day or just today? I shifted in my seat. Good grief, he had a nice butt. Besides Phill I'd never seen any man nude. Well, a few times, I had spotted a few guys parading in hammock thongs in Miami Beach (when they *really* shouldn't have) but I blocked that image out of my memory.

I was five pages into the chapter but couldn't recall anything I'd read. Did I even read it? Was he still swimming? I got up from the sofa, clutching the book to my chest, and edged to the door to peek outside.

Hunter had returned from the beach—with his shorts on—several feet away from the porch. I hurried back, dropped the damn book in front of the couch, snatched it up, sat down, flipped it open, and pretended to be immersed in it.

"How was your swim?" I asked without lifting my gaze when he came in, my palms damp at the thought of what was hidden under his shorts.

"Fine." Hunter retrieved a brown sack of rice from the cabinet near the couch. "You should have joined me."

My breathing increased, and I hummed my answer. My focus was glued to a page with an image of some odd structure, but from the corner of my eyes, Hunter's chiseled torso taunted me.

He crossed the room to the door. "Must be an interesting book."

"Yes, very informative." I regarded Hunter's broad shoulders, saltwater clinging to his tan skin.

"Easy to read?" He turned, meeting my eyes.

"Yes, why?"

His mouth curled into a smile, the corners of his eyes crinkling. "Because you're holding it upside down."

Damn it. I flipped it around.

Today, May 31
Ha! I'm up before you
6:15
Thanks for a nifty sundial.
When did you do it?
7:06
You know the rule:
whoever is up
makes the fire and
breakfast.
7:10
I didn't know it
was a rule. You
need to teach me how to
make fire first.
7:15
Ready for BIG
reveal today???

Chapter Twelve

"Pull harder!" Hunter yelled from the other side of the boat.

The question "Where is your 'please'?" teetered on the edge of my tongue, but this was day five of Operation *Reely Nauti* Rescue, and we both were overtaxed and a little edgy with anticipation. To haul a vessel full of water that was equivalent in weight to an African savannah elephant wasn't exactly easy and straightforward. Blisters covered my palms, my muscles ached from too much pulling and lifting, and my ass sported a large bruise from an unfortunate tumble I performed when a rope broke the day before.

Over the last few days the progress with the boat had been much better than with decoding the message. By now, I could recite those digits like my social security number. We'd spent our evenings playing with them, and not a single idea had worked so far. It was becoming more apparent to me that either I wasn't as smart as I thought or whoever created it was a mastermind. Or the answer was hidden in plain sight, and we were looking too hard.

But right now, I wasn't focusing on the message because, at the moment, Hunter and I were trying to lift the boat upright using the hoist frame we had built yesterday. I wasn't an expert, but the boat appeared intact. At least all three sides of it that we saw so far. I couldn't stop praying for the damage to be minimal, so that in a few days, we could ride to civilization. Yet, since this morning, a tight feeling pinched my chest each time I pictured saying goodbye to Hunter at the airport, like I had a large fishbone lodged in me, not letting me take a deep breath.

"Sydney! Pull!"

"I'm fucking trying!" Clenching my teeth, I tightened my grip, wrapped my thighs around the rope, and climbed on the cable, hoping my entire body weight could help.

"Why are you swinging on the rope?" Hunter's voice came from somewhere behind me.

"Isn't it obvious?" I rolled my eyes. "I'm playing The Floor Is Lava." I twisted to look at him over my shoulder, and the slow motion made me spin a full circle. "I can't pull anymore and don't know what else to do."

Hunter's expression was tired, though a tiny flicker of amusement lit his eyes. Part of his bangs were plastered to his face, falling over his left eyebrow. And he was shirtless again. The man didn't know how to keep his shirt on. A sheen of sweat covered his skin. Sweaty men were gross, right? Yet, he looked like a GQ cover model.

This wasn't the first time I'd seen him only wearing shorts, but for annoying reasons the sight had turned me into a mass of hormones. If shirtless man was a fetish, then I certainly had it. My mouth turned dry, and an unshakeable craving for lime and tequila overcame me. I wanted to groan. Why couldn't he look like Danny DeVito?

"I thought you said you are pretty strong?" he teased with a smile.

I gave him a warning glare. "The strongest muscle I have is my middle finger. I'll prove it in a second."

"And here I thought it was your eyeballs because you roll them so much."

My hands grew weak, the sore blisters burning, but I held on as if my life depended on it. "Well, are you just going to stand there?" I demanded, not hiding my irritation at … why was I irritated? I woke up annoyed. Physical exhaustion was definitely a partial cause of my mood, but there was another nagging reason. Not a very clear reason, but it was there.

Hunter stepped toward me, and my knees pushed into his taut abs, as he reached for the rope and his fingers looped around the cable above me.

Our faces were on the same level, our noses a few inches apart. I stared into his blue eyes. My stomach did an odd flip—probably due to poor diet and over-exhaustion. It was rude to stare, but it was hard not to with him being in my personal space. Hunter hadn't shaved in days, his stubble masking a tiny mole above his cupid's bow and another at the corner of his mouth.

"You look as if you want to say something." His heated gaze locked with mine.

"You're in my face."

His lips curved up, and his arm muscles tensed. He yanked on the cable. My knees crashed to the ground, my face now at his crotch.

"Is this better?" he asked.

Bastard.

I backed away as if he had burned me. Without losing momentum, he changed the positions of his hands and heaved once more. The *Reely Nauti* swayed and rocked, slowly lurching off its side and sliding into the holding stand with a loud swoosh.

Hunter looped the rope around a tree trunk and tugged on it hard. He placed his right foot against the trunk and groaned, pulling on the cable. His skin glittered, his back and arm muscles flexing and rippling with each movement. I averted my gaze from Hunter's juicy, round ass that should be illegal for any man to have.

Hunter tied a knot and looked at me, his hands on his knees, catching his breath. "Well, this is the moment we were waiting for. You ready?" He straightened to his full height and marched around the boat.

My chest hurt again, and I rubbed it. Of course I was ready. This was what I had wanted ever since I opened my eyes for the first time in Hunter's hut: to go home. I jumped to my feet and rushed after him to face the moment of truth.

Chapter Thirteen

And the truth was a total fucktastrophe and we were utterly screwed.

"Oh God." I covered my gaping mouth. "It's huge."

"That's what she said," Hunter said in a low voice as if to himself, his eyes assessing the damage.

"I'm glad one of us still has a sense of humor."

The giant hole facing us sucked in the last hope I had to get out of there. The *Reely Nauti* looked like a prop from *Jaws*. The rupture started from the middle of the starboard and ran at least five feet to the stern. One part of the opening was wide enough for me to slide through it easily. How did this happen? I looked at the bay with boulders sticking out in the distance, but the boat was secured to the dock, so it shouldn't have a ravine.

Swallowing, I turned to Hunter. "Can you fix it?" Why did I even ask when I knew the answer was *are you kidding me?*

He raked frustrated hands over his hair, then linked them on the top of his head. "Only with magic."

I wanted to cry. Like really hard. Like a tired toddler. And I was tired. So, so physically exhausted. Never in my life had I done as much manual labor as I had in the last week. And it was all for nothing. We might need to play more "get to know you" games since we were screwed for an indefinite number of days.

"Can we at least try, please?" There was no hope in my tone, just desperation. "Stuff the hole with life jackets or those fishing buoys."

He cast me a tired sideways look, his jaw clenching as if he was on the edge of impatience, before turning on his heels and marching into the shadows of the jungle where his workshop was.

My feet moved to follow Hunter, but I faltered. Perhaps he needed some time alone, a space to process our circumstances. Just like me, he had a life and business to get back to, and the Grand Canyon on the side of the *Reely Nauti* was a mega drawback. I had to find a quiet place where I could come to terms with the fact that I was stuck on this island until we could catch a ride on some random passing boat or seaplane.

I padded down the coastline toward the hut, my feet sinking into the warm sand. In the heart of the horizon, the sun hung low, its amber rays skidding upon rolling waves. As I neared the leaning palm tree, a bright green object perched on the black rocks stole my attention. The color looked similar to the washed-up toddler lifejacket we found yesterday while cleaning the beach. Changing my course, I walked to the water, concentrating on the piece of trash.

The closer I got, the slower my breathing became, and then my heart jolted when I recognized the floating bag holding the urn with my father's ashes. Excitement rippled and a startling new hope shot through me: I haven't failed my father. I could finish his mapped-out sailing trips, spreading his ashes. I could learn how to sail and buy a good boat with the money from the house sale. I didn't have to do it all in one year. Or maybe I should? Take a gap year or two and say "screw it" to my job. Okay, I may have gone too far there.

I hesitated, turning to see if I could find Hunter first, but then a wave hit the rocks, its white talons grazing the bag.

Without further thought, I waded knee-deep into the water but stopped short. The wave had wedged the bag much higher than I could reach without first climbing the darn rocks. To this day, fear of the water snakes had kept me away from that foot of the mountain. I'd watched Hunter wade into the ocean up to his thighs and disappear around the corner only to reappear a few feet higher, climbing on large stones, before sliding between two rocks and vanishing from view again. Not once did he get hurt. Maybe the snakes moved out or died, and the crabs ate them.

The wind was calm, but the waves crashed hard, reaching the bag's bottom. A wave could push the bag off at any moment, and it would be lost in the sea forever. The right decision was to wait for Hunter, but I couldn't lose my dad's ashes again. I took a deep breath and approached the area in the same way I'd seen Hunter do many times before when tides were low.

I closed in on the spot, my eyes searching for snakes in the water and on nearby rocks. None so far. A school of bright fish darted around my legs. My heart thumped hard against my chest. This was a bad idea. Green seaweed blanketed a broad area with a large rock providing a great stepping stone to get higher. I stepped on the slippery rock, the algae carpet soft below my feet, and quickly crossed to the flat slab. I stopped, checked for snakes, and climbed on it. From here, the path wasn't straightforward, just chunks and bits of the mountain piled up as if, at some point, the wall had collapsed. Passing between stones, I ascended to the next level. After another inspection pause, I maneuvered to improve my footing and went higher.

Then I shifted sideways with my chest and stomach pressed hard against the boulder, the rays of sunlight warming my skin. With my fingers digging into the cracks, I navigated around the ledge, the unsympathetic surface of the stone abrading me. The bag was within my reach. Almost. My body trembled as I rose on my tiptoes, one hand holding onto the side of the rock and my feet close to sliding off its slick surface. I stretched as far as I could, reaching for the bag, my fingers hovering near the edge of the green plastic, so close yet unreachable. Unable to grab it, I rested my head against the stone. If Hunter saw me now he wouldn't be happy, but I was sure he would understand later why I had to do this. Once he'd stopped being mad at me.

Another wave slammed into the boulder, spraying me with cold, salty mist. I took a breath and tried again. My fingers brushed a corner of the bag and then pinched it. With a gentle yank, the bag fell, but my grip didn't let it go.

"I got you," I whispered. Happy tears ran down my face as I drew the bag to my side and shuffled back. My mind swirled with the belief that everything in my life was coming back on the right track. Not all was lost.

"What the hell are you doing there?" Hunter shouted, walking toward me.

I lifted the bag, triumphantly. "This is my dad."

"Just stay there. I'm coming."

"I'm okay." I scrambled down, jumping from one rock to another, to the next one, and then—

Two black snakes with a dark red stripe along their length struck my leg.

Once.

Twice.

A scream tore through my throat. Fear and pain pierced through me like a spear, and then a numbing sensation spread like wildfire over my body. My fingers let go of the bag, and I tried to grab the edge of a rock, but I missed it and stumbled face-first into the sea. Water rushed into my nose, my mouth, and pooled in my ears. The sandy bottom was within my reach, and I knew what to do. I needed to get up, but my arms and legs didn't respond.

I couldn't move. I was drowning. An image of Bambi in the storm flashed before me. Her eyes swam with fear when she knew her fate. My throat clogged.

Strong hands yanked me out of the water and carried me to the shore.

"Why would you go there?" Hunter demanded, his voice distant.

Every breath was a struggle.

Was I even breathing?

He eased me onto the sand, then disappeared from view, leaving me staring at the purple skies with amber hues. Hunter reappeared and took my face into his hands.

"Blink if you can hear me."

I closed my eyes but couldn't reopen them. My chest was heavy, and at the same time, a sensation came over me like I was falling through space.

"Sydney, goddamnit, look at me!" Hunter shouted.

My eyes fluttered open.

Hunter moved my hair off my face, his eyes full of concern. "Damn you. Don't scare me like that." He collected me in his arms, then pushed to his feet and carried me to the hut.

"If you continue getting hurt, I'll run out of medication before I can send your annoying ass back home." He lowered me onto the bed and propped my head on the pillow. "Keep looking at me. Watch what I'm doing. Listen to my voice."

The fear of dying and poison (literally) paralyzed me. Bitten twice. Was it bad? An overdose of venom. I couldn't deny that, aside from the horror of this situation, I felt weightless and relaxed. My eyes closed again. If death finally found me, this was a peaceful, painless way to go. Well, sort of.

The weightlessness vanished, and I plummeted through the darkness. A flicker of gold flashed like a match struck in the night. The arrows on Hunter's tattoo caught and sliced my skin on my shoulder, my arm, the side of my torso. My back collided with a three-masted ship topgallant yard. Pain. So much pain. My limp body slid down the topsail. I twisted and turned, my hands grasping slacks, but they slipped through my fingers like sand. I crashed on the cold metal of the magnetic needle of the compass. Nausea threatened to overtake me as the needle spun out of control, making meridian lines blend, but the etched digits of two, three, six, and nine over the cardinal directions flared on the gold sundial.

2. 3. 6. 9.

N. E. S. W.

Chapter Fourteen

Blinking in a dimly lit room, I took a breath, expanding my lungs as much as they would go. I wiggled my toes. The fabric rubbing against my skin brought me great relief. I could move. I could feel. I was alive.

Hunter slept next to me on his back, his left hand rested on his chest, and his right arm stretched out and under my neck. The light of a nearby lantern on the nightstand cast a serene glow on his dirty-blond hair and days of stubble. My fingers wanted to trace his face, but I was afraid to wake him, so I allowed my eyes to do it instead. I'd been in his arms yesterday, but sadly, I hadn't been able to appreciate the touch of his skin to mine.

Stupid snakes. Well, stupid me. My eyes flickered to the green bag with my dad's ashes safely stowed on the desk by the window. Hunter had rescued it. I smiled and nestled my head into the hollow of Hunter's shoulder and placed my hand on his chest. Night birds cooed, and the wind sang a lullaby, chaos replaced by peace. I was content.

I stirred, then awoke abruptly, alone in bed. The sun spilled into the room. Breeze tugged at the journal pages on the desk and played with pink and purple flower petals in an aluminum mug. This was a déjà vu. Only now I knew where I was, and the enormity of my gratitude for the handsome man who lived here was impossible to encapsulate.

Ignoring the throbbing headache that drummed beneath my temples, I slowly sat up and looked at four small red openings with purple outlines on my ankle. Hunter had saved my life for the second time. I had to thank him, but a wave of nausea pushed me back onto the bed. This could wait. I closed my eyes and tried calming the feeling of sickness by listening to the birds and the ocean. The porch step creaked, and familiar footsteps approached.

Hunter perched next to the bed, holding a cup. "Hey," he said in a low voice. "How are you feeling?"

"This feels like déjà *poo* of how we met." I gave him a weak smile. "How many days have I been out again?"

"One. I brought you some water." He helped me lift my head and held the mug to my lips. After a few sips, he lowered me back down. He placed his hand to my forehead, the cool touch of his palm bringing short-lived comfort, and heat blossomed in my chest like a flower at his attentiveness. "No fever, that's good."

"Aren't you going to lecture me?" I squinted one eye at him.

"Maybe later."

"Did I dream it or does your boat have a huge…?"

Hunter's face creased with pity. "Sorry."

My initial reaction was to jump out of bed and work on the plan of what we could do to get the hell off the island, but a tidal wave of fatigue held me down.

Before my mind whisked me into nothingness, I whispered, "Thank you for saving my ass."

Hunter was silent for a moment then his hand cupped the side of my face. His calloused thumb gently traced the corner of my mouth, tugging at my bottom lip. His eyes tracked his movement, then he leaned in, saying, "Anytime," and pressed a kiss to my brow.

For one, two seconds.

At the touch of his warm lips every pressure point in me became a living pulse as if someone poured pop rocks candy into my bloodstreams. When Hunter pulled away, his eyes held shock, like he had done this on impulse, and it had surprised him. It had sure as hell surprised me.

"I…" he said, closed his mouth, and opened it again. I eyed him quizzically, waiting for an explanation. The act was sweet. It was kind. It was sincere. It meant nothing but a friendly gesture. "I was double checking for fever."

"I understand."

He backed away and quickly left the room, and as I watched him leave, I couldn't stop a smile from pulling at my lips.

Aside from the light discomfort in my ankles the next day, I was back to normal. At noon, judging by the sun directly above, I found Hunter in the kitchen. I leaned against the tree and surveyed the soft-spoken man, removing fish wrapped in leaves from the hot coils. Hunter was a reserved, manly man, yet if he lowered his guard, he could be funny and, at times, flirtatious. But most of all, he was a kind, gentle man. The flutter in my chest accelerated at the thought of yesterday's tender kiss. My chest expanded with the warmth of appreciation, and then guilt gutted me open, letting out all the warmth. I shouldn't have climbed the black rocks and made him worry.

I felt dwarfed by my ignorance. "I'm sorry I went there."

Hunter looked up. "You should have taken my advice and let the snakes bite you while I was present," he said calmly, raising his eyebrows as if to say *I told you so*. "I thought you were going to die."

"Am I immune now?"

"Immune to what? The snakes or your stupidity?" A smile teetered on the edge of his mouth.

"Hey." I scowled at him. "Don't be an asshole. Tell me you never did stupid shit someone warned you not to do?"

"Sorry. You're right." Hunter crouched beside me, and his fingers gently glided over my sores, then his hand followed the bruises up my calf and to the back of my knee, making them go weak. "You are not exactly immune to the venom, but you'll handle it better next time. One or two more bites, and you should respond the same as you would to a bee sting. It will hurt for a while. Luckily, they didn't strike your heel. It happened to me once. It didn't heal properly for a long time. I limped for weeks." He stood up and inclined his head toward the table. "Let's get some food in you."

Not having eaten anything for two days turned me into a growing teenager. Hunter was halfway done eating white flaky fish with mango salsa when my plate already had no evidence of lunch.

"Do you want some of mine?" He slid his plate to me, the compass on his forearm reminding me of my strange dream. Without asking for permission, I reached for his arm and rested it on the table between us, peering closely at his tattoo, noticing details on the sundial that I could swear weren't there before.

"I think I know the answer. Well, not the answer, but I know primers that could help us to find answers." I gently traced the dial on the tattoo, Hunter's skin warm and soft under my fingertips. "This sundial was never meant to be used to tell time. Think of any horizontal sundials you have seen. The numbers are grouped mostly on the top half, with a large gap on the bottom because the shadow never crosses that part during the day. On this compass, the digits are arranged like a regular clock. Notice that each cardinal point is precisely under '12', '3', '6', and '9', and only the '2' in '12' has the same thickness as '3', '6', and '9'."

Hunter peered at his forearm as if seeing the tattoo for the first time. "I'll be damned."

The artist he hired did an extraordinary job capturing the tiniest details. If I was right, we could crack all the messages in no time. An hour at most.

"We were too busy overthinking and overlooking details that were right in front of our noses. These are the keys we need to find the placement of letters in the alphabet. Based on these, we'll know where to shift the rest."

"If you feel well enough, do you want to try it now?" Hunter asked.

"Yes, but let me take a quick wash first." I scratched my arm, then my scalp.

In the hut, I grabbed clean clothes and gathered my shampoo, soap, and a towel. Halfway to the lake, I approached a scene I wasn't expecting to see. Hunter had secured the blue drum above three bamboo walls. Just like I described to him, he'd attached the watering can to the hose and elevated it by a rope that was tied up to a hook screwed into the tree. My mouth agape, I walked into the outdoor shower with a bamboo floor. This was better than I'd imagined. This was an Instagram-worthy outdoor shower. The upsurge in Hunter appreciation hit me so hard a burst of laughter laced with a squeak of sob slipped between my lips. I didn't deserve his kindness. More than ever now I wanted to be right about the numbers on the dial and help him crack the message as a thank you.

I set my toiletries on a small shelf nailed to the trunk and stripped off everything, not caring that there wasn't a door. After days spent alone with Hunter, he'd earned my trust.

Holding my breath, I untied the string and lowered the hose. Like a gift from God, warm water rained down, pulling a loud sigh out of me. I stood with my face skywards, soaking in this luxury. Unhurriedly, I soaped up my body and let my hand travel over my skin. This was a dream. The dream in which my fingers kept turning into Hunter's as they were reaching the most sensitive places.

I had to thank Hunter.

Feeling reborn, I walked into the hut with one purpose in mind. Hunter stood by the map on the wall, removing colorful pins from it. Without saying anything, I moved to him, set my stuff on the bookshelf, pulled on his hand until he faced me, and wrapped my arms around his waist.

"Thank you for everything," I said, pressing my face into Hunter's broad chest. It took everything in me not to burst into tears. His attentive and empathetic personality was too much for me. "Especially for the shower. It is the kindest thing anyone's done for me in a long, *long* time."

Hunter encircled his strong arms around me, his palms engulfing so much of my back. "You're welcome." He rested his head on the top of my wet hair. "It was an exceptionally well-designed idea."

Waves whispered against the shore as we embraced, neither of us taking the first step to let go. We fit together too well. I was aware of how hot his skin felt against mine, how fast his heart pounded in his ribcage, mimicking mine, how his scent of citrus and sunshine was forever embossed in my mind. And I'd miss him so much when I had to go home. I wished there was a way for me to convince Hunter to return to the States. Because I had to admit I really liked him, and would have loved to take a chance to date him. But would he want to date me? Hunter was a versatile jack-of-all-trades and resourceful problem-solver who most likely was looking for a partner like him, and not a software nerd who didn't know how to hard-boil an egg until she turned twenty-seven.

Reluctantly, I relaxed my grip and stepped out of his hug. "Ready to crack these numbers?"

"More than ever." Hunter went to the table covered with paper and pulled two chairs out.

"All right. Assuming these are four separate number-to-letter encrypted sentences, and the bolder digit is a key number, we need to create four separate tables with twenty-six columns with two rows. Once we have new alphabets, we can replace each number in the message with its corresponding letter." I took my seat and opened a journal to a new page. "The first row will be letters. The second row will contain digits." I drew the first chart, filling the top row with letters A to Z, then scribbling 2 under N because cardinal point North was under twelve with only 2 in bolder font. "In English, the second letter of the alphabet is 'B'. In our case, it's 'N'. That makes 'M' be the first letter. With this, we consider the alphabet is shifted by twelve."

I wrote three under "O", four under "P", and continued filling out the rest of the empty boxes, stopping when I penciled in the last number under "Z", which was fourteen. Then I returned to the blank cells and wrote twenty-six under "L", and kept filling them in until I reached the "A" column and scribbled fifteen under it.

A	B	C	D	E	F	G	H	I	J	K	L	M	N	O	P	Q	R	S	T	U	V	W	X	Y	Z
15	16	17	18	19	20	21	22	23	24	25	26	1	2	3	4	5	6	7	8	9	10	11	12	13	14

Crouched over papers on the table, we created other charts, matching the given keys to numbers: three corresponded to "E", six matched to "S", and nine went under "W". After that, we filled in the remaining empty slots.

Breaking the code wasn't hard once we knew what to do. The air around us crackled with excitement and joyful certainty. Laughing at some of his or my puns and silly suggestions of what it could be, his shoulder bumping mine, my hand landing on his arm more than once. And, good Lord, his laugh made the thought that we were stranded on an island evaporate into nothingness.

With the first several unraveled words, we high-fived and whooped, the thrill pushing me to write the next one even faster. Several words went quick—okay, fine, I cheated and mostly guessed them—but the word I had to decode letter by letter, 'Achilles', slowed me down. Hunter's hand moved as fast as mine. The more words he jotted down the more muttered curses escaped his mouth, indicating that he was just as baffled as I was as we unraveled sentences. And then, finally, I scribbled down the last word: *place*.

Chapter Fifteen

After days for me, but years for Hunter, of battling these numbers, at last we had our message. Or, in our case, four riddles.

Strong but hollow alive but dead inside
In natures fortress wade into deep before you seek
When the ocean bows low it exposes Achilles fatal flaw
When you face to face with death you are in the right place

"What the hell is that supposed to mean?" I asked, securing a messy bun on my head with a pencil.

Hunter dragged his hand over his face. "Riddles."

"I know they are riddles." I rolled my eyes. None of the sentences made sense, but it wasn't a surprise that a pirate made it extra hard. I scratched my ankle where the snakes bit. "This is confusing as fuck."

"Indeed."

We stared at the written messages in silence. What bothered me the most was the last one that mentioned facing death. Did Captain William Thompson mean metaphorically, or did he hide it somewhere we would literally have to risk death to reach?

"Are these four different locations," Hunter said, "or steps that lead to the location?"

"That's an excellent question." I tilted my head, thinking. "What do you think?"

Hunter hummed, pressing his lips together and puffing his cheeks. After a deep exhale, he said, "If it was me, I would separate my loot." I had the same thought. Not the best idea to put all your eggs into one basket.

"Then we should treat them as separate entities." I pushed loose hairs out of my eyes. "Okay, which one sounds like a place we know about and could easily crack? 'Wade into deep' obviously means water, and 'fortress' probably is the island. So what do we have here that matches this description?"

"The lake with the waterfall is deep. The pond by the giant tree is only waist deep and too small to hide anything in."

"Okay, what else?"

"Bow could mean a curve," Hunter said, pulling a map of the island from under the pile of papers and spreading it on the table. With the pencil, he circled several places where the island's shoreline bent. "These would be easy for us to explore on foot, but these four," he pointed at the northern side, "are impossible to reach without a boat."

"It says 'ocean bows low.' Maybe it means it's on the southern side of the island, so we could ignore these locations. Okay. We have several potential places to explore." I reread the other two riddles, which both had hostile words. "What do we know of that could kill us or is already dead, but apparently is also a zombie because it's still alive?"

Hunter chuckled. "Your guess is as good as mine."

I was smarter than this. I could crack this. I got up and walked around the room, playing with words. Strong meant powerful or forceful. But it also had to be hollow, which could be empty or soulless. "I think I got it. The hill on the island is made of a rock. It's lifeless, it's dead. But the jungle represents a breathing, living organism."

Hunter's mouth quirked. "Are you saying it means the treasure is hidden somewhere on this island?"

My shoulders slumped. With a sigh, I dropped onto my chair.

"How about we continue brainstorming as we check out a few potential locations while it's still bright outside?" Hunter said.

"Where do you want to go first?"

"The easiest one would be the lake."

I groaned. After the warm shower I'd taken, my hope was never to set a foot into that icy pool again. "I was afraid you'd suggest that."

We gathered Hunter's snorkeling gear and strolled to the waterfall. First, we examined the area behind it (a sheer rock wall), and then we identified several suspicious boulders deep in the water before diving in. The lake was crystal clear, and from the shore, the bottom appeared much closer than it was. Hunter swam with ease to the deeper area, whereas I had to surf up and gulp (yelping and cursing at the same time) more air since the shock of cold water knocked my breath away. It took me several tries before I reached the bottom, just long enough to explore for a few seconds before I had to go back up.

Winded, I crawled out of the water and lay flat on my back, my goosebump-covered skin sucking up warmth from the rock that had baked all day in the sun. I trembled after spending close to an hour in Lake Baikal junior. It would be a shocker if I didn't get hypothermia after today.

Hunter dropped next to me, his cold shoulder touching mine. He released a deep breath.

"I have permanent brain freeze," I said, my teeth chattering.

He faced me, lips blue, cheeks red, and wet hair sticking up in different directions after he'd removed his mask. The corners of his mouth turned upward. "This lake is so damn cold 'blue balls' is taking on a whole new meaning to me."

I let out a breath of surprise and then a guffaw erupted from me. Hunter was full-on laughing, too. For a long minute, we were two idiots, shivering and cackling. Once the funny bug left us, I was exhausted. And ravenous, so damn hungry I could eat a cow. We ventured back to the hut, where Hunter and I swapped wet clothes for dry and he disappeared to start making dinner, while I stayed to ponder more about the riddles. Monday jumped on the table as soon as Hunter left, and I didn't bother to shoo him away or set him back on the floor. He would only jump up again.

One of the other options for the second riddle was the fishing lagoon. Though I wasn't sure if the surrounding area counted as a fortress if a considerable part of it was a low barrier made of a reef. I moved to the next line. Achilles. Why him? My eyes searched the bookshelf until they came across D'Aulaires's *Book of Greek Myths*. I pulled it out, opened it to the table of contents, and ran my finger down, finding nothing. Then I turned to the index at the end of the book and looked up "Achilles 106, 180, 184."

I flipped pages, my eyes scanning the words, reading about the greatest Greek warrior, raised by the wise centaur after his mother, Thetis, went to the sea and never returned. The reason for his weak spot was how she held him over a sacred fire while making him almost immortal—by his heel.

Because she held him over fire, the riddle could mean we had to walk on something hot. Sand was hot during the day, but there was much of it. The rocks got hot, too, and again, there was a lot of space with bare stone.

Monday rubbed his nose on the tip of the pencil in my hand then gingerly tried to bite it. "No." I booped him on his nose. "That's not food."

My stomach growled.

"Is there a cat on the table?" Hunter pressed his shoulder into the doorway, arms crossed.

I smiled innocently. "Nope."

"Oh, okay. Do want to take a break and join me in the kitchen?" He wiggled his eyebrows, his face conveying peculiar excitement. "I have a surprise for you."

A dead chicken—that was his surprise. Not sure what I was expecting: a bottle of wine, a pair of sunglasses, a comfortable pillow—ideally faux goose down—but the lifeless bird wasn't it.

"Oh, dear." I grimaced at the sight. "Did you kill it?"

"I thought you'd like something besides fish."

It would be a nice change from our daily meal of fruit, avocado, fish, sticky rice, or undercooked beans. I wanted to suggest to Hunter that he soak beans overnight to soften them like my mother used to, but it wasn't my place to tell him what to do. He was kind enough to host me, so I appreciated any food he served.

"I'll be honest with you." I wrinkled my nose in disgust and gestured at the lifeless bird. "I don't know how to pluck or gut that."

"No worries, I'll do it," Hunter said. "Tonight, for dinner, we'll have grilled chicken."

My mother was against waste, so she found ways to get the most out of everything. I might have never helped, but I'd had the privilege of watching her cook while I did my homework in the kitchen.

"Why don't we cut off bigger pieces, grill them, and use the rest to make a soup?" My eyes landed on a gigantic carrot on the picnic table, covered with dirt. I palmed the enormous root, testing its weight and feel. "Wow, that is huge! My fingers don't fully wrap around ... er ... what do you call it? Its root? Shaft?"

Hunter threw a look at me over his shoulder, an eyebrow raised. "I don't think carrots have shafts, but I've held larger things in my hand," he deadpanned, but then a slight smile curved his lips into a full-on smirk. I shook my head, and my entire body burned with embarrassment because my mind couldn't undo the image of Hunter holding his dick. "Why are you blushing?" he said. "I was talking about an eggplant. What did you think?"

Laughing, I left the vegetable alone and smoothed loose hairs off my forehead. Hunter reached for my face and lightly brushed his knuckles over my cheek. All my nerve endings telescoped to the one spot he touched.

"You have pen ink everywhere," he said.

"Oh good." I stepped to the mirror on the tree and gasped at my reflection. Blue streaks covered my face as if I was back in tenth grade writing a five-thousand-word essay on why physical education shouldn't be part of the standard high school curriculum. I groaned and rubbed spots with my finger. "You should have told me I looked like this."

"I didn't notice it until now." Hunter took a sharpening stone and moistened the top with water. He angled a knife and slowly drew the blade down and across the stone in a smooth motion.

"Phill would've pointed that out right away," I said. Phill's only talent was to find everything negative before he saw anything positive. I braced for the old anger to bubble up as it used to, but it didn't.

"The good news is I am not Phill."

Hunter had no idea how good that news was. If I had to spend an hour on a deserted island with my ex, I would've swum to the next dry land to get away from him. I wetted the towel and scrubbed my skin harder.

Hunter's hands paused, and he looked up at me. "Do you mind if I ask you why you married him?"

I wished back at the high school senior prom, I didn't think just because he was on his way to graduating as valedictorian —just like me—and headed to the same university, it was our fate to be together. "I thought I could have what my parents had since they were college sweethearts." I sighed. "I was an idiot."

"I have a strong feeling *he* is an idiot. Not you." The muscles on his tan forearms flexed when Hunter flipped the knife to the other side and used the same motion. Then his hands changed blade sides again and repeated the same skillful and capable movements five times.

I tore my eyes away and rolled my head around, cracking my neck like I was getting ready for a ring fight. "My dad needed a lot of attention. I felt bad leaving him alone with a nurse. I quit my job and took care of him. Phill was unhappy that we were running through our savings because I stopped working. I suggested he get an actual job instead of waiting for a management position for the past five years. That didn't go well. He also didn't like that I spent so much time with my dad. Our house had a spare room, and I wanted my father to move in with us so I could look after him, but Phill said no. I wasn't going to beg, and gave him an ultimatum: either my father moved in, or I moved out. By the end of the day, I moved out." I gave Hunter a weak smile. "Two months later, I was served divorce papers."

I scoffed at the memory of how surprised I'd been to open the door, thinking it was my lunch DoorDash delivery, to find a short young man with a letter. I didn't even know why I was shocked. Somewhere deep down, I'd known that this would happen. Only I suppose I was hoping it would be me who filed first.

"He based his divorce on spousal abandonment. Which was, on some level, true. He got a good lawyer and robbed me of half of everything, including my 401k, never mind that since we got married, I had been the only one who had a job. I was tired and didn't fight at all during our divorce. I just wanted it to be over. And to top it off, Phill lied to me about the debt he ran up online gambling. I couldn't do anything about it because everything was in my name." Close to three years had passed, but talking about it again made me feel like I was back there, my life being sucked out of me.

Hunter took a large pot and placed it under the pipe with running water. "Do you want to know a fun fact?"

"Um … sure."

"When humans develop in the womb, the anus forms before any other opening. Which basically means at one point everyone was nothing but an asshole," Hunter said, looking at me. I had no idea where he was going with this. Then he added, "I have a feeling Phill never developed beyond that stage."

I blinked at him, then burst into laughter. "This is the best." I wiped at my eyes. "Tina said, 'You can't fix stupid, but you can divorce it.'"

"And she is right." Hunter nodded.

She also was sure Phill suffered from SPS (Small Penis Syndrome) and couldn't handle my success. He wasn't like that when we were in school. His personality only worsened after we graduated from university. I already had a job, and he couldn't find one. I jumped at the first opportunity to get my foot in the door, but he waited for something better. As my career rocketed, his deep envy of me increased. Each time I got a promotion or a bonus, he wouldn't talk to me for a day, sometimes longer.

Shaking out my hands and letting the pent-up energy out of my body and into the earth, I smiled. "All right. No more talk about the douchebag. Now it's only fair since you asked about him, I get to ask you a personal question."

"Do your worst."

I already knew a lot about Hunter, but my craving to learn

more grew stronger with each day we spent together. I looped some of my hair behind my ear.

"Did you have a girlfriend before you moved here?"

"Yes." Hunter lifted a pot full of water; his biceps bulged, forearm muscles tensed. He carried it to the fire pit. Hunter had remarkable arms. And ass too. I looked down at my flip-flops before he could notice my prurient watch.

I wanted him to elaborate. But he picked up the next knife and started sharpening it. I stared at him until he caught my eye.

A shy smile pulled at his lips. "You look like you have questions."

About a million of them. "What happened?"

"We met at the bar where I was celebrating my twenty-third birthday. Dated for about three years. I got laid off and couldn't find a job in finance, so I worked two jobs to support us. Jolie was busy with medical school, and when Edward offered good money, I thought, why not do it for half a year and then come back. Jolie wasn't happy about it at first, but then I convinced her that extra cash would benefit us since we both had huge student loans. She was okay with me leaving to work with Edward." He concentrated on the stone and blade. "And then I really liked it here. I liked the people and life in Rarotonga and the weather. I called Jolie and tried to persuade her to move here." He chuckled. "That didn't go well. She said no. I took a few weeks to think about it, and when I decided I had to return to her, she told me she had met someone else. And that was that." His voice was without melancholy. Did he regret coming to help Edward?

"Did she meet that someone else after you asked her to move here or…?"

His eyebrows went up like he'd never thought of that. "I don't know, and it really didn't matter. Jolie was done with me. She's married now." I could detect some pain in the last statement.

"How do you know?"

"I saw it on Instagram."

"You have an Instagram account?" I couldn't picture Hunter as a guy who would post or follow anyone on social media.

"Of course I do. Who doesn't?"

"Castaways who live on a deserted island, that's who. Actually, I can see it being a huge success." I dramatically raised my hands, palms out like I had a vision. "Half-naked, hunky single man living on a tropical island with two cats doing manly things every day. Millions of followers. I can see cat food and Speedo sponsorships." Why did my mind right away have to go to teeny-weeny bikinis? I could have mentioned a sunscreen brand.

He playfully rolled his eyes. "It is not my personal account. It's for my business. You'd be surprised how many bookings Edward and I got through it."

"So, you social media stalked her?"

"No. Two years ago, she reached out just to say hi."

Illogical jealousy seized me like an octopus gripping its prey. I bet Jolie did it to rub it in. Or maybe she was still pining for Hunter. Why was I thinking about all of this? I shouldn't care. I was too much of a damsel in distress for Hunter to be interested in me. Yet, I wished I had my phone—and electricity, and the internet—so I could check out what she looked like.

"Are you talking to her?" *Please say no.*

"I didn't reply to her."

"Good," I blurted, too fast and way too pleased. "I mean, it's good that you moved on and started dating others. Right?"

I didn't need to know that bit of information. Of course not. I was trying to be polite and show my concern about his well-being and nothing else. No hidden subtext—just plain politeness. And yet, I held my breath, waiting for his answer.

"I dated some." At that point, our eyes connected. Hunter's face relaxed, and his features faded to thoughtfulness, then something complicated. "I'm still looking for *the* one."

I wished he would smile because his stare was downright intimidating and unapologetic, a mix of emotions of primal possession and tenderness. And it stirred an involuntary throb in me that was now in need of satisfaction.

"Are you a hopeless romantic?" I asked.

"Are you not?" he countered.

I scoffed. "Probably not. Love brings pain. People divorce you or die. In the end, you are left with a broken heart."

"A wise man or woman, I'm unsure, said, knowing both love and loss is what makes humans alive. Without love, there is no meaning in life."

The way he grasped my gaze sent waves of anticipation through me. When was the last time I felt like this? It wasn't wise to start something with Hunter. We were roommates, island-mates, and it should stay like that. Uncomplicated. But a match had been struck in my lower core, and that was a borderline dangerous feeling.

I had to find a question that would put us back in a fun and playful mood, and away from thoughts that had no business existing in my head. We'd started the "get to know you better" game, and I had to come up with a better question to get to know Hunter on a deeper level. A million questions, like a school of fish, all scared in different directions when I tried to pick one.

"Who's your celebrity crush?"

I wanted to face-smack myself. Seriously? That was the best I could come up with?

The randomness of my question puzzled him at first, but then he smiled. "That's easy. Heidi Klum." Hunter rinsed the knife under the water, scrubbed carrots of dirt, then handed me everything. "Peel these, please."

I pointed the blade at him. "Not Gal Gadot?" I had to tease him, even though it sounded like I was asking him if he liked me since she could be my twin.

"She's hot too," he said, retreating, raised arms in surrender. My cheeks grew warm with the compliment. "What about you? Who is your celebrity crush? And if you say, Henry Cavill, I'll howl."

I ran the knife over the root, scraping off its delicate skin and watching it fall into a bowl on the table. "Well, then you better start howling because Henry is fucking fantastic. Only a bit short for my taste."

"Isn't he like six one?" Hunter lit the logs and threw the used match into the growing fire.

I shrugged, *what can I say?* "Yeah, if he were a few inches taller, I would totally marry him."

"You have a thing for tall guys?" He wiggled his eyebrows, straightening his back and squaring his broad shoulders.

I ran my eyes over Hunter's statuesque figure. I *had* a thing for him, but not just because he had the greatest physique and, God, that handsome face—no, it was more. His humor and kindness. Something about him was so calm. He was sure of himself, confident, and I couldn't deny that I found it attractive. All of it. And there were also small touches like his cute text message notes, and the fresh flowers that appeared in the hut and on the picnic table, that made this rustic place feel like a glamping second cousin. Hunter also gave very good forehead kisses. Okay, there'd only been the one, but it was flawless.

I shrugged again. "You'll do," I said in an indifferent tone, willing my lips not to curl up at the corners.

"You're all right too." He winked and picked up the bird by its feet. "Now, do you want to learn how to pluck a chicken?"

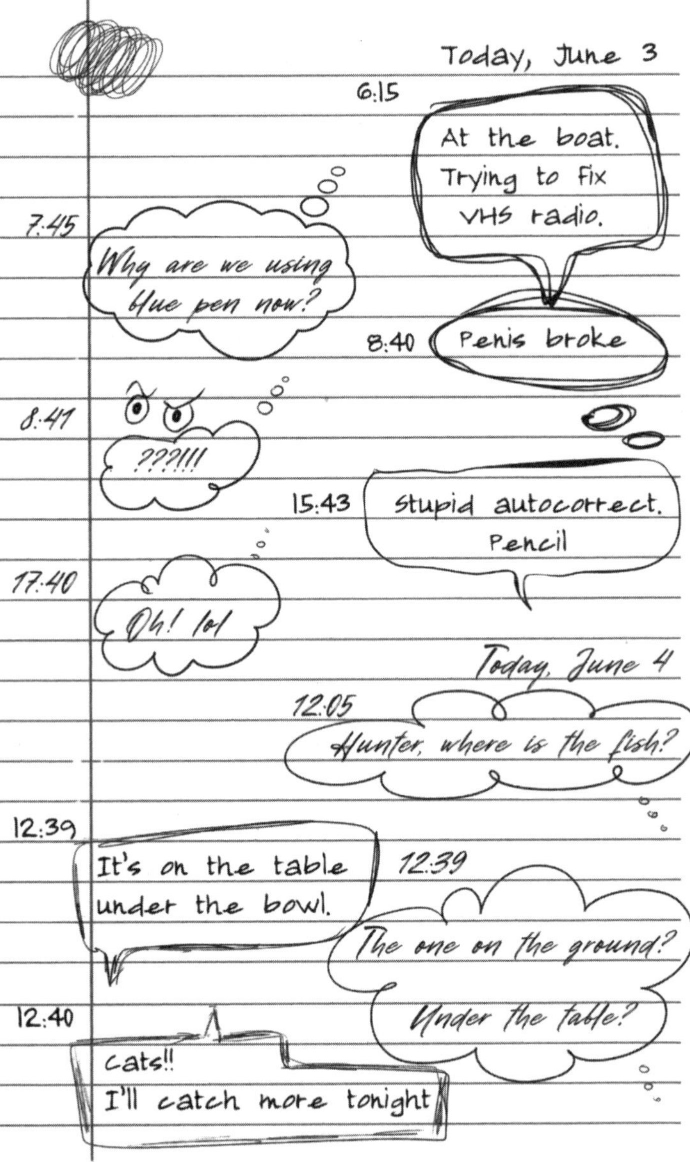
Today, June 3
6:15
At the boat. Trying to fix VHS radio.
7:45
Why are we using blue pen now?
8:40
Penis broke
8:41
???!!!
15:43
Stupid autocorrect. Pencil
17:40
Oh! lol
Today, June 4
12:05
Hunter, where is the fish?
12:39
It's on the table under the bowl.
12:39
The one on the ground? Under the table?
12:40
cats!!
I'll catch more tonight

Chapter Sixteen

The next day, Hunter and I decided to only focus on the riddle *"When you face to face with death you are in the right place,"* which led us to the idea to poke around the skeleton and see if John was onto something but possibly triggered a trap (thereby facing his death) before reaching the treasure. Since the pit wasn't large enough for all three of us, and *just* in case something went astray, only Hunter climbed with a shovel into the hole, and I stayed up. As Hunter dug, he placed most of the fresh dirt into the lowered bucket, and I pulled it up. We dropped that idea after digging about three feet down, with only extra blisters on my palms to show for it.

In the late afternoon the following day, I studied the island map on the blanket in the shade of the leaning palm. I couldn't take another minute in the hut, so I moved my "office" to the beach. I chose to work on the *"When the ocean bows low it exposes Achilles fatal flaw"* riddle. My idea was to find Achilles' shape in the island's contour, but the more I studied it, the more it felt like a waste of time.

"You are not your usual self today," Hunter said, plopping beside me.

I didn't sleep because my back and shoulders hurt from yesterday's John Keating bootcamp. And I might have been a tad bit cranky because of that. "And what is my usual self?"

"Cheerful, full of annoying questions and suggestions." A smile quirked Hunter's lips, and his eyes glistened like the ocean on a bright day, and they held an essence of affection. He often looked at me like that, sometimes averting his eyes as if he wasn't staring. But on some days, he kept my eyes locked with his for what seemed endless time, unafraid to show his vulnerable yearning.

"This morning, I thought of something, but after staring at the map for too long, I think it was a dumb idea."

"What was it?"

"What if the outline looks like a Greek god or the island had the shape of a foot. And if I could find the part that resembled a heel..." I shook my head. "Never mind, this is stupid."

"No. I think you are on to something." Hunter shifted closer, his knee bumping against mine, his chest pressing into my shoulder, as he leaned to look at the map in my hands. A slow, dazzling warmth spread across my skin at the touch, enveloping my entire body. He hummed as he thought, rotating the map one way, then another. Then he made a notable "hmm" sound. Hunter had seen something I didn't notice before.

"What?" I peered at him. His face was so close I could graze the tip of my nose on his stubbled cheek.

"We are looking on the island from the above, but if we

were out in the sea." Hunter pointed into the ocean. "Coming from Southwest. It would look something like this."

He grabbed a pencil and notebook, flipped to a fresh page, and sketched. After a minute, I was presented with a pancake, a pile of something on top of it, and a large foot that hung in the air to the right from two smiley human and cat stick figures.

"This is you, me, and two cats on the beach." Hunter circled the obvious.

"I got it. Explain the foot with…"—I counted—"six toes."

"Sometimes you can be so judgy." Hunter's tongue peeked at the corner of his mouth, as he erased one tiny circle. "Happy? May I continue now?"

I chuckled. "Yes, please proceed."

"If you catch the side of the hill just from the right angle, it does appear like a bare foot is about to leap off." Hunter dropped the notebook and got up. "Come on, let's check out that area. Put on your swimsuit."

"We're hiking. Not swimming. Why would I need to change?"

"Once we are done exploring, it's a great spot to jump off. Have you ever dived off a cliff into the ocean?"

"No," I said. "But I guess it could be fun."

Most likely not, but I'd also thought sailing wouldn't be fun, yet I had enjoyed it—until I almost drowned and turned into an extra in the *Cast Away* movie. I wasn't miserable, but quite happy and relaxed most days.

Dressed in swimsuits, we walked on the beach until the sand line disappeared, and the calm waves brushed against the jungle undergrowth. There, we turned into the woods. When the route went up the hill, Hunter took the lead, allowing me uninterrupted time to admire the width of his back. Eventually, the path became steeper. Hunter climbed like a mountain lion, barely breathing heavily, whereas I puffed hard, sweat running down my neck. Joining Hunter on his long morning swims could do me some good.

At some point, the path traveled along the hill's edge, with waves crashing below. I clutched Hunter's arm for security. And an excuse to touch him was also a bonus.

We paused at a narrow pathway that led down to a smaller rocky beach.

"The spot isn't far. After you jump, swim around the corner to that cleared area and follow the trail up," he said.

"Who said I'll jump?" I eyeballed how high we were. A hundred feet? More?

From there, he veered into greenery again, and we meandered up the hill some more through the jungle. The trees, vines, and thick bushes became rare, exposing the bare mountainside. The discoloration in the stone layer—a light brown deposit—bowed to resemble an arched foot from a distance. The area yielded no hidden entry nor any carved-in messages.

We went farther up. I was winded when we reached the flat, grassy area near the cliff's edge.

"Are we under the heel?" I looked up at the solid sheer mass of rock before me, my eyes following the distinguished lighter layer, until it curved and went straight up.

"Yep, this is the place."

Hunter and I scrutinized the wall for some time, closely inspecting the line where grass butted against the rock, prodding cavities, and reaching shoulder-deep into some cracks. In the end we came up empty. We stood, hands on our hips, now facing the endless ocean, the constant breeze turning into a stronger gust from time to time. Day three of our search, and it was once again fruitless.

Taking measured steps, I crept to the brink, my fingers digging into Hunter's wrist as I peered down.

"Don't you dare push me," I warned him, though I didn't think he was the kind of person who would do such a thing. My mind whirled, trying to measure how far up we were. Too far.

"I'm not sure I can do this," I said, stepping back and letting go of Hunter's arm.

Not a second later, he rushed forward and jumped.

I gasped, dropped to my hands and knees, and crawled just in time to see Hunter plunge into the water, legs first, disappearing into the ocean.

My heart throbbed with worry. It felt like an eternity before Hunter finally burst through the surface.

"Jump!" he yelled and waved his hand.

"Never!" I shouted, then laughed.

Hunter swam to the small beach and edged his way up the steep incline of the footpath. I scrambled away from the cliff's brink and sat on the grass. Leaning on my hands, I took in the vast, beautiful view of blue hues. I enjoyed the sense of untroubled happiness. I couldn't remember the last time I felt so content.

Hunter reappeared between the trees and shook his hair, showering me with cool droplets. "Come on, Wonder Woman. It's only terrifying the first few times."

That was a poor tactic to convince me.

"Exactly. It's te-rri-fying."

"You don't know what you're missing." He stepped to the edge and turned his back to the open water.

"Where did you learn how to do it?"

"I was on the high school diving team." He flashed me a broad smile and flipped backward.

Shaking my head, I lay flat on my back.

His daredevil attitude not only pushed my blood faster through my veins, but also sparked an unwanted heat deep inside of me. The late afternoon sunlight was soft on my face, and the salty breeze playfully caressed my sunkissed skin. Seagulls glided high up, their wings a flash of silver against the bright blue sky. Up here, I felt as free as they were. Free of all the world's problems. Free of my troubles. Free of past hurt. I wanted to stay in this moment and feel like this for the rest of my life.

A few minutes later, Hunter towered over me, the sun's last rays gleaming in water drops on his defined muscles. It was no longer possible to ignore changes in my body chemistry at his proximity, turning me into dynamite and my nerve endings into lit fuses. I had a major crush on him. And I had no idea what to do with myself.

"If you give me a heart attack, you better know what to do. All that mouth-to-mouth and pushing on my chest stuff." It was my stupid attempt to say: *I like you so much, would you please kiss me?*

"Are you going to try this?" he asked. "I can hold your hand, and we jump together."

We could hold hands and jump, me screaming my lungs out and not letting go of him as we broke the water. We'd surface up, laughing, and swim back to the small beach. Breathless, dropping on small rocks and caught in the moment, he'd kiss me. With a rush of adrenaline and exhilaration of sexual energy, we would strip off our clothes and make love right there and then. The image was so clear. But could I do it? I rolled onto my stomach and stared at the ocean below.

Not. A. Fucking. Chance.

"Let's go back to our beach and swim." I squinted at him. I'd have to find a different way to steal his kiss.

"Okay. Meet me where the path forks." Hunter balanced with no apparent difficulty on the edge. He stretched out his arms. "Watch this."

"Nothing good follows a statement li—"

With a powerful drive, Hunter pushed off the ground. His body rotated a few times downward, entering the water seamlessly. My mouth dropped open in awe.

When Hunter swam to the shore I rushed to meet him. I caught up to him at the dirt path's midpoint and my flip-flop caught on an exposed root, tripping me forward. Hunter grabbed my wrist, swiveling me around. My right foot slid on small rocks, and the left went straight for his groin. He turned to block it but lost his balance. We barreled down the hill deeper into the woods, stumbling over soft grass clumps, small twigs catching on my skin and hair. We rolled into a bed of ferns, and I sprawled on the ground, my legs and arms stretched out, and Hunter's big frame landed on me. Without lifting his head off my shoulder, Hunter let out a full, throaty laugh, his body shaking. Laughter burst out of me, too.

"Are you laughing at me?" I wiped the tears from my eyes.

He shook his head, chuckling. "You should have seen your face when you almost kicked me."

I snorted, which only made us laugh more. Hunter buried his face in the crook of my neck, his breath warm against my skin. When his laughter ceased, he rested his weight on his elbows, hovering over me, and our gazes connected. Ocean droplets fell off his hair, landing on mine as he stared at me. A new sense of nervousness left me breathless.

"I tripped you," I said, mesmerized by the feel of him on me, his hot skin pressing against mine.

"I'm aware of that." His voice was low.

My hands found his back. I wanted to slide them down so I could reach and squeeze his butt, but I ran my fingers upward. Hunter's body became rigid, and it seemed he stopped breathing. A storm of emotions passed through his eyes. Heat fluttered against my ribs, and my heart beat so fast, I swear Hunter felt it. My nipples were hard, poking through the thin fabric of my bikini top. I was sure he felt them, too.

His throat worked, and his gaze dropped to my lips. "Anything broken?"

My heart—if you don't kiss me right now.

I slid my foot down Hunter's leg and curled it around his calf. An expression flashed over his face faster than I could read. Fear? Regret? Restraint? Hunter's chest heaved, and his eyes closed briefly. Then he took a breath, exhaled slowly, and met my eyes. "Sydney."

The way he said my name was enough for me to never want to leave this place. I quivered with anticipation for the next moment. He looked at my mouth. I tipped my chin up, inviting him. Breath was the shortest distance between our lips.

A rustle of dry leaves took Hunter's attention. I twisted to look. With a green lizard in his mouth, Monday stared at us, his yellow eyes round as if surprised to find us in such a compromising position. Tuesday darted from under a fern and pounced on Monday. They pranced around, blended into an orange, white and black fur ball, and rolled behind a curtain of overgrown vines. The lucky lizard scrambled away in a hurry.

"Did you see that?" Hunter got up, leaving me instantly cold. The moment we had was broken. "There's an opening."

Needless to say, I didn't give a damn if there was or wasn't an opening. We had been about to kiss. Was it possible to misread everything about Hunter's lingering gazes at me, gentle touches, and constant glances at my lips? The state of his dick was a huge indication Hunter had precisely the same thoughts as I did.

But Hunter pulled me to my feet as if nothing had just happened between us and stepped to an enormous fallen tree that leaned against a stone wall. He dragged large branches out the way, ducked under the trunk, and pushed some overgrown vines aside, exposing the gateway into the mountain.

I swallowed my pride and stepped beside Hunter, leaving some distance between us. He kept his gaze forward, and I forced myself to do the same. The second my eyes took in our new discovery my jaw went slack, but then my lips turned into a grin. The markings of hand tools used to carve larger spaces in the rock loudly signaled that Hunter and I had finally discovered the right place. My mind swirled, excitement exploding beneath my breastbone.

"Hunter," I whispered, but I really wanted to shout. "This is it."

He glanced at me with an unabashed smile, eyes wide and

bright, full of anticipation, a tiny twig stuck in his hair. "I can't believe I've searched this entire island and never noticed it."

I nudged him with my elbow. "I guess it's a good thing I'm clumsy."

Hunter's face broke out in a grin, and then we walked into the mouth of the cave.

Chapter Seventeen

"Do you think there are bats?" I trailed after him into the dim, confined space, just about wide enough for two people to walk side by side. Thick tree roots ran along the edge of the floor and crept up on the walls.

"I don't know, but watch out for this." Hunter tapped on a low-hanging rock, ducked, and passed under it. With my height I didn't have to worry, so I walked right under it.

A sharp blast of wind whipped between us, sending shivers down my body. Light curved around the bend about twenty feet deep, and we came out in a vast enclosed grotto.

The majestic dome inside of the mountain was like nothing I'd seen before. Directly across from us, the daylight filtered through a large natural skylight high above the water. The ocean surged through an opening to the outside at the bottom, where, I had no doubt, during a low tide a small boat could easily travel through. This was the perfect location to hide treasure.

"In nature's fortress wade into deep before you seek," I said. "Hunter, this is one of the riddles. We cracked it." By sheer luck, but who cared.

"We sure did."

Steps, some organic and others hand-chiseled, led to a narrow sand and rock beach. Monday weaved between our legs and ran down the path as if he owned the place. On the last step, he paused and scratched his ear. He and Tuesday probably roamed over this area all the time; those cats probably knew every inch of the island. Too bad they couldn't tell us what they knew. Hunter held out his hand for me, and I took it. We descended the stairs and walked along a bank where the waves gently kissed the sand. His hand still held mine. I was fully aware he hadn't let go.

My eyes traced the stone fortification that encompassed us until they stopped on a cleft about four feet long and shoulder-width wide, a foot above the waterline.

I pointed. "Do you think that leads somewhere else? 'Wade into deep' could mean go deeper into the mountain."

"Wait here." Hunter relaxed his grasp on my hand and trod water knee-high to the crack in the wall. He carefully stepped on slimy rocks coated with algae, grabbed the edge of the rock and planted his right foot on the wall. Pulling himself up, he slipped into the dark hole without a care, obviously not worrying about what creepy-crawly could lurk inside.

"See anything?" I called out.

Hunter reappeared. "Too dark to see. We need to bring flashlights with us."

"Seriously? You have flashlights? I could have used one on my way to the outhouse at night."

Hunter lowered down on his ass as he eased back toward

me, his foot slipping on a rock, but he kept his balance. "It's only for emergencies."

Going to the bathroom in the middle of the night was an emergency in my book. "Where do you keep it?"

"In a wooden container on the porch." He raised his eyebrows. I blinked at him. I had no idea what he was talking about. "Closer to the kitchen ... where my hammock is. I use it as my nightstand."

I raised and dropped my hands in surrender. Evidently, I didn't pay much attention to my surroundings. Not the best quality for a person on a treasure hunt.

Standing in the shallows, Hunter checked his watch. "It's after six. We pack tonight and return here at first light," he said. "If Captain William Thompson hid something here, it would be deep in the water."

With the first flush of the morning Hunter and I returned to the cave, bringing a rucksack stuffed with fruits and boiled eggs, two bottles of water, and a prybar. Fitted with flippers and masks, we explored the waters while bright sunlight fell through the openings in the grotto's ceiling and the gap out into the ocean. The tide was low, making the sea passage large, letting in more daylight.

Below the surface was a thriving underworld as deep in some places as the cave was high. Closer to the surface, a vivid rainbow of colored and striped fish broke up and darted away from us as we snorkeled. Some larger fish swam unbothered, watching us investigate the area bejeweled with aquatic plants and barnacles. In the rainforest of the sea Hunter passed between rocks, diving deeper between the long kelp strands. I followed him, checking out thick beds of seaweed, marine growth, and anything resembling wooden cases or manmade objects while carefully avoiding anything that could sting, bite, or eat me.

After a half an hour search, Hunter and I agreed to fan out in separate directions to cover more of the ocean floor. As Hunter was a much more experienced diver than me, he went down much deeper, studying the undersea outcrops, while I tackled the shallower sections. Soon, we parted far enough that I lost track of him in the serene sway of tall seaweed. Wearing an inflatable yellow belt pack, I explored the waters slowly, floating on the surface, pedaling with my flippers, each of my breaths in the snorkel sounding like Darth Vader. Through the semi-fogged mask, my eyes examined the magnificent spectrum of color below, searching for anything out of place in color or shape. Colorful starfish neighbored the urchins tucked in undersea rocks. Fish sparkled and glimmered where they caught the light, and rich oceanic life changed from dark to bright green as it waved at me.

I worked my way closer to the portal that led out. Hunter had warned me to stay away from here and not chance getting sucked out into the open ocean. The undercurrent pulled on me with an invisible force, but not to the point where I couldn't fight it, yet my breathing labored, and I kicked faster, giving my lungs and legs a good workout.

The sun came out from a passing cloud, and the waters became clear, exposing plants and coral growth. In two hundred years many plants, corals, and vibrant sea anemones had taken root and reclaimed every hard surface, masking everything from my untrained eyes. We were looking for trunks, but by now the chances were the wood had disintegrated and the chests could have fallen apart, the treasure inside them drifting out into the open water and forever lost to any treasure hunter.

I stopped swimming and pulled the mask off, rubbed the skin where the rubbery skirt left its mark, then spat into the glass. *Gross. I know.* It was the old trick to keep it from fogging up. With mask back on, I traveled in the direction we hadn't explored yet. I was close to giving up when a group of stacked rocks of the same exact sizes, with distinct right angles, came into my view. My heart skipped a beat.

I tried to dive deeper to check it out, but the belt yanked me back. I finned fast to the shore. Once my feet found ground, I unbuckled the orange strap and flung the floating device onto the dry, rocky beach. Hunter's head popped out of the water on the opposite side of the cave.

"Hey! I found something," I shouted. He twisted in the water so fast I had no doubt he felt a whiplash.

"Where?"

"Maybe thirty feet to the left from that opening."

Without waiting for Hunter, I swam to the spot, took a few deep breaths, and dived. Whatever it was was at most twenty feet down, and reaching it took little effort. My eyes rounded with excitement when I recognized the outline of wooden cases coated with barnacles and algae, their braces eaten through with rust. I moved deeper for examination, my fingers pushing seaweed threads out of the way and my face coming close to the ill-fated skull. I drew away as a scream erupted from my throat, bubbles rushing in front of me. In an instant, saltwater pooled into my mouth, and I swallowed it. My stomach revolved as I floundered, my arm and leg working out of sync as I desperately pushed upward.

My head broke the surface. I gagged and gasped. A sudden

touch on my shoulder pulled another scream out of me, and I lost my grip on the flashlight. *Crap.*

"Sydney!" Hunter called, his voice urgent.

I spun around. "There's a dead body."

Hunter plunged his face into the ocean, his arms treading hard to keep him up float. He looked back at me. "Where?"

"Near the trunks. I saw a skull."

"Oh," he said, as if it was yesterday's news. "I thought you meant like a real body."

"It was a body at some point." I spat seawater out of my mouth.

His mask fogged up. "You found trunks?"

"Yes. Maybe four."

He took several deep breaths and submerged, his fins kicking up water as he swam. A minute later, he resurfaced, grinning ear to ear. "Come with me."

We swam to the shore, and while he walked to pick up the prybar, I sat in the shallow waters, giving myself a moment to compose myself. It was just a skeleton, nothing big, but seeing it in the water made me think of Bambi and how her body probably was lost in the ocean. And my chest hurt. I took my mask off and wiped my eyes.

"Are you okay?" Hunter lowered close to me, and the sudden warmth of his body made me realize how cold I was. His mask sat atop his head, drops of water clung to his eyelashes, and red creases ran over his cheeks and forehead. No doubt my face sported the same imprints.

"Just a bit shaken up by the surprise of another…" I waved in the direction of where the cases were stored under the water.

"You're thinking about Bambi?" he asked in a kind voice.

"I should have done more to save her." My face creased and my eyes stung with saltwater.

"Hey, you did what you could." Hunter pulled me in, his arm coming around me, offering me the comfort of his broad body. "She's probably alive. Searching for you right now."

"Then why hasn't she found us?" I said, my cheek smoothed into his warm chest.

Hunter took a deep breath then said on exhale, "Because there are many other islands spread out over a hundred square miles. It takes time to find someone. It's only been two weeks. If you didn't know where you were, and she could have drifted farther in the opposite direction before someone picked her up..." He pressed his lips to my head for a long minute. And I tried not to think what this meant. He was a caring person. This was what they did. They kissed on foreheads and into wet hair. "Bambi is looking for you, but just in the wrong place. She'll find you soon."

I understood he said that to make me feel better, but I wanted to believe him. He held me for a long time, allowing me to calm my heart down. Today was about Hunter's triumph uncovering the Treasure of Lima, and not about me feeling sorry about my tragic sailing trip. I pulled away from his warmth. "I'm ready to go back," I said.

Armed with the prybar, we returned to the water. Keeping my breath in and my panic at bay—it was just a collection of bones—I examined the frozen-in-time skeleton. A trunk pinned its lower half, the remnants of his clothing long gone, only a leather belt with its corroded buckle looped around its waist. The flashlight I dropped earlier emitted a bleak light from the split in the seabed. I swam closer to retrieve it but was too afraid to immerse my hand into it.

Something toothy or poisonous could be hiding there, and in any case, it appeared like it would be out of reach even if I tried to get it.

I came up for air and then went down again. Hunter took hold of a padlock on the top case, and it broke off without a fight. He passed it to me, then placed the prybar where the top and bottom had fused by time and algae. With one push, he pried it open, sand and green muck slid off the lid, and sediment stirred up, clouding the water around us.

Bubbles rushed up around my face as I briefly squealed with delight. My mind ran over the treasure list in Edward's diary. Gold coins. Gemstones. Candelabras in gold and silver. Probably not the 780 solid gold statue of the Virgin Mary with Baby Jesus, unless they'd cut it into chunks, which would be a pity if they had. Hunter took my hand, and we finned up to the surface again.

"Oh my God, Hunter. We found it." I looped my arms around his neck, my mask hitting his, our bodies sinking for a split second. His hand circled my waist, his chest pressing into mine. Our legs knocked at each other occasionally as we kicked them to keep afloat.

I peeled myself away from him just enough to look at his handsome (masked) face. For a moment we stared at each other, breathing hard. The moment called for a celebratory kiss but with bulky objects on our faces that would be beyond clumsy and awkward. Yet, if Hunter were to grab and yank me to him, I wouldn't fight it.

"Do you think they're full of gold coins?"

He grinned. "I hope so."

"Should we go see now?"

Hunter pulled the mask over his head and smoothed his

face with his hand. "Give it another minute for the sand to settle."

We grinned at each other, our chest heaving from excitement and not hard work treading waters.

"Thank you," Hunter said, looking at me intently.

"For what?"

"For believing me and not letting me search alone."

"I'm having a good time," I said. And it was the truth.

"Me too." He lowered his mask. "Ready?"

Taking several deep breaths, we went under.

As the sand settled, so did the disappointment that sank into the pit of my stomach. The first case had a collection of embossed leather books that contained a muck of emptiness; the second held the same; the third one had fragments of fabric, perhaps silk, that disintegrated as soon as I touched it; and the fourth held gunk and filth.

"This couldn't be it," I said, as we withdrew in defeat and slumped on the rocky beach. "The riddle describes this place. So, what the hell?"

Hunter tossed his mask on the sand and pulled water bottles out of the bag. He gave me one. I drank half of it, some freshwater drops escaping my lips, mixing with saltwater, and running down my neck.

"That was not the treasure. Maybe import documents, government secrets," Hunter finally spoke. "They must have made a mistake and confused chests. This is the only explanation I can come up with. They meant to hide something else here. Something that wouldn't turn into soot." He ran a frustrated hand through his hair. "Fuck."

I swallowed hard. "Sorry." I wasn't sure what else I could say to comfort him. It really sucked. I barely slept last night, anticipation keeping me up and constantly checking if it was dawn. If anger and disappointment had crushed me down like a heavy boulder, what Hunter felt must have been ten times worse. I'd searched for treasure for a few days, whereas he'd spent years roaming the ocean looking for it.

Hunter shook his head, and lay on his back. "It's fine," he said, staring up at the skies through the opening in the ceiling above us. "I don't think I told you that my grandfather and Edward weren't the only two obsessed with treasure hunting."

I tore my eyes from his toned body, where abdominal muscle flexed with each breath he took, and looked at his face. "They weren't?"

"No. Unfortunately, two of Edward's brothers met their tragic demise while also searching for this godforsaken treasure. The older brother, Kevin, died after a grey reef shark attacked him during a dive in the unexplored territory between this island and Bora Bora."

I sucked in a breath. "Fuck, that's horrible."

"The younger brother, Joseph and two of his friends, ventured for a two-month-long expedition before his thirtieth birthday. Their fates remain a mystery to this day. My aunt blames Holden's family curse, like we're some kind of Kennedy family of the oceans." He rubbed his face, muffling a groan. "When Edward and Annie took full custody of me, she made him give his word that he would never drag me into this bloody treasure-hunting mess that put my grandfather into a madhouse and took so many away from the Holden family. She made him stop searching for it too. When I left for college, Edward left to live here, and Annie divorced him because she wasn't going to be the widow of a crazy man."

I reached out and squeezed his forearm. "Now you have proof they weren't madmen."

"Sort of." Hunter eyes cut to me, mouth lifting at one corner. "What we found is dust."

"Yes, but we found proof that the riddles are real. And now *we* know that treasure is real and somewhere hidden on Teaku. We have three more chances to find the rest. Hopefully, it will be in solid form."

Today, June 5
7:05
...
7:45
Are you composing your txt or just left your cursor on the paper?
Wow! Very nice txt bubble. How long did that take you?
18:53
Too long.
Thank you for doing the dishes
19:00
A good friend tells you the meal was delicious. A great friend does the dishes.
Who's that?

Chapter Eighteen

That afternoon, Hunter and I cooked lunch and went over everything we (mostly he) knew about the island, debating about the next best place to look. The island was several square miles, mainly mountainous, and the possibilities for hideouts camouflaged by nature were endless.

We tried to think like the captain who'd arrived here two hundred years ago. He could have easily noticed the entrance into the grotto while scouting, as it most likely hadn't been overgrown with vines and flowering bushes. Or perhaps he'd uncovered the cave as he passed the island on his ship, during low tide, when the gap on the ocean side was wider. The ocean level was probably also much lower back then. Were there other caves easily accessible from the water? The island's outline curved outward, making it impossible to see the mountainside from the land. Hunter and I needed a boat (that we didn't have) to go around the island and look closer at the cliffs from the water.

We had to work with what we had: the jungle. A lot of it.

Some areas were so dense with vines and trees that it was impossible to see through. The thick, perpetual canopy stripped the day of its sunlight, throwing an extra layer of dark shadow over the ground, but at least it provided cool relief. And that was what we agreed to focus on. The more challenging the place was to reach, the better our chance of finding something there.

"Let's work on the two riddles that mention death or dead," Hunter said, offering me a palm leaf with a fish fillet and a small amount of rice. "Snakes are not deadly, despite your wrong opinion, so we can dismiss them. The other deadly creatures around here are sharks and possibly sea urchins, but those are in the ocean."

"What if a huge boar lived here when the captain arrived?" I blew a wisp of hair out of my eyes. "From what I know, it can be very deadly when you come face to face with a wild pig."

Hunter's hand paused midair to his mouth, rice pinched between his fingers. "How would a pig get here?"

I shrugged. "I don't know. How did snakes get here?"

"They could have been water snakes at first." Hunter arched an eyebrow.

"Wild pig could have evolved from merpigs." I stuck my tongue at him, and he snorted. "Okay. Fine. What if death or deadly doesn't mean a live creature but the way to get to the treasure," I suggested. "Another trap. Difficult journey. Or a challenging journey full of traps. Why did John fall into the pit? What was he looking for in that area? Since he was the captain's friend, he might have had more insight than riddles. The captain could have simply left him directions that said, 'Travel west until you reach a big rock, then turn right. Bring a mate because it's a lot of crap to carry back.'"

"Yet, his friend fell to his death into the trap?"

"John could be like any other man and didn't read the instructions." I smiled, earning an eye roll from Hunter.

"We should inspect the area once again," Hunter conceded. "One doesn't leave a trap without good reason unless they were protecting something."

Our conversation continued until the day gave in to the evening, and the sun touched the horizon. By now, the water in the barrel was at its perfect warm temperature, so I excused myself to shower.

While standing under (limited) heated happiness, I blindly searched for the shampoo bottle and squeezed more than I should have. Reality washed over me as I massaged my scalp: Hunter's bottle was half full, and mine was nearly empty. Soon, I'd run out. We had one extra, but in all this time, not a single boat had passed us, and at this rate, it wouldn't be enough for both of us. My knowledge of what natural resources were used for personal hygiene was restricted. I have seen coconut or avocado masks for sale, but those weren't for cleaning but for improving hair condition. Could I use eggs or mangos? Mom used lemon to clean the kitchen. If applied just once a week, the acidic juice wouldn't damage hair, would it? I cursed under my breath, turned the water off, and reached for my bikini, knowing what I had to do.

In the kitchen, holding my unsure gaze in the mirror, I untied my wet, messy bun, gripped my hair at the base of my neck with determination, and brought scissors to it. I didn't want to do it. All my life, I had had long hair. What if I didn't look good? Phill scorned women with hair cut above their shoulders. I needed a good forehead slap. His opinion shouldn't matter anymore, but somehow, it echoed somewhere deep inside, quieter but still there. What would Hunter think about it?

My mom had constantly experimented with haircuts, and my father had worshiped her even if she didn't pick the right style. When I was in high school, she arrived home with an unflattering blonde pixie cut that washed out her stunning features. I had covered my mouth with my hand and said, "Are you having a midlife crisis?" but my father didn't say a word, only gave her their regular hello kiss and a pat on her butt as if nothing had changed. Standing on a tropical island with the knowledge that their beautiful and uncomplicated love ended too early broke my heart.

"Hey, what are you doing?" Hunter carried logs and dropped them on an elevated stand.

I looked over my shoulder. "A makeover."

"Why?"

"If I cut it as short as yours, we might make the shampoo stretch for an extra few weeks." I recollected hair back into one thick bundle. Water drops ran down my back.

"Okay." He brushed off bark bits stuck to his shirtless, sweaty torso and approached me. "Let me do it."

My eyes met his in the mirror. "Are you a barber?"

"Are you?" He removed the scissors from my grip, his fingers brushing over mine. "It's probably easier if I do it."

I dropped my arms at my sides. Hunter stood behind me, his eyes heavy with some emotion I couldn't understand. He hesitated. "I might do a terrible job."

"It doesn't have to be a work of art." I shrugged one shoulder, knowing I could avoid the mirror at least for a few days.

He ran his fingers through my hair, lightly tugging it,

making me roll my eyes from pleasure, as shivers raced down my spine. "Are you sure?"

I gave him an encouraging smile with a nod. "Hair isn't teeth. It will grow back."

Hunter chuckled. "Tell that to anybody bald." He untangled strands into three parts and brought cold metal up. "Any hairstyle in particular you would like? Mohawk? Mullet? Buzz cut?"

"Not any of those, please." I laughed. "Just make it short like yours."

I pinched my eyes shut when the scissors touched my shoulders. The blades came together, snipping my hair. Once. Twice. Several times more. Soon, a heavy weight I didn't know I carried fell away from me.

"These are not the best ones to cut with," Hunter said, almost to himself, brushing something off my back. "Is it good enough? If you like it, I'll try to even it out."

Swallowing my apprehension, I shook my head, the hair ends skimming my shoulders. "Shorter."

"Shorter?"

"Yes."

"Let's sit down." He gently gripped my shoulders and guided me backward to the picnic table. We straddled the bench, Hunter behind me. He continued his task, lifting and trimming parts of my hair. Once in a while, his arm bumped my shoulder, or he would take hold of my head and level it straight, correcting my posture. "Stop pushing your head against my hand like a cat," he said, a smile in his voice. But it was impossible to control because each time his fingers ran over my scalp, his transcendent touch sent me into complete bliss, and I wanted to moan.

"It feels so good when you do that."

"What? This?" He massaged my scalp, pressing his fingertips into my skin, releasing delicious swirls inside me.

"Hunter." I moaned.

He coughed. "Don't say my name like that," he said in a low, husky voice. "Please."

I stifled a laugh and let him continue his work. Several moments later, he asked me to turn around and face him. I did as I was told. Leaning, he reached out but then pulled back. "That won't work. Scooch closer."

I looked down at the three feet between us, our legs barely touching. "There isn't any space."

"There is too much of it. Get closer."

I hopped once on my bottom to him, my knees jammed into his wide-open thighs. "Better?"

"Now, hold still." Hunter raked my hair with his hands, pushing some of it on my forehead, obscuring my view of his handsome face. "Don't move, or it won't be even."

The metal touched the bridge of my nose, and hair clippings fell between us. Hunter pushed my hair to the side, then off my face completely. I pried my eyes open. Hunter had his eyebrows pulled together and was biting his bottom lip, concentrating as if working on some masterpiece. Small clippings mizzled on my eyelashes, and I blinked them away. I sat statue-still as he brushed my hair a few times, his fingers on my scalp sending a warm current through me. His hair was longer than the first day I saw him; it curled behind his ears and at the nape of his neck, and my fingers itched to run over it, to feel its softness. I wanted to reach out and push his bangs off his forehead.

"Maybe I can give you a haircut." I gently scooped up a

lock of his hair and pulled it down to his nose bridge to show him how long it was. He smiled, the lines around his eyes creasing, and his large palms enveloped my head and straightened it.

"Hold still." His gaze caressed my face briefly before returning to my hair.

"Is that a no?" My lips pulled at the corners, but I dropped my hands on the bench, my fingers immediately picking at a minor groove.

"Don't move, or you'll look like lightning zapped you in the ass."

I started giggling, but Hunter again took hold of my head and gave me a playful, stern stare. His gaze dropped to my lips, my grin faltered, and I was very aware of my blood traveling from my heart through my body and back again.

I tried to focus on the gentle sound of the ocean or a raspy buzzing of bugs instead of Hunter's red, slightly parted, and moist lips. I couldn't help but wonder how he kissed. Were his kisses slow and languid or hungry and zestful? I shouldn't think about that, and instead I counted only the golden-colored stubble on his jaw. That might take a while. I blinked a few times and instead counted the number of laugh lines around his eyes—a total of six—and deep lines around his remarkable mouth—one on each side. One small mole in the center of his Cupid's bow. My lips tingled with the need to kiss it.

I didn't think cutting hair was sexy or erotic, but here I was, getting a wave of heat through me. It could be because Hunter wasn't wearing a shirt. If I were an artist, I would want to paint beautiful landscapes of his face and body. But I wasn't an artist. All I could do was commit every nanoscopic and vital detail of this gorgeous man to memory.

My gaze roamed over his exposed sun-kissed skin, noticing every ripple of muscles on his chest, taut abs, and a trail of dark hair disappearing into the top of his shorts. And I wanted to hook my finger over the waistband and see his reaction. Would his hands loop around my hips and drag me flush against him—well, I might get splinters in my ass if he did that —but would he gather me to him and let me feel his skin on mine? Or would he tell me to stop, like when he asked me not to say his name? I had to curl my hands into fists to prevent them from doing something stupid and embarrassing.

When I looked up, Hunter's eyes, rimmed with thick eyelashes, were heavy on me. My stomach swooped like I was free-falling. His hands were no longer near my face but resting on his thighs. Had he caught me staring at his crotch?

His Adam's apple bobbed as he swallowed. "I think this is a good stopping point. It's a bit uneven, but it doesn't look like I used a lawn mower."

I wanted to say thank you, but a small clump of hair stuck to my lip. Before I inhaled it, I tried to push it off with my tongue, but it only stuck to me more. Hunter's lips curved to a side, and his hand moved to my mouth. He pinched the tip of my tongue between his fingers, catching the annoying hairs, and my pulse found a new permanent location to throb. Hard and fast.

Hunter's thumb grazed my lower lip, then he dragged his hand against the side of his shorts. He gently brushed hair clippings off my nose and shoulders, his fingertips stumbling over my bikini strings.

He exhaled a slow breath as if he were losing a battle against his self-control. "You probably want to dip in the ocean to wash off."

I wanted to yank his hand and place it at the base of my throat, where my pulse thrashed like a bird caught in the net, but instead I touched my hair, getting used to its short feel. "Thanks again."

His darkened eyes never left mine, smoldering me to ashes. I was in emotional purgatory. Stay still and wait for him to make a move or take matters into my own hands? Literally. Take his face in my hands and crash his mouth to mine. He would be the second man I ever kissed. The second man to have me.

"Will you go for a swim with me?" I asked.

"With this sexy haircut, I'll never want to let you out of my sight."

"Yeah?" I patted my head subconsciously again, pulling on short strands. "You think I look good?"

"Of course." He smirked. "Why wouldn't you? I gave you this cut."

With a roll of my eyes, I pushed on his shoulder. "You're so full of yourself."

At the beach, I was waist-deep into the warm sea when Hunter barreled by my side and quickly submerged himself in the water. It was long before his head popped out a fair distance from me.

"Aquaman," I said to myself and swam to him.

It was exhausting to keep myself afloat by the time I reached Hunter. He was in deeper water, where my feet couldn't reach the bottom. Taking a deep breath, I relaxed and sank under.

"You tired?" Hunter asked when my head broke through the surface.

"Do you mind if I join you in the morning for a swim? I need to get better at swimming."

"Not at all."

He took my hand and pulled me in closer. His hands grasped my waist. My body bumped against his, and I rested my hands on his shoulders. Closing my eyes for a moment, I relished his proximity—his warmth, the softness of his skin. I brought myself to his eye level, looping my legs around his torso and linking my ankles. Once again, I thanked the universe for the laser treatment. My legs and underarms responded well, but my bikini area not so much. Alas, now my down south didn't have a landing strip exactly, more a savanna grassland—land at your own risk. And I bet Hunter wouldn't mind taking a risk.

An electric current shot up my spine when my center smacked against Hunter's firm stomach. The need for him blinded me. It took all my willpower not to move my hips and grind against him. His gaze swept over my face, and when he paused at my lips, the eagerness for what could come next sent a zing straight through me. I stared at his mouth, waiting, not breathing. We swayed with the push and pull of the ocean.

"Sydney"—his throat bobbed—"if I kiss you, I'm afraid I won't be able to stop."

"You don't have to stop." My fingers played with soft curls on the nape of his neck.

His eyes flickered to mine, water droplets clinging to his long eyelashes. "Sex complicates things."

Our relationship had an expiration date, and we were both well aware of it. Was he afraid to fall in love? Was I? Of course. I already had a crush on him. But if I kept in mind that this was a short-term affair, I wouldn't develop anything more than a little crush. As for Hunter, he would move on after we had a good time. Perhaps he worried if we had sex, and it turned out to be awful, we risked cohabiting in awkwardness. Was he insecure? I could boost his confidence and make it easier for him by admitting that Phill was vanilla. An only on Sunday and Thursday kind of guy. And besides my ex I had nobody else to compare to.

"Hunter, it doesn't have to be anything serious. It can be just a fun time between two consenting adults."

"I don't think you are someone I can just have fun with." Hunter's fingers moved on my back, pulling me closer, my breasts pressing into his chest. His eyes flitted across my face. "I already like you too much. It'll hurt when it's time for us to go our separate ways."

I understood what he meant. The same fear pushed against my ribs, but I was also out-of-my-mind horny, and that was enough for me to take a risk.

Our breathing was quick and shallow. His pulse throbbed in his neck, the tempo no doubt matching mine. He was nervous. He was scared. And for that, I wanted Hunter even more.

His grip strengthened on my back, and he tilted his head, lips parting. The distance between us was a scant breath. My eyes went over his shoulder, and my heart stopped.

"Shark." I choked on the word, fear knotting my throat. My right hand shot out to point at a black fin in the water about a hundred yards away from us.

Hunter tensed and twisted around. "Fuck."

With me in his arms, he lunged us forward toward the dry land. When the water reached his waist, and my feet found the ground, I slipped out of his grasp. He gripped my hand and pulled me with him. My feet sank into the hot sand, but I didn't stop and bolted to where the jungle encroached on the beach as if the shark would chase me this far.

"Oh my God." Catching my breath, I hugged the leaning palm tree and pressed my forehead on its bark.

Hunter sunk onto the tree trunk, his chest heaving. "It's probably the same blacktip reef sharks that have been visiting once in a while. They like to lurk around those rocks."

"And after all these days, you just now tell me about it?" I peered at him around the tree.

"They are not bad. They're friendly."

I scoffed. "I didn't see you staying in the water."

"Well," he chuckled nervously, "I wasn't exactly keen on finding out if I'm right."

My stomach hollowed. That Hunter wasn't sure about the type of shark it was only made my anxiety worse.

"No more swimming for me." I flung my arm out toward the ocean. "I'm not going back there ever again. Knee-deep, and not an inch deeper."

Hunter waved his hand dismissively. "Swimming in the ocean is overrated anyway."

Once my breathing subsided, I slumped next to Hunter, our thighs touching, my eyes on the black dot circling in the water. "No doubt this island has treasure because all kinds of things that want to murder intruders guard it. Snakes. Sea urchins. Sharks. You name it." I laughed, but Hunter didn't. I glanced at him and caught him looking at me. His eyes were soft and curious.

"What?" Feeling self-conscious, I smoothed my hair and looped some of it behind my ear. I hadn't had a chance to check out my new haircut before we spun to the beach. So, for all I knew, I might have looked like Gollum (and Hunter was *my precious*).

"Stop fidgeting with your hair," Hunter said, wrapping his fingers around my wrist and taking my hand away from my head.

The spot where his thumb touched ignited, and heat threaded its way through my muscles, electrifying my body. Hunter's eyelashes lowered as his gaze dropped to my lips. When he lifted them back there was an unspoken question in his darkened eyes. My breath stalled.

"I'm going to kiss you now," he said, his voice low, deep, and thick.

"Please." I managed.

Hunter cradled my face in his hands and bridged the distance between us, pressing his hot mouth over mine. The feel of his soft lips sent my world off its axis. A sigh escaped my throat. God, his mouth. His gorgeous, seductive, incredible mouth.

My lips parted, inviting him to deepen the kiss. He tasted of ocean salt and need. Hunter kissed me confidently, no second-guessing. He groaned with satisfaction. Ungovernable happiness erupted in me, and I twisted my fingers in his hair, tugging him closer. His breathing grew labored, and he gathered me to his body, his large palms fitting perfectly against the valleys of my back and setting my every sense on fire. Hunter kissed me like I was the only woman he'd ever wanted to kiss, like he'd die if he didn't. I was drowning in a sea of pleasure and need, and I clung to him like a lifeline. I could have guessed kissing Hunter would be earth-shattering, but I didn't know it would feel like a luscious, wild dream. I moaned and came up for air when he pulled his mouth away.

Hunter smiled against my lips. "The sounds you make will echo in my head for the rest of my life." His breath was a flutter on my lips, and then his mouth was moving against mine.

His arms came around my waist, and I wound my arms around his neck, pressing my chest flush against his, desperately seeking closeness.

He coaxed me onto his lap, letting me feel how much he liked me and my sounds. The feeling of his hard length unleashed a shudder in me. The thought we could, we would, we should have sex turned me into a frenzy, and my insides melted as if I'd stepped on a hot wire.

"More," was all I could say before he kissed me with an unquenchable hunger I craved. And I returned it. He angled my head and deepened the kiss. Arousal throbbed in my core, and I yearned for more. I needed more than his kiss. I needed more of Hunter. I needed all of him.

Chapter Nineteen

It was a blur how we made it to the porch. Hunter cupped my bottom and lifted me off my feet. I wrapped my legs around his waist, and my arms encircled his neck, pressing my mouth to his. Our kiss was sloppy, impatient, clumsy. Tongues tangled. Lower lips bitten. Teeth may or may not have been chipped.

He carried me up the steps but stopped before entering the hut.

"Should we take it slow?" His voice was a husky growl.

I covered his face with kisses, rubbing my hips against him, my center swollen with lust. "I'll pretend I didn't hear that." I licked his bottom lip, then nibbled at it again.

"Sydney, I don't have condoms," he murmured, nuzzling my neck, his breath hot on my skin, "but I'll do everything to make you lose your mind."

"I have an IUD." I bit and sucked his earlobe. "I haven't been with a man since before my divorce." My lips found his.

Hunter wrapped his arms tighter. My back crashed to the wall, his weight ramming against me. His fingers tightened on my butt, and he kissed me over and over again.

He broke our kiss, pulling an irritated moan out of me. "I got tested after my last relationship, and we're good to go."

That was all I needed to hear. "That's the hottest thing you've ever said."

Hunter groaned, sending scorching heat straight down to the spot I wanted him to touch. He leaned slightly to avoid hitting our heads on the door frame and stepped inside. We stumbled toward the bed, falling and laughing, his body sinking on top of mine. He lifted on his elbows, framing my face, and his blue eyes darkened as they roamed over me.

"It drove me mad, being unable to touch you all this time." He moistened his red lips. "I've never wanted anybody as much as I want you."

I ran my hands over his shoulders and back, arching against him. Everything that I was burned for him. "Please, put me out of my misery."

"I need this to be perfect. Tell me how you like it." He brushed the strands of hair from my eyes, then dipped his head to leave a trail of tender kisses along my jaw. His tentativeness was hot, but it annoyed the hell out of me. "Tell me what you want," he repeated.

At that point, I wasn't sure how I liked it. My skin quaked in anticipation of his lips exploring every inch of me. I longed for him to do whatever he desired to do just so I could feel him inside me. To have a release. To feel well taken care of.

"I don't know." I blew out an irritated breath. In all the books I read, the lover made his partner see stars when they came. All I had seen with my ex was a lazy rotating fan in our bedroom. I wanted to see stars, too; I wanted to experience the Big Bang. And I believed Hunter was capable of delivering it.

"However you like having sex, I'll like it too. So please," I threaded my fingers through his hair, gripping it tight, knowing and ignoring that I hurt him, "stop talking and make me come."

His lips traced a path down to my neck as his large hand slipped down my sides to my ass, then went up. His fingers, gently, as if he wasn't sure if he was allowed, brushed over my wet bikini top, drawing my nipples tight. Then his mouth captured mine again with a deep kiss, his dick straining against his swim shorts and pressing hard into me.

"I have to warn you," he said, his breathing labored, "I will devour you like you're my last meal, and I've been starving for ages."

My fingers traced every hill and valley of his sculpted muscles, then worked beneath the elastic waist of his swim trunks, reached for his ass, and squeezed it. It was firm, just as I thought it would be.

He pushed aside the triangle of fabric on my left breast and took my nipple into his mouth, sucking on it, scraping his teeth on it. A shudder ran over me. His hand tenderly glided to my nape and tugged loose the knots of my bathing suit top. When it came undone, I curved my back to help him do the same with the second knot. With the top loose, he pulled the material off me and threw it on the floor. Heat went through me at the feeling of his wet mouth, and the tease of his teeth on my skin. Moans escaped me as he drew in my nipple more while he teased my other peak with his thumb, driving me out of my already overheated mind.

Hunter's mouth found its way back to mine, and he kissed

me hard, our tongues entwining. I bit his bottom lip, pulling on it as he withdrew.

"I'm going to fuck you first." His hand coasted down over my stomach. "Then I'll make love to you." His fingers slid under the band of my bottoms and found me wet and ready. He hummed, closing his eyes for a moment. "Once I start, there is no pulling back until you are spent to my satisfaction."

What did I care what he would do with me as long as he made me come? Preferably hard. Bringing myself to orgasm was never enough. I wanted to feel full. I wanted to feel pain mixed with pleasure. The way I felt right now was close to hysterical ecstasy. My heartbeat drummed in so many parts of me: my lips, the tips of my breasts, my thighs, below my knees, my fingers, my toes.

He palmed my swollen sex, moistening the tips of his fingers, then slowly traced them along my folds, making me lose my mind. "You feel like silk," he mumbled into my lips as he slipped a finger inside me, then two. I moaned at the fullness. His thumb slowly roved over my clit, then pressed down, making me close to going over the edge. He dipped his tongue into my mouth simultaneously with his fingers. I needed to get swept away, lost in this pleasure, and never be found. My insides blazed, and I was so, so close to realizing my dream of seeing shooting stars.

"Hunter," I said breathlessly, arching into his touch. My hand moved to his shorts and rubbed his cock, pulling out a low growl from deep in his throat. "Please."

"Not yet." Hunter sucked my neck and then scraped his teeth on it. He moved down and licked my nipples, first the right one, then the left one. He pulled his hand out from under the fabric, and I whimpered with disappointment.

Hunter tugged on my bottoms, and I lifted my hips to help him free me from them as he moved off the bed. Kneeling on the floor, he drew me to the edge and parted my legs, opening me to him. I lay bare in front of him, my chest rising and falling fast, my pulse beating hard in my throat, and my body ignited with want. Before today, a month, a year ago, I would've been embarrassed to be so exposed, so out there, but Hunter's silent wonderment and the hungry look on his face gave me so much power I ached to ask him if he wanted to taste me.

"You're so beautiful," he said, his hands running over my legs, starting at my feet and moving slowly up to my thighs. He dropped gentle kisses on my ankle, knee, and up along the inside of my thigh.

With each kiss closer to my center, my orgasm drew closer. Hunter moved to my other leg, pulling a curse out of me and a low chuckle from him. His breath caressed my heated skin as his mouth hovered over my center. I moved my hips up as an invitation, and he took it.

Hunter's tongue slowly stroked through my folds, and a hungry groan broke through his lips. He kissed my clit, then his tongue flicked it before he sucked it. He pushed his tongue inside me and, in a curling motion, massaged sensitive spots I never knew existed. Digging his fingers into my thighs, he dived in deeper. He consumed me like I had seen him eat a ripe mango, his lips encasing it, teeth grazing succulent flesh, sucking on it. An embarrassingly loud moan escaped me.

Hunter laughed. "That good, huh?"

I sighed, throwing my head back. "Do it again."

Then he flattened his tongue against my pussy and dragged it up, turning me into a whimpering mess. I loved the way he moved it with vigorous precision. He slid his fingers inside me and began moving his hand, my arousal pulsating against his lips.

My hands grabbed the sheets, and I couldn't keep my hips in place. Hunter pressed down on my stomach to keep me steady and added another finger in, stretching me. At first, his fingers were going slowly in and out, but when my breathing became frantic, he swirled his tongue around my clit and deepened his thrusts.

Incoherent sounds and murmurs passed my lips, and an orgasm ripped through me. Pleasure rushed over me like a tsunami, sweeping me into euphoria. Hunter's movements slowed as he kept licking me softly, giving me extra time to dissolve and melt.

When my body went limp and still, I took in a deep breath for what seemed like the first time in a long time. I draped my arm over my eyes, and a nervous laugh vibrated through me. It was either that, or I would cry. At the age of thirty, I'd finally had someone's mouth on me. "Thank you. That was amazing," I panted, perching on my elbows. "I think I wouldn't mind experiencing that every day, but if you don't get inside of me right now and show me your other talents, I'll die from spontaneous combustion."

"Scooch up," he said.

Holding my gaze, Hunter stood, and a self-assured smile grew on his face. He took off his shorts, revealing his erection —and it was certainly nothing to be shy about. He was perfect. He crawled on top of me, dragging his pelvis over my clit, pulling an additional moan out of me.

"I love the sounds you make." He kissed me, his cock playing at my entrance. I wrapped my hands around his back and pulled him down, parting my mouth so his tongue could drive farther. I tasted myself in the kiss. Another thing I'd never done. Our kiss turned from soft to hard, then back to soft. He nibbled on my lower lip and looked at me, his face awash with an unreadable expression, his eyes tender rather than erotic abandon.

"What is it?" I asked, seeing this new vulnerability replace his earlier cockiness.

"I've never had sex without a condom before."

In some way, that meant I was his first. A sinful smile broke out on my face. "Are you afraid you won't enjoy it?"

"No," he said, his breathing coming faster, "I'm afraid I won't last."

"That's fine." I moaned, my fingers tightening in his hair. "What are you waiting for?"

Hunter pushed his hip, slowly guiding his cock into me, stretching me more and more. My smile dropped, and my breath hitched.

"Is that all right?" He paused, and I could feel his heart thumping against my breasts.

"Yes." I opened my legs wider, allowing him to go even deeper, welcoming all of him in.

Without breaking eye contact, he thrust his entire length into me, and I gasped with pleasure.

"Good God," he groaned, burying his face into my neck and nipping my shoulder. He moved with unhurried, long strokes. "So tight," his restrained whisper caressed my ear. I tried to speak, but all that came out were gasps.

"You promised to fuck me." My words were impatient and needy.

"I want to take my time," he said, pressing his lips to my jaw.

An orgasm mounted again at my core. "Move faster, please."

Cursing, Hunter pulled my left knee to my chest and changed his angle. He rocked his hips hard, delivering pain and pleasure that overpowered me, making me struggle to breathe, making me claw at his back, and making me beg for more. He increased his rhythm, sweat collecting on his face and shoulders, and the sounds that tore from my throat were nothing but pure animal.

"Sydney." He exhaled.

The way he said my name was like warm honey on bare skin, sweet and sticky and so delicious, and that was all it took to push me over the edge, forcing another white-hot sensation to rip through me. My inner muscles clenched against him. Another hard thrust and a groaning sigh of relief left his body. His hips slowed their movement, and his strokes grew gentler. Letting my leg fall, he collapsed on me.

"Jesus Christ." Hunter turned his face, pressing his lips into my hair. "I think my soul left me when you came around my dick."

I wasn't sure why that made me laugh, but it did. "I think I lost my mind for a minute there."

He raised on his forearms, his gaze searching my eyes. I waited for him to climb off me and disappear outside to shower and wash off my stickiness as Phill had each time he finished.

Hunter dropped a long kiss on my forehead. It was such a gentle gesture after what we had done and the filthy promises he had made. If I wasn't already lying down, I'd have swooned.

"I want to learn how else to make you lose your mind," he said.

Today, June 6
6:10
Would you go on a date with me tonight?
7:10
I'm free after 6 pm. What's the plan?
7:25
You. Me. Fire on the beach. Star gazing
7:34
Your such a romantic
7:35
You're
7:35
OMG! Your so ducking annoying
7:40
You're

Chapter Twenty

Last night, I'd screamed or moaned various words, mostly praising, begging, or cursing. We'd made love—I shouldn't call it that, it was more like I had joined a Cirque du Soleil show—several times as if we couldn't satisfy our hunger for each other, confined only by our lust. I was afraid to ask where Hunter learned so much about sex and how in the world a man could be so limber. I made a mental note to do some stretching.

I had nestled beside Hunter in the bed, his arm wrapped around me. It seemed natural to press my body against his. I was content and relaxed, but my mind started navigating the ocean of uncertainty. Would I find closure if I followed Father's sailing pipedream, spreading his ashes? Should I invite Hunter to do it with me? Would he agree? Or should I return to my old life of never-ending battles against AI or a fourteen-year-old Russian hacker and forget altogether about this idea?

I thought of the words on my father's urn, "Follow me at your own risk." I knew it was a farewell joke from him, but what if it was also a sign that he knew I would find his journals and he wanted me to follow his dream to experience and appreciate the world around me? He often said that I was spending an unhealthy amount of time indoors, staring at a monitor. His notes showed he hadn't forgotten about his sailing plans because he had updated the boat types and routes within the last ten years. I couldn't fathom why he never spoke of it. Was he afraid I would think he was out of his mind, or did my mother not want me to know? They hadn't spent a day apart. Did he give up something so plainly vital to him just to be with her? What did she sacrifice to be with him? What would I sacrifice for love?

The early morning promised the day to be hot, with a little breeze and calmer waters. I rummaged through drawers of clean clothes, looking for a shirt. I pulled on my Mind the Gap T-shirt and buttoned up my jean shorts. Hunter, in all his naked glory, walked into the hut with breakfast, his hair wet from his morning swim. His bottom lip sported a minor bruise where I sank my teeth too hard yesterday. He slid a Plumeria flower behind my left ear, his fingers gently tracing the side of my face. "You do not know how often I thought of doing this."

"I love it." I smiled, touching the petals.

He offered me a mug, and I peered inside it. "No coffee?"

"Unfortunately, we are out. From now on, only orange juice or coconut water. And I know how much you love … let me think, what did you call it earlier … a turd-colored fruit?"

"Actually, I don't mind coconut now." Either my taste buds gave up being prejudiced against the flavor, or being with Hunter had cured their associations with my ex.

"I think you are overdressed." He kissed me, his hand slipping up my thigh, and the tips of his fingers curling inside my shorts. "Your body is stunning. You should always be naked."

"What if someone comes here?"

"Then we'll get dressed." He traced his tongue over my bottom lip, then nipped on it.

"And would you be able to focus on anything but sex if we were naked all the time?" I asked.

Hunter's fingers made their way around the fabric and found my aching-for-attention center. "It doesn't matter. I can't focus when you are fully covered either."

That morning, we didn't do much island exploration. By lunchtime, Hunter once again was very familiar with every inch of my body. In the afternoon, we finally made it to John's trap for broad investigation, but not ten minutes later, my butt was propped against a mossy rock, legs hooked around Hunter's waist, his hot mouth on my neck while he slid in and out of me.

We took the rest of the week off, and spent it like we were on our honeymoon, barely talking about *work* (aka treasure) and learning more about each other, having sex in every position I could and couldn't imagine. In the mornings, Hunter dragged his bare ass out of bed and went for his swim, leaving me in sheets soaked with sweat and sex, my need satisfied. When sunlight crept deeper into the hut and the smell of wood burning filled the space, I finally rolled out of the bed. Dressed only in my bikini bottoms, I washed my face in ice-cold water, brushed my teeth and landed a kiss on Hunter's shirtless back, tasting ocean salt on his skin. During breakfast, we didn't bother with using separate plates—just one extra dish to wash—and shared our meal out of the same skillet and bowl. Hunter would burrow his face into my neck, palm my naked breast, and murmur dirty ideas he'd planned for us later in the day. This was our new routine. And I was in a tropical paradise.

Five days later we returned to the location entirely intending to finish what we had started. No sex. Not even touching. Till we were done with work for the day, of course.

"Where do we begin?" Hunter stood on the opposite side of the hole from me. The farther he was from me, the less I felt the gravitational force that pulled our bodies together.

"We need to keep our minds and eyes open for anything that is strong, hollow, alive, dead, Greek god related, and or could kill us," I said, staring at the skull's hollow expression. Poor guy died here alone. I hoped his death had been quick. A giant brown spider crawled out of John's open jaw, and I stepped away from the trap, my shoulders shaking off the feeling of the spider's eight legs on my skin. Cats and an army of lizards in the hut kept the spider population in check, but it was a different story here in the deep jungle.

"Are there any poisonous spiders on this island that could kill us?" I walked to a tree with a complicated web between two branches. Perhaps if there were (much to our regret), we had to search for a dark place like a cave where these spiders lived.

"I don't think so," Hunter said, "but it doesn't mean there aren't." He tapped the machete we'd brought to cut a thick network of vines, ready to clear a new way for us to walk. The plan was to explore the overgrown and hard-to-travel places at the foot of the mountain, starting from John's hole and going up north. With any luck, we would uncover another unexplored cave or a suspicious burial site with a tombstone or rock formation in the shape of something related to the riddles.

It was a man and a woman against a tropical wildness for the next nth hours. Well, it was more of a man against it and a woman trailing behind, appreciating the man. Hunter worked hard chopping branches and vines, and I carried a backpack with provisions we needed when it was time for a break. After several minutes, Hunter's sweat-soaked T-shirt clung to his back, exposing the strength of his muscles and taking too much of my attention away from the treasure search. At some point, while admiring Hunter, I sighed so loud that he stopped and turned to look at me with a confused face.

"Are you okay back there?" Hunter pushed the bangs off his forehead, slicking his hair back. I loved it when he wore his hair like that, especially right now, when his face had a few days of stubble. He reminded me of Chris Hemsworth, and heat pooled at the base of my spine. A week ago, I couldn't act on my desire, and now I could, but not right at this moment because we'd agreed to focus on our work first.

"Just thinking of how proud Edward would be of you. You kept your promise and made sure Holden's family name will be forever in history as the discoverers of the Treasure of Lima," I said, too embarrassed to admit the meaning behind my horny sigh.

Hunter eyed me briefly before turning back and breaking off a long aerial root that grew down from the branches of a tree that could be easily mistaken for a dense forest of lean trees.

"Edward didn't make me promise," Hunter said.

"Oh?" I stopped. "I was under the impression you were doing it because he asked you."

"No. I'm doing this because I don't want the man who

raised me like his own to be a laughing stock for those who thought he was a lunatic, just like his father and two brothers."

"Shit!" A kamikaze bug flew into my ear, and I slapped the side of my head, trying to get it out.

"You alright?"

"Yes. Bugs. When did Edward tell you about the treasure?"

"When I arrived here, he didn't tell me for the entire fishing season, but when the bookings slowed and Jolie broke up with me, he saw an opportunity to bring me on board. I was a grown man who could decide for himself if I wanted to be part of the Holden family curse." He chuckled, shaking his head. "There are no curses, just decisions we make that turn out to be bad ones." His expression dimmed, and he looked past me. "So many bad ones."

I wondered if Hunter was talking about his uncles and grandfather or himself. What bad decision had he made? Somehow, my mind kept returning to Jolie, and Hunter's regret at leaving her and coming here.

"Now you have proof that the treasure is real, and Edward wasn't crazy. I bet your aunt will feel guilty for not supporting him."

Remorse slithered down my throat that I'd also thought Hunter was mad when he told me what he was doing on this island the morning I found him waist-deep in the hole. In my defense, at that time, I had known Hunter only for a few days.

Hunter grunted, trying to break a thick vine. It snapped, and he pulled it out of our way. At the speed we trudged, it would take us several hours to follow a curve of the hill that should have led us to the hidden cut-through with the giant tree and bat cave.

"If not for your help," Hunter said, "I'd die a lonely old

man who told pirate tales to random strangers at the Avarua marina."

"And now you'll die a rich man surrounded by his children and grandchildren who love to listen to the tales of your adventures."

Hunter side-glanced at me, a dimple forming on his cheek. His blue eyes were so beautiful I could get lost in them. "Thank you," he said.

"For helping with treasure or illustrating a different life for you?" I smiled back at him.

"Both."

The afternoon weather turned sticky, hot, and muggy. In four hours of our search, we found several dark openings in the mountain that didn't go deep and were, unfortunately, empty. Hunter and I reached the spot in the narrow gorge with the bat cave and the cool pond. Hunter stripped off his clothes and stepped into the water. I followed his lead, goosebumps running up my body. I nestled between Hunter's legs and pressed my back against his chest, relishing his body heat. He wrapped his arms around my waist, pulling me even closer.

"Remember when you showed me this place for the first time, and a bunch of bats flew out?" I nodded at the dark cave opening near the tree. "You protected me with your body. And I enjoyed it so much I fantasized about many other situations where you would do it again."

"Since we're being honest with each other right now, I'll admit that I've visualized you against me at least a hundred times every day since that evening." He outlined my breast with his finger and pressed a fervent kiss to the side of my neck. "When you wore my T-shirts over your bare body, I had to walk the entire time with my dick half-mast."

"I saw your naked butt when you went swimming on your own last week."

"I know you did." His hand traced down my stomach and disappeared between my thighs. The hardness of his erection prodded into my back.

"How?" I huffed the question.

"You were acting strange when I returned and couldn't look at me during dinner," he whispered, teasing my earlobe with his teeth. I wouldn't be able to meet his eyes now because he worked two fingers into me, and my eyes rolled back into my head. I clenched around them and moaned. "You're so soft and hot inside." He added another finger, stretching me and making me gasp. I widened my legs for easier access, propping my feet on the slippery rocks, pushing my body into Hunter's.

"You are so beautiful when you come undone," he said in a husky voice, amplifying my throbbing lust. His fingers were deep inside of me. He teased and stroked me, applying just the right pressure, at a torturously slow pace, as if he were spelling a secret message, a spell. My breath hitched, and pleasure clenched deep within me. My muscles coiled around his fingers as my orgasm mounted higher.

Just a few more strokes. I readied to get lost in oblivion, imagining myself facing Hunter as I'd slide down his cock as soon as I reached my—

"Fuck," he said, and not in a sexy way. The movement of his fingers stopped. "I know the answer to the riddle."

He pulled his fingers out, and I crashed landed from my lust ride. "Which one?" I said, winded.

"When you face to face with death, you are in the right place. It's the bat cave."

Fingering me made him think of the bat cave. Lovely.

"Why do you think that?"

"Because look at it." Hunter's hands grasped my shoulders, and he gently guided my body to my right.

Behind the tree, the bat cave appeared as it had before: a sheer mass of rock with a dark, large entrance at the bottom and two large, round-*ish* cavities above.

"I'm not sure what I'm looking for," I said, narrowing my eyes in the hope of seeing what Hunter saw. I closed one eye, then opened it and closed the other. Nothing.

Hunter leaned in, his mouth close to my ear, and whispered, "It's the front of a skull."

As soon as his words left his mouth, the three dark holes morphed into a nasal cavity and two eye sockets. No jaw. The nasal passage was the bat cave.

"Holy shit!" I turned to look at him. "But you said it was empty."

"Yes, but I also didn't go too deep inside of it."

"Oh, my god. Now you tell me that?" I climbed out of the water.

"What are you doing?" Hunter asked as I grabbed my shirt and pulled it over my head.

"What does it look like? I want to look in the cave."

"I hoped we would—" He wiggled his eyebrows, hinting with a nod toward the water. Lovemaking with Hunter was a slice of heaven, but this was too exciting.

"Not now." I picked up his clothes. "Come on, let's go look."

Chapter Twenty-One

We peered into the open mouth of the cave. "Are you sure you want to go in?" Hunter asked.

Nope.

"Yes." My body tightened.

"I'll go in alone. Wait for me here." He took the hammer we brought with us out of my hand in case we had to bash something over the head. Hunter stole a kiss and stepped into the cave, murkiness consuming his body.

"No. I'm going with you."

We plunged into the cave, Hunter leading the way with the bright light and me tiptoeing after him. The opening was large, with the damp ground and vegetation creeping as far as sunlight could reach.

I grimaced and pinched my nose from the assaulting smell. "What's that?"

"Probably bat scat. Look." Hunter nodded to stalactites and small fuzzy creatures clinging to the rocky ceiling. It was hard to say how many were there, maybe a hundred or more.

My muscles turned into stone. I was expecting them at any second to act chaotically which would make me act chaotically too, but they didn't move.

Hunter squeezed my hand. "You go back and wait for me outside."

After what I'd experienced with the snakes, I could handle anything. "I can do this."

We crept further, following the musty pathway. My flip-flop sank into mush, and my foot slipped out of it.

"Shit," I hissed, balancing on one foot. "Light, please."

I let go of Hunter's hand, twisted, and bent to pick up my shoe. My knee wobbled, and I tumbled forward. My foot swung and kicked the flashlight out of Hunter's hand, sending it flying into a wall. Everything around us went dark, only the dim light from the entrance curved around the bend.

Hunter uttered a snort. I was glad one of us found this funny. My palms and knees sank into bat-crap goo. Failing to suppress his laughter, Hunter helped me up, then picked up the flashlight and hit it once at the base. Light returned to the cave.

I rubbed my hands on a wall to remove some concoction of the dirt and crap, then yanked my flip-flop out of the mud and placed it back on my foot.

We continued navigating the cave, and soon, the passage tapered until we could barely stand side by side. From there, the cave split into two paths. We went left but shortly faced a dead end. Hunter and I searched for anything out of place, inserted our hands into small cracks, and moved around odd rocks below our feet.

Disappointed, we returned to the fork and tried the other corridor. Dark space with dense air contracted as we pushed further in, eventually cramming our bodies sideways. We stopped. My breathing became quick and shallow as a suffocating thought that we could get stuck and die in here crossed my mind.

"Hunter." I touched his arm. "I don't feel good about being here. I can't breathe."

"Let's go back," he said.

Holding my hand in his, Hunter walked me out, planted a kiss on my forehead, and then disappeared back into the cavern. I sat cross-legged under the tree, my back resting against it. The bat cave was the right place to search, but I had a feeling we were looking at it in the wrong way. The passages were too narrow.

Not much time passed before Hunter appeared out of the darkness, his hair a mess, his shirt covered in dirt beyond recognition, his eyes downcast.

He slumped next to me. "Nothing."

"Do you think John and his friends have already found it?"

Hunter shrugged.

I propped my right shoulder against the tree and faced Hunter. "We found proof that it is here. We just need some time and maybe extra help. If we bring a professional in to help, can we still claim the finder's fee for the total value?"

"I'm not sure. But I need us to find it all. I need to do it for Edward and my family."

A feeling of dread came over me, tightening a knot in my stomach. It was important to me to finish my father's sailing journey, and it was vital for Hunter to honor the man who raised him. And then Hunter and I would go our separate ways. A question burned inside of me. "Once this is over, will you really stay here?"

Full of sadness, his eyes searched mine, and he took a deep breath. "I'm sorry."

I shouldn't have been upset about it, but my emotions were overpowering me. Hunter made it clear earlier that he wanted to stay in the South Pacific. This was a fun time, and the sex was out of this world fantastic, but this wasn't my life. And I'd promised myself I wouldn't get attached to him—or worse, fall in love.

Maybe when I returned to spread my dad's ashes, I could stay at Hunter's resort and see him again. Make love to him again then if he wasn't involved with someone else. I swallowed the lump in my throat. But right now, no boat waited to take me home, and I could pretend Hunter and I were meant to be together forever.

"This is the right place." I rose and offered Hunter my hands. "The day is still young. Let's go back inside and search some more. It's hidden in there, and we just missed it."

An hour later, I sat near the cave's opening, taking a brief break. I placed the flashlight next to me and took a sip from my bottle, then offered it to Hunter.

He gladly accepted my offer. "I think someone found the loot before us." He wiped his mouth with his hand and gave me back the bottle and leaned against the wall opposite me. "Or there is another death-looking place."

Come hell or high water, I couldn't consider quitting when we were this close. Shifting my butt on the rock, I nudged the flashlight, and it rolled off the stone and dropped, casting light on Hunter. There was something unnatural about the way the crack in the wall went up and around, making a large, jagged arch around him.

"Do you see how it has a lighter color than the rest of

them?" I moved my finger up and down in the light, letting its shadow run the length of the split in a stone.

Hunter traced the line with his finger, then he pulled a knife from his back pocket and picked at the seam.

"I'm not a geologist," he said, "but I think this is not original to this cave."

"Is it possible they deposited the loot here and then constructed a wall?"

The unequivocal confidence of this idea steadied my heart race. If my hopeful imagination was right, then, holy shit, Captain William Thompson hired brilliant stonemasons as his sailors. And, no doubt, the two hundred years wait only helped to disguise the faux barrier.

"One way to find out."

Grabbing the hammer, Hunter swung it wide and hit the flat rock hard. Every muscle in my body vibrated from the first blast. The sound bounced from wall to wall, and then the cave swallowed it and then breathed out a shrieking noise. Hunter and I flattened to the ground, covering our heads with our hands, waiting for hundreds of bats to rush above us. Once the screeching and swooshing air stopped, we got up.

"You okay?" Hunter asked. I nodded in response and returned my focus to the wall.

Zigzag lines ran from the center of the first blow. Hunter continued to hit the rock repeatedly until he made a hole. Chipping off more rock with his hands, Hunter enlarged the opening. I handed him the flashlight. Through the fog of dust and stone particles stored deep inside the cavity, trunks stacked on trunks came into view. A feeling of pins and needles coursed through my body as I stared at our discovery. My mind grasped that it wasn't a hallucination from dehydration or exhaustion and that I wasn't looking at a mirage that could vanish in the blink of an eye. It was real. And we finally found it.

"Finally," Hunter whispered.

The rest of the wall crumbled with ease as our greedy hands pulled on the edges and enlarged the entrance. Dust suspended in the air reflected the light as we entered the damp chamber. My eyes widened, taking in what I hoped wasn't a figment of my imagination formed through spending too much time dreaming of this moment.

"Please pinch me," I said. "Wow. Just wow."

Eight large wooden trunks crowded the space, lightly dusted with dirt. Some chests were filled to the brim with gold and silver candelabras, their lids not even closed.

Hunter opened a chest, exposing swords and daggers. He laughed, the sound equal parts disbelief and exultation, then threw the next one open to find more relics embedded with gemstones.

"Come look at this," I said, walking to a spot where five large tapestries were propped up against the wall. Grabbing the hem of the antique fabric, we revealed a colorful scene framed by a rich decorative border of scrolling foliage of a woman on horseback alongside two huntsmen, a pack of dogs trailing after them, a landscape with palm trees and vines, and a clearing in the trees revealing a flotilla of ships out in the sea. Even in the semi-darkness, it was stunning.

Hunter picked up a dagger and weighed it on his palm as he studied it. The unpolished metal shone. Hunter lifted his head, and his glistening eyes found mine. "Sydney, we did it."

My chest expanded with pride and thrill. Not only because of what we discovered tonight, but because in the short few weeks, I'd changed so much that the old me wouldn't recognize me now. And I wouldn't have done it without Hunter.

I was physically and mentally stronger (spending many hours in the sun was cruel for the skin, but the abundant boost of Vitamin D was much better for my mental health than sitting in my dark office in front of a 24-inch iMac). I was living an adventure (not by choice, but I loved it now). I got a new haircut (sort of by choice). Most importantly, I took a risk of having feelings for someone I knew had no place in my other life. Not because I didn't want Hunter in it, but because he stated he wasn't going back from the start. This was his home now. And my home was Florida. And it wouldn't have been fair for me to convince him to leave. Just as it wouldn't have been fair for him to convince me to stay. My eyes burned with tears.

"What's wrong?" Hunter's eyebrows pulled together, and he dropped the dagger. "You don't look happy."

I pulled a smile. "Oh, I am happy." The happiest I'd have been in a very long time.

"Then, why are you crying?"

I snorted and wiped my eyes, scraping my skin with dirt. "Because I'm really happy. Look at yourself. You are crying, too."

"Come here." Hunter stretched out his arm, and I took his hand. He drew me close, and in an instant, my body melted into his. "This is all because of you, Wonder Woman," he whispered into my hair. "Thank you for being so incredible."

He pulled away just long enough for me to see his face in the dim light. His lips parted, and his eyes searched mine. I stood stock-still, waiting. My heart pounded in my ribcage, no doubt its sound reverberating inside Hunter's chest. The emotions flooded me the way he stared at me. *What?* I wanted to ask. *What is it?* But Hunter pulled me back into him and let out a deep sigh. "Only two riddles left to solve."

A heave of disappointment wrenched at my heart. It made no sense for me to dare him to say something that would abso-fucking-lutely mess with my future judgments. That wasn't what he was going to say earlier. Was it?

Today, June 13
18:35
Sex on the beach?
18:40
As in drink?
or...
19:03
Find me on the beach, and
you'll find out.
XOXO

Chapter Twenty-Two

Later that evening, as the last sunbeam dissolved in the ocean, we finished our dinner near a small fire on the beach like a married couple, happy to be in each other's company after a hard workday. Monday, with his yellow eyes barely open, faithfully waited for me to share a leftover piece of fish, while Tuesday chased small crabs at the edge of the water unbothered by the sneaky waves which once in a while touched his feet.

"Today is incredible. I still can't believe it," Hunter said. He had changed into a clean pair of shorts, and I wore his light green T-shirt and my bikini bottoms. "I wish Edward were alive."

Hunter couldn't stop grinning all evening long and had all the right to do so. He'd finally found what he sought, and I was glad I'd played a role in it. And it did something to me. A wonderful feeling twirled through me and rooted itself in my chest. And I knew that moment that whenever I'd find myself on a beach in Florida or anywhere else, it would always bring me back here. To this month. To this day. To Hunter. The feel of the sand or the sound of the rolling waves forever would all be a living memory of our time together.

"He would be very proud of you," I said, tossing orange peels into the fire. The flames flickered different colors as the fruit skin caramelized and caught fire, a smoky Old-Fashioned fragrance filling the air momentarily. *Add this smell to that living memory too.*

"I'm eternally grateful to you," he said and kissed my inner wrist, stubble grating my skin, then his attention fixed on my face. He had that look again he'd had earlier. His expression was so vulnerable, unguarded, his parted lips on the verge of revealing a private secret. A wave of butterflies erupted in my stomach as if he had just confessed his love for me.

I let out an exaggerated sigh and waved my hand at him. "It's a team effort. We work well together. Like we are Superman and Batman."

He arched an eyebrow, smirking. "Did you use the Superman reference because Cavill is in it?"

"What? Oh, good grief. No. I didn't even remember he was in that movie."

That was a fat lie. My favorite part of the movie was when Henry was shirtless, in the rain, stealing clothes. I'd rewatched it countless times. Shoot. Maybe that was *Man of Steel*. All the Henry Cavill shirtless moments blurred into one. (Okay, so shirtlessness was my Kryptonite)

"I'm glad I'm a few inches taller than him. Otherwise, I would be dying of jealousy and fear that one day he would swoop in and steal you from me." Hunter gave me a cheeky grin, his dimples deeper than usual.

"You have nothing to worry about." I laughed and rested

my head on my pulled-up knees. I cataloged the man next to me on the beach blanket.

My crush on Hunter had developed into something that would cause pain in the near future. And maybe that was precisely what I needed as a reboot to my system. To let my heart soar high with feelings just to crash back down to earth. I could get over Hunter. Miami had close to half a million people. No doubt one of those people was a man just as kind and funny as Hunter, a jack of all trades who was also good-looking (which shouldn't matter), taller than Mr. Cavill (which also shouldn't matter), and a *seriously* talented lover (which Hunter really, *really* was).

"What are you thinking about?" he asked.

"I'm thinking we have unfinished business that we started in the lake, but someone had to be rude and blurt out the riddle answer." Drawn by his gravity, I leaned in and brushed the tip of my nose against his. "What are you thinking about?"

A mischievous smile curved Hunter's full lips, and his fingers pinched my T-shirt, tugging me to him. "How about I show you now."

Our mouths explored each other as if we had never kissed before, our tongues teasing and coaxing for incalculable minutes until we were both ready to drown in sweet nirvana.

Hunter laid me on the blanket without breaking contact, settling on his left elbow. He hummed as he kissed me, and a sound sent sparking tingles across my skin. He bit my lips, then my jaw, his fingers going for my bikini and trying to take it off. I lifted my hips, helping him.

My body freed, Hunter massaged my center with an open palm, lighting up all my nerve endings.

"Show me how much you like me," I demanded, and a pleased grin took over Hunter's face.

"Trust me. I like you a lot."

My fingers wrapped around his shaft, eliciting a soft "fuck" from Hunter. I loved the heavy feel of his dick in my hands, and my mouth watered at the thought of sweeping my tongue around its smooth crown, sucking its head, and taking him into the back of my throat, but my selfish, needy side demanded Hunter inside my core, making me cry out his name until my voice was hoarse.

"You make me so fucking hard." His throaty voice and dirty talk made my toes curl, turning my body into a quivering mess.

"Please get inside of me already." My tone now was a plea. Hunter's pupils dilated with hunger. He palmed my neck with gentle pressure but kissed me hard.

"Take off your shirt," he said against my mouth. "Then get on your hands and knees."

I pulled the shirt over my head and did what he asked. He folded over me, nudging my legs apart more, his dick hot and stiff against me. His lips trailed kisses at the nape of my neck while his free hand stroked my damp curls.

"I love how wet and slippery you are," he said, positioning the head of his cock at my entrance and creating a scorching point of contact.

His talented fingers glided down my spine and over my ass, slapping it once lightly, then moving up again, torturing me with anticipation. Before I could beg, he buried himself with one long thrust, filling me completely and making me cry out.

"You feel so good," Hunter grunted, finding a steady

rhythm of slow strokes. I sucked in a breath as Hunter rocked his hips and crashed against me again, his fingers digging into my flesh. Heat gathered at the base of my spine as his fingers found their way down and stimulated my center. Sex with Hunter was so much more than I ever thought it could be. I wanted him to make love to me for the rest of my life. My breathing was frenzied with too much arousal.

"I'm close," I whisper-moaned, struggling to speak. My hands clutching at the blanket as I bucked, demanding more. "Harder."

Hunter's hands took an iron grip on my hips, and he began driving inside me deeper and harder, his movements rough. The slap of his pelvis against my bare ass and sensitive sex made my blood run faster. The crash of waves against the shore mingled with the crash of our bodies against each other as the air around us was filled with greedy noises and growls. Pressure built inside me, and I begged him not to stop. Lightning struck somewhere near, or maybe it was my imagination. I shattered, letting out strangled swearwords punctuated by his name. I saw fireworks instead of bright stars on the canopy of the night's sky above us.

The guttural sound Hunter made within his throat and the feel of his thickness as the orgasm tore through him could have easily pushed me over the edge one more time. He slumped on top of me, our bodies fused together. His large hands covered mine, that gripped the bunched-up blanket.

Hunter's heart drummed against my sweaty back, in sync with mine. He pressed his mouth into the nape of my neck, then exhaled a heavy breath, warming my skin.

"Sydney," he said softly, and there was an unspoken

question in my name that released shivers through my humming body.

"Yes?" I turned my face to him.

Hunter's lips brushed against my temple then the shell of my ear, and he repeated my name in a whisper. I hummed in reply, closing my eyes. My stomach twisted with knots of pleasure, anxiety, and anticipation of what he would say next.

"You are the best thing that has ever happened to me," he said.

Part of me was glad he didn't say what I hoped and feared he could say, and part of me was disappointed.

"I know." I smiled the smile I would for the rest of my life each time I thought of him. He huffed a laugh and landed a last kiss on my back.

Later, we rolled into the bed and Hunter pulled me close to his solid body, my butt tight against his crotch, his legs curving under mine. He whispered good night, his lips brushing over my shoulder in a kiss, and the exhaustion quickly overtook him. But not me.

While Hunter was deep asleep, I lay wide awake, staring out of the open window. The area around the hut was tranquil, night birds were silent, and a breeze didn't play among the trees. Cogs turned in my head as I went over the last two riddles.

Strong but hollow alive but dead inside
When the ocean bows low it exposes Achilles fatal flaw

Sailors liked superstitions. Hunter didn't strike me as a superstitious person, but Bambi had worn gold hoop earrings because she thought it brought good fortune. So much for that.

What was dead and alive? My mind sifted through different mythical creatures. A harpy was a human vulture who took people to the underworld and tormented them. Mermaids were beautiful monsters, luring sailors with a song to the ocean's depths. Tritons were fishtailed sea-gods. Why Achilles? He had nothing to do with water. In books and movies, pirates always believed in mythical sea monsters, and ships sailed off the edge of the ocean or were sucked into giant whirlpools, but nothing to do with Greek gods. But Captain William Thompson hadn't been a pirate. He'd been the commander of a merchant ship who became a criminal.

Achilles' heel meant weakness, a vulnerable spot. But did it mean literally a spot on a human body, or was it some kind of temptation? The only temptation on the island was Hunter. Maybe I was missing something about Greek mythology. I groaned—quietly so as not to wake up Hunter. Alexa or Siri would've been so helpful right now.

I woke up in the middle of the night. Moonlight found its way through open shutters, casting silver shadows across the desk where Monday lay spread out on the journals. Hunter lay on his back asleep, breathing peacefully, his arm dropped over his eyes.

Soundlessly, I slipped into bikini bottoms and the T-shirt I'd thrown on the sofa last night. I tiptoed out of the house, heading for the beach, Monday trailing behind me. After three weeks on the island, the fear of darkness and lurking shadows in the jungle no longer followed me. It was fair to say I'd grown accustomed to this life, yet I missed many things about my life in Miami. I missed Tina, my home, and my Nespresso machine.

The waves caressed the shoreline, and the black canvas

unveiled the limitless universe. It was hard to say where the sky stopped and the ocean began. The moon seemed closer than ever, as if I could stand on top of one of the boulders and touch it. In the middle of nowhere, without city lights, the skies were an open window into the universe, with billions of stars and galaxies visible to the naked eye. So much was unknown. It was breathtaking, and I felt as if this island were a flowing part of the cosmos, a fragment of its mystery.

I spread the blanket I brought with me on the sand and sat. Monday kept on walking along the underbrush line. He stopped a few feet away from me, dug in the sand, turned around, and squatted over the hole.

"Nice," I said, pulling my knees to my chest. At least one thing was the same here as in Miami: beaches were gigantic litter boxes.

I looked up at the sky and tried to pick out constellations. But besides knowing the names of the twelve that made up the zodiac, I didn't know what I was looking for. Bambi had talked about stars a lot. Showing me how to find the Southern Cross by locating the two brightest stars (she used names, but I didn't remember them now) and drawing a line between them, then extending it all the way to the horizon, and where the imaginary line crossed was the South.

She had tried to teach me more about how to identify different constellations, but I brushed it off even as I politely listened to her. Now I wished I had paid closer attention. She mentioned the North Star was a part of the constellation Ursa Minor, Little Dipper, and Big Dipper. Bambi also explained that she could measure angles between the stars and the horizon if she needed to figure out the latitude. She must have known what she was talking about if she had guided the *Bloody Mary* for two weeks without GPS toward the Cook Islands. She'd made a mistake somewhere because it took us nine days instead of seven, yet she brought us close to Rarotonga before the storm. If Bambi hadn't gone overboard and had guided the boat through the storm instead of me, we would have landed in Rarotonga, I had no doubt about it. I steered the *Bloody Mary* in the wrong direction, to the wrong island. Yet, nothing about it felt wrong anymore.

"Why aren't you in bed?" Hunter's voice startled me.

"Jesus." My hand flew to my chest. "Don't sneak up on me like that."

I patted the spot next to me.

"Do you know anything about constellations? Isn't one of them a hunter?" I asked, toppling sideways and resting my head on Hunter's shoulder. The night wasn't cold, but I welcomed the heat radiating off him as he nestled near me.

"All I remember from the astronomy class is that constellations shift seasonally. Some are unique to the northern or southern hemisphere. The Southern Cross is only in the Southern Hemisphere. I think Orion is in both."

"Can you find it for me?"

Hunter chuckled. "No."

"OMG, Hunter Holden. How can you take tourists on deep-sea fishing tours if you don't know your constellations?" I said in a teasing tone. "What would you do if your modern navigation system broke?"

"I guess we would remain lost forever." Hunter's sigh turned into a yawn, and he rubbed his eye. "Why are you out here wondering about all of this?"

"I couldn't go back to sleep. I was thinking about Achilles' heel. Greeks associated the constellations with mythological gods and mythical creatures. Achilles wasn't a god. He was a hero. Is Orion a god?"

"Well, Zeus is the king of the gods, and Hera is the queen of the gods. And if I'm not wrong, Athena is the goddess of war."

I shot him a confused glance. "Wait, I thought Ares was the god of war."

"He's a god, and she's a goddess." Hunter kissed my temple. "Like you."

"I'm a goddess of war? I'm a very peaceful person."

"You're a goddess of beauty and all that is good in my life." He lightly squeezed my thigh. "Let's go to bed."

"Wait. What about Achilles? Is there a constellation named after him?" I stretched my neck's stiffened muscles.

"Tomorrow, check the Greek mythology book in the hut. Maybe it mentions something about it." Hunter yawned again and glanced at his watch, four twenty-seven lighting up on a green backlight. "Correction, you can check it today."

"I already read it. There is nothing helpful." I reached down and scratched around the snake's bite on my ankle, trying not to scrape too much of the healed area.

"Does it still bother you?" He smoothed his warm palm over my ankle, gently massaging my skin.

"It's a bit itchy."

"Did I tell you about when a bastard snake bit me on my heel? It took weeks for it to—" His hand halted.

"Shit," Hunter and I both said at the same time.

"Hunter," I said with urgency, catching his eyes. Excitement shot like a pinball and bounced inside of me. "It makes sense now. He hid it with the snakes, or at least somewhere near them."

"The ocean bow must have something to do with the water

level. When the tide is low, it exposes more of the black rocks," Hunter said.

I smiled so wide my jaw hurt. "Should we look now? Go get the flashlights."

"It's better to wait for the sunrise. We barely have any oil left for lanterns and we should preserve our batteries. In the morning we'll look, but right now let me take you to bed."

"To bed as in…?" I leaned into him, inviting him for a kiss.

"Follow me and you'll find out." He kissed the words into my lips.

Today, June 14
7:45
I think you spelled SOS backward on the beach.
7:55
Nice try

Chapter Twenty-Three

At the picnic table, over fruit salad and cups of coconut milk (undeniable proof that I was a changed woman), Hunter and I discussed where we should start our search.

"I assume I'd be okay if a snake bit me again, but I think I'd rather avoid it if I can," I said.

"I'll search the black rocks alone, and you can explore the surrounding area."

"Or we, and by that, I mean you, could try to remove all the twisting beasts out of the way first, and we can look together. Didn't you say you have some special stick to catch them?"

"It's broken."

"Well, what about this?" I pointed at his three-pronged fishing spear. "You can hit the snakes with that."

Hunter arched an eyebrow. "We are not killing snakes." He stepped around the fire pit and dropped his used mug into the tub with water. "Let's look in the shed and see what we can find."

On the way there, we foraged in the jungle until we picked

two long, sturdy branches. Inside the shed, we collected two ten-gallon buckets with lids, a gardening hand trowel, an extra hammer, and a large shovel.

At the rocks, Hunter began searching for nasty creatures. I stayed in the knee-high water, in a ready-to-missile-out-of-there position, in the event a rogue snake escaped and swam to me. I assumed the snakes knew how to swim, at least for a short distance, otherwise Darwin's law would have taken care of them in the last two hundred years. And it was great that it didn't because we wouldn't have figured out the riddle.

The bucket sat on a lower rock, and, using the sticks, Hunter tried to pick up a snake and drop it into the container. Each time he pulled one up, it fell. At first, Hunter cursed under his breath, but by the end he shouted all kinds of profanity, jumping backward like a mongoose in a dance with a cobra.

Twenty minutes later, we had only one snake secured under the lid. Hunter tossed the stick, shifted between rocks, and bent. He cursed, then rose back up, gripping two snakes by their necks, their bodies twisting over his arm. He opened the lid and shook them off into the bucket, then shut the lid back down. Blood dripped off his arm.

The crushing panic knocked the breath out of me. I rushed to him, but I stopped by the bucket as he opened it and dropped another snake.

"You okay?" I asked.

"Never been better. Grab another one of these buckets from the shed. Take this one to the beach."

I grimaced when he handed me the bucket. The top was secured—I hoped—but my breakfast threatened to make a second appearance.

"Please don't catch any more until I'm back," I said. "Rest a bit."

I returned as fast as possible with another ten-gallon drum, and Hunter repeated his bare-hands-catching technique. Nine snakes later, Hunter checked the area for more but couldn't find any. He extended his bloody hand to me and helped me climb the rocks. Both of his arms and ankles bled, and the spot between his thumb and index finger had bloody holes.

"Hunter, you got…" I counted all the bites, "six doses of—"

"I'll be okay." Hunter pressed his back against a wall. "I just need a minute." He closed his eyes and exhaled heavily.

"You aren't okay."

"Nah, just give me a few to rest." He slid down and dropped his head to his knees.

I took the third bucket to the beach and then climbed over the rocks where Hunter was. "You should've listened to me and brought your fishing pole. Snakes are nasty animals."

Hunter didn't answer, just groaned from pain or maybe from my nagging. I sat next to him and stroked his back. Lazy waves lapped over the rocks with a steady pulse, and the warm breeze carried the scent of the salt. We remained there for some time, Hunter resting while I stared into the sea, the blue, cloudless skies above promising of a nice day.

When the blood stopped running down Hunter's legs and hands, we started by throwing the smaller stones into the sea. Some of Hunter's wounds started bleeding again. With all the manageable rocks out of the way, we studied the area. Nothing looked out of place, and we tried to think of where Captain William Thompson may have hidden the fortune.

"You think it could be under this enormous stone?" Hunter

pointed at two giant stone slabs. I shrugged and handed him the hammer and the large screwdriver.

No matter how many times Hunter smashed it, the block stayed in one piece. He dropped the tools, positioned his back against a rock wall, planted his feet on the stone, and pushed. The slab gave in and moved a fraction of an inch. I joined him, and together, we forced it off its spot, but not far enough to easily see what was under it. The water spilled from under the slab each time a new wave hit.

"There must be an open space," he said. "I'll try to pull this end up, and you look underneath."

He wiped the sweat off his forehead, leaving a red mark from his bloodied arm, and stood above the stone with his legs wide apart. Groaning, Hunter lifted the hunk of rock, and I hunched down, prepared to peer inside. Water splashed into my eyes, and I recoiled, rubbing them. Blinking rapidly, I tried again to look into the void below. Another wave hit, covering what possibly looked like two wooden trunks. My heart skipped a bit with excitement.

"I see it," I shrieked.

"Watch out!" Hunter yelled.

I jerked back as he dropped the stone.

"What was there?" Hunter panted.

I smiled wider. "I think there are chests."

Hunter twisted on the spot, his eyes searching for something. "We need to add round rocks under the slab and roll it off. I will lift it, and you put them under." It was a good idea, but Hunter's hands were visibly shaking.

"Your arms are tired," I said. "We know where it is. We can come back later."

Hunter shook his head, breathing hard but grinning. "We're so close. I have to see it."

He'd been searching for years, so I couldn't blame him for not wanting to wait any longer. And I couldn't rob him of this moment. I hoped the trunks held a genuine fortune this time, not the gunk of centuries-old papers.

Hunter stepped down and reached into the ocean. He splashed water on his face and washed his arms. Meanwhile, I climbed higher and found two soccer-ball-sized rocks to use as wheels. I brought one down. Then I returned to get the next one, and out of nowhere, a black snake struck my wrist. An awful scream escaped me. I staggered back, clamping my hand around my right forearm, tears stinging my eyes.

Hunter sprinted to me and pulled me into a hug. He kissed the top of my head. I sobbed into his chest, not so much from pain as from the shock of attack. My ears rang as a slight tingling sensation prickled in my fingers and toes. A heavy fog rolled into my head.

Hunter let me out of his embrace, but his hands kept a grip on my arms. "How are you feeling?"

"A little dizzy." I checked the two punctures on my arm, the skin swelling around it.

"It should pass soon," Hunter said. He helped me lower myself to the rock in the shade. Dizziness washed over my body and the teeth marks burned like hell. Hunter rested against the wall, stretching out his legs.

"I'm so sorry I didn't catch them all," he said in a low voice.

"It's okay." I lay down, using his muscular thigh as my pillow, closing my eyes. Hunter's fingers gently stroked my head and ran down my back.

After some rest, I sat up, swayed, and blinked a few times to regain my focus.

"Any nausea or pain?" Hunter took my injured arm and examined the bite with dry blood around it.

"I feel fine." The battered skin looked irritated and swollen, but the earlier brain fogginess wasn't there anymore, and I was determined to finish what we had started. Shaking off the discomfort in my arm, I said, "We have unfinished business."

Hunter gave me an "are you sure" look but rose at the same time as I did. He fetched the other rounded stone and then took up his position, placing his long, strong legs near the slab, his large hands gripping the edge. He raised the immense slab. I tried to stuff a rock under it, but it wouldn't go.

"Higher," I yelled.

Hunter grunted, lifting the slab higher. I plunged deeper and placed the first stone beneath it. If he dropped the rock, it would've been the end of me. I was shoulders-deep beneath the six-hundred-pound slab, pushing the second stone under.

"Sydney!" Hunter roared in warning.

I drew out just as Hunter's hands let go. He staggered back, breathing hard. "What now?" I asked.

"We need to push it off and repeat until we have enough space to go down there."

Exhausted, covered in blood and sweat, enjoying the strange, brutal ecstasy of finding a part of the treasure, Hunter and I sat cross-legged on the beach sheltered from the scorching sun by the palm tree, a handful of gold coins and a colorful rain of cut gems of different sizes and shades between us.

I was mesmerized by the glimmer and unable to believe what I was witnessing. Underneath the slab in a large cavity, we discovered three chests filled with doubloons and leather pouches full of precious stones. Hunter picked up a smaller bag and tipped it over. Clear, polished stones fell out, their sparkles blinding me. He swirled his finger in the gems, turning them over. When they caught the sunlight, they shined an even more beautiful, radiant glow.

"This is amazing," I said. I couldn't wait to find the last hidden part of the treasure, the seven-foot solid gold statue of the Virgin Mary with Baby Jesus. But not today. Hunter and I deserved rest. I gestured to his and my bloody arm. "Let's take a break for a day or two to heal and then continue our search."

"Okay." Hunter rubbed his swollen hand over the bloody dots. "You take some of these to the hut, and I'll free the snakes."

"Are you sure? Can we just let them eat each other?"

Hunter shook his head, unimpressed with my suggestion. "No. It's their home."

Fine. Hunter was right, but after today, I would never want to come even close to that place.

"Should we get the chests from the hole first?" I asked, touching an aching spot on my arm.

Hunter glanced at the black rocks, pulling his lips to the side, thinking. "It's safer to keep them hidden there for now. We have enough to take back with us as proof we found the Treasure of Lima, or part of it at least. We will use the contacts that Edward gave and bring the right people on board to excavate it."

I sighed, handing back a doubloon to him. "I'll help you push the slab back into its place."

Today, June 15

7:15

Where are you?

Chapter Twenty-Four

I found Hunter in the icy lake. His head rested backward against the flat rock, eyes closed, skin pale. Something was wrong—very wrong. A panic coiled around me like an anaconda. I dropped to my knees next to him and placed my hand on his wet forehead. It was like touching hot coals in the firepit.

"You are burning up," I whispered. "You should be in bed, not here."

Hunter rolled his head to face me, grunting, his jaw clenched, teeth grinding together. After a long second he exhaled, the contour of his face altered by agony. "I need to bring my temperature down," he said, and a shiver ran over his body either from the cold-ass water or it was fever chill.

"What do you think is wrong with you?"

He drew a sharp breath. "Just an infection."

Hunter brought his left arm out of the water, and horror drained the blood out of my face. Last night, the bite on his hand had been red and slightly swollen, but now his hand was brick-red and three times its usual size. The punctured holes were penny-sized and ripped at their edges, the skin around them blackish-blue. The gruesomeness of it wasn't easy on my stomach, and it roiled with nausea. I clamped a hand over my mouth and took a deep breath through my nose.

What did people do in the movies in this situation? In *Outlander,* Claire Fraser amputated someone's leg or arm to stop infections from spreading. Fuck. I twisted back, launched to a nearby bush, and threw up. I would make the worst nurse. I groaned, embarrassed by my weakness, and wiped my mouth with a shaking hand.

"So sorry," I said, swallowing the foul taste down my acid-burned throat, and returned to my original spot. "What can I do?"

My eyes welled up, and my heart drummed with worry that if we didn't get Hunter's infection under control, he might die. I scrunched up my face, trying not to sob at that thought. I couldn't lose another person I deeply cared about. I wouldn't allow that.

"Wonder Woman." Hunter a weak smile pulled at his lips. "Don't cry. I'll be okay."

The medical field was an unmapped territory for me. I cared for my father close to two years, but he wasn't physically sick, he had no open wounds that I had to redress. My tasks were ensuring he ate, drank, took his medications, and I changed his diaper and bathed him.

"Didn't you put antibiotics on it yesterday?" I asked. Last night, Hunter rinsed his wounds with an antiseptic solution, and I used the remaining on mine. I was fine today. Why wasn't he? Sure, the spots on my arm were sore, but they looked fine.

Seeing my strong and energetic Hunter like this was unreal. And nerve-racking. My breath hitched.

"Tell me what I can do?" I said, my voice wobbling with emotions.

He sighed. "Just sit with me for a while and don't let me drown."

I folded my legs under myself next to Hunter's head and sat quietly, gently running my fingers over his scalp and trying to remember if we had a first aid book.

In the hut, I helped Hunter get into the bed, gave him acetaminophen pills, and covered him with all our towels and blankets, which wasn't a lot because no one needed covers on a tropical island. For an hour, every five minutes I changed a wet washcloth on his forehead, careful not to wake him up. Hunter's chest rose and fell with shallow and rapid breaths. Every so often, a soft whimper fled his lips. All-consuming panic spread like a poison within me, and a lump formed in my throat. I didn't want Hunter to be in pain. I would give anything to help him.

Stepping away from the bed, I ferreted the medical box out again but found nothing useful. I located the book on first aid, studied the sections about open wounds, and snake bites, and read a chapter on natural antibiotics: garlic, honey, ginger, goldenseal, and myrrh. What the fuck was that? It didn't matter. We probably didn't have it on the island, just like we had nothing else on that list.

Sometime during his sleep, Hunter pushed off all the coverings, allowing me to check his exposed body for anything else that could have been infected. All the other cuts and wounds looked fine.

Seeing Hunter frail and vulnerable threw me back to the last days of my father. My throat constricted as my mind pivoted back to that dark place, and I couldn't let it drag me down. I fled to the beach, stopping when my bare feet reached the hot, soft sand. Closing my eyes and lifting my face skyward, I concentrated on the constant soundtrack of waves rolling onto the shore, birds chirping, and bugs buzzing. For every time my mind shoved aside a morbid thought, another would take its place.

What if Hunter dies? No, not thinking about that.

Would he suffer long before his last breath? Fuck. My brain was persistent.

An animal-like growl erupted out of me. "He'll be okay," I said out loud so I could hear myself. Everything would be okay even without garlic or ginger. Hunter was a healthy man who had me to help him. I wouldn't let another man I cared about die. Not on my watch. I wiped my wet cheeks and repeated the breathing exercise: breathe in through your nose for four seconds, hold breath for seven, and then exhale through your mouth for eight, repeat three more times.

My heartbeat slowed down, and so did my thoughts, pausing on the image of the shed and the pile in the far corner of stuff Edward's girlfriends left here. I went over them weeks ago, pulling out some clothing, a hairbrush, and dried-up body lotion (I diluted it with coconut water and it lasted me for a few days). There was also a small bag with some boxes and pills. I shied away from it, uncertain what it was, fearing it was some illegal drugs, something I shouldn't have discovered. But now I wasn't scared.

Before sprinting to the shed, I checked on Hunter. He was asleep. The washcloth on his forehead slid sideways, and his damaged, blazing-red hand rested near his hip.

I kissed Hunter's brow just as he did when I was sick. I replaced the dry washcloth with a new, cold one and left the hut.

In the shed, I found the suitcase and opened it. A musty smell wafted in my face, and a few bugs darted away. Unbothered by the spiders, I rummaged through the luggage until I dug out the small container I had come for. Inside, it contained multiple blister packs filled with various pills. There were no long-ass paper instructions on how to use any of these medications, and most of the names were unfamiliar to me. One of them, though, was Penicillin 250 mg. Besides the tablets, there were also tiny glass bottles. Penicillin G Benzathine and Tetanus Toxoid.

"Thank God," I said, keeping my happy tears at bay.

When I was in high school, I brought a stray cat to our house as a gift for my mom. The surprise cost my parents over five hundred dollars when something spooked the cat, and he bit my father's forearm. The following day, he had to go to the urgent care because his arm ballooned with an infection overnight. The doctor gave him two injections, Penicillin and Tetanus, and sent him home with some painkillers and more antibiotics.

I could do the same for Hunter. Only after further inspection, the container had no disposable syringes or needles. Damn it. The medical box in the hut had antique-ish-looking glass syringes probably used for who knows what but I could work with that. Stuffing everything back in and taking the entire box, I hurried to the hut.

How long medication could last in the hot tropical weather and what dosage to give were good questions, and I had no answers. I could poison and kill Hunter, but there was also a greater chance the infection would spread and eventually kill him. I decided to take my chances with medication. A rescue boat or plane would be very much appreciated right now.

I flipped the first aid book to the part where it talked about doing injections. Vein. Nope. Not doing that. Muscle. Yes. I could do that one. It had a warning about some patients' allergies to penicillin. I glanced at Hunter, and pity coiled inside me. I had to wake him up.

"Hey," I said in a low voice, running my hand over his hot face. "Hunter, look at me, please." After a few tries of me talking to him, his eyelashes fluttered, then he opened his eyes. I smiled. "Hi," I said. His eyes rolled, and his eyelids started to close. "No, Hunter, wake up. I need to know if you are allergic to Penicillin?" He opened his eyes again, some sharpness that had always been in them returning for a slit second. "Penicillin. Are you allergic?" I said words louder this time.

He shook his head, closing his eyes, his lips moving. He was trying to say something, but I couldn't hear. I leaned closer to his face. "What?"

He swallowed, a ghost of a smile on his lips. "I'm right here. You don't have to yell."

Unclear why it made me laugh, but it did, I started crying. It was a good sign that Hunter was joking, wasn't it? I wiped my nose on my shoulder.

"What about tetanus? When was your last shot?"

"Don't know," he rasped, then swallowed. "Water?" That put an end to my giggles and set me into action. Supporting his head, I helped him drink. Then I made a fire and boiled water with the glass syringe and needles. I washed my hands with the same water, burning my skin, but it was the only way to sanitize them.

"I need to give you two shots. Okay? I'll explain later where I found it."

To my surprise, my hands were steady when they hovered over Hunter's thigh as I readied to play the role of his Guardian Angel or Angel of Death.

"I'm so sorry," I whispered an apology in advance for hurting and perhaps murdering him. Clenching my teeth, I jabbed the needle into his leg. Hunter groaned, and I winced as if the pain shot through me too. Turning his head to the side, he mumbled something like *chic*, or *sheet*, or maybe *shit*. Definitely *shit*. Then I repeated sanitizing (I had only one needle) and stabbed Hunter's other thigh with a tetanus injection.

After tucking towels and a blanket over Hunter, I spent the entire night on the chair near the bed, watching Hunter shiver and moan, either getting better or dying. I smelled like a sweaty horse's ass, and my shirt stuck to my skin, but I wasn't willing to leave him, only getting up to bring fresh pots of cold water for the washcloth. My mouth had an acrid taste, and I remembered my earlier episode in the morning by the lake and that I hadn't had any food all day. I pulled my legs to my chest and set my chin on my knees, watching Hunter's chest move reassuringly up and down.

The cats curled up by Hunter's side and slept near him until Hunter had to lean over and throw up in the bucket I'd prepared earlier (the first aid book mentioned this in the side effects of Penicillin).

By morning, Hunter had stopped quivering and sweating,

his breathing had normalized, and while the swelling in his hand hadn't gone down, his forehead felt cool to my touch.

I disposed of the bucket contents I left on the porch overnight, started the fire, took a quick shower, and changed into clean clothes. Hunter slept through the day, only waking up when I gave him antibiotic pills with some water.

It was closer to midday when Hunter shifted in the bed with a groan and pulled himself up against the headboard.

"Hi," I said, dragging my exhausted body from the couch and finding a spot at the corner of the bed. "How are you feeling?"

"Very tired."

"You can't be tired. You slept for two days," I said with a smile, my gaze sweeping over Hunter's face. It had gained back some of its normal color, but his eyes were sunken in, and purple moons underneath them could easily be mistaken for bruises.

"Thank you for saving my life."

"I had to return the favor, right? You save my ass. I save yours. Now we are even."

His eyes crinkled at the corners as he smiled, dimples appearing on his stubbled cheeks. "If I recall it correctly, you owe me one more favor." He rubbed his eyes with the heel of his good hand, then looked down at his damaged one. "Damn, that's not very appealing."

"I don't want to jinx it, but I think the swelling went down a bit." It was most likely my wishful thinking, and my tired eyes playing a trick on me. "Does it hurt a lot?"

He moved his fingers and sucked up a hiss through his teeth. "Not at all."

I laughed. "Are you hungry? I have coconut water, filtered like you showed me, fruit salad, and boiled eggs."

"Not a grilled fish?" he said in a teasing tone.

"Um, no to that. You haven't taught me how to use the spear, and there is no way in hell I'm going near those snakes." I nodded at his hand. "The last two days weren't fun at all."

"Boiled eggs and fruit sound great."

Over our meal in bed, I filled in Hunter on everything I'd done in the last days. He shared with me the unhinged dreams he had, and that he could hear me talking to the cats and lizards.

Leaving our dirty dishes on the table, I climbed onto the bed next to him. My hand held his undamaged one, our fingers interlocking. I closed my eyes with the thought that tomorrow I'd try to get a fish for us. It would be a surprise for him. And for me for sure.

In the early morning hours, Hunter was halfway back to normal. His hand was sore, the skin looked like he burned it, and agonizing pain shot each time he moved his index finger and thumb, but he was mobile. While he was in the shower, I walked to the beach with the spear, determined to catch a fish —but in the regular bay and not the small lagoon. Debating if I should first go for a quick swim, my gaze scanned the calm ocean. And what I saw took my breath away. A sailboat.

I jumped, lifting my arms and waving them like a maniac. "Help!" I shouted with all the power in me. There was no way anyone on that boat could hear me. I needed something to get their attention. It would take too long to build a smoke signal. I needed something quick.

"Hunter!" I yelled, twisting to look at the jungle and then

back to look at the ocean. "There's a boat!" I called louder, backing into the line of trees and sprinting to the hut.

Hunter had promised that Bambi would come looking for me. It was her. She had come to rescue me. I needed to send a distress signal to the boat and not let it leave without us.

Dropping the spear on the porch, I rushed back, yanked on my shorts and the first shirt I saw on the couch. "Hunter!" I called out again so loud my throat hurt.

Throwing the top drawer open, I rummaged through all the crap inside, searching for the flasher pistol. Slamming it closed, I opened the next one and tossed shirts out onto the floor until I found an orange gun at the bottom.

I bolted down the stairs and back to the beach, my feet stumbled over each other as if I were drunk. The boat was on the horizon, but closer to the curve of the island.

"Shit. Shit. Shit." My hands trembled, and I dropped the cartridge. I picked it up and tried again. I shoved the flare shell into the barrel, closed the gun, cocked the hammer, aimed the loaded pistol at the sky. Turning my face away, I pulled the trigger.

Nothing.

With my eyes shut, my finger pressed again.

Nothing.

Panic surged through me as the boat skimmed the curve of the island, barely visible behind black rocks. Damn it. I studied the gun and noticed a button on the side. I pushed it, threw my arm up, and discharged the flare, its boom deafening me for a brief moment. The bright yellow flame burned for less than ten seconds and died out. There was no way someone could have seen that. I reloaded the gun and sent out another one for good measure. I knew I shouldn't use more and saved the other two shells for the next time.

The boat receded from view, and I held my breath, hoping and begging for it to turn around. The tight, scared feeling wedged in my ribs that the people on the boat hadn't noticed my signals. Each second moved at a glacial speed, obliterating any hope of mine. I readied to run to the cliff and try the gun again, but dread gave way to relief as the boat returned.

Chapter Twenty-Five

Ankle-deep in the water, I jumped and waved my hands, excitement coursing through my body, not letting me stand still. We were going home.

"Sydney, what are you doing?" Hunter called out to me.

"Look. Our ticket off the island!" I pointed at the white boat, then waved my arms above my head again, bouncing up and down before leaping to Hunter.

He rested his shoulder on a palm tree, his good hand gripping the towel around his waist, water running in multiple streams from his soaking wet hair. Hunter felt somewhat better, but he needed to go to a hospital for proper evaluation by a medical professional and probably get the correct medication. His face had a hint of paleness. He shouldn't have moved too much yet.

Shielding the sun from his eyes with a hand, Hunter peered at the now anchored boat. A figure standing at the stern was watching us through binoculars. Even from this far, it was obvious that it wasn't Bambi but a tall man. Who cared who it was? This person was here to save us. I could practically feel the wind on my face as we raced back over the waves to Rarotonga, hear Tina's voice when I'd call her, and explain what the hell happened to me. *Eugh.* I also could feel the headache of wrestling with bureaucracy to get my legal documents so I could go home. Something resembling regret yanked on my heart, and I did my best to ignore it.

"I'll be right back." Hunter left me on the beach and marched to the hut.

My feet carried me back to the water, skipping and prancing like a kid hyper on sugar, and it was time to open birthday gifts.

Hunter returned dressed in a shirt and cargo shorts. I sprung to him, wanting to jump, hug, and kiss him, but I thought better of it. I didn't want to bump his hand accidentally.

We watched the figure descend into a lowered dinghy, and soon, it zipped toward us. Hunter snarled a grunt of disapproval.

I pinned Hunter with my stare. "Do you know him?"

"Yes." His brows were drawn tight together. "It's Tom."

"And we like Tom. Right?" I kept my eyes trained on Hunter, reading his stony expression. "Talk to me, Hunter."

"Let's pack and leave with him as quickly as possible," he said in a low voice, as if the man—Tom—could hear us. "Do not mention what we found."

What did Hunter take me for? A goddamned ditzy woman who would run up to the first individual she saw and say, "Hey, guess what we found? Lots and lots of gold and treasure that is worth over two hundred million dollars."

"Of course I won't mention anything," I said, not hiding

my irritation at his comment. If we had time, I would chastise him and make him apologize, but the dinghy hit the shallower waters. Tom grounded on the beach. The motor killed off.

The man was tall and broad-chested, his blond dreadlocks twisted into a bun on the top of his head, making him look even taller than he was. He wore a white shirt with ripped-off sleeves and lightweight pants. He was around Hunter's age. And despite his bright smile, there was darkness in his attractive, tan face.

"Hunter, my mate, finally I found you," Tom called out, jumping into the sand and trudging toward us. He had an accent, maybe British or Australian. "I started to get worried that you bailed on me with my money." Polarized sunglasses covered his eyes but didn't hide his leer at me. He stretched out his arm to me. His fingernails were painted black, his hand covered with tattoos. "I don't think we've met before. I'm Tom."

He seemed like the wrong person to owe money to. I threw a questioning glance at Hunter, then focused back on Tom.

"I'm Sydney." I hesitated at first but then shook Tom's rough, wet (or sweaty) hand. I should have added *nice to meet you*, but it felt like a lie and died in my dry mouth.

"Pleasure to meet you," he said.

Tom took his sunglasses off and hooked them behind his neck. "You know how hard it was to find this place? The lady at the Roster Bar sent me to an apartment in Avarua, but they told me Edward hadn't paid rent in months. I asked around more, and it turned out you lived on a boat, and the old man had some secret island." I recognized the similarity in his and Bambi's accents. He was Australian. I wished it was her talking to us now and not this troublesome-looking man.

"Sydney and I have been stuck here for weeks," Hunter said, his tone neutral. "We would appreciate it if you gave us a ride to Rarotonga right now."

Tom placed his hands on his hips and gazed around as if to appraise the location or to see if more people were with us. "So, this is where Edward lived? Looks nice. By the way, sorry about his passing," he said matter-of-factly, like he was letting us know not to forget to drag garbage to the curb. His green eyes squinted into the distance at Hunter's broken boat. He sucked in air through his teeth. "Fuck me, look at that hole. When did it happen?"

"About a month ago," I said, shifting on my feet.

"Do you mind helping us? I need to see a doctor." Hunter lifted his damaged hand.

Tom hooded. "Damn, man, that's nasty. Did you do that to him?" He looked at me. "He didn't get you off, and you smashed his hand." Tom laughed at his own joke. What a douche.

Clenching my teeth, I grinned, my skin hurting with tension. "Yep, don't mess with me."

"Do you mind taking us now?" Hunter said. "My hand fucking hurts."

"I gotcha, mate, but give me a minute. I just got here. I want to check the place out first." Tom wiggled his eyebrows, stepped around us, and followed the path toward the hut. If he went inside, he would see the journals sprawled on the table and a pot with coins and gemstones on the floor. But if Tom first visited the kitchen, I could use that moment to say I had to change clothes and hide everything out of his sight.

My stomach sank like a rock when Tom went up the stairs and disappeared inside.

"Wait by the dinghy," Hunter said and trailed after our no-longer-welcomed visitor.

I glanced over my shoulder at the small boat on the sand. An impulsive idea of taking it to the anchored sailboat and leaving cut through my mind. Treasure be damned. The problem was, I couldn't leave Hunter. We were in this together now, whether I liked it or not. The second problem was I didn't know how to sail. I should have asked Bambi to teach me the first day we set off. It was a pity that I had a way to get off the island, yet I was trapped. Only now, besides snakes, we had to deal with a dodgy man.

I regarded the orange flare pistol I held. It looked like a toy gun, but loaded, it wasn't a toy. Squatting, I laid it on the ground at the base of the palm tree and covered the plastic with dry leaves and twigs. Just in case.

Dusting the sand off my hands, I marched to the hut. I was a grown woman who deserved to know what kind of trouble Hunter and I were in and not be told to sit and wait by the boat. When I reached the door, Hunter and Tom stopped talking and turned their attention to me.

"I thought I asked you to stay on the beach," Hunter said, his posture stiff as if he'd swallowed a sword.

"I came to get my stuff." I arched an eyebrow and moved to the shelf with a drawer where I kept the very few things of mine. Which was my T-shirt and nothing else.

"Sydney, how did you meet my friend?" Tom moved around the room, picking at random items on the shelves. How much should I share with him? Honesty was the best approach. Fewer lies to remember.

He stopped at the hutch on the opposite side of the couch from me, picked up an old, broken Wenger watch off the shelf, and, after a quick inspection, slid it into his pocket. Nice. He had the manners of a head louse. He was aware we were watching him, and he didn't give a damn. Or was it a running joke between him and Hunter? I took yours, and now you must take it back sort of game.

Tom's foot bumped the pot on the floor, two books piled on top of it serving like a lid. Hunter had placed them there to stop Monday from trying to fish coins out of it. If Tom discovered gemstones and gold coins, he wouldn't leave or take us back until we gave up everything.

Tom looked down.

Cold sweat rolled down my back.

"About a month ago I got shipwrecked here during a storm," I said loudly, pulling Tom's attention to me.

"Shipwrecked? That's wild," he said, forehead wrinkling, and continued his patrol around the room.

I let out a nervous laugh. "Yep, something you don't hear every day. Hunter nursed me back to life."

Tom glanced at Hunter, his teeth sinking into the smirk on his face. "Mate has a caring heart and tends to care for sick people." The way he said that didn't sound like a compliment. "Where are you from originally?" Tom perused the titles of the books on the bookshelf near the bed. Was he going to steal one of them, too?

"Miami, Florida. I was scattering my father's ashes in the South Pacific."

"Alone? That's a long journey from Miami."

"I chartered a boat in Australia. My captain died in the storm." I caught Hunter's eyes and tilted my head slightly at the pot, rounding my eyes, trying to communicate with him that we should wrap it up and go.

"Shit, that sucks." Tom walked to the table and narrowed his eyes, scratching his unshaven neck. "What's this?" He reached for the papers where we had old charts with numbers and letters. And now we were screwed. He lazily fingered through the journal, pausing on the page with a sketch of this island. Multiple ideas about where the treasure could be penciled in all over it, including the bat cave but not the black rocks or the secret grotto.

Tom pulled the chair out and sat as if he was in no hurry to leave. His pose was relaxed and lazy, his legs stretched out, showing off black-painted toenails. "This is what you have been doing while hiding from me all this time?"

"I wasn't hiding," Hunter said. The sweat glistened above his eyebrows and on his temples. He looked more drawn than ten minutes ago. "Sydney and I are trapped here."

"What is this?" Tom tapped his finger on the journal.

"Just some ideas." Hunter swallowed. Too visibly.

"We should probably go." I pulled the rucksack off the top of the bookshelf and set it on the couch, flipping the top open. My mind tried to gauge how to take the coins and gems with us and not leave them behind. "Look at Hunter. He is not well. He needs immediate medical attention."

As if he didn't care (which, of course, he didn't), Tom continued flipping through the notebook, finally stopping at the sheet with a drawing of the coin his uncle found. Edward's artistic talent impressed me before, but now I wished he didn't have it. Tom sat upright, his undivided focus on the journal in his hands. "The compass Edward lost to Spencer had numbers on the back. Did you figure them out?"

It became clear that Tom was in the loop about Edward's treasure hunt. Either he was part of Edward's crew, which

Hunter forgot to mention, or he searched on his own, or he just happened to be present when Edward gambled away the compass to Spencer. Which one was it?

"You know what they are. They are coordinates." Hunter kept his voice light, but sweat soaked the T-shirt on his back and around his neckline. I was unsure if he too was worried or if he felt unwell again.

"Then why do you have them in the tables with letters? What are these sentences?" He dropped the journal and lifted the smaller notebook. A coin slipped out and clanged on the floor, spinning. My breath vanished, and I bet the color of my face matched Hunter's. Tom reached down and picked it up, and brought it to his face, his eyes going wide.

"I thought you found nothing?" Tom's tone was cold, and he shot us a cunning glance.

"It's Edward's," Hunter and I lied in unison.

"Edward gambled the ones he had." Tom's fingers curled around the gold. "I think you both are full of shit, but we can continue this conversation while on our way to Rarotonga." His face rearranged into a sham of delight. The tension in my muscles let go (a bit). He was taking us to the main island. "You don't look very good, Hunter. Once you get better, we can search for the gold together. But I'm keeping this." Tom pocketed the coin and picked up the journals and notebooks.

"Why are you taking these?" Hunter asked, taking a step to the table.

"You wouldn't want to leave these here while you are gone, would you?" Tom said, screwing up his features with a mocking concern. "What if the wrong hands get hold of them?" I had a feeling that the wrong hands already held our notes in their iron grip.

"Of course not." Hunter's smile was as taut as a string about to snap and hit someone in the eye. Ideally, Tom's.

"Good. Pack your shit, and I'll see you at the beach." Tom quickly exited and descended the stairs.

Hunter made a move to leave, too. "Come on, we don't need to take anything with us."

I grabbed Hunter's arm. "Wait," I hissed and jerked my head to the pot. "What about that?"

I could offer to stay and let Hunter go, but how safe was it for him to be with Tom in his condition? How safe was it for me to stay here alone, unarmed? We were in the wolf, goat, and cabbage brain teaser, only we had to cross an ocean by boat, not a river. How could we reach safety without Hunter, me, or both of us being eaten? My heart pounded painfully against my ribs. Hunter needed medical assistance, and I had no trust in Tom. Hunter and I must both go. There was no other way around this.

"Fuck," Hunter muttered, and his eyes darted around the room. "There is no time to hide it." He took the books off and stuffed the gems and coins into his side pocket. Water soaked the fabric of his shorts, not helping us at all.

"I don't like your friend," I said, grabbing my father's urn from the desk. It was the only item I cared to not lose again.

"He is not my friend," Hunter said, rising from kneeling and quickly grabbing the table's edge for balance, but using the wrong hand. "Jesus!" he roared, wincing and clutching his hand to his chest. "Fucking hell, that hurts."

"How dangerous is he?" I stepped to Hunter and helped him get up. "What if he has guns on his boat?"

Hunter looked me in the eye. "We'll be okay."

I wanted to point out that he had avoided answering both

of my questions, but we also had no choice. Hunter needed a doctor. I could take the flare gun with us.

The boat's motor roar sliced through the air. Hunter and I stumbled to the porch.

Tom skidded over the waves toward his sailboat with his back to us. *Shit. Shit. Shit.* I threw the urn into the bushes and ran to the beach.

"Stop! Please." I chased after him, waving my hands like an idiot. I was a fool. How stupid of us not to walk with Tom back to his fucking boat. "Come back, you, asshole!" I screamed, dropping to my knees in the water.

Chapter Twenty-Six

"You should have told me your friends are a bunch of modern-day pirates," I said as I walked into the hut, dragging in sand on my legs that I didn't care to shake off before coming in. I yanked my soaked shorts off with so much anger the fabric scorched my thighs.

"They are not pirates. They are just"—Hunter exhaled, shaking his head—"people Edward and I should have avoided."

Hunter sat on the end of the bed, elbows pressing into his knee, the good hand gripping his hair. He hadn't looked up at me since I returned.

"He is coming back, but not alone, right?" I asked, discarding the wet T-shirt I wore on the floor. Back on the beach, I had sat unmoving in the water, watching Tom getting on his boat, lifting the dinghy to it, and the asswipe had the nerve to wave me a farewell. I should have flipped him off, but my arms were heavy with dread.

Hunter lay back, rubbing his face and exhaling a long sigh. "Yes. And probably soon."

From where I stood, it was apparent Hunter needed rest, and maybe I shouldn't be grilling him right now, but goddamnit, I was mad and scared. "What does *soon* mean? Tonight? Tomorrow? In one week?"

I couldn't believe this was actually my life right now. It must be because I didn't forward all those chain letters to my friends years ago, and now the promised curse had caught up with me. First, I barely survived the storm, then almost overdosed on snake venom (okay, fine, that one was on me), and now I had to deal with a questionable man who had no decency to help people in need and stole from us.

"I don't know."

"How much do you owe Tom?" I asked, crossing my arms over my chest.

"A little over one hundred thousand."

"That'd better be rubles and not dollars."

He released a weak chuckle, which was followed by a low curse. It was unclear if it was because of the pain in his hand, or this situation, or both.

For a brief moment, I debated whether it was safe to give Hunter another penicillin injection. Instead, I pressed an antibiotic pill out of a blister pack, shook out two Tylenol from a bottle, and sat them on the nightstand next to the mug that still had some water from the morning. "Take the meds and lie in bed."

Neither of us had eaten since yesterday evening, and even if hunger wasn't clutching my stomach (fear was doing enough of that job), Hunter and I needed to replenish our strength. I rubbed the skin of my face with my hands and pulled them over my head, tugging on my hair with frustration. Anger at Hunter for not being honest with me bubbled up in my chest, but seeing him unwell tamped it down.

I exhaled an aggravated breath like a dragon releasing its steam. "Why didn't you tell me about that?" I said, keeping my tone cool with difficulty.

"Because you shouldn't be here. You shouldn't have met Tom. Ever." Hunter slowly sat up, and his bloodshot eyes looked everywhere but me. "Who I owe money to is none of your business."

Ouch. That hurt, but I could deal with it. Hunter had all the right not to tell me everything about his past. When I asked him what he planned to do once he found the treasure, Hunter mentioned he wanted to pay off the debt. I just assumed it was credit cards, school loans, or a mortgage, the normal things people owe money on, and not a debt to some thug.

"Maybe your financial situation isn't my business, but you should have warned me about someone searching for you and the treasure. I specifically remember asking if someone else was looking for it, but you didn't answer my question. You deliberately hid it from me. You owing them money puts me in danger because I'm stuck on this damn island with you." I walked to the door but stopped before exiting. "When Tom returns, we'll be outnumbered and utterly screwed. You should have been honest with me about it from the start."

"And what would you have done differently if you knew about Tom and my debt to him?"

Nothing. I wouldn't have slept well at night that was for sure.

"I wouldn't have used a flare pistol to bring his attention to us."

Hunter shook his head, then looked at his swollen hand. "It wasn't you. He was on his way to the island. If not today, he would have come another day."

I nodded slowly, because Hunter was right, it wasn't my doing that brought Tom here. And now he had more reasons to come back. If he was on his way to Rarotonga, that meant we had at least eight hours before he returned.

"I'm going to make us something to eat," I said, and left the hut.

I snatched the spear I had thrown earlier and went to the beach, planning to let out the frustration on the fish. I walked to the dock where a lot of fish liked to congregate, hoping it would be easier to stab one.

What else didn't Hunter tell me about his life? Were there more people he owed money to? Dismay pooled in my gut at the thought I'd let myself fall in love with another man who lied about debt. Why did Hunter need such a large sum of money? The apple didn't fall far from the tree, and just like Edward, he could have poured all the money into the treasure search. Or worse, gambled it away.

"You're so stupid," I muttered.

It took all my strength not to return to the hut and yell at Hunter. It wasn't the best time for that. Tom was coming back and not alone. Hunter needed to get better so he could help me make a plan—any plan—defensive, offensive, or escape.

One saving grace was that the journals contained no information about what we found, but just a lot of tables with numbers and letters, pointless charts, erroneous markings on the sketched map, riddles, and numerous ideas about where the treasure could be hidden on the island and in the water. The black stones overrun by snakes camouflaged trunks with doubloons and cut gems, but the bat cave, crammed with loot, was out in the open. Sort of. They had to find it first.

I waded into the water waist-deep and lifted the spear over my shoulder, watching fish meandering near me, ignoring their looming danger. My eyes darted from one fish to another, unsure which one I should try to catch. The shaft wasn't light, and its weight pulled on my muscles. If I waited any longer, I would drop it. With a quick move, my arm went down, my body bent forward, my chest hit the water. A wave smacked me in the face.

"Fuck."

I straightened and wiped saltwater out of my eyes. The prong missed the fish and stabbed the sand. I tried again. And again. Several times more. Yet no fish, just a pulled muscle in my shoulder blade. The irritation at Hunter now was replaced with annoyance at my inability to catch our fucking dinner. We needed protein. Eggs would work, but I wanted fish. Or chicken. I squinted at the beach, where a brown hen pecked at something near the lower underbrush between palm trees. Nope. I cringed. For some reason, I drew the line at killing a bird. Fish was okay, but not chicken. Go figure.

Closing my eyes, I went back to the time when I watched Hunter fishing here. He walked into the water slowly, and after he took his position, he became statue-like, patiently following the prey only with his eyes. With a quick jerk of his arm, he sent the spear into the water. Hunter didn't bend. He also mentioned that refraction caused fish to appear in a different location than they actually were.

Drawing out my arm slowly halfway, I scanned the water

for my target, my fingers firmly gripping the shaft. My eyes stalked a slow, large fish. Heart rate quickened. Breathing slowed. I broadened out my arm and readied for the attack.

"Aim lower," I whispered Hunter's advice. "Strike just under where you think the fish is."

I discharged the pole in a quick move, letting it completely out of my fingers. The sharp metal tips pierced the fish.

"Oh my God!" I shrieked with excitement but then scrambled to grab the pole before I lost our dinner to the ocean. I wished someone besides the chicken on the beach had seen me doing this. Maybe it was beginner's luck, but I didn't care, and the proud feeling inside my chest swelled to the size of a hot air balloon. I caught the fish. With a spear.

I grinned, briefly forgetting about Tom and the trouble coming our way, and lifted my proud catch out of the water. "I'm badass," I said to the fish. "And you are my dinner." Shoot. Perhaps it was time to get out of here before sharks smelled the blood, and *I* turned into *their* dinner.

I popped into the hut to share my achievement with Hunter, but he was asleep. If he hadn't been sick earlier, I would have woken him up so we could debate what to do about the earlier visitor and his unavoidable return. But Hunter needed rest to get better, so I let him sleep.

The fire I'd started earlier in the pit became the perfect grilling coals. I gutted and cleaned the fish, stuffed it with lemon and orange slices, and placed it, wrapped in banana leaves, over the coils. I couldn't stop smiling as I collected mangos and avocados, then peeled and diced them. The fishing triumph boosted my mood, and nothing felt impossible now. If I could catch dinner on my first try (well, not try, but on the first day), there was nothing stopping me from standing up against Tom and whoever he brought with him. Unless he showed up alone but with a gun. Or worse. Not alone, but still with guns. With Hunter's current condition, it was one and a half against them (however many that would be).

I flipped the fish over. The smell of cooked meat with citrus waffled in the air, and my mouth watered. Money wasn't worth more than a life, so letting them take all the loot would be easier. We could show them only the bat cave and say the coin was from there. But what guarantee did we have they would leave us alone and alive? What if they demanded more until we gave it all up? We should give up everything right away to make them happy. My chest ached. Loss of the treasure meant Hunter wouldn't be able to claim the discovery. I removed the fish from the grate, my earlier pride and excitement perished.

My thoughts on escaping the island or fighting off Tom raced like loony animals, one madder than the previous one. The first week I arrived here, I hid a knife under the mattress, and now I needed to hide others in the bushes around this place. Hunter also had a Swiss Army knife. It was small, but I was willing to use anything in self-defense. I shouldn't have ignored Tina's invitation to join her Krav Maga class.

In the hut, I ran my palm over Hunter's face, gently waking him up, his skin cool to my touch. At least he wasn't burning up with a fever. "Hunter, I caught fish."

He opened his eyes and grunted, sitting up. "I had no doubt you would," he said, his voice thick with grogginess.

My hand went around his back, helping him lean against the headboard. "Let me help you."

"No, it's fine. I want to eat at the table."

"Are you sure?"

"Yes. I think whatever you gave me earlier is working. I feel better." He swung his legs off the bed, breathed in, and got up.

It was weird to see the table empty of the papers and journals—a silent reminder of a vital topic Hunter and I had to discuss. Tom left about two hours ago, so we had about six or more hours.

Or less.

Uncertainty was the only sure thing.

Hunter stared at the filet and salsa next to it for a long minute, his hands resting on each side of the plate.

"Is something wrong with your food?" I asked, around the piece in my mouth. A small bone stabbed my gum, and I picked it out.

He shook his head, lifting the fork. "It looks good."

We ate without speaking at first, concentrating on picking tiny bones out of the fish (so I didn't stab the greatest fish, but it was juicy and sweet). Monday and Tuesday sat on the floor at my feet once in a while begging, meowing and pressing their paw into my thigh. Hunter had a rule not to feed them at the table but today felt like a good day to break it. I dropped two large bone-free pieces to each cat.

Hunter cleared his throat. "I'm sorry I wasn't honest with you."

Meeting his eyes, I leaned against the chair's back, crossing my arms. My earlier anger had eased, but I wasn't ready to forgive him.

"I don't think there is anything that I haven't told you about my life, so I'd have really appreciated it if you were honest with me and told me about Tom right away," I said. "Whatever happened in your life it won't change how I feel about you." That was an overstatement. If he murdered someone, I would have to work on my feelings for him. "What happened to the money you owe Tom?"

I held my breath, willing myself not to jump to any conclusions and to keep an open mind. I had known Hunter for only a short time, and I had (needed) to believe he was a good, kind person and that whatever reason he had for that money, it wasn't selfish or base. Hunter wouldn't break my heart.

"I suspected Edward wasn't healthy for some time, but I didn't know how bad it was. He had no health insurance, but needed a better medical examination and treatment. I suggested he fly to the States anyway and do it as self-paid. Edward had no money, so I paid for his flights there and back, as well as all the medical bills using all the cash I saved up while working with him. Doctors told him he had six to fifteen months." Hunter looked away, lost in his thoughts, then squeezed his eyes tight, shaking his head. "How do they come up with that number? Six to fifteen. Why not sixteen or fourteen?"

"I'm sorry," I said in a low voice.

Hunter rubbed the wetness under his eyes. He took a deep breath and let it out slowly, perhaps to gather the courage to say the next words. "Edward wanted to continue to search for the Treasure of Lima as if nothing had changed. We did for nine months. But then he got worse pretty fast, and he was in so much pain. The man raised me as if I was his son. I needed to help him, but I was broke. A few years back, Edward and I had a month-long job in Samoa, where Edward introduced me to Tom and Spencer. And even though I knew it was a risky and bad idea, I went to Tom and asked for a loan. Edward and I flew to Atlanta, where he spent some time in a hospital, and then they moved him to a private hospice, where he died two months later. But at least without pain. I made sure they kept him comfortable. He didn't know where I got the money from. If Edward knew, he would have made me give it all back."

My heart squeezed tight at his agony. It was cowardly of me to think Hunter had gambled or wasted that money. The pain of seeing someone you love slowly dying and not being able to do anything to stop it was too familiar to me. I circled the table and looped my arms around Hunter's shoulders, careful not to bump his damaged hand.

"Where did he think you got the money?" I asked, leaning my face to his shoulder.

Hunter pressed his head to mine. "I told him Jolie helped me to find a nonprofit organization that covered all the costs."

He moved his arm around, and I climbed on his lap to give him a stronger embrace.

"Is Tom also looking for the Treasure of Lima?" I asked.

"He wasn't until Edward gambled away the coins he had. Then word reached Tom that maybe the treasure was real and was somewhere in these waters, not off the shore of Costa Rica. Tom wanted to partner with us, but Edward knew better than to do any deals with him."

Unlacing my hands from Hunter's neck, I looked into his blue eyes, rimmed with redness. "We must figure out what to do when he returns here."

"I have a plan that could work," Hunter said. "Tom most likely will beach in the same spot. We hide and wait for them in the woods. When he and his guys—and I know he won't come alone—reach the hut, we use that opportunity to go for their dinghy. We steal it and take it to the boat."

"And what if there is someone on the boat?"

"I will deal with it when we get there."

I pinned him with a stare. "And what if we are caught stealing their dinghy?"

"Then we come up with Plan B, and I might have an idea for that too."

Chapter Twenty-Seven

Hunter and I stood on each side of John's hole, readying to cover it up. Our Plan B was simple (sort of) but risky: take Tom here under false pretense, and he walks into the trap.

"Is he gullible enough to believe we're taking him to the treasure without a fight?" I said in a low voice. If Tom did arrive while we were here, he wouldn't know where to find us, but we talked in hushed voices as a precaution. I bent to grab a long, dry palm leaf.

"Yes." Hunter dragged a large branch to the dugout and laid it over the opening.

We worked on camouflaging the hole, going separate ways to collect more debris, coming together to drop it off, and then repeating the process many times. The space wasn't huge, but we had to disguise it well to fool Tom and whoever he brought with him.

"How exactly do we do this?" I pressed my hands on my

hips, arching my back for a quick stretch until some joints popped.

"When we get close to the last turn, you and I run. We go around the trap." Hunter wiped the sweat off his face with the hem of his T-shirt. "They shouldn't see us doing it, and if we are lucky, one or two of them will go right in the middle of it and have little time to react to avoid the fall."

"What about the rest of them?" I wished we knew how many people were coming. Hunter said that Tom's crew was four people, so we should expect at least that many.

"They either stop to help whoever fell, or they keep going after us. Either way, we know this place better than them, so we don't stop moving until we reach the boat."

"What if they shoot at us?"

"You duck and run," Hunter said with so much calm in his voice that it sounded like he took it as a joke.

"What if we get separated?"

"You keep running. I'll catch up with you. At the beach, you take their dinghy and motor out to the bay."

I shook my head, feeling an unwelcome twinge of nerves in my ribcage. "We shouldn't get separated."

"Sydney, you get into the boat," Hunter said, his tone firm but kind.

I didn't like this plan at all. "I get into the dinghy, and then what?"

If I took it to the sailboat, I couldn't navigate the boat alone to get us help. I wouldn't even know where to begin. Maybe if I had many hours on my hands, but not under pressure and with time shorter than a lit bomb fuse. Damn it. Once I was back at home, a sailing course would be the first thing I'd sign up for.

"You know how to start an outboard motor, right?" he said. I nodded. "Take the dinghy out far enough and only come back when you see me on the beach. Alone." Hunter wrapped his arms around my waist, pulling me flush against him.

"And what if you don't come back?" My voice cracked on the last part, and I hugged him tighter.

"I'll come back." He kissed the top of my head.

"Playing Hunger Games through the jungle might only work if your condition doesn't decline again like it did this morning. Maybe you should rest and let me do all the work? Save your strength for healing."

I let go of Hunter and scrutinized our trap. This was bad. A five-year-old could build something better. "This is way too obvious."

Hunter walked around, rubbing his neck, then cursed under his breath. "This looks like total shit. Let's get more leaves and branches. We should start covering the path much earlier, so it all blends into the point where we wouldn't even know where John is."

"I'll do it, you sit," I said.

"Sydney, I'm fine."

I rolled my eyes, shaking my head at his stubbornness. "Then we need some clue as to where the center is so our asses don't fall in."

Hunter raked his good hand over his hair while he stood thinking and looking around for a minute. He stepped off the path and bent, his hand gripping something behind a low bush. Together, we dragged a bucket-size rock to the back side of the pit, aligning it in the middle.

"This is our indicator," Hunter said.

We worked for an hour, pausing a few times to listen if we

heard something. Soon, for anyone who had never been here, the path looked like an untouched part of the jungle, which was probably what it had looked like when Johnny the skeleton stepped into this trap.

Hunter and I walked back to the hut quietly, ensuring if someone was waiting for us, we heard them before they heard us. I couldn't stop thinking about worst-case scenarios: we fall into our trap, they separate us, they hurt us, or worse, they… I banished that last thought out of my mind. Nothing would happen to Hunter and me because our first plan would work, and we'd sail away into the sunset, or whatever time of the day, and he and I would take control of their boat.

The area around the kitchen and hut was empty, and the bay was free of boats. It was a huge relief to know we had some time to find a good hiding place and perhaps come up with extra plans. It was better to be over prepared than underprepared.

"Should we hide in the grotto?" I found a Ziploc bag in the desk drawer and handed it to Hunter. If Hunter couldn't find the enclosed alcove after all these years, it was guaranteed (if we stayed silent) that Tom wouldn't find it, either. "Let's take food and fresh water and wait for them to leave. How long can they possibly stay here? A few days? A week at most?"

Hunter added coins and gems to the bag. We were going to hide it and retrieve it later when we could bring help with us.

"And then what do we do?" Hunter said.

"They leave, and we build a raft, Tom Hanks style, and paddle away." I smiled.

He chuckled. "We'll be sitting ducks. They know we are somewhere on this godforsaken island. It will be just a matter of time until they catch us. We have to deal with Tom right away." Tossing our small fortune on the desk, Hunter stepped to me. "Sydney, they are cunning thieves, not murderers."

"Are you sure?"

Hunter's forehead wrinkled, and his shoulders sagged. "No, but I'll do everything in my power to take care of you." I believed him.

His gaze held me in place, his features softer, not tired anymore. His hand cradled my jaw, and he softly brushed my cheek with his thumb as if I were made from porcelain and the moment I left him, I'd shatter into a million pieces. "I know back then in the water, we agreed this would be a short-term thing, and no feelings involved, but I was in love with you already." His words were a caress on my skin. My breathing slowed, and a light feeling took over me, pushing away exhaustion and fright. "I could have said it then, but you were firm on this just being sex, so I thought it was best to keep my feelings to myself." His eyes searched my face like this was the last time he would see me. "I'm not asking you to love me back. I'm not asking you to stay here with me. I just wanted you to know that I love you, and I'll be a wreck after you leave and probably never get over you, but that is something for me to deal with later."

My heart leaped out of my chest and landed in his hands, where it would stay forever. I felt it, too—the love for him. It pained me to think that in a day, a week, or a month, we were heading back to our other lives. I wanted to scream, "Come with me," but I knew it wasn't fair.

"I love you too," I blurted out. I felt more happiness, emotional security, and commitment in my with-an-expiration-date relationship with Hunter than with anyone else.

"You do?" he whispered, his lips turning up at their corners.

"I do." My words came out more like a croak, tears running down my cheek. I wanted to take the sound back and try again, respond with a much sexier sound, but Hunter's face broke into an unhinged smile, and his eyes glistening with so much happiness as if I were Hunter's treasure, and he'd searched for me all this time. I brought my hand to his neck and gently tugged him closer until his warm mouth caught mine. His lips parted, and he kissed me soft and slow, as if we were kissing for the first time. So tender. So sweet. I turned into a puddle and swayed into him.

I was still here with Hunter, but I already missed him. I wanted to split in the middle, one part of me to stay here and the other to return. If I said that out loud, it might give Hunter false hope that I might have changed my mind. This wasn't the place to build my new life. And it fucking destroyed me. Hunter released a sigh of pleasure or relief, or both. With his good hand on the side of my face, Hunter angled my head and took my mouth again with a devouring kiss, his stubble scratching my skin, his other arm wrapped around my back tighter, putting me flush against him.

The moon might have gone around the Earth thousands of times, and when we parted, Hunter's lips were red and swollen, no doubt matching mine. Hunter pressed his forehead to mine, his eyes closed.

"All I want right now is to strip you of your clothes and show how much I love you, but…" He exhaled a quiet laugh.

"We should continue getting ready for the unavoidable," I finished his thought, then added with a teasing smile, "Maybe later?"

"Then we'd better hurry." Hunter brushed a brief kiss on my lips and then snatched the Ziploc bag off the desk. He walked backward, his eyes locked on me, smiling.

I buried the plastic bag in the sand under the stairs, and then we found a hiding place in the jungle on the beach's border, ten yards from the leaning palm and the path toward the hut. A pandanus tree with its complex roots and branches and thick shrubs with fragrant flowers around it concealed us so well that even if we had fallen asleep and missed the unwelcome guests' arrival, they wouldn't find us easily.

We stared at the bay through the screen of branches and leaves for a long time, small rocks and shells biting into my legs. I brushed crap off my skin and faced the jungle, leaning my back against the roots. Across from us was a tree similar to the giant near the bat cave, only this one was baby-size in comparison, and its trunk quickly forked into two. The more I studied it, the more I became aware that, whereas the giant's leaves had small, pale green, maple-like leaves, this tree's leaves were dark green and shiny on top, almost like a laurel oak. One part of the tree broke off at the base and leaned against its neighbor. Something was off about this. I dropped a twig I'd been twisting between my fingers and crawled over.

I poked the dead trunk, its bark hard to the touch. I lay on the ground and carefully peeked through its bottom (hoping nothing would jump out at me from there) and recognized the blue skies on the other side. It was hollowed out. It had been broken for a while, completely cut off from its nutrient system. Why were the leaves green? I grabbed one of the slim branches, and my gaze followed its length up the trunk and over the tree it rested against, then it reached the other tree and got lost in its canopy. Only then I understood. This was a network of vines. The same vines I have seen throughout the island. The tree was dead, but it looked alive.

"Do you need anything from the hut?" Hunter asked.

We brought food, meds, water and two kitchen knives. I shook my head. "Nothing I can think of."

"Stay here. I'll be back." Hunter moved between the bushes and disappeared toward the hut.

A few minutes later, he returned with towels and a beach blanket. "We should have brought these with us right away."

"It's a slumber party, not a hideout," I said, smiling and taking the towels from Hunter. The small space was enough for one person to semi-stretch out while the other had to sit at their feet or lie snuggly on the top of them. I helped Hunter arrange everything, and he dropped onto the makeshift bed, reaching out his arm to me.

"What are you doing?" I asked as he pulled me to straddle him.

"What does it look like?" His hand came around the nape of my neck and pulled me for a deep kiss before his lips trailed to my jaw. "A man in possession of a good fortune must make love to a woman he's confessed his love to."

"Your fortune sucks," I said, laughing.

His fingers gripped my hair, and he pulled my head back, exposing more of my neck to him. I closed my eyes and whimpered when his hot mouth landed on the sensitive spot, his stubble leaving a path of small fires. My hips moved involuntarily against his hardness, the greedy need for release quickly building inside me. Everyone grieves differently, and the same could be said about stress relief. Some took yoga. Some punched walls. We were going to have sex, and I wouldn't oppose it.

"Take off your shorts," Hunter said, then scraped his teeth on my earlobe.

"Who is going to watch the bay?" I asked, my hands already working on the button and the zipper.

"We'll hear them if you're quiet." Hunter fiddled with his own shorts. He exposed himself just enough for me to sink onto him. He groaned with pleasure, and I swallowed a moan as I took him in, inch by inch, until I was full of him.

I looked at him, and for the millionth time, my thoughts stammered, rapt in awe at how handsome he was. Especially when he looked at me like I was the only woman for him. I blinked to restart my brain function, then said, "Are you sure this is a good idea right now?"

"It is always a good idea to have sex with you." His voice was low, and the edge of his mouth hitched, his palm cupping my ass. "Our space is limited here, and my hand is—"

"We'll manage." I captured his mouth with mine and moved slowly, my soft noises of need escaping with gasps. His groan vibrated in his chest, and I felt it in every part of my body. It scared me how much I wanted this man and how easily I could lose myself in him. I tried not to think of the future and only focused on this moment. On us. And how good he made me feel. How much he wanted me. How much I wanted him. Our kiss went from hard to soft, then back to hungry. Hunter tasted of salt and citrus, and his heart pounded against mine when I looped my arms around his neck and began working him faster.

"You feel incredible," Hunter said breathlessly. He sucked and bit the base of my throat.

His word spiraled through me, making me want to change my mind. To stay with him. To trust my heart that it was what

I needed. I rocked back and forth with a slow rotating movement, dragging my clit against his pelvis, its coarse hairs creating a perfect sensation, sending waves of pleasure at our contact.

"Let me get behind you," he whispered.

"No," I insisted. "I want to be in control." I squeezed tight around him and a rugged exhale rippled through his throat. Hunter pressed his head back on the tree, closing his eyes.

My thighs grew tired in a few minutes, and I was getting out of breath, but I needed to chase my relief and help Hunter to reach his. I was so close. We were so close.

Hunter sensed my exhaustion, and his left hand snaked between our joined bodies. His fingers massaged my clit, his hips rhythmically driving into me deeper again and again. His mouth found my ear, and he demanded in a seductive whisper, "Come around my cock, sweetheart."

Maybe it was him calling me by nicknames he hadn't before, or maybe it was his goddamn command and the way he growled it, but that was enough for me. My inner muscles tightened, gripping him, and with a muffled cry into his mouth, I unraveled. And so did Hunter, with low curses mixed with my name. My body slacked against Hunter's, and I smiled into his shoulder, totally happy, totally in love, and totally not sure if returning home was the right decision.

Later, Hunter assumed the first watch while I attempted to fall asleep. It wasn't easy. Pesky bugs buzzed (and crawled in places of my body they shouldn't), not letting me relax. Perhaps it was how I sat: my knees were drawn up to give Hunter more space at my feet, as he watched the beach. By now, Tom had had enough time to reach Avarua, gather whoever he needed to bring, and return to Teaku at any minute. So rest was the last thing on my mind, even though I knew I needed it.

Today felt like the longest day of my life. My overstimulated brain overthought everything that happened: Tom's visit, Hunter admitting he loved me, uncertainty about what would happen to us when this was over, us hiding in the bushes, the dead trunk looming above, my back against its alive twin. I slapped a pestering bug on my shoulder.

Strong but hollow alive but dead inside.

The last riddle kept flashing in my mind like the lightning of a passing storm in the distance. You smelled rain, felt an electric charge in the air, yet you couldn't feel wet fat drops, but you knew it was coming your way. The answer to the riddle was within the reach of my fingers. Still, I couldn't grasp it.

The gold statue was seven feet tall and Captain William Thomson would've needed a gigantic space to store it. On the printout the illustration showed it was slim. It could have been lowered into an opening in the mountain because the rock was strong and dead, but the trees on the top were alive. Well, damn it. There was a lot of the mountain here. It had to be something a bit more obvious. Something that was here two hundred years ago but already big and strong. The giant. It was far from the beach, well hidden from view and weather elements. It could be dead for years and never bothered by storms and strong gusts. It could be the answer to the riddle if it was also hollow.

"Hunter," I said. "What if the last riddle means the giant tree near the bat cave?"

"You're supposed to be asleep," Hunter said without looking at me.

"No, listen." I straighten up. "It looks alive, but it's ancient, and for all we know, it could have been half dead when Captain Thomson found it. He probably stuffed the statue into its trunk. It is so huge he could hide two statues inside if he wanted." What little energy levels I had flared to life. "I want to check it out."

Hunter twisted to look at me, his forehead wrinkled. "Now?"

"Yes. It's still light outside. I'll check it out and come back."

Chapter Twenty-Eight

Leaving Hunter to monitor the bay, I skittered through the jungle, tripping over a root once and suffering a minor heart attack when Tuesday darted out from under bushes. Dumb cats. When I reached the tree, I quickly realized getting to the top wouldn't be as easy.

"Crap," I muttered, eyeing the tree limb about ten feet off the ground.

I circled the trunk once and then again, debating how to climb it. The distance between the tree and each side of the mountain was too far for me to climb by spreading my limbs like a starfish. The trunk's width prevented me from wrapping my arms or thighs around it, and the bark, while ridged, didn't provide enough grip for my toes or fingers. There weren't enough manageable-sized stones to move and build a stepping base. I needed a ladder.

The sound of someone moving quickly over the rocks sent my mind into a panic, rooting my bare feet to the ground.

Hunter appeared, and immediate relief flooded my ribcage but then a new panic hit me.

"Fuck. Are they here?"

"No. But we shouldn't separate. If we do something, we do it together."

It sounded romantic, but we were on borrowed time. I sized Hunter up. He was six-three and built like a gladiator. I was five-five. If we made a human pyramid, I could reach it. The only question was if I could climb once he lifted me. About six years ago, Tina secured two passes to a new state-of-the-art indoor climbing facility and dragged me along with her. She made it to the top—twice—whereas I fell off the wall after making it a quarter of the way—in my defense, it was still high. The highest point was a hundred feet. When I landed, I twisted my ankle, and that was the end of our fun. Well, it wasn't the end of the fun per se; we just moved it to a much safer place. A margarita bar next door.

I took a deep breath. "I need to stand on your shoulders to reach the first branch."

Facing the trunk, Hunter crouched and held out his good arm to me. I placed my right foot on his shoulder, grabbed his hand and placed my other foot on his left shoulder. This was a bad idea.

"Don't get up just yet. I need to be stable." I rested my palm on the tree for balance. "Okay, you can get up now. Slowly." Hunter's body shook under my weight. "Hunter?"

"One sec. My thigh muscle is cramping up," Hunter said through clenched teeth, then gingerly rose. I wobbled and let go of his hand, pressing my other palm on the tree. My hands walked its trunk as I got higher and higher, and my legs trembled, finding stability.

"I'm fully up. Can you reach it?" Hunter asked.

I stretched my arms up, my hands going round the branch. I couldn't fully circle the branch with my arm to pull myself up. What if Tom's boat had appeared on the horizon the second Hunter turned his back to the bay and ran here? I had to do this faster and get back to the beach. Or maybe it was best to give up.

"I don't think I can do it."

"Yes, you can." Hunter's hand found my right foot.

With one powerful push, he lifted me higher, and I threw my arms up. My hands wrapped around the bough, my nails digging into the bark. My legs dangled, gravity (and defeatism) pulling me down. Rough bark bit and scraped my forearm and biceps. I swung my body and tried to find traction with my bare feet against the trunk. Sweat started building all over my body, my toes found friction, and I worked my left leg up, and my left calf caught on the top. With another push, I circled my right leg over. After taking a few labored breaths, like a sloth, I climbed the branch toward its end, squeezing my thigh muscles until they shook from tension.

My body trembled, my muscles telegraphing the urgent message that they wouldn't hold on for too long. It wasn't too late to jump off.

Between heavy breaths and unseductive groans, I maneuvered my body around the branch, its bark scratching my legs, arms, and stomach raw. I anchored on the top of it. This was only the first branch. Without losing more time, I slid down backward until my ass pressed against the tree trunk.

I lifted my gaze skyward and examined the network of branches above me—a good thing I wasn't doing it at night. Vines climbed and looped around some limbs, the color of their bark blending in with the tree. They appeared as one entity from the ground, but up close, it was clear that the green leaves didn't belong to the tree. Parts of the tree seemed dead, bare of leaves, and missing bark in some places.

"Do you see openings?" Hunter asked.

"Not yet. It seems like the tree splits into three thick stems. Maybe the center is hollow."

"Is it easy to get to it?"

Some tree limbs were more reachable, and some weren't. "Depends on your definition of easy."

On that day when I climbed with Tina, I didn't really fall. Well, I did. Sort of. I remembered looking up and thinking there was so much wall left to climb and doubting my ability to make it. I had relaxed my fingers and given up without trying.

Right now, I didn't want to give up. I had made it this far and wouldn't stop; curiosity compelled me.

I placed both feet in front of me. Fear gripped my shoulders, but I slowly stood up, my back never breaking contact with the bark. My legs wobbled, but I regained my balance. What was I afraid of? Spilling my ass on the ground or being wrong about the riddle?

All of the above.

I pulled myself over the next branch and kicked my legs out, bringing my upper body over and to the side. My skin stung like hell, but I pushed further. Adjusting my stance and blinking away the micro crap that trashed my eyes, I established the best bet on where to move next. I carefully placed my foot on a smaller branch to get extra leverage and push off. Four levels high, I neared my target. One more branch, and I could check out if the tree was hollow but not empty. The hopeful thought that we were about to discover the last and paramount piece of the Treasure of Lima sent a wave of enthusiasm through my body but the tingle of awareness crept up my spine that if I fell, there was a good chance—I didn't even want to know how far—I would plunge to my death. So I really hoped this labored risk wasn't all for nothing.

Securing a firm place with my feet, I gripped onto a branch and pulled with my weight on it. It broke off. My heart lurched. With a loud yelp, I reeled backward, my arms windmilling. My entire life flashed in front of my eyes. No, not my entire life. I only saw my dad, frail and pale, in the last days of his life. Dead inside and barely alive, his soul searching for its way out of the jail of his body to reunite with my mother. A white rage shot through me. He didn't love me enough to live. He lost the love of his life, but I was his daughter. I should have been reason enough for him not to die. He could have told me about a sailing trip, and we could have done it together. I wouldn't be alone. I wouldn't have been on a fucking tree on the island in the middle of nowhere.

My fingers caught an offshoot, pivoting my body to the right, and my shoulder slammed into the trunk, my feet rooted in place. My chest heaved, and I focused on my breathing, trying to get as much oxygen in as possible. In and out. In and out.

"Are you hurt?" Worry carried with Hunter's voice.

"All good," I managed between ragged breaths.

As my heart rate slowed down, my anger abated. It was embarrassing how fast I blamed my dad for my mistake. Dad never asked me to do this. It was all on me. But without the brainless decision to charter a sailboat, I wouldn't have met Hunter. And despite some unpleasantries—fine, a lot of them

—these weeks had been the best ones of my life. Being high up on the tree was not okay for me. But I was okay. I was better than that.

"Do you want to stop?" Hunter asked. "We can come back another time."

Hell would freeze before I quit. "I made it this far. I can go a little further." Saying words out loud gave me a needed boost of energy. With my pulse painfully drumming in my throat, I attempted to climb the last limb (first, prodding it with my finger for any soft places to make sure it wasn't rotten).

It seemed like my entire body burned with millions of scrapes I had collected while climbing. A bug ran up my leg, and I flicked the little bugger with my finger, sending it somewhere into the air. A thought hit me. What went up had to go down. Me. I had to go down. Damn it. Whatever Captain William Thompson stowed away in this tree better be worth the pain and risking my life. I straddled the branch, gathering my strength and courage to get up and see if my efforts weren't for nothing. Swallowing a lump of fear wedged in my throat, I edged closer and peered over into a large, dark, gaping hole in the center.

A hybrid of a sob and a squeak escaped me. Wrapped in a brownish, weathered cloth and covered with dry leaves, dust, and bird or bat poop, something was crammed inside.

I leaned over, my body seesawing on the thick outer layer of the trunk, my legs in the air. Ignoring a discomfort under my breastbone, I stretched my arm down and dusted off the dirt, exposing discolored and stained fabric. I snatched my hand back, my elbow hitting a funny bone. What if it was some sort of odd pirate ritual to bury friends? Or enemies. Bandaged like a mummy and stuffed into a tree. My marbles were getting loose in my head. The riddles were about treasure, not anything else. Carefully, I knocked on the surface. A solid sound. It couldn't be a skull. Not that I'd knocked on a skull before.

I scraped my nails on the top until they caught on the fabric's edge. Pinching it between my fingers, I pulled on it. The cloth easily gave in and ripped. I dug more until I peeled off the last layer, and gold glimmered. I grinned wide until it hurt.

"It's Mary," I whisper-yelled to Hunter, then slapped a dirty hand over my mouth. No need to announce our discovery to the world. There was no way Tom would be near us even if he had arrived the moment Hunter left his post. But better to be safe than sorry. I began my careful descent.

If the records were correct about everything Captain William Thompson had stolen, then Hunter and I had found the entire treasure. All that remained for us was to contact the right people interested in the Treasure of Lima.

I was on the ground in Hunter's arms in no time. My mind didn't recollect the descending journey just like in my past when I arrived home after a long workday, unsure if I had stopped at any red lights or yielded to incoming cars. All I knew was that I was in my safe haven.

The space was much darker now, but Hunter's grin was bright, the corners of his eyes crinkling. His exhilaration mirrored mine.

"We did it," I said, unable to contain my happiness. I was drunk on a hormonal cocktail of endorphin and dopamine. I had a sudden and overwhelming urge to dance or just jump around.

"It's all you. Your cleverness is what was missing all these years. I love you, Sydney. It will hurt so much to say goodbye to you," Hunter said into my hair, his embrace on me tightening.

A twinge of pain went through my heart like someone stabbed it with a hot iron pole. I didn't want to say goodbye either. My mind and heart struggled to determine the right decision for me. To leave or to stay. But this wasn't the time to debate. I would think about it later. Once we escaped and reached the main island. Unharmed.

Chapter Twenty-Nine

Early in the morning, Hunter's low curses jolted me out of my sleep like someone had lit a fire under me. A distant ache echoed in my muscles and bones from sleeping on the ground. I rubbed my eyes and then focused on Hunter. Tension laced his forearm as he gripped the binoculars. I didn't have to ask what was wrong, and my insides twisted with a visceral fear. The time on his watch was six-thirty in the morning.

I slowly crawled to him and looked over his shoulder and through branches. The skies were the color of a bruise, and thunder rolled somewhere in the distance. A dinghy with two men quickly approached the shore. One of them was Tom. My heart hammered faster the closer they got. In my mind, I repeated our simple plan: we run to the dinghy as soon as they reach the hut.

"Do you see anyone on the big boat?" I whispered, zeroing in on the sailboat in the bay. It looked different from the one Tom had arrived on the previous time.

"No, and it's strange," Hunter whispered back. "Tom would have brought more than just Garry."

"Maybe he couldn't find anyone else at short notice, or they are on the boat hiding." I closely watched the larger boat in the bay, trying to see if I'd notice anyone on it. It appeared empty. They wouldn't be hiding. What did Tom care if we knew he brought more men with him? So maybe it was our lucky day, and once we reached the main boat, it was ours without a fight.

"By the way, that's my boat," Hunter grumbled.

"That's the *Nauti Guy*?"

Hunter's jaw ticked. "The shithead stole my boat."

They killed the motor in shallow waters, and soon, the dinghy beached exactly where Hunter and I expected it to. It was a little further for us to run, but we could make it in under fifteen seconds. The two men hopped out of the boat and pulled it to the dry sand.

The second man, Garry, was a heavy guy. He wore a bandana around his bald head, long navy pants and a T-shirt with a red scuba diving logo. Tom hadn't changed his clothes from yesterday. He and Garry surveyed the area. I couldn't see if they had any weapons with them. Then Tom said something, pointing toward the path that led to the hut. My breath hitched as they walked in that direction.

Hunter touched my shoulder and moved in closer until his mouth was near my ear. "As soon as they step inside, run." I turned to look at him, and he gently clasped my face in his hands and brought his lips to my forehead. "We'll be okay." He smiled, but it was apparent he wasn't sure about the words he said. I didn't feel brave and wanted to hide in here until they left.

Last night, Hunter and I had closed the window shutters and made two human shapes under the flat sheet in the bed in the hope it would fool Tom for a split second that we were asleep inside and buy us extra time to steal the dinghy. I watched through the leaves, their figures slowly approaching the porch.

Tom stopped at the door and tilted his head as if listening for the sounds inside. Then his hand went to the handle, and he slowly opened the door. After another few seconds, they walked inside. My heart hammered in my chest to the point it was about to explode. It was now or never.

Hunter and I broke through the bushes.

Eyes trained on the boat.

My feet worked hard against the cool sand.

Hunter was several feet ahead of me.

My heart rattled in my ribcage.

The boat was twenty yards away.

Did they see us?

Ten

Were they out of the hut?

Five.

Were they after us?

Three.

Fuck.

A scrawny man lay flat on the bottom of the boat, pointing a gun at us.

Goddamnit. I wanted to scream and cry and kick the sand with my feet. I should throw sand in his eyes. Knock the gun out of his hand. Tackle his skinny ass down. Drag him with us back into the boat if needed and then throw him overboard later. Yet, in shock, I stood there frozen, my heartbeat thundering in my ears. Sneaky, fucking Tom. How did we not think about this scenario? We were fucked.

"Hello, Hunter," he said, sitting up.

The man was short, with greasy, thinning, sandy hair and a face resembling a taxidermy gone wrong, with one of his eyes bulging out. His outfit was similar to Tom's, but it was all black. The man gave me a once-over and made a low whistle.

"Jack, at least now I know you're good at something." Hunter shook his head with a humorless laugh. "You can hide in a small boat."

Jack glared at Hunter and jerked his hand with the gun. "Move back."

I lifted my palms up as we stepped back. Jack got out of the boat and stuffed the gun into his pants, his eyes drifting to something behind us. Or someone.

"Did you really think I would let you just take my boat?" Tom called out, his voice like sandpaper against a raw wound. He and Garry sauntered to us, both grinning like sharks.

Up close, I could see that Garry had a face made for radio, with a potato nose and a huge bottom lip swallowing a nonexistent top. His T-shirt was two sizes too small and exposed a sliver of hairy belly.

Tentacles of terror clasped tight around my stomach as my eyes focused on one, two, three handguns visibly stuffed in their shorts. This situation had turned into a shitstorm sandwich fast, and we were dead smack in the middle of it.

"Why did you have to take my *Nauti Guy*?" Hunter asked.

"Until you pay me back every penny, that is my boat," Tom said. "And now the interest is doubled."

"Unbelievable," Hunter muttered. "Is Barry on the *Nauti Guy*?"

Tom scratched his unshaven jaw. "It didn't work out between us. He owed me money, too, you know."

What the hell did he mean by that? Barry was either fish food or no longer associated with Tom. Probably the former. I bristled, feeling the blood drain from my face. But then the idea struck me. If Barry wasn't here, did that mean that the bigger boat was empty, and that there were only three of them, and they were all here on the island? A small hope flared within at me. If our Plan B worked, the *Nauti Guy* would easily be ours.

"Are you ready to give us a ride to Rarotonga?" Hunter said, straightening his broad shoulders. "At least let me take Sydney back. She is not part of it."

"Mate, you sound like a broken record," Tom said with an air of reproach, bending and grabbing a backpack from the boat I hadn't noticed before. "I'll take you and her back, but only once you show me what you found."

"I told you. We haven't found anything here. It's all in the sea."

"Let's discuss our business like civilized people over a cup of coffee and some breakfast." Tom lifted the bag, smiling. "I came bearing gifts."

My senses prickled with awareness. The story in the Bible had three wise men who visited the infant Jesus, bringing gifts. Garry and Jack looked more like dull-witted savages than wise, but the number of the men standing before us matched. And yesterday, we found the Virgin Mary with baby Jesus. This was a sick joke. The heavy man jerked his head, signaling us to follow Tom.

Chapter Thirty

In the kitchen, Tom pulled out a blue thermos and two trail mix granola bars out of the bag and placed them on the table. Then, he grabbed the aluminum mugs off the shelf as if this was his place and poured brown liquid into them. The smell of coffee quickly hit my nose. I didn't want his coffee. He could have added drugs to it.

I pushed past him and marched to the running water. I cupped my hands, plunged them into cold water, and then splashed them onto my face. I wanted to dunk my head into the bucket and scream.

"Greeks say not to trust enemies who bring you presents." Hunter accepted a mug from Tom.

"Why would Greeks say that? Have a seat, Sydney." Tom motioned to the bench like a polite host, inviting me to sit down. Without drying my face with the towel, I sat beside Hunter, my arm brushing his.

"Heard of a Trojan?" Hunter retorted.

"Of course we have," Jack said. "It's a popular condom brand."

Wow. That's the sperm that won.

"I'm not talking about condoms, but your father should have worn one," Hunter said, placing his hand on my knee to stop it bouncing. "I'm talking about the Trojan horse."

"Uh, that story," Tom said, offering me a cup full to the brim with coffee.

I eyed the mug, inhaling the sweet aroma, my mouth salivating. When I met Tom's eyes, he gave me a quizzical stare.

"Please don't tell me you think I have poisoned it."

I shrugged. "Hunter has a point."

Tom clicked his tongue. "Oh, for fuck's sake," he said as he set the cup on the table, untwisted the thermos cap, and poured the remaining contents into it. Then he lifted his hand in a cheers and drank it all down. He made a mocking, satisfied sound. "Now drink and eat."

I choked out thanks and picked up the mug. No sugar, no milk, no problem because it was a good, strong coffee, and I missed it so much. Hunter and I ate in the layers of silence, not looking at each other. I hated that I enjoyed the sweet and salty taste of the breakfast that Tom had brought.

Tom leaned on a tree that held one corner of the stretched canopy, then glanced at Jack and nodded, signaling something that they must have agreed. An awful feeling replaced my bone marrow, and my body turned heavy as a rock. This couldn't be anything good for us. Tom had returned more prepared than we were. Jack folded the knife he used to carve his name into the picnic table and walked away in the direction of the porch.

The racket of drawers slamming and furniture moving reached us. Hunter soared to his feet. "What the hell, Tom?"

Garry stepped closer to us, meaty paw resting on his gun tucked in the belt of his pants. He reeked of cigarettes, mildew, and a hint of yesterday's binge drinking. I crinkled my nose at the stink.

"Why so jumpy?" Tom raised his eyebrows. "Nothing to worry about if you have nothing to hide, right? Sit down and finish your coffee."

I tugged on Hunter's hand. "Let him look for whatever they think is there."

The coins and stones from the pot were now hidden in the sand under the steps. Burying it near the house was a good spot for grab-and-go when we were on our way to take the dinghy when we would escape during our Plan B. The plan that Hunter and I needed to find the right time to execute.

Jack trod to Tom and whispered something to him, showing him the kitchen knife I hid in the hut when I first turned up here.

Hunter twisted to look at me. "Where did he find the knife?"

"Under the mattress," I said over the rim of my cup. "I intended to use it on you." He drew back with a shocked expression. "What? You can't blame me. I didn't know you that well at first."

"Fair."

Tom's eyes cut to something on the beach, and then he cast them down to the cold, sharp metal in Jack's hands.

"Garry, watch these two," Tom said.

He and Jack walked away, so we couldn't hear their

conversation. They glanced at us several times. My gut feeling was that whatever they talked about wouldn't play out in our favor. Then, to my surprise, Tom shoved Jack, sending his skinny ass over the teakettle into the low ferns.

"What do you think is going on over there?" I asked Hunter and crumbled the wrapper.

"There seems to be a power struggle between those two." Hunter peered over his shoulder, swallowing the last of his coffee. "It looks like they're disagreeing on something. Garry, should you be taking part in that conversation?"

Tension simmered around Garry. His jaw tensed, and his nose flared as he scrutinized Tom and Jack, who were having what appeared to be an urgent conversation. But just as he was told, he didn't move and stayed like a well-trained guard dog. A breeze cut through, bringing the stench of mildew off his clothing.

If we were in a movie and Hunter were Jason Statham—only much better looking, with hair, and taller—he would knock all these thugs out, and we would run away. But this wasn't a movie. Hunter's hand was sore. And there were three of them with guns against one without a weapon. I wasn't a fighter, so I didn't count myself.

"Okay. Let's get to business," Tom said, tightening his dreadlocks into a bun as he approached us. He pulled out the journals and notebooks he stole from us and dropped them with a thump on the table. "Now tell me where the fucking gold is."

"There isn't any here," Hunter said flatly, as if it weren't a lie at all.

With an amused expression, Jack, arms crossed over his

chest, propped his narrow shoulder against a post. "And I'm telling you, you're both liars."

"There is gold, but it isn't here," Hunter said, his voice urgent but absent of panic. Hunter pointed out to the beach. "It's in the ocean. Let's get on my boat, and we can continue to search. Edward and I were getting close to finding it. You have as much information as we did, so I'm sure you were close, too."

Tom released a harsh laugh. "I searched high and low where Edward told us and came up empty. I spent over eighty thousand fucking dollars looking for it just this year." His fingers curled around the gun's handle. "For the last time. Tell me where it is, or someone gets hurt," Tom said in a low, menacing voice. The chill in his tone made my hair stand at its roots.

Hunter faced me and his eyes bore into mine. He gave a subtle nod, just enough for me to notice. I wondered if any of them would notice the wild jounce of my skin near my windpipe. This was it. We were taking them to the trap now. I took a breath for what felt like the first time.

"Fine." Hunter stood up and jerked his chin to the left. "It's this way."

Tom ran his tongue over his teeth, his nose wrinkling. "Wait a second." He opened the journal to the page with the island map sketched with several locations marked. "Nothing is in that direction. You need to take us here." He pointed the nose of his gun at the bat cave on the map. "If I am right, it is…" He picked up the journal, held it to the ground, turned, and faced the way to the garden. "There. It's that way."

My heart spasmed. Tom wasn't as stupid as we'd thought, and at the game of scheming he was one move ahead of us.

Tension ridged Hunter's body, and he swallowed thickly. "Yes, but we should go this way first. It's easier. Where you want to go is harder to get to."

"No. I want to see this one first." Tom stuffed the gun into his shorts. "Lead the way."

Chapter Thirty-One

Hunter and I walked first, and everyone filed after us. Instead of picking a quicker, straight shot to the bat cave from the kitchen, Hunter led everyone past the garden and the shed, where we turned into the thick screen of the jungle and meandered our way half a mile until the path inclined and soft dirt turned into rock. Thirty-five minutes later, we approached the majestic tree and stopped at the cave. Jack struggled to catch his breath. He pulled out an inhaler from his side pocket and puffed on it. Garry was the least fit among us but showed little exhaustion.

Tom surveyed the area, his eyes stopping at the giant tree. A low whistle passed between his lips. "Look at this huge bastard. A bird shits a seed, and this massive hulk grows here."

"It's inside the cave." Hunter gestured at the dark opening. "You need a flashlight."

"Did you bring one?" Garry said, wiping sweat off his round face. Hunter shrugged as in sorry, not my problem.

Tom strolled to the cave entrance and stopped where

sunlight drew the line next to the darkness and the derby of the freshly broken wall was barely visible. He peered inside, then edged deeper. The dimness swallowed his body, and he vanished from my view. His whoop echoed out, and a second later, a scratching sound of bats followed it. A gunshot went off. Four of us staggered back as a dark, squealing cloud jetted out of the cave. Jack yanked his gun and sent several rounds at the hundreds of bats flying out in a frenzy.

Hunter pulled me down and enveloped me with his body. I clamped my hands over my ears. The noise ricocheted between faceless stone walls—my only hope was that the bullets wouldn't do the same.

The noise stopped. Several lifeless, black creatures dotted the ground.

"Who the fuck was shooting?" Tom came out of the cave. Garry inclined his head at Jack. "You could have hit me, you idiot."

"You shot first," Jack yelled.

Tom inhaled through his nose, his face turning into disgust. Stuffing the handgun into his shorts, he walked to the opening that led to the drop-off. "What's that way?"

"A dead end," Hunter said, helping me to my feet.

"Okay. The cave has tons of shit inside. It'll take some time to bring it all to the boat. Each of you, grab what you can carry." Tom gestured at Hunter and me. "You two go first and start dragging things out."

"Why should we help you?" I said, crossing my arms. "You're robbing us at gunpoint."

"I'm not robbing you. He," Tom pointed at Hunter, "owes me money. I'm taking what is mine."

"The agreement was that we show you where the treasure

is, and you give us a ride to Rarotonga," Hunter said. "You can come and get it on your own later."

Tom sucked on his teeth as if trying to get a piece of stuck meat out. "I changed my mind." He gave the coldest stare at Hunter. A lurch of foreboding in my gut was as painful as a snake bite. "You help us get it all to the beach. We take it to the boat. And once everything is out of here, we take you to Rarotonga."

"That's days' worth of work." Hunter threw his arm in the direction of the cave. "Those are heavy, and you need more men to carry them. She isn't strong, and my hand is injured."

"Do you have a plane to catch?" Tom said. "You've spent weeks here. What is another day? Now, move your arses."

I shuffled inside the cave first, stumbling on the rocks, my eyes slowly adjusting to the darkness. I wrapped my arms around one of the rolled-up tapestries and tugged on it. It probably weighed as much as me, if not more.

With a groan, Hunter and Tom picked up a trunk and immediately dropped it. Then they tried again. By the time they hauled it out and set it by the tree, they were both out of breath. This was going to be a very long and miserable day. So far, nothing had gone according to our plans, and all I could do was wait for Hunter's signal that we were ready to take them to the trap. Again.

"This will never work," Hunter said, pressing his hands on his knees. "The chest is too heavy."

"We unload more of this shit into that." Tom nodded at the tapestry next to me. "She can pull it."

"That would damage it," I said, not hiding my anger.

"Do I look like I care?" Tom glared at me. "Unroll it."

I hated this guy.

Grabbing the hem of the antique fabric, I unrolled it. My heart squeezed. Soon, its beauty would be lost to the world.

While I dragged the fabric bundle up as a sack filled with heavy monstrance adorned with gems, Hunter and Tom carried a half-empty chest. Garry and Jack took a smaller trunk with silver and gold relics. We stopped several times to catch our breath and let our limbs rest.

When we reached the beach, the sun was at its highest point in the sky, making the air impossibly thick to breathe in. Sweat soaked every fiber in my clothing, and the scrapes burned and itched under my shirt. Leaving things on the dry sand, we marched back to get more.

Hours bled into each other. With only a quick break for lunch of a cold canned soup Jack brought from the boat, we made multiple trips from the cave to the beach until I couldn't move my feet. Hunter and I didn't get a moment alone, so I wasn't sure of our plan. It was well after midnight. Tom, Jack, and Hunter went inside the cave to retrieve the last few items, but Garry consistently stayed out to keep an eye on me. There was something vile in the way he constantly looked at me, the way his eyes slid from my face down to my legs. The large flashlight on the ground cast the light behind him, making him look like a horrendous beast.

I sank to the ground by the tree, drawing my knees to my chest, and pressing my head to them. I smelled him before I saw him stepping close to me. Garry's arm was outstretched, the sharp point of the sword inches away from my nose.

"What the fuck." I recoiled, standing up and pushing my back flat against the tree. My stomach twisted with anger and fear. Garry scraped the sword tip down my neck, over to my chest, stopping in the center of the valley of my breasts.

Hunter's hand came out of nowhere and gripped the blade. "Don't," he said through his clenched teeth. Their eyes locked. If Garry moved a fraction, he would slice Hunter's hand open. And then both of his hands would be damaged.

Not letting the metal out of his grip, Hunter pushed the sword down, and I slipped out of its reach. When I was far enough away, Hunter uncoiled his fingers and stepped aside. Garry just laughed, throwing the blade on the ground.

I took Hunter's hand to examine a bleeding cut across his palm, but it was hard to see well. I thought (hoped) the cut wasn't deep and, in my humble medical opinion, didn't need stitches, but we needed to bandage it.

"You shouldn't have done that," I said, looking up at him. "It's good that you are up to date on your tetanus vaccination," I teased.

Hunter wrapped his arm around my shoulder and pulled me to his chest. He buried his face in my hair. "Sydney," he whispered. The quiet but urgent way he said my name made my pulse gallop. "Take off your sandals." With caution, my legs moved to do what he said, the soles of my feet finding the cold stone under me. "I'll start a fight. You run."

I jerked to look at him, a burning sensation developing behind my eyes. "No," I rasped, my voice creaking, knowing he wouldn't take no for an answer.

We agreed not to get separated. It was suicidal for Hunter to stay with the three of them. I felt petrified. Tears spilled, and I shook my head.

"Yes."

"I'm too tired."

"You can do it." Hunter took my face in his hands and brushed his lips against mine in a gentle kiss. "I love you," he whispered. "I'll be right behind you."

He smiled, letting go of me, and marched to Garry, his right hand, the good(ish) hand, made into a fist.

Chapter Thirty-Two

My heart beat triple time as I charged through the jungle, branches clouting my face, my toes hitting roots. I picked the shorter path to the hut, the one that we hadn't used today. My heavy breathing and pulse flooded my ears, blocking any other sounds. Was anyone after me? Perhaps I should have pivoted to the right and run toward the trap. Hunter didn't say where I should go. We didn't agree where we would meet. The beach? The trap? Like a knife, heavy and sharp, worry about Hunter twisted in my gut. I should stop and wait for him or return to the cave and help him.

My ankle twisted and I tumbled face first, sliding on my chest and stomach into low ferns. I pushed off the ground and stiffened. Someone else moved fast through the woods. How long had they been following me? Was it Hunter?

They stopped. My breathing ceased. There was a complete cessation of sound.

My eyes were adjusted to the night, but I couldn't recognize who it was.

I wanted to call out Hunter's name, but fear (or self-preservation) took a firm grip on my vocal cords.

Panic pulsated in my neck, sending a vibration all the way to my toes. My heart drummed inside my ribcage to the point whoever it was probably heard it.

If it was Hunter, he wouldn't stop running. If it was Hunter, he would whisper my name.

It was one of the three thugs.

A twig broke too close to my left. I sprinted. I abandoned the idea of taking a straight pass to the hut and changed my course. Trees whipped my face, setting my skin on fire. My mind rushed over every idea of how to lose the chaser. They didn't know this island as well as I did. High levels of adrenaline diluted the pain from stabs of rocks and twigs under my feet. I made unnecessary turns and passed the garden.

If I reached the shed, I could grab the gardening tool, and if I reached the workshop, I could snatch a hammer. If only I could make it.

Why wouldn't they yell at me so I would know who it was?

My foot slipped on a grassy patch, splitting my legs into a half-split and pulling my inner thigh muscle. Fuck, that hurt. Without looking back, I scrambled up and kept running.

At the last turn, I bolted toward the shed area and hid behind the mound of plastic garbage. Breathing through my mouth, I waited. The jungle was quiet. No one was after me. I had either lost them, or it was Hunter. Where was he? He could have steered to the boat, or to confuse Tom's men, taken off in a different direction from me. Damn it. The workshop was a short distance from here. Crouching, I left my hiding spot.

In the blackness, it was anyone's guess where the fucking hammers were on the workbench. With stealthy hands, I palmed the surface, only twisting once to see if anyone was advancing at me. My fingers brushed over the cold metal of the hammer's head. I seized it.

Teaming up with the jungle's darkness, I hid to catch my breath, my eyes trained on the lone sailboat in the bay, its lights twinkling in the distance. I wished I knew where Hunter was. The thought that he was hurt, or worse, made the hairs on my arms stand up. I should have not listened to him and stayed to help. But I had to believe Hunter was fine. He was smarter and stronger than all three morons, and he knew the island better than any of us. He would meet me at the beach, like we decided. I had to move forward with our original plan.

Taking a breath, I readied to run the last stretch to the dinghy—about four hundred feet. I stepped out from the woods. My dirty white T-shirt reflected the moon's light. I retreated. The moon wasn't full, but it was too bright for me to race freely on the beach. Anyone could spot me.

Gripping the hammer's wooden handle, I crept in shadows outside the jungle, where the sand mixed with pine needles and low creeping vines. Soon, the outline of piled loot on the beach came into view, and near the waterline, the dinghy patiently waited for someone to take it out. That someone was going to be me. It was another hundred feet before I could reach it.

I made it to the spot where Hunter and I had huddled

behind trees earlier. Only thirty yards left to go. I licked my dry lips and took off.

A body slammed into me, knocking me off my feet sideways.

The hammer flew out of my hand.

Curse words punctuated their labored breath as they drove the side of my face into the sand, seizing my arms behind my back. A devastating mix of panic and anger filled my veins, and I wrenched my arm out, only to get pushed deeper into the sand. A heavy weight crushed my ribcage. He didn't reek like roadkill in summer days. Tom? Jack?

I spat sand out of my mouth and hissed at the pain in my arm. "Let me go."

Jack laughed and yanked me to my feet. He was awfully strong for a small man, or I was too tired to fight.

"Tom wants to talk to you," he said.

"Where is Hunter?" I asked, digging my feet into the sand.

"Just walk." He shoved me forward.

"Where is Hunter?" I repeated.

Before Jack had tackled me, the hut had been dark, but now light oozed out of the closed shutters as we approached it, shadows shifting inside. I paused the last step, my eyes meeting Garry's, who stood at the door, holding a flashlight and blocking most of the entry.

"Can you move?" I asked, shielding the bright light with my hand. He didn't step away. Asshole.

"Go on," Jack urged me with a shove.

The porch planks groaned as I squeezed by Garry, avoiding any unnecessary contact, my heart beating unpleasantly hard. This was the first time I had seen the room after Jack had raided it yesterday. A flashlight on the desk threw a direct light into the space. Bookshelves and drawers were mostly empty, their items thrown on the floor, and the bed moved away from the wall, its mattress crooked.

"Sydney," Hunter said, and I turned, my eyes landing on him standing by the sofa. He sported a bloody bottom lip, and his right cheek was swollen. My body went weak as if I had seen a ghost, and I wanted to cry. My shoulders sagged with relief that he wasn't hurt—badly.

"I almost reached it." I hid my face into Hunter's chest, wrapping my arms around his waist. A multitude of brown and green marks covered his beige T-shirt as if someone had dragged him through a grass field.

"You were very brave," he said, embracing me.

"Next time we run together," I whispered.

His low chuckle vibrated in his chest. "Okay."

"I'm a little disappointed that you took all day to finally run away," Tom said, walking in. He took the same spot at the table as the last time, lit the lantern, rotating the knob until it didn't turn any further. The flame spitted and sputtered, and after a few seconds, the wick flared to life, throwing a gloom of light at his face, where a streak of blood ran down its side. His eyes were cold and calculating and held a lot of anger.

"I don't know how you didn't go blind reading all this shit," Tom said and stacked his feet on a chair, crossing them at the ankle. Then he lowered the gun next to the journal and flipped through the large notebook until he stopped on the page with a sketch of the island. A second later, he turned and squinted at the map on the wall with all the pins we had forgotten to remove.

Jack moved to the desk and picked up my father's urn.

"Please don't touch that," I said. "That's my dad's ashes."

The man's eyebrow stippled with false pity, his one good eye focusing on me. His hand unscrewed the top and took it off. "That's so sad that your daddy is dead." He flipped the urn upside down. "Oops."

The ashes spilled out on the floor, my father's ghost wafting under the bed and around Jack's filthy feet. Fresh grief throttled me. I felt sick to my stomach, my throat closing in.

"Dickhead!" Hunter crossed the room in the asshole's direction. Garry grabbed Hunter's shoulder, but he shook off the hand. Wrenching the urn out of Jack's hands, Hunter kneeled and cautiously scooped ashes with his palms. He dropped what he collected inside the vase, then rose to his full height and placed the urn on the desk. "You touch it again," he said to Jack. "You'll lose your second testicle."

Jack's face tightened with irritation, and his hand went for his gun.

A single shot went off to my left. My hands flew to my ears as I hunched down, a horror unfolding in my mind. For the second time today, the guns had become extremely real. There was a hole in the wooden floor near the table. My chest hurt as if a panic attack had taken up residence there. Hunter and I were going to die.

"Can we go back to the business?" Tom snapped, bringing everyone's attention back to him. His hand held the pistol.

"Sydney, are you okay?" Hunter unpeeled his back from the bookshelf, his chest rising and falling as fast as mine. I gave him a curt nod and straightened on my shaky legs.

"The Treasure of Lima is worth hundreds of millions of dollars. What you showed me isn't worth that much. Explain to me the pins. The red one is where we have already been. What about the rest?" Tom asked.

There were ten pins. The purple, pink, white, black, orange, and light blue marked places that had all turned out to be a bust. But the red pin was the cave, the blue was the grotto, and green was the fishing lagoon, but its real meaning was the snakes' spot. The yellow was Johnny the Skeleton. This was our chance to try again to lure them into the trap. Hunter's gaze flickered to mine, communicating that the show was about to start.

"And before you come up with a lie, tell me where you found these?" From under the journals, Tom withdrew the bag with coins and gems that I had buried in the sand.

WTF!

I swallowed, the spit scraping my dry throat.

"Where did you get it?" Hunter said, the stiffness in his body unmistakable. I, too, froze to the point my muscles ached.

Tom sneered. "Jacko found it earlier today when the black cat dug at something. And he found a kitchen knife buried there, too." Tom's eyes cut to me, and he tsked. "I assume that was yours, Sydney?"

Goddamnit. Tuesday, the traitor, had utterly screwed us.

"Do not take me for an idiot!" Tom slammed his fist on the table again and the lantern rattled, making me jump. "I knew all along you were both lying. The gold is here. No one is leaving the island until—"

"We tried to take you there this morning," Hunter raised his voice, "but you didn't listen."

Tom's arm was casually draped over the back of the chair as if we were just having a friendly chat. "Because I assumed you fed me bullshit, but now I'm ready to listen."

"I told you they lied to us," Jack said.

"Shut up, Jacko!" Tom waved his hand with the gun at Hunter. "How much is there?"

"Four trunks," Hunter said. "Take us to the main island. Tomorrow, you'll get it yourself."

"Hunter, do you hear yourself? Take us to the main island ... get it yourself," Tom said in a mocking tone. "I'm the one who has the boat. I'm the one who has a gun. I say who goes where and when. Why isn't the location marked in the journal?"

I wiped my nose on my shoulder, the sand scraping my skin. "Because that's where the gold is. And there isn't any need to mark it in the journal if we both know where it is."

"Okay. Let's take a look now." Tom scratched his scalp and got up. "Garry, find something to tie her up."

My thoughts became turbulent, a whirlpool of horror and uncertainty. My eyes jumped from Hunter to the open door to Tom. No one was supposed to be tied up, especially me.

"This is unnecessary." Hunter walked around the table and inserted his body between them and me. "Tom, Sydney walks with us."

Tom shook his head. "She stays here. Garry, you and I are going to check it out. If everything is good, we'll all go to Rarotonga."

"What about him?" Hunter asked, nodding at Jack.

"Jacko returns to the *Nauti Guy* and waits for my signal."

There went our plan to steal the boat.

"What signal?" I clung to Hunter's arm like he was my lifeline. Everything was going against us.

"The signal to come back." A cruel smile starched across his face. "You think I'm stupid enough to leave the dinghy on the beach for you to take if something goes awry? You already tried to steal it twice."

"I can stay with her," Garry said, unmoving from his original spot by the door.

I would rather be in a box with bats and snakes.

"Did I stutter?" Tom said with an irate tone. "Go find something to tie her up."

Garry grunted and marched out of the hut.

"You don't need to do this. Jack is taking the boat to the *Nauti Guy*. Where do you think she would go?" Hunter said, our fingers interlocking.

Tom's calculating eyes studied the map on the wall. "It isn't about where she could go. It's just a precaution to prevent her from doing something stupid, like finding another kitchen knife. How many did you hide around here, Sydney?" He looked at me with a sneer, but I didn't care to answer. Let him think we had more knives stashed around here.

Garry returned with four pieces of thin rope that once held the kitchen tent. He advanced in my direction, but Hunter put his free hand out. "Let me do it."

"Get lost." Garry reached around him for me, and Hunter knocked his arm away. Garry pulled the gun out and forced it under Hunter's jaw. "Move."

Fear stunned me like a scorpion. Garry's small eyes, with their wickedness and instability, made it clear to anyone that the deranged man wouldn't hesitate to pull the trigger.

"It's fine. Let him do it." I cupped the side of Hunter's face with my hand and moved it so I could look him in the eyes. "Show them where the rest of the treasure is and return to me. Okay?" I rose on my toes and pressed my trembling lips to his, then with my chin up and an expression of indifference, I walked to the chair where Tom had sat earlier.

Taking the seat, I aligned my ankles with the chair legs and draped my arms around the back of it, leaving some space. With any luck, I could wiggle my arms out of the rope grip and break free. And also manage to not throw up from Garry's appalling reek.

Chapter Thirty-Three

Good news: I didn't barf. Bad news: Garry did a remarkable job of tying me to the goddamned chair.

Ten seconds after they left, my right foot fell asleep from blood circulation cut-off. But no worries, I had a plan in place for how to get myself out of this tight situation. I just needed to get across the room to the desk's junk drawer that was ajar and get the Swiss Army knife. Easy peasy. Of course, it was hard to open the blade one-handed, but I'd cross that bridge when I got to it. Both my wrists were (sort of) loose, so everything was possible.

The main goal was not to tip over.

If I tip over, game over.

With ridiculous body jerking movements, the chair wobbled inch by inch in the correct direction. Hot survival instinct coursed through my bloodstream, and my heart worked harder than a twin-turbo engine. Raw spots developed on my wrists and ankles where the rope rubbed against my skin.

Near the table, halfway through the room, the chair leg caught in the hole in the wood floor. I jerked harder, but the chair didn't budge. I blew my bangs off my sweaty forehead and tried one more time, jolting to the right with furious impatience. The chair leaned, wobbled, and I flew sideways. Oh shit. My shoulder smashed the table. The lit lantern at the edge jumped, tilted, fell, and hit the floor, its glass shattering.

The spilled oil ignited. The sheets fell off the table and landed in the oil. Flames licked them, and woosh, they were lit up. And like magic, the flood of fire overtook the raggedy hut.

Fucking fuck.

"Fire!" I yelled. "Fire!"

White smoke rose from under the mattress, and like in a nightmare, red flames crept up the sheets.

I wiggled my legs and arms as much as I could to loosen the grip of the cable, ignoring the painful bites of the coarse fibers. My right foot freed more, and I pushed off and set the chair upright. The smoke stung my nostrils, making it hopeless to take a breath. Frantically yet not to overdo my efforts, I moved the chair inch by inch to the front door. There was no time to get the Swiss Army knife. I was one step from hell and had to get out.

"Fire!" I yelled again and broke into a horrible cough. My chest burned as if a hornet's nest erupted in my ribcage, stinging me within.

I jerked. I wiggled. I used my toes to drag the chair, closer and closer to the door. The closer I got, the harder I worked. Adrenaline in my bloodstream launched me over the threshold. My knees hit first, easing the blow to my head. Scraping my legs and forehead on the porch's rough wood, I moved to the stairs and tumbled down the steps, pain hitting my body at different angles.

I landed on the dirt path, and the back of the chair fell off. My arms were free. Unable to untie the ropes around my ankles, I used all my anger and jiggled the chair legs until they broke off and the ropes were easy to remove.

My chest felt heavy as if a ton of weight was pressing on it. Hunter's IDs and cash were inside. Father's urn. I was losing it all over again. Panic snaked through my veins. I hurtled up the stairs, wanting, needing to rescue it. At the door, the billowing smoke stopped me, and I staggered back, shielding my face from the hellish heat. I ran to the kitchen, tripped, got up, then finally reached it and grabbed a bucket. I scooped water out of the tub we used as a sink and turned to rush back.

"Sydney." Garry stepped out of the darkness.

"Help me put the fire out." I tugged on the bucket, spilling half of the water as I carried it, its heavy weight banging my shin.

He grabbed it out of my hand and threw it to the side.

"What the fuck?" I shouted.

"The piece of shit house is gone."

Smoke rolled out the windows, and red and yellow flames blazed inside the house. His lips pulled into a predatory grin, and it stirred an awful feeling inside of me. He was so obnoxious.

He was alone.

The pulse in my neck hammered to the point of agony. Garry shouldn't be back. Something had happened to Hunter. I stepped back, bumping the shelf with plates and utensils. My hand went behind me, and I fumbled for the three-pronged spear. My clammy grip tightened around the shaft, and I wielded it in front of me.

"Why don't you put that down before you try something stupid?" Garry pulled the side of his shirt up, revealing the gun and an unnecessary piece of hairy belly.

I dropped the tool. "Where are Hunter and Tom?"

"They are none of your concern," he said slowly and deliberately. I steered around the picnic table to insert some barrier between us.

Garry crept deeper, his eyes narrowed on me. "You look scared."

Did Hunter and Tom make it to the dug-out? What if it didn't work? I maneuvered around the table again, my back to the clearing in the jungle that led to the garden. I could bolt and hide somewhere. No. I should run to the trap.

"Why are you here?" My voice was hoarse.

"To save you from the fire."

I doubted Hunter would send Garry to check on me. He would've come himself. We made a full, slow circle around the table. The devilish dancing shadows of roaring fire made him look crazed. We stopped.

I needed to find Hunter, but first, I had to eliminate Garry. I could take him deep into the jungle or to the shed and somehow hurt him and run. But that meant we would be alone. In the darkness. Even farther away from Hunter. Or … I could … my muscles went rigid, agonizing goosebumps prickling my skin as I thought of the black rocks.

No.

Think of something else.

This was the best idea.

Was it stupid of me?

Yes, but it was a risk I was willing to take.

"I know where more gold is," I blurted.

Garry cocked his head as if he had misheard me. "What?"

"I found more gold. And diamonds. Lots of it. Hunter doesn't know. I was going to keep it to myself. Come back and get it later." My breaths came in quick and shallow.

"Bullshit."

"I'm serious."

He jerked his chin. "Why are you telling me this now?"

"Because if you help me get out of here, I'm willing to share half of it. Tom won't give you a fair share. He is a lying thief, and I'm an honest nobody who got dragged into this shit show. Just think about it. Tom thinks he calls all the shots, but it's only because you let him believe it, but you're manipulating him to do what you want to do. Am I right?"

I had no idea where all this word vomit was coming from. I was gambling. Garry narrowed his eyes, but the change on his face—the change that all brainless, gullible men show when they gobble up praise and flattery—gave him away. I had him.

"Tom is a fucking idiot."

Just like you.

"I agree."

"*Nauti Guy* is mine. Because Tom sank my *Sugar Daddy*. He owes me. And I told him Bazza was stealing from us. He didn't believe me."

I didn't give a rat's ass who Bazza was. "Exactly what I'm talking about."

"I did all the dirty jobs for that Australian big mouth, and how much respect did he show me?"

All righty, Garry had proven his point that he was upset

with Tom. Enough of that. I needed him to ask me to show him the gold. I straightened my posture.

"So, I have your word that you won't hurt me? We split the money fifty-fifty once we return. Yeah?" I asked. He slowly nodded. "Okay. Can you signal Jack to come back now?"

"No. I'm not an idiot." Garry bared his teeth in a grin, and I willed myself not to cringe. How could smiling make someone uglier? "You show me where the gold is first," he said.

And Garry fell into my trap.

"Of course. It makes sense you want to see the proof first. I understand," I said, grateful it was too dark for him to notice my hands and legs shaking. I wasn't sure if I could walk. "Follow me."

A dark, cloudless sky with a light of fading stars was a promise of a calm day, but inside my chest, worry stormed. We walked out to the beach, and the peering boulders in the bay became recognizable on the inky canvas. In the distance, the lights of a sailboat bobbed in the water. For a brief moment I wondered what Jack was doing out there. Why he wasn't noticing the bonfire.

A breeze tugged on the hairs around my face. Waves lapped the beach but crashed harder around black rocks at the end of the cove. I walked waist-high into the water, then waited for Garry to catch up with me.

Garry stopped at the edge of the water. "Why are you going there?"

"We need to go up there and move through the opening at the top." I pointed up, even though Garry most likely couldn't see the crack in the rock wall. "After that, it's not far."

I moved deeper and inched around the first big black stone.

"You wait here. I'll go alone and get some gold to prove to you it's there."

"No. I'll go with you." Garry was knee-deep when he pulled something out of his pocket. A second later, a bright light came on. A cellphone flashlight.

Damn it. He could notice the snakes.

I had no option but to move forward. He followed me, holding his phone. As we slowly trod over the rocks, my blood pounded in my ears, muting the sound of waves beneath. Hunter had better be right about becoming immune to snake venom. Because if not, I was—

A sharp sting burned my ankle. I halted, clenching my jaw to stifle a scream.

"What?" he asked, the light of his phone blinding me. "What's that face for?"

"I can't take responsibility," I said through gritted teeth, "for what my face does when you're around me."

Another stabbing pain struck my ankle. We were in the right spot. My legs wobbled, and I grinned.

"What the fuck is wrong with you?" Garry's eyebrows pulled down, and his nose wrinkled in disgust and confusion. He ran his light from my face downward to the black swirling around us. "Fuck." He jumped back.

With all the energy left in me, I steered behind Garry and pushed him on his back. He stumbled, then tripped and fell to his knees, losing a grip on his iPhone. The phone perched sideways, projecting light on Garry. He shouted and struggled to get up, but the look on his face froze in horror. His body jerked once, twice, and then he stilled.

My hand trembled, and my leg ached, but I could move. I took in a wheezing breath, grabbed Garry by his shoulders, and sat him upright, his face away from the water. He was a worthless person, but I didn't want his death to be on my hands. Deep down, I was a spiteful woman, but not a murderer.

Moving carefully around him, I found his gun and threw it into the water. Well, I shouldn't have done that. Stupidity must be contagious.

"Garry, I'm not an expert on these snakes, so just know that you might die," I said, looking at his wide-open eyes.

The hut was a blazing mess, sending smoke signals to the world. And to Jack, too. My eyes scanned the bay for the approaching lights of the smaller boat. The coast was clear. He must not have seen the BBQ party with his good eye. Or maybe, just like Garry, he had an ulterior motive too and was gearing up to leave us all on this island. Or he was asleep.

Exhausted and dehydrated, I crawled out of the ocean onto the beach and fell on my back. My legs throbbed with pain. Saltwater burned my wounds, assuring me I was still alive. There was no time to rest, but I had no energy to move. Hunter. I needed to find him.

And then I heard him calling my name.

"Hunter!" I pushed off the sand and rushed toward his voice.

At the line of the jungle, Hunter appeared near the leaning palm tree. My knees buckled when I drew near him, and he caught me by my forearm, wrapping his strong arms around me.

"You're okay." Hunter pressed a kiss on my head. I nodded, sobbing into his chest. He leaned back to look at me. "Did Garry hurt you?"

I shook my head.

"Where is he?"

"Snakes," I croaked, hot tears slipping into my mouth. "I took him there."

Hunter pulled me into a hug again. "I'm so sorry I didn't stop him."

I wiped my nose on his dirty shirt. "I can take care of myself."

"I have no doubt. What happened to the hut?"

"Remodeling." I joked, and Hunter chuckled.

God, I was so glad this was almost over. All that remained was to wait for Jack to come back—if he was coming back—and take over the *Nauti Guy*.

"Hunter, we should move off the beach if we want to surprise Jack. He is still on the boat."

The boom of the gun ripped through the air. Then the gun went off again. We were too late. Jack had spotted us.

"This way." I pulled Hunter into the jungle.

Hunter jerked me to the left on the beach. "No. This way."

We were white targets against dark woods. Even with one bad eye, Jack could see us.

"You are dead!" Tom yelled, then broke into the harrowed cough.

What the hell? Tom wasn't supposed to be here. He should have been in the hole. Hunter's head whipped around to look over his shoulder. Gray smoke made it impossible to pick out any movement in the jungle. The gun went off again, and this time, something—a bullet—struck the palm tree. Could Tom see us, or was he firing at random?

Hunter yanked on my hand, and this time, I followed, running after him along the beach, staying close to the edge of the woods. I twisted to see a figure running out of the jungle and charging in our direction.

Hunter turned into the darkness of jungle and pulled me with him. Was there a plan? Or were we just running? When we reached the workshop, I skidded to a halt.

"Hunter, wait." I bent, planting a hand on the side of my stomach, where the cramps hurt the most. "We need to find a tool or something."

"We need to lose him." He tugged on my hand.

"Let's hide in the grotto." We would be cornered rats, but that was fine. They couldn't stay on this island forever. "Please," I pleaded, choking on the word.

The snap of the branches nearby and the rush of a body through the woods gave a shove to our feet. Taking an extra zig-zagging turn to confuse Tom, we ran toward the undisclosed cave. The path inclined. The taste of blood coated my throat with each deep breath I took. Our safety was within reach.

We neared the entrance, and Hunter gripped my hand and pulled me behind him up the hill until we were out of the jungle. Fright soared through me. He kept taking me higher. We reached the cliff jumping spot.

I dug my heels into the ground, wrenching my hand out of his.

Hunter swiveled around, his chest heaving just as fast as mine. The wind lifted strands of his tousled hair in a chaotic dance. "Do you trust me?"

"Yes, but—"

He pointed down at the ocean. "This is the way out."

A breeze battled with the hem of my shirt. Chills ran up my skin from the morning air or was it Hunter's suggestion.

"We have to jump?" I squeaked.

The early sun's golden threads seeped into the night, bringing optimism with it but also a reminder that it was harder to hide in daylight.

"We jump and take my boat. Look." The small vessel quickly moved away from the *Nauti Guy* to the beach. Jack was on his way to save his friends. Or hurt them. If Jack looked up to his right, he would spot us. I wasn't sure I could do this.

"You are a strong swimmer," Hunter said, firmly. "The distance from the cliff to my boat is shorter than from the beach. We have some time, but not much, soon it will be bright enough for anyone to see us. If we jump now, don't scream. Sydney, please. This is the way."

After weeks of living here, I had proved that I could do things that before had seemed unimaginable to me. I looked at the tall man I loved with messy hair and a face covered in dirt and scrapes, wearing clothes that resembled a zombie apocalypse survivor, and laced my fingers through his.

"Do you want to count to three?" He squeezed my palm as we inched to the edge.

I swallowed a hard lump of fear. "Just say that you love me."

"I love you," he said.

I took a deep breath and took a leap.

Chapter Thirty-Four

My eyelids clamped together all the way down, and my free hand pinched my nose. I went into the bitter ocean water like a rocket. And then I let out a scream. Like a giant wave, emotions of rapture, sadness, regret, and contentment without warning crested against me. A shock of cold water was like a restart to my system. I felt reborn and ready to embrace the new me and my new life. And I did dare to say it; I was ready to live an adventure. Once we got to safety.

When my head broke the surface, it took the last of my willpower not to shout with excitement. I was breathless but had never felt more alive. I'd done it. I jumped.

Hunter held my hand while treading water, looking at the *Nauti Guy*. I relaxed my fingers around his and began swimming to the boat. With confident strokes, my strong muscles propelled me forward. My breathing matched my arms' movement—breath in and breath out. With each push, I was closer to my escape.

The *Nauti Guy* slowly swayed, waves going around and under it, making gurgling sounds. I slowed as we approached the boat. I thanked the stars it wasn't any farther because my energy was running dry. Hunter reached the stern and climbed on board, then he extended his arm and helped me up the ladder. As soon as I was out of the water, goosebumps rushed over my skin, and salt bit into every scrape and cut on my skin.

We collapsed on the deck, my chest heaving from the long swim and the thrill of escaping Tom and his crew. Against the morning skies, a large seagull soared high, its wings spread wide. Free bird. We were free, too. We had made it. We were safe.

Hunter rolled on his side, facing me, and I used this opportunity to pull him by his shirt. His lips brushed against mine softly first, and then then they pressed firmer. His fingers found their way through my hair, and he rested his full length over me. After a swim in a cold ocean, I welcomed his warmth, melting into him. I loved his weight on me. Elation expanded my soul. Pressed against Hunter so comfortably, I indulged in the alleviation.

I wound my arms around Hunter's neck, my face brushing his stubble as I hugged him. I loved everything about Hunter, and I loved that he had helped me discover a new me—a strong, capable, and, most of all, resilient me.

Hunter rose on his elbows, his lips pulled into that toe-curling smile I had come to know so well. He opened his mouth to say something, but jerked his head up to look straight ahead.

"What?" I asked, my body going rigid, picturing Tom and Jack on the dinghy racing toward us.

"We should go."

Hunching, Hunter moved to the front, pulled the anchor, and slipped into the helm. I flipped on my stomach and craned my neck to peek through the rails. No one was after us. The *Nauti Guy* motors came to life, and I mustered the energy to get up and face the island.

A small figure, Jack, ran on the beach, waving his arms and yelling. My left hand gripped the railing as I raised my right in farewell.

The fire wasn't blazing anymore, just a spiral of gray smoke rose into the air like a ghost of everything that had happened in that hut. Me waking up for the first time after the storm. Hunter and me hunching over journals for hours. All the sweet and dirty vows Hunter whispered in my ear when we were tired before we fell asleep, his arms around me. Us making love countless times on the bed, against the walls, on the mess of papers on the floor. All that sex. Raw and hungry.

The boat picked up speed over the waves, and I slid down on the floor and lowered my head onto my knees. A million emotions flooded my heart. Overwhelmed, I let myself cry.

I cried for Bambi. I cried about losing my dad's ashes (twice). I cried for how exhausted I was (I could close my eyes and sleep for weeks). And I cried because I was finally going home, where my friend, my job, and my fast new life awaited me. And it all felt wrong.

Hunter concentrated on navigating us back to Rarotonga, and I tried to figure out why each time I thought of going home, unease dragged me down like a boulder. We cruised for a long time without talking, until eventually he slowed the boat not far from the Avatiu Harbor, then killed the motors. He slid next to me on the floorboard, his large hand coming over my small one, engulfing it in warmth.

A tired smile pulled at his lips, and this was when it became clear my home wasn't in Miami. For days, I had questioned whether this was the right decision for me. I searched for reasons it was important for me to return, and I couldn't find any. I loved my job, but nobody said I couldn't do it remotely. Tina was my only close friend, but I couldn't (and shouldn't) build my life around her, and she would want me to choose love (and the greatest sex ever) over her. And when I searched for reasons why I should stay here, on the Cook Islands, I only came up with one absolutely-no-fucking-doubt vital reason: Hunter Holden.

My home was anywhere Hunter was. It was scary to abandon my old life and start anew in a new place with a new person, but everything we went through in one month was like speed dating on steroids. And we turned out to be great together.

"Why are you so quiet?" Hunter asked, his thumb making a gentle circle on my skin.

"I want to be with you."

His eyes met mine with so many emotions that my chest tightened. "You don't need someone as messed up as me," he said.

"I don't think you're messed up. Owing money to criminals is"—I sucked in a breath through my teeth—"troubling, but you did it for a good reason. And you'll pay them off and never have to deal with them again." I turned my hand palm up to his and laced our fingers. "I don't want to go back."

His eyebrows pulled together. "Why?"

I shrugged, smiling. "Because there is no place in the world I would rather be than with you."

"Are you sure?" he asked, voice low but hopeful. His lips

seemed to fight a bigger smile. "It will take a long time to get the reward. Years. Or it might not work out with a finder's fee at all, and you'll end up with a broke fishing boat owner whose house is a pile of ashes."

"I don't care about that. And we can rebuild the house. It was a piece of crap anyway, had horrible air conditioning, and the plumbing was awful."

He threw his head back and laughed. I loved his rich laugh, and I would hold tight to that sound for as long as my memory allowed.

"What about your battle to fight cybercrime?" he asked.

"I can fight it from any place in the world."

"You might grow bored with me. There are no more mysteries to solve, no secret messages to break. You'll be the girlfriend of a guy who takes tourists to catch fish."

"What about the resort you want to build?"

Hunter rubbed his face, releasing a muffled groan of exhaustion, then looked away to where the highest pick of the reef-protected volcanic island came into view over starboard. "You were right. Teaku isn't the perfect place, and I know nothing about running a business."

"You know how to run the charter business."

"That's because Edward taught me how to do it."

"You could always learn how to do something else." I bumped his shoulder with mine. "I'll help you. We could also go sailing for a while. I don't have my dad's ashes with me or his diary, but I have a list of all the islands he wanted to visit imprinted in here." I tapped a finger on my temple. "I think that would make him happy. It would make me happy, too."

"I'd love to do that." He pressed his forehead to mine.

"Wonder Woman, I don't think I ever lived before you walked into my life."

"You mean shipwrecked into your life?"

"Yes," he said, his lips brushing against mine softly. "I wanted to tell you that I loved you for days. It was like a ticking bomb inside my heart waiting to go off. I should have said it when I knew it."

"And when was it?" I smiled.

"The day we were trying to lift the *Reely Nauti*. I came around the boat and saw you hanging on the rope."

"Really? When I was sweaty and angry, hanging on the cable like a kid who was about to fail their PE class."

"You were so determined and not afraid of work, and so beautiful, and good God, you were so snappy when you were tired. And my heart was in deep, deep trouble." He kissed me again. "I need to be honest with you. When I saw the *Reely Nauti's* damage, I was relieved and scared all at once. It meant I had more time with you, but I knew I'd only fall in love with you more, and it would be torture to say goodbye to you when you left." His eyes crinkled from the smile.

"Some people say falling in love is like cliff diving—exhilarating and stupid—and others say it's like falling asleep slowly and then all at once, and I don't know how it happened to me, but…" I smiled. "All I know is when I thought of home, I saw you instead, and that's when I knew I loved you."

Hunter kissed my temple and hugged me. "I love you, beautiful."

The man saw me when I was near death, bruised and dirty, with greasy hair, not even wearing a lip gloss, and Hunter still found me attractive.

"If you think I'm beautiful, wait until you see me all dolled up. You'll pass out from lack of oxygen to your brain because your blood will drain down south too quickly."

He chuckled. "I have no doubt about that." He pulled away, eyebrows slightly furrowed. "I don't think you ever told me your middle name?"

"Louise. It's my mom's name. What is yours?"

"James."

"Mmm, I like it. Hunter James Holden," I said, brushing my lips against his.

A blast of a boat horn jolted us from our happy bubble. We got up and watched a cabin cruiser approaching us. It wasn't a coast guard, but a large, gray boat.

"Do you know who it is?" I asked.

"Yes. Liam McKee. He runs a deep-sea fishing rental."

"He is your competition. Do you owe him money, too?" I said, pushing his arm with my shoulder.

"No." Hunter laughed. "He is a good man. But he shouldn't be here. He usually goes back to Ireland until October."

The boat dropped its speed and slowly came closer, the newly created waves making the *Nauti Guy* bob more with excitement. It turned, showing large lettering on its side, making me snort. *Feck Orfe*.

"Does anyone out here give their boats normal names?" I said, laughing.

"What fun would there be in that?" Hunter raised his hand and waved.

When the *Feck Orfe* came closer, a tall man in his late fifties (though, with fishermen, it was hard to tell their age) wearing sunglasses came out to the helm, and was followed by a shorter person wearing an orange life jacket.

I shielded the sun with my arm to take a better look, and my heart soared when my eyes landed on Bambi. My vision blurred. Unable to form any word, I slapped my hand over my mouth to smother a sob of relief. Bambi was alive. Someone saved her.

"Bambi." I gripped Hunter's forearm. "That's Bambi."

"The woman with Liam?"

"Yes." Warmth radiated all over my skin, and the morning sun had nothing to do with it.

Their boat was now several yards away from us. Bambi's face broke into a huge smile, matching mine. I could imagine what thoughts went through her mind when she saw us. Hunter and I wore dirty and torn clothes. Hunter's sleeve had bloodstains from grappling with Tom. His right cheek had a hint of a bruise. I smoothed my short hair on the sides as if that would help my appearance.

"How's it going, Holden?" Liam McKee called out.

"What are you doing here, McKee?" Hunter shouted.

"I'm just helping my new lady look for her friend," Liam said, inclining his head to Bambi, listening to her.

"I found you, babe," Bambi said loudly. That nickname had made me cringe so often when she used it, but now it was the best one anyone had called me by.

The boats came close, and she climbed over the gunwale and jumped from the *Feck Orfe* to the *Nauti Guy* like a teenager. I moved around Hunter and hugged her petite frame before she could protest. Without hesitation, she threw her arms around me.

"Oh my God," I choked out through my sob. "I'm so happy to see you. I thought you were dead."

Easing my iron grip on her, she stepped back and looked

over me. I wiped my nose with my forearm and grinned. Bambi appeared healthier than before. Her hair was as short as mine, and she wore small sailboat-dangling earrings instead of her golden hoops.

"You look great." I squeezed her bony, but warm hands. "And these earrings suit you."

When she smiled, her face wrinkled with a million lines. I missed those lines. "Liam gave these to me."

"They're lovely."

She glanced over my shoulder at Hunter. "I wouldn't mind getting a hug from him." She winked at me, and I snorted a laugh. "Who is he?"

"That's Hunter. My boyfriend."

Aww, that felt so good to say it out loud.

Bambi looked me up and down with puzzlement, and her smile faltered. "Babe, you look like shit. What happened to you?"

"It's a long story."

Liam climbed on board too and Hunter and I briefly told them what happened to us, starting from the awful storm, the time Hunter and I shared on the island, and about Tom and his crew's attack. Bambi told us about how the Coast Guard found her two days after the storm, holding on to the unidentified life ring about twenty kilometers from Muri. The life ring that I threw to her. She spent a week at Rarotonga Hospital. By mistake, she told them that she and I were heading to Mangaia when she went overboard, so they conducted a rescue search around that area. After the search was called off, Bambi returned to Australia only to come back here because she realized her oversight. By that time, the Coast Guard didn't want anything to do with her, so she charmed Liam into helping her.

Bambi apologized for the error she made and also for putting us into a pickle by stealing and selling my navigation system and satellite phone, but more importantly, she wanted to apologize for failing as a captain when she started drinking. She had been sober since that horrible storm. I forgave her.

A little after ten, Hunter radioed to Avarua, requesting permission to enter the harbor and arrange for a dock. Before docking, we went over drawers and found some of Hunter's identification documents and money he had stashed away for a rainy day. Liam and Bambi gave us a ride to the local police station. Avarua welcomed us with the wharf sidebars, shops, and open-air markets where folks bargained for handmade jewelry, art, and souvenirs. Some people wore a flamboyant head *ei* made out of flowers, and all of it against the vivid rainforest background.

At the station, still wearing bloodstained and torn clothes, we reported Tom's attack. We learned that Tom, Garry, and Jack were wanted for racketeering and burglarizing a dozen boats and marinas in Samoa, Tonga, and the Cook Islands. The night Tom stole the *Nauti Guy* and someone else's boat, he and his crew left a security guard and a dispatched police officer in critical condition during the robbery.

Hunter provided the island's location and warned that the men were armed. I notified the police about the black rock snakes in case Garry was still there. We also mentioned the discovery of the Treasure of Lima. There wasn't any reason to hide it because when police arrived, they would see the loot on the beach.

It must have been a slow day because the chief of police

asked us to wait while they gathered a team with a K9 crew to Teaku to make the arrest. This morning, when we were on our way to Avarua, I had suspected I would be back on Teaku soon, I was just not thinking it would happen on the same day.

While Hunter finished filling in the paperwork, I borrowed an iPhone from a detective and video called Tina on WhatsApp. When her excitement, punctuated by cursing, subsided, I gave her a short version of what had happened to me, and I promised I would provide more details soon. She complained that involving local authorities and Interpol in a missing person case in international waters was more complicated than filing taxes. I felt guilty for making Tina lose her mind with worry, so to make her feel better, I flipped the phone camera to Hunter and she instantly asked if he had a single brother.

Later, Bambi brought us a lunch of fish sandwich and fries, and a change of clothing, and took us to the hospital.

"You should go with Bambi to Liam's place and wait for me there," Hunter said, lacing up his shoes he had taken from the *Nauti Guy*.

"We agreed that we don't get separated." I dried my hair with a towel after showering.

"Aren't you a bit sick and tired of me by now?" he asked, his finger tugging on the new elastic bandages around his hand.

"Never." I threw the towel on the bench.

In the afternoon, two boats with armed officers and three German shepherds raced to Teaku. We followed them on the *Nauti Guy*. They instructed Hunter and me to remain on board until we were granted clearance to go to the island.

When we arrived, the dinghy was beached on the sand, and

the island appeared to be deserted, minus Garry. The first thing I noticed as we entered the bay was the red scuba diving logo on Garry's shirt against black rocks. He was there, probably afraid to make a move in the snake trap. It didn't take much time for the dogs to find Tom and Jack, hiding in the shed. They gave up without a fight, and police escorted them off the island. When everyone had left, Hunter and I stayed in Teaku bay because we couldn't just leave the loot on the beach for anyone to grab. *Feck Orfe* with Liam and Bambi bobbled near us. They came to help keep an eye on the Treasure of Lima.

Under the night sky, the *Nauti Guy* swayed in the water, lullabying us. Hunter held me close, his hand on the curve of my waist, my head tucked against his shoulder. I wanted to live my new dream of exploring the still-vast ocean. Only this time, I wouldn't venture out unprepared. And I wouldn't be alone—Hunter would be by my side.

Someone once said that love could be found in unexpected places. Sometimes we went out searching for what we thought we wanted and ended up with what we were supposed to have. Only in my case, I got caught in a crazy storm and nearly died before plunging onto an island and straight into Hunter's life. And now we were bound for life by blood, sweat, saltwater, and a touch of bat poop. What the future held for us was a puzzle, but together, Hunter and I would overcome challenges as deep as the ocean and perplexing as endless caves.

Epilogue

THREE YEARS LATER

The Caribbean morning sun warmed my skin through a tinted window of the *Treasure Hunters*. I blinked several times, staring at Hunter's face, edged with hope and excitement. I couldn't believe my ears when I heard his proposal. We talked about it many times, but I didn't think he was seriously considering it. His eyes searched mine, and I was afraid the longer I didn't give him the answer, the more he would think I was against it. I wasn't. I was just surprised. And a bit scared, too. And a whole lot excited.

We were in St. Thomas Bay with a beautiful sliver of white sand lined with dozens of palm trees. The waters were always calm, providing the perfect spot for swimming and wading. The beach had a Shore Thing bar, and Just For Fun, a small place that rented umbrellas and chairs, SUPs and kayaks, and snorkeling gear.

"Are you sure you want to do this?" I asked, leaning over

the table in the gallery and taking his hands in mine. "This is a huge commitment."

"Of course." The corners of Hunter's lips turned up. "I think it will be great for us."

"Well, yeah." I laughed. "Let's do it."

I slid from the booth, careful not to bump my five-month pregnant belly on the table corner, and circled to Hunter's side, where I climbed on his lap to kiss him but stopped.

"Wait a minute, why are you suggesting it now?" I peered into his eyes, my hands loosely looped around his neck.

After Hunter and I had placed the Treasure of Lima discovery into motion with officials and found a good lawyer to represent us, we left the Cook Islands. He sold Edward's business, and I sold my parents' house, and we bought a new home—a sixty-five-foot sailboat, the *Treasure Hunters,* and explored the world. By the way, three years ago, I knew diddly squat about sailing, and now I was an exceptional captain.

As soon as news broke about the discovery of the Treasure of Lima, Hunter received numerous offers to buy Teaku. Per the original purchase agreement, he couldn't sell it for another few decades, so he leased the island for a handsome sum of money for the next ten years to a treasure enthusiast who built a small eco-friendly adventure camp with an option to renew it. A third of the profit it brought us, we donated to several ocean cleanup nonprofits.

My phone vibrated on the table, its screen filled with Tina's smiling face, wearing sunglasses and a large beach hat. With some regret (because it was rude to disregard friends), I pushed the ignore button because Hunter and I were having a vital conversation that could and would change the course of our lives.

"So tell me why we are talking about this now?" I asked, looking back at Hunter's handsome face.

My phone came back to life again. Tina. The universal rule of calling twice in a row in case of emergency applied to our friendship.

"Go ahead, answer it." Hunter smiled and tilted his head at my iPhone, relaxing against the seat's cushioned back as if we were discussing a grocery list and not our future.

"Hey, are you okay?" I answered the call.

"Yes. Are you?"

I glanced around the tidied-up galley, then at the calm aquamarine ocean outside the window. "I think so," I said suspiciously. "Why are you asking?"

"You usually text me to have a safe trip before my flight. And I'm almost at my gate, and still nothing from you," she said, her breath huffy as she speed-walked through the airport. Tina spent all her vacation days with us, flying to meet us wherever we were.

"You haven't taken off yet, have you? So technically, I have time." I smiled.

"I can't wait to see you and your cute belly," Tina squealed. "We haven't hung out since my visit to Italy. When was it? Five months ago?"

"Yes," I said.

"When you got pregnant after seeing Henry Cavill," she said, and if not for the airport hubbub, I would hear her snickering.

Tina and I have an ongoing debate about whether I got pregnant the same evening we caught a glimpse of Henry Cavill (fine, we watched him for about an hour) filming his movie in Sardinia because my ovaries were overly excited.

And yes, he was just as handsome in real life as on TV, but my Hunter was much better looking.

I rolled my eyes, shaking my head. I needed to wrap up this call since it was obviously not an emergency. "Hey, I need to go right now. You have a safe and good trip, and I will see you in about four hours."

"I take an Uber to Emerald Beach bar like last time?"

"Yep."

"And your rats are still with you?"

Tina wasn't a huge fan of cats, but Monday and Tuesday were our faithful companions since we had left Teaku, so she would have to get over her cat-erade for the next two weeks.

"They can't wait to see you," I said, running my palm over Hunter's cheek, enjoying the soft feel of his freshly shaved skin.

"Okay, see ya soon." Tina hung up before I could say bye to her.

I blew air through my pursed lips, loosely draping my arms on Hunter's shoulders. "So, where were we?"

"Remember the house you liked on the top that overlooks the bay?" Hunter said, his palms skimming my back. He was holding back something, and I was afraid to let my hope soar high until I knew where he was going with it.

"Yeah," I said warily, but anticipation fizzed through my veins like champagne bubbles.

His expression was unabashed bliss. "It came up for sale yesterday, and it can be ours if you want it."

And now my stomach was full of butterflies (it could also be a baby moving). I arched an eyebrow. "How? It's a bit out of our price range."

"This morning, I received a call from Lisa Browne's firm..."

he said, his smile widening, cheeks showing off his cute dimples.

"Oh my God." I shrieked. "Is it really done?"

"Yes. It's done."

"Done?" I repeated, shocked to my core this day had finally arrived.

Hunter nodded, and I entwined my hands behind his neck. He buried his face into my shoulder crook, his chest expanding in rhythm with mine.

After three years of waiting, we had given up on the idea that our finder's fee would ever be granted to us. It turned out that the finders-keepers rule only worked in elementary school and didn't apply to multi-million-dollar historical treasures. The process of receiving the "thanks for locating the long-lost treasure" payment was not as easy and straightforward.

"It's eight and not ten percent as we initially were promised, but I think we will be okay," Hunter said, his gaze tracing my face as his fingers gently smoothed hairs out of my eyes. "If you still think we should buy Shore Thing and Just for Fun and settle here, now we can."

When we came across this slice of paradise three years ago, Hunter and I were on our honeymoon voyage, and we fell in love with it. While having drinks at Shore Thing, we befriended the owner, Brad, who was considering retiring soon and wanted to sell his beachfront property with both businesses. At that time, Hunter and I weren't looking for a place to anchor yet, but we knew eventually we would need to pick a spot to call our home. With a baby coming on board soon, it was time to think about where we would want to land and start our family.

"I already know which room will be our nursery."

I released a happy breath and kissed Hunter's stubbled cheek. "Can we go see it today?"

I was already on my feet, reaching out to pull Hunter onto his.

"Of course," he said, wrapping his arms around my waist and pulling me closer so he could press a kiss to my belly. My fingers worked their way into his sun-bleached golden hair. My heart was impossibly full. I conjured a rich image of us chasing our little ladybug on the green lawn in front of the house, her blonde curls bright against blue skies, and her giggles so loud I could hear them right now. I wanted that so much.

Hunter looked up at me, his blue eyes catching sunlight. "I love you." I bent and brushed my lips against Hunter's, saying it back. His hand slid down and grabbed my ass, and I was glad we didn't have an appointment with a realtor that morning because we would certainly be very late.

DON'T MISS *DIGGING DR JONES*
A LAUGH-OUT-LOUD SPICY ADVENTURE ROMCOM

A surprise gift is exactly what Adriana Jones needs to improve her vacation, and a bracelet with gems will do the trick. Except once it's on, she's faced with two problems:

1. The bracelet is actually meant for Andrew Jones – the renowned and utterly gorgeous archaeologist.
2. It will not come off, no matter how hard she tries…

There's only one solution: Adriana must accompany Andrew on his quest to find an ancient lost treasure deep in the jungles of Colombia. This was *not* on Adriana's vacation agenda, but an adventure with the very sexy Dr Jones might just be the treasure she's been seeking…

AVAILABLE IN PAPERBACK, EBOOK AND AUDIO!

Acknowledgments

Kind words cost nothing, but the power they have is priceless.

I wasn't a troublemaker kid (and as an adult, I'm mostly well-behaved too). I struggled with academics, but I wasn't a terrible student. Later, in my thirties, I found out that I have dyslexia, but back then in Russia, people didn't diagnose students with anything; they considered you either a smart student or a stupid one. When I was leaving my high school, the parting words of my principal were, "You'll never achieve anything in your life." I'm not sure who peed in her borsch that day, but those callous words have stuck with me even now. I don't think her words were meant to inspire me to be a better person; they were intended to be cruel and to hurt me. Often, they have spawned imposter syndrome, but they have also propelled me to try harder.

Hunter's Treasure was the second novel that I wrote years ago, and over the years, it has undergone several evolutions. Backstories rewritten, characters removed, characters added, the plot line thrown out and a new one added. The only parts that stayed the same (except for line edits, of course) are the first chapter and the last paragraph. *Hunter's Treasure* was the first manuscript I queried my agent, Helen Lane. It didn't win her heart, and she sent me the kindest rejection email, which only made me want to query her again with the novel I was writing at that time, *Digging Dr Jones*.

Helen, thank you so much for not automatically deleting my second query. 😃 You're not only the best advocate for my writing career, but you're also the most talented editorial agent. Thank you for always telling me (kindly but without sugar-coating) what I need to change in the novel to strengthen it. Also, thank you for your patience with me regarding my next book. 😬 I promise I'm working on it. Soon you'll get a hot mess in your inbox from me.

Thank you, my wonderful editor, Jennie Rothwell, for taking a chance on this novel after only reading the first few chapters and a brief synopsis.

Thank you to Kara Daniel, Grace Edwards, Chloe Cummings, Katie Sadler, Ciara Briggs, Sofia Salazar Studer, and other amazing One More Chapter team members who have worked on this book. Thank you to Lydia Mason, Caroline Scott Bowden, and Victoria Oundjian for ensuring that my written sentences were converted into proper English and for ensuring all the the's and a's were accounted for.

Thank you, Tanya Agler, for setting me on the right path in the romance genre. Years ago, Tanya was one of the judges for the Maggie Award of Excellence. After *Hunter's Treasure* won first place in the contemporary romance category, I received my pages back with the judge's comments. The kind and helpful notes blew me away. I reached out to the Georgia Romance Writers and asked them if I could send a thank-you note to this judge and see if they would like to read the rest of the novel. A week later, Tanya contacted me. She read my entire manuscript and told me everything I was doing right and all the things I was doing wrong. To this day, I practice all the writing guidelines she gave me and reread the books she recommended on writing craft.

Huge thank you to my critique partners and writer friends: Christine Kelly, Toni Bellon, Kim Catanzarite, Lauren Connolly, Kim Conrey, Kathy Hamdy-Swink, Joanna Jelen, Tricia LaRochelle, Jeremy Logan, Megan Benoit Ratcliff, Branda Sevick, John Sheffield, Kristen Terrette, AWC Romance Critique Group, and Atlanta Writer's Club. As always, if I have forgotten to mention someone, please forgive me and know that I'm forever thankful for your help.

I'll never stop being thankful to Bianca Marais, Carly Watters, and CeCe Lyra at *The Shit No One Tells You About Writing* podcast. Even after I've sold and published books, I still look forward to listening to your episodes and reading your newsletters; you always give outstanding advice about writing and publishing.

Huge thank you to Lucy Bennet and Leni Kauffman for creating a beautiful cover. I thought nothing could beat the stunning *Digging Dr Jones* cover, and I'm glad, Leni, you proved me wrong. 😃

Thank you, my incredible family and friends, especially Kelly, Krista, Sarah, Tamara, Tanya, and Tiffany, for your endless cheerleading and for showing up at my book events to make sure I'm not there alone.

To my mom and dad, once again, my apologies for whatever a translator app translates to you when you try to read my book. And Dad, thank you for buying multiple copies of my books to give away to your friends.

My beautiful, kind children, Alexander and Catherine, thank you for your love and for bringing me snacks when I don't appear from my office for long hours, and also for cleaning the kitchen when I'm in crunch time.

And at last, thank you to the handsome leading man in my

life, Burke. Everything I know about love and romance is because of you. Thank you for your encouragement, and thank you for taking the time to listen (or at least pretend to) to my ramblings about the publishing industry, writing, and books. Thank you for answering all my annoying questions about sailing, boats, maps, or "what do you call that thingy again?" You are the most remarkable man I know, and I wouldn't mind getting stranded on a tropical deserted island with you. Think of all the "naked Saturdays" we could have every single day. I love you. 🥳

The author and One More Chapter would like to thank everyone who contributed to the publication of this story...

Analytics
Imogen Wolstencroft

Audio
Fionnuala Barrett
Ciara Briggs

Design
Lucy Bennett
Fiona Greenway
Liane Payne
Dean Russell

Digital Sales
Laura Daley
Lydia Grainge
Hannah Lismore

eCommerce
Laura Carpenter
Madeline ODonovan
Charlotte Stevens
Christina Storey
Rachel Ward

Editorial
Rosie Best
Kara Daniel
Charlotte Ledger
Lydia Mason
Jennie Rothwell
Sofia Salazar Studer
Caroline Scott Bowden
Helen Williams

Harper360
Emily Gerbner
Ariana Juarez
Jean Marie Kelly
emma sullivan
Sophia Wilhelm

International Sales
Ruth Burrow
Bethan Moore
Colleen Simpson

Inventory
Sarah Callaghan
Kirsty Norman

Marketing & Publicity
Chloe Cummings
Grace Edwards
Katie Sadler

Operations
Melissa Okusanya

Production
Denis Manson
Simon Moore
Francesca Tuzzeo

Rights
Ashton Mucha
Alisah Saghir
Zoe Shine
Aisling Smyth

Trade Marketing
Ben Hurd
Eleanor Slater

The HarperCollins Contracts Team

The HarperCollins Distribution Team

The HarperCollins Finance & Royalties Team

The HarperCollins Legal Team

The HarperCollins Technology Team

UK Sales
Isabel Coburn
Jay Cochrane
Leah Woods

And every other essential link in the chain from delivery drivers to booksellers to librarians and beyond!

One More Chapter is an award-winning global division of HarperCollins.

Subscribe to our newsletter to get our latest eBook deals and stay up to date with all our new releases!

signup.harpercollins.co.uk/join/signup-omc

Meet the team at www.onemorechapter.com

Follow us!

@onemorechapterhc

Do you write unputdownable fiction? We love to hear from new voices. Find out how to submit your novel at www.onemorechapter.com/submissions